Author Bio

Jerry Dye lives in Dundee, Scotland and is married with two grown up children. Now retired after nearly forty years in the construction industry, Island Wars is his debut novel.

Find him on jerrydye.co.uk

ISLAND WARS
Copyright © **2025 Jerry Dye**
All rights reserved.

No parts of this publication may be reproduced, stored in a retrieval system, or transmitted in any form or by any means, electronic, mechanical, photocopying, recording, or otherwise, without the prior written permission of the copyright owner.

This book is sold subject to the condition that it shall not, by way of trade or otherwise, be lent, resold, hired out, or otherwise circulated without the publisher's prior consent in any form of binding or cover other than that in which it is published and without a similar condition including this condition being imposed on the subsequent purchaser. Under no circumstances may any part of this book be photocopied for resale.

This is a work of fiction. Names, places, events and incidents have been used fictitiously or are the product of the author's imagination. Any similarity between the characters and situations within its pages and places or persons, living or dead, is unintentional and co-incidental.

ISLAND WARS

By

Jerry Dye

Dedication

Huge thanks go to my family for humouring me throughout the writing process and for tolerating my many periods of self doubt.

Also, apologies for making you buy the book!

Chapter 1

October 2021 – London

The trees lining her street murmured in the nippy evening breeze while shed leaves swirled amongst discarded plastic bottles and snack wrappers, creating a vortex. I kept my hood up and head down. I reached the entrance door to her building which led to a common stairwell, accessing three of the four flats, but the twelve steps down to her basement flat provided cover from the debris spray above, not to mention I was hidden from prying eyes.

She lived in the well-heeled area of Bishops Park, Fulham. Once working class, now a wealthy and desirable area to live, Fulham was home to many a famous face. Tonight, I was only interested in one of them.

Sarah O'Neill slowly opened her front door to find me on her doorstep. Her initial shock and curiosity quickly turned to terror when I buried a six-inch kitchen knife into her heart. Unable to react, the TV and radio presenter stumbled backwards and died before hitting the floor. I calmly walked in and closed the door.

I cleaned the sharp knife and placed it, and my nitrile gloves, in my sports bag. After snapping on a new pair, I surveyed the enormous open plan space. The pristine leather corner suite was new. A huge flat screen television dominated the bay window, the adjacent wall featuring a top of the range sound system. A display cabinet adorned the dining area with several photographs of Sarah posing with famous people. A large mahogany look table and matching chairs overlooked the modern white kitchen with chrome appliances, handleless units, granite worktops and an island with a high level spotlight.

The place was immaculate. Orderly and clinical with no unwashed dishes or scattered magazines lying around, no dirty cups or glasses waiting to be rinsed.

Just as I remembered.

Sarah's relentless organisation made the search of her cupboards relatively easy. Everything had its place. The drawers of her display cabinet were uncluttered. Notepads and pens in straight lines, three stacked jigsaw boxes, each with several hundred pieces. I doubted any of them were missing.

But, nothing important.

I searched her office, which doubled as a second bedroom. A small desk was home to a closed laptop and another notepad. Underneath I found a box containing two binders, organising her life neatly and alphabetically. Energy bills, insurance documents, water, council tax and incidentals were in one. I quickly found and retrieved what I needed.

The other, heftier file contained her financial records. For my own amusement I had a peek. Boy, did she have a lot of debt. Two credit cards maxed out at the £15,000 limit and a Gold card currently at £25,000 and rising. She seemed to be making the monthly payments but the threatening letters from the bank about her £700,000 mortgage explained where she was falling behind. She'd taken some payment holidays but now the bank was rumbling. From what I read it wouldn't be long before they started the repossession process. Oh well, she doesn't have to worry anymore!

I stripped in the living room and donned a new set of clothes and disposable overshoes before respectfully giving her lifeless body a wide berth and gingerly climbing the external steps. With my hood up and scarf tightened over my face mask, I pocketed the overshoes before strolling to the main road, past rows of retail units and fast food outlets. People paid no attention to me. Another invisible person minding their business.

Next to the bins behind a Chinese takeaway, I changed again. A different jacket and a baseball cap before jumping on a number eleven getaway bus into the city.

Chapter 2

At the same moment Sarah O'Neill was being murdered, a man hunched in the doorway of the Boots store on Clapham High Street, his weary eyes intensely scanning every passing car. He cared not a bit about his wild sandy hair and crumpled clothes. An hour earlier, he'd received a text with an attachment, showing a blurry video of a girl and boy, hands tied and blindfolded. Despite the mask he recognised his nineteen-year-old daughter Amanda. The text instructed a meeting time and place but warned - no police.

Relief came from Amanda appearing unharmed but a hundred scenarios raced through Detective Chief Inspector Angus McIntosh's mind. A strong, rugged man, tonight he resembled every one of his fifty years, and more.

Regardless of how this scenario played out, he knew who the target was. Some bastard was going to pay for this.

He cared not about the murderous vibes he clearly exuded to several passers-by who glanced at him then sharply away as he stared right back. At 7.35pm a sleek black Mercedes illegally parked outside the store. McIntosh stayed put and no movement was forthcoming from inside the car. The stand-off lasted a couple of minutes until the front passenger door opened and a man rolled out. Barrel shaped and huge in stature, if not in height. The gorilla motioned for him to get in the back seat.

He walked unsteadily, legs buckling, head throbbing and a mass of cold sweat clumped on his back. Gorilla helped him with a not so gentle shove.

A cheery voice said, 'Hello, Detective Chief Inspector, long time no see!'

'Terry, I swear tae God if you touch her, I'll fuckin kill you myself.'

Terry Johnson had recently played at the kiddie's criminal table but had steadily climbed the tree and now had links to Eastern European organised crime gangs. He'd been immersed in the last major EIU investigation, an armed robbery at a French diplomat's residence but, as usual, steered clear of leaving any incriminating evidence. His local knowledge and muscle plus Albanian OCG funding should have made the job a slam dunk. Things didn't go to plan.

'Relax, this is just a friendly chat. Seemed to be the best way to get you focused. I'll let them go tomorrow,' Terry said.

'Why'd you kidnap them and anyway, who's the laddie?'

Terry laughed. 'Oh oh, is that your daughter keeping secrets? I don't know. They were together and my boys waited as long as they could but he seemed so attached and wouldn't leave her. They got fed up and grabbed them both. Also, kidnap's a strong word. Let's just say I borrowed them. You're going to do something for me and there are consequences if you fail. You need to see how easily I can get to you and your family.'

'What d'ye want?'

'Simple, lose the evidence incriminating Matthew.'

McIntosh was not entirely surprised. 'Cannae do it. The evidence room is monitored and every coming and going is recorded. Nae chance of removing evidence.'

'You better find a way, now you know what's at stake. I'll be watching your family's every move so don't think about moving them. And don't let that famous Scottish temper get in the way. It's time to keep a cool head.'

McIntosh tried to buy time. 'I cannae promise but when you let her go tomorrow I'll see what I can do.'

'Not good enough, Chief Inspector. Maybe you can't promise but I can.'

'Aye okay, let me talk to Amanda and get her to send her mother a text to say she's staying with a friend, or she'll report her missing and half the Met will be looking for her by the morning. Get the laddie to send the same to his parents.'

'Fair enough, by the time you get to your car I'll have her call you and send that text. Nice to do business, Chief Inspector!'

Gorilla opened the rear door and bundled McIntosh out before the car sped off. He walked back to his car in a daze, hands buried deep in his jacket pockets. The chilling wind attacked his thumping head and by the time he dejectedly slumped in the driver's seat the intense pain made him feel sick. He fished around the glovebox for his emergency stash of painkillers and chucked three down his throat. When his phone rang he jumped. A few seconds later his crying daughter appeared on screen.

'Dad, dad, what's going on, what do they want?'

'Amanda, just keep calm you're going to be ok,' McIntosh dispensed with any niceties. 'Have they touched you or hurt you in any way?'

'No, just tied and blindfolded us. I don't understand. What's this about?' she sobbed.

'Don't worry, they're using you to get to me. Do what they say. Who's the boy?'

'Lucas, a friend from college. We were walking towards the tube station when a van pulled up and four men jumped out and threw us in the back.'

'Listen, they're releasing you tomorrow and I'll collect you. They'll get you to send a text to mum to say you're staying with a friend. So she won't worry, but I'll let her know what's going on. Lucas will have to do the same with his mum.'

'Will you let his parents know?'

McIntosh gulped. 'I can't, not until you're both safe. I can't risk them calling the police. Once you're back I'll explain to them that he innocently got caught up in something.'

'Ok dad. Will you get into trouble?'

'Nah, it'll sort itself out.'

The connection ended abruptly. A knuckle dragger must have heard enough. He'd tried to remain upbeat so Amanda wouldn't see his concern.

His phone pinged….an incoming text. He imagined Debbie getting the same one.

'Hi, I'm at Sophia's for tea and going to crash here. See you tomorrow. Xx'

His agitation wouldn't allow him to settle until his daughter was home. Should he speak to someone? His boss? No, not that detestable bastard. His team? Not fair to involve them. No, he'd keep quiet, at least till Amanda was home.

He moved to the next problem. His missus. He'd never excelled at lying to her. She'd always seen through his bluster and bullshit. It was one of the things he'd always grudgingly admired about her. Only this time it involved their precious daughter. Her radar would be on high alert. He'd have to wing it and hope for the best.

It started badly.

He arrived at his Shepherds Bush home, softly closed his front door and tiptoed into the hallway. Three steps in, his wife appeared from the living room, a confrontational look on her face.

'What the fuck have you done?' she said.

Chapter 3

Debbie McIntosh loved her husband but she knew, Detective Chief Inspector or not, she was the boss in their relationship. Two fiery Scots, who'd met and married twenty-one years ago in London. She'd helped her husband through several highs and lows and was the glue that kept their marriage on an even keel.

She was not to be taken lightly.

'What are ye on about?' he said, hesitantly.

'I've been online, paying some bills and saw our windfall. Want to talk me through it?'

'I've nae idea what you're talking about.'

'Oh, just the £25,000 that magically arrived in our bank account. Wondered if you might have an inkling where it came from?' Debbie's face reddened and her eyes widened.

'Fuckin hell,' McIntosh knew he needed to come clean. 'Look, let's sit down and talk. There are things I need to tell you. It's Amanda.'

Debbie immediately became wary and defensive, 'What about Amanda, what's it got to do with her?'

'There's nae easy way to say this. Amanda's been kidnapped, along with a young laddie.'

McIntosh watched his resilient wife crumble, tears cascading, hands over her mouth trying to take it in. He knew she'd react this way. He was a distant second in Debbie's scale of favourites. He was okay with that. She'd had a miscarriage not long after they were married and complications forced her doctor to recommend that she never have children. For a year the devastated couple had resigned themselves to a childless existence until

Debbie found she was expecting. The accidental pregnancy was fraught with difficulties. Several hospital stays, long bed rests at home and a distressing birth made Debbie silently vow to protect Amanda at all costs.

For the first time she felt unable to keep that promise.

'Look, I've spoken to her, she's fine, they're getting released tomorrow,' he said.

Debbie visibly tensed. 'Tell me everything, no bullshit, no sugarcoating. Everything, NOW!!'

'Ok, whoa,' McIntosh raised his hands in surrender. 'I got a message earlier tonight with a video showing Amanda and a boy, tied up and blindfolded.' He produced his phone and passed it to his wife

Debbie winced while watching the video, her tears continuing to flow. 'Oh my God, she looks so afraid.'

'She's ok, I calmed her down when I told her I would pick her up tomorrow.'

'Who's the boy?'

'Some laddie called Lucas. Has she mentioned him?'

'Em...well...yes.'

'Hells Bells, why am I the last to know everything?'

'Duh! I'm sure she wants you involved in her relationships? Anyway, they're just friends. Think Amanda might like it to go further but she's taking it slow. So, what happened?'

'The message said to go to Boots in Clapham. A car appeared and I got in. Terry Johnson was inside.'

'That bastard's got our daughter?'

'Aye, he said he wants me to lose evidence in the armed robbery case. Told me not to involve the police.'

'Wait a minute, you said Amanda was being released tomorrow. You couldn't do anything by then.'

'Johnson took Amanda to show how easy it was and how easy it would be to do again, if I dinna do what he wants. The laddie was in the wrong place at the wrong time. Terry's letting them go tomorrow. When I got back to the car Amanda FaceTimed me.'

'How was she?'

'Upset and crying but unharmed.'

'I don't understand. If they release her before you do anything, couldn't we just disappear?'

'Johnson made it very clear he'd find you anywhere and I believe him.'

'Where does the money fit in?

'I honestly never knew about the money until you told me. He must have deposited it to frame me if he needed to.'

'Tell someone about this, before it goes too far.'

'Not until Amanda's safe. Then we'll decide. We cannae do much else till morning.'

'What about Lucas's parents? They'll need to know.'

'They can't, at least till we get them both back. Then I'll explain it to them. Hopefully, they'll keep quiet. The last thing we need is publicity.'

'I'll never manage to sleep with all this going on,' Debbie said.

'I've got to try. I've got an early start and I cannae go in looking like a dog's breakfast.'

Chapter 4

At 5am, McIntosh finally abandoned the pretence of sleep. He took a long hot shower, brushed his teeth and dressed quietly, in darkness, to avoid waking Debbie. He recalled a draught around 2am and guessed she'd finally succumbed. He leant on the black kitchen worktop listening to the coffee machine's lazy rumble, contemplating this fucked up situation. His stomach churned but he daren't eat. He sipped his coffee, staring blankly at the walls. His buzzing phone jolted him from his trance.

'Yes.'

'Boss, we've caught a bad one,' DI Simon Bayford said. 'Woman stabbed to death in Fulham.'

'Fuck!' He needed this like a hole in the head. 'Where?'

Bayford gave him the address. 'Me and Heather are already here.'

McIntosh gently shook his wife awake. 'Debs, I've got to go, murder in Fulham. I'll let you know as soon as I hear about Amanda.'

'You better, and remember, tell someone about the money,' she replied, yawning.

Even at that time in the morning, traffic was heavy, jostling for position. He waited patiently at the Shepherds Bush Road lights before crossing the Hammersmith Flyover onto Fulham Palace Road. He ignored the horn tooting and road rage going on around him. He imagined the state of people arriving to start a day's work.

As he was directed through the police tape into Windsor Street he could see DI Simon Bayford and DS Heather Walton chatting with a couple of local PC's. He parked and walked over.

'Morning boss, dress in the dark did you?' Bayford said, smiling.

McIntosh never normally fussed about his appearance but today his dishevelment was particularly evident. Not in the mood for banter, he looked up at his handsome, bearded Inspector. 'What've we got?' he growled.

Bayford sensed his boss's icy mood. 'Female victim, lying in her hallway with one stab wound, looks like through the heart.'

'ID?'

Bayford and Walton exchanged a glance. 'It's Sarah O'Neill,' Walton said.

McIntosh clocked the look. 'Is that meant tae mean something tae me?' he said gruffly.

'TV presenter, now a morning DJ on Electric FM. It's why they called us,' Bayford said. 'She's due on the radio anytime now.'

'Shite,' he said, as concerned about the inevitable media explosion as the poor girl lying dead. 'Who found her?'

'Her driver, Trevor Broad,' Walton said. 'Collects her at 5am every morning, texts her to say he is outside but today she didn't reply. He called but she didn't answer so he peeked through her letterbox and saw her on the floor. He dialled 999 but also called Electric. We've told them to keep it quiet until she's been identified.'

McIntosh pointed to a middle aged man, conversing with a policewoman. He wore a long overcoat, woolly scarf, white trainers and beanie hat. 'Is that Broad?'

'No, that's her agent, Paul Greenwood,' Walton said. 'Broad contacted him too. Broad took a panic attack. Couldn't breathe, so an ambulance has rushed him away to hospital.'

'How long before the media gets here, do you think?' Bayford said.

McIntosh thought back twenty-two years to the shooting of Jill Dando, in a street not too far away. That press and media frenzy did not bode well, nor did the fact her murder remained unsolved.

'Soon, if it's not already common knowledge. Preserve the scene and let forensics do their thing. You and Heather take a look inside. I want to talk to her agent.'

'Not wanting to see the scene boss?' Bayford said, surprised.

'Nah, I'll hang aboot here. You two go on ahead.'

Before the two detectives descended towards Sarah's flat, Bayford turned to look at McIntosh. 'Does he seem ok to you?'

'The boss? He's fine, remember he's not a morning person. It's too early for his sparkling repartee.'

Chapter 5

Before entering the flat, Bayford and Walton donned protective jumpsuits and immediately saw Sarah on the hallway floor. The blood pool around her body and the large chest wound suggested an obvious cause of death. Still, Evelyn Marsh knelt over the body, carefully examining every inch.

In her late fifties with short brown hair tinged with grey, the forensic pathologist enjoyed a reputation for being unashamedly inappropriate when dealing with corpses. Behaviour that was tolerated due to her expertise. A fellow Scot, Angus McIntosh had a lot of time for her.

'Ah, McIntosh's band of Bravehearts, minus your glorious leader,' she said, looking over her glasses. 'I wondered if this one was up your street. Though it's a bit extreme to murder the poor wee lassie for her shite choice of music.'

Bayford sighed. He liked Marsh as well but kept his snappy comeback to himself. 'Is this it?' he said.

'This is it, Inspector. One fatal blow, no frenzied attack and no other apparent injuries. We'll have a better look back at the lab but it looks like someone stabbed her through the heart, about turned and walked out. Nothing broken or over turned although I'm sure you'll have a more thorough look round. Have you not had any breakfast, Sergeant?' she said to Walton, attacking a hangnail. Walton laughed nervously before removing the nail from her mouth.

'I'll leave you to it,' Marsh said.

Bayford and Walton examined half the flat each but told the same story. Spotless with zero clutter. Chair cushions and pillows plumped out and aligned and a duvet cover with an exact overhang round three sides. Not one item where it shouldn't be. Underneath a desk Walton discovered two folders containing Sarah's household documentation. She had a quick flick through before bagging the folders as evidence, along with her laptop.

'Anything?' Bayford asked.

'Nothing to get excited about. Couple of folders with her paperwork. She was in some amount of debt though. Either she received a ridiculous salary for presenting a radio show or she was in way over her head. Also, I think she may have had OCD. I know the phrase gets bandied about but it's the neatest and tidiest house I've ever seen.'

'No forced entry,' Bayford said. 'Maybe someone she knew? Crime of passion? Except they tend to happen as someone's leaving. This one happened as someone walked in.'

***

'Paul Greenwood?'

'Yes.'

'DCI Angus McIntosh. I'm in charge of the investigation.'

An ashen Greenwood looked ready to heave. Shivering uncontrollably, despite several layers, his teeth rattled which made it difficult to talk. 'You....you.... you're Scottish.'

It was a recognised fact within the Metropolitan Police that Angus McIntosh's accent grew coarser and more aggressive when someone pissed him off. He'd been delicately advised of this many times over the years but still couldn't really see it. Nevertheless, a calmer approach was called for.

'Aye, is it a problem?'

'N..n..n..no, sorry, just an observation.'

'Ok, can you tell me how you knew Sarah?'

'I'm her agent..em.... was her agent, for around five years or so. I just can't believe this happened.'

McIntosh softened his waspish brogue. 'When did you last see or speak to Sarah?'

Still shivering, Greenwood's speech became steadier. 'Just under a week ago. We went to an event in the west end, some homeless charity appeal. Sarah thought charity events made her more appealing and likeable, as well as raising her profile.'

'Did she need to be more likeable?' McIntosh said.

Greenwood hesitated. 'Well…she had a reputation for upsetting people in the public eye.'

'Give me a for instance.'

'While she was a TV presenter, she interviewed the Irish actress Madeleine O'Connor. It didn't go well, developed into an argument. Last year, on the radio, she was asked who her worst ever interviewee was. Of course, she said O'Connor and went into a rant. O'Connor responded on Twitter and the spat lasted for days. Sarah didn't know how to let things go.'

'She wasn't shy about letting people know what she thought of them?'

Greenwood smiled. 'That's an understatement. But the general public seemed to like her fine.'

'Because they didn't know her very well?'

'Possibly,' Greenwood said, miserably.

'Did you normally go to events with her?'

'Since her divorce. Before that she would go with her husband or other celebrity pals.'

'When did she get divorced?'

'About two years ago.'

'Was it a happy marriage?'

'Not really, volatile for as long as I knew them together. Mostly screaming and shouting, nothing physical I was aware of. They both suspected the other of having an affair.'

'Were they?'

'I honestly don't know. Sarah flirted a lot with famous, handsome men. It wouldn't have taken much for her to stray. If she did, she didn't tell me. I couldn't tell you about David.'

'The ex-husband?'

'Yes, David Blain.'

'So he escaped as well, eh? Do you have his contact details?

McIntosh's attempt at humour was lost on Greenwood. 'Not on me, it's in Sarah's personnel file. There's no one in the office yet but I'll get it as soon as I can. This surely couldn't be David?'

McIntosh shrugged. 'You know him better than me. Let's see what he says. One last thing Mr Greenwood. Where were you last night?'

'I had dinner with my wife and son around 6ish, then out at 7.30 to collect my daughter from studying at a friend's house. Then home again for the rest of the night.'

'Ok, remember to call me with David Blain's number.'

'I will,' Greenwood said, dejectedly shuffling away.

Chapter 6

The Elite Investigations Unit answered directly to the Specialist Crime Commander and operated out of a suite of offices on the first floor of Charing Cross police station. The name referred to the status of the crime. If the victim, or perpetrator, was front page newsworthy the EIU got the shout.

In 2018, faced with what seemed like a wave of crimes against celebrities living in London, the Met decided to establish a unit dedicated to investigating said crimes. Inspector Angus McIntosh was promoted back to Chief Inspector and became the unit's first SIO.

He deliberately chose a small, loyal band of detectives and handpicked his team on the word of several trusted sources despite never having met or worked with any of them. To date there had been no changes in personnel, aside from additional support as and when.

It's two junior members, DC's Glenn Myers and Joanne Findlay were busy scouring CCTV cameras around the area where Sarah lived. Their desks faced each other, a dividing partition purporting an element of privacy. Being the younger generation, any inexperience was offset by energy and enthusiasm. They brought different qualities to the team, consistently impressing their boss.

'Fancy a drink later?' Myers said.

'Not a good idea Glenn.'

'Just a drink. As friends. No need to make a big deal about it.'

An attractive, petite brunette with close cropped hair, Findlay knew Myers liked her but she discouraged him as often as she could. He was a handsome, genuine guy and, in different circumstances, she might have been interested in his athletic body but her private life played second fiddle to her career and she knew a friendly drink could lead in a direction she didn't want to go. 'I just don't want to get involved,' she said, picking up the phone.

Before Myers could respond, McIntosh, Bayford and Walton strode into the open plan squad room, takeaway coffee's in hand, discussing the morning's developments.

'What did you make of the agent boss?' Bayford said.

'Flustered, but to be fair, his client had been brutally murdered. Glenn, speak to his wife and check his alibi,' McIntosh said, handing Myers a piece of paper.

'Ok, do we have a time of death?'

Bayford interjected. 'No, should find out later today. We'll get the forensics report as well but I'm not expecting much. I've seen sterilised operating theatres dirtier than that crime scene.'

'Any further info on the ex-husband?' McIntosh said.

'I asked Joanne to locate him,' Walton said, glancing at the young DC speaking on the phone, an animated expression spreading across her face.

Findlay ended her call. 'You'll never believe this boss, he's missing. That was his girlfriend. He disappeared last night and she hasn't seen or heard from him since.'

'Right, first things first. Take a statement from the girlfriend. Find out where he hangs out, who he meets, is it normal for him to stay out all night. We need to find this guy. Did he kill Sarah before going into hiding or is he another victim?'

***

McIntosh slouched in his swivel chair, the bespoke lumbar support trying, and failing, to mould itself to his position. Hands interlocked behind his head, he closed his eyes and breathed deeply. His ten-foot by ten-foot office had white painted plasterboard walls on three sides and a clear, acrylic Perspex window on the other, overlooking the squad room. A small bookshelf and a hard wooden chair completed the furniture, apart from a roller blind for privacy.

He purposely chose the smallest office. The incident and meeting rooms were both larger but he never actively welcomed too many visitors. Harder to get rid of.

However, the small space suddenly felt claustrophobic.

Subconsciously, he headed downstairs towards the evidence room. Carl Stanley, the young duty PC, clocked him coming and immediately stiffened. He hadn't seen a DCI here before. They normally sent a lackey to do their dirty work.

In his mid-twenties and relatively inexperienced, Stanley only had two years on the job and despite a reputation as diligent and conscientious, most of them had been spent carrying out humdrum tasks upstairs or stood behind this cheap wooden counter with a glass frame and a small opening. During his first six months on the street, he'd routinely questioned a suspect in a violent house invasion, believed his story and unwittingly sent him on his way. Later, undisputed proof of the man's guilt was found but, by then, he was in the wind. A warrant for his arrest was still outstanding but the man was a ghost and Stanley carried the heavy burden on his back.

Keen to make a better impression but never getting the chance, he wondered if he was cut out for this line of work. If not for the uniform, he could have doubled as a bank teller. Maybe a better option? McIntosh sensed Stanley's unease and realised, despite his own crusty mood, he'd need the friendly approach.

'Morning Carl, how are you today?' he said, brightly.

'Yeah, fine thanks sir, everything ok? It's not often we see you here,' Stanley said, inwardly shitting himself.

'Aye, need to check some details on the Johnson case. The CPS have asked a question and I need to make sure what we have matches their requirement. The rest of the team are busy.'

'Ok sir, you need to sign in and I'm supposed to accompany you.'

'Hardly necessary Carl, what do you think I plan to do?' McIntosh said, with a level tone.

'Nothing sir, obviously. Just procedure. Don't want to get into trouble.'

'Ok Carl, whatever.'

McIntosh knew the procedures well but if he ended up doing this for real, he planned on being alone.

The large, airless evidence room had a musty scent of old paperwork. The rickety wooden door and antiquated ceiling downlighters practically touched the stacked boxes and suggested an operation indifferent to recent technological advances. Despite the uninviting ambience, he could see a system in place and prayed the fresh cases were the most accessible. A bored Stanley gazed at anything other than what McIntosh was doing and was oblivious to the audible sigh of relief at finding the relevant case box at floor level.

'Will you need much longer sir? I shouldn't leave the desk unmanned for too long.'

'A minute or two Carl, just double checking a couple of things.' McIntosh produced an old CPS headed letter he'd found lying in his office. He'd already spotted the evidence he was interested in but continued to poke around, occasionally grunting while looking at the meaningless letter. Eventually he let out a satisfied nod.

'Ok Carl, I'm done.'

'Everything in order sir?'

'Seems to be, you know what the CPS are like. Everything needs double and triple checked before they'll set foot in a courtroom.'

'Yes sir, very pedantic but better safe than sorry,' Stanley said, ignorant to the workings of the CPS.

'Thanks for your time Carl, have a good shift.'

'Thanks sir.'

McIntosh ambled back to his office, a little happier than when he'd left twenty minutes before. If he needed to, stealing evidence was doable if he got a minute alone. He had to conceive a plan to make it happen.

Concern turned to Amanda. Nearly 10.30 am and he hadn't heard a thing apart from three missed calls from a clearly panicking Debbie. He'd give it another half hour.

He made himself a coffee and returned to slouching in his chair, unable to concentrate. He sipped away, staring blankly until his phone pinged at exactly 10.58am.

'lock ups longton terrace 11.30 dont be early'

Chapter 7

He checked Google Maps before grabbing his jacket and heading to Elephant and Castle. He wouldn't contact Debbie till he had Amanda back. Nothing to be gained except earache.

It was a straight road, over Waterloo Bridge and joining London Road but it was a fraught journey, not helped by a moron who'd lost his indicators, jumped red lights and constantly switched lanes but he barely noticed the several angry horn blasts aimed in his direction.

At 11.32 he drove slowly along a quiet Longton Terrace. Deserted, except for two open lock ups, one a mechanics workshop, the other being loaded with boxes from a small panelled van. The two men unloading the van stopped and pretended to chat as he drove by, hiding the boxes from sight. Illegal activity? He didn't care. There were no other vehicles.

He reached the end of the road, turned around and parked. On cue, his phone buzzed.

'Go to 22A. Door is unlocked'

He drove a hundred yards, getting dirty looks from the dodgy guys at the van and parked outside Unit 22A. It's metal roller shutter and old, side hinged timber door were both closed. He snapped on a pair of disposable gloves. Better safe than sorry. The side door was unlocked and he cautiously stepped into a sea of blackness.

Unable to see his hand in front of his face he brushed the side wall, feeling around until he found a switch. It was connected to a fluorescent tube fixed to a ceiling joist. Although the dim light barely lifted the murky gloom, the large rectangular space was empty except for two blindfolded figures rigidly standing against the back wall, like prisoners waiting for a firing squad.

The temptation to shout to his daughter was strong but he resisted, fearing an ambush. There were two recesses where shadowy dark clothed assassins could easily have been lurking in wait. Jesus, was he getting paranoid or what. He checked them out. No assassins. When he felt confident enough he hollered. 'Amanda, it's me!'

'DAD!'

McIntosh removed the blindfolds and untied the young couple's hands before hugging his daughter. Seeing her father opened the floodgates and the pretty, dark haired teenager clung to his arm while Lucas's top lip began trembling. McIntosh put his arms round both teenagers and led them from the lock-up.

They stood on the pavement outside the empty unit, trying to adjust their eyes to the brightness. Amanda wouldn't let go of her father, while Lucas attempted to control his lip and show some bravado. McIntosh stifled a smile. 'What happened after I saw you last night?' he said.

'Nothing much. They gave us some food but nobody really spoke to us. We tried to sleep but it wasn't easy.' Amanda said.

'What about this morning?'

'They tied our hands, blindfolded us again, and put us in a car. When it stopped they shoved us in there and told us to stand and wait, without speaking. We didn't know if anyone else was there so we've been silent for about half an hour.'

'Aye, sorry I got stuck in traffic.' He looked up the road and the van was gone. Probably Terry's boys.

'What's going on, tell me the truth.'

'It's complicated, I'll take you home and explain it there. Get in the car and call mum, let her know you're ok. I need a quick word with Lucas.'

He studied the young lad in front of him. Late teens, a bit scrawny with unwashed bleached blonde hair and an unkempt demeanour. He tried to figure out if that was the prisoner look or his normal appearance, or was McIntosh just getting old. Shite, he was subconsciously assessing if this laddie was good enough for his daughter.

Lucas sensed the evaluation and looked more terrified than when he was tied up but he managed to whisper. 'I don't understand any of this Mr McIntosh.'

'Aye son, I know. I'm really sorry you've been caught up in this. You were just in the wrong place. You're not in any danger but I need to say something really important. You can't tell your mum and dad what happened.'

'Why not?' he said, indignantly.

'Your parents would likely get the police involved, which would be understandable, but it would put Amanda's life in danger.'

'But you are the police!'

'I know son, but in this case I'm just another member of the public trying to keep his family safe. Once it's over, I'll explain the situation to your parents and tell them how you helped Amanda. For now, I need you to promise you'll keep this to yourself.'

Lucas pondered for a few seconds. 'Ok, I suppose so, just for Amanda though. I want to make sure she's safe.'

'Good man. Now get in and I'll take you home,' he said, envisaging a situation where he might have to actually like this laddie.

***

After dropping Lucas at a spectacular mock Tudor house in Ealing, the McIntosh's returned home. Mother and daughter embraced in a warm tearful hug. McIntosh made tea while Amanda told her mother the whole story. After more tears and hugging, Amanda ran upstairs to jump in the shower.

'She looks pale. That's taken a lot out of her,' Debbie said.

'She's always pale. She'll be fine.'

'I don't know Mac, I'm worried about her.'

'I know, let me try and sort it.'

'When will you speak to Lucas's parents?' Debbie said.

'Hopefully never!'

Debbie eyed him suspiciously. 'Mac, you can't not tell them. That's out of order, even for you.'

'I spoke to the laddie, told him to keep schtum. If they know now it'll get blown out of proportion. Once it gets sorted, I might conveniently forget to tell them.'

'Christ, I hope you know what you're doing?'

Me too, McIntosh thought.

Chapter 8

Glenn Myers walked into the squad room and dumped a load of first edition newspapers on a desk. 'They're having a field day,' he said.

'TV'S SARAH SLAIN!' the Sun emblazoned on its front page. The sub-heading read, *'TV show curse strikes again!'*

'EXECUTED ON HER DOORSTEP' was the Mirror's offering. *'TV and radio presenter stabbed to death.'*

The Star went with 'SARAH STABBED THROUGH THE HEART'

The more reserved broadsheets stated the facts as they knew them, leaving the wild speculation to the tabloids.

'What did you expect?' Findlay said. 'It's pretty respectful just now but wait until the conspiracy theories start emerging and they hear about the ex-husband.'

'What's this about a curse?' McIntosh said.

'The Sun is reporting that Sarah is the third dead celebrity from a reality TV show. The other two were an accident and a suicide,' Myers said.

'Check it out, find out if there's a connection,' McIntosh said.

Commander Jonathan Beswick walked into the squad room and the chatter evaporated. The stylish Saville Row suit and shiny brown leather Oxfords did not complement his dark thinning hair and creepy eyes. 'I see you've all seen the papers. DCI McIntosh, can I have a word in your office?'

Beswick sat in the spare uncomfortable chair. McIntosh loathed the man. Beswick's only commitment was to achieving his own career goals. He had zero interest in supporting his fellow officers. The rank and file universally despised him.

He and McIntosh had previous.

'I shouldn't need to tell you about the pressure from above. The DAC is already on my case about the press,' Beswick said.

'No sir. I take it we'll be getting additional resources?'

'You'll get whatever you need, just don't fuck this one up.'

McIntosh bristled and silently counted to ten. 'We didn't fuck anything up. We solved the case and got a result. There's an upcoming trial, in case you've forgotten.'

'A man died!'

'He was one of the armed gang!' McIntosh's voice got louder, couldn't help himself. 'He was posing as a FUCKIN SECURITY GUARD.'

'NO ONE WAS MEANT TO DIE. As SIO it was your responsibility. You planned it badly and cost a man his life,' Beswick said, storming out.

McIntosh closed his eyes, massaged his forehead and breathed deeply. More than anyone in the world, that man could rub him the wrong way. Seven years earlier, while at Islington, he'd loudly and publicly insulted Beswick, then a Chief Superintendent, resulting in subsequent demotion back to Detective Inspector.

After a transfer to Wood Green he quietly worked away for four years before regaining the DCI rank, coinciding with an invitation to lead a new Central London task force, specifically created to deal with crimes involving celebrities.

His new team gelled quickly and was busier than McIntosh expected but it was a breath of fresh air. He was given a freedom to make decisions, without constantly looking over his shoulder.

However, good things never last and his freedom and the unit's growing acclaim was shattered when Jonathan Beswick, the ultimate arse kisser, and his arch nemesis, acquired promotion to Specialist Crime Commander, thus resuming their fragile relationship.

'Simon, you got a minute?' McIntosh shouted.

Bayford sat, sipping tea. 'Beswick being his usual self?'

'Aye, times a hundred. He's a tosser who'd have no problem dismantling our team, just to get one over on me again. We cannae give him the satisfaction.'

'We've got extra bodies coming tomorrow. A DS from Hammersmith and two DC's from Notting Hill.'

'Do we know them?'

'New to me, DS Chris Dolan and DC's Stuart Strong and Kelly Arnott. Heard of them?'

'No, ask around, see if anyone knows them.'

'Ok boss,' Bayford made to leave.

Acting on instinct, McIntosh decided to take a punt. He wouldn't call Simon Bayford a friend. He didn't claim to know much about him as a person apart from being a Northern lad who lived in Wood Green with his wife Rachel. Oh, and he was a tall, good looking bugger and a great detective who's calming influence rubbed off on him…sometimes. Bayford came highly recommended from a Sergeant at Islington who'd seen his work at close quarters. McIntosh trusted him implicitly.

'One last thing Simon,' McIntosh breathed deeply. 'Shut the door, I've something to tell you and it doesnae leave this room.'

Bayford nodded solemnly.

'My daughter and her friend were kidnapped yesterday. They were tied up and blindfolded but released this morning, unharmed.'

Bayford sat open-mouthed. 'Jesus Christ, what's going on?'

'Terry Johnson. He wants me to do something for him. Kidnapping Amanda was a stunt to let me know how easily he can get to my family. Taking the laddie was a blunder. He's nothing to do with this.'

'Fucking hell, what does he want you to do?'

'Destroy the evidence against Matthew.'

'Shit, you have to tell Beswick.'

'No chance. D'ye think he'd be on my side? No-one outside this room knows and it stays like that. Understand?'

Bayford nodded, 'Sure boss, whatever you want.'

'Thanks, at least till I devise a plan. If I go AWOL, cover for me. I'll try and keep you in the loop but we've got this fucking murder to contend with so you might have to be in charge more than usual.'

'No worries boss, I'll handle it. I thought you were a bit off this morning. That explains it.'

'Aye I know. I had other things on my mind and, for the record, I did get dressed in the dark and, believe it or no', I wasnae worried about my appearance.'

Bayford shrugged. 'Don't know what you're talking about. I thought you looked the same as normal.'

'Cheeky bastard!'

Chapter 9

Ten minutes later McIntosh addressed his team. 'We're getting three warm bodies tomorrow but until then, tell me what've we got so far?'

Myers spoke first. 'I've made a couple of calls regarding the TV show. It was called Island Wars. The other dead celebrities are Andrew Harvey and Ben Edwards. Harvey was a newsreader who drowned in a Majorcan swimming pool last month, apparently on holiday with his gay lover. Edwards was an ex footballer. He committed suicide a few weeks ago.'

'Jesus, I remember that on the news,' Walton said. 'I didn't know they were on the same show.'

'I've put a call into the show's producer, Peter Robson. Hopefully he'll give us some background,' Myers added.

'Good,' McIntosh said. 'If the show's a dead end let's quickly rule it out. What did we get from David Blain's girlfriend?'

'Not a lot boss,' Findlay said. 'Went out late on Wednesday. Didn't tell her where he was going. Never came back.'

'Was that normal behaviour?' McIntosh asked.

'He's been known to go missing from time to time. He's a serious poker player. She assumed it turned into an all-nighter. I asked her to call as soon as he gets home.'

'Anything else?' McIntosh asked the group, who responded with shaking heads.

'I'm going over to pathology,' Bayford added.

'I'll come with you,' McIntosh said. 'See what our friend Evelyn has to say. If we don't get something soon these new bodies will be sitting around scratching their arses.'

***

'Good to see you detectives,' Evelyn Marsh said. 'I wondered when you'd put in an appearance, Chief Inspector.'

McIntosh thought she looked smaller behind her desk. Maybe his imagination. She certainly looked bushed. Maybe the early start after a heavy night? He knew she liked a tipple. You can take the woman out of Scotland....

'Couldnae stay away too long Evelyn. Anything of note?'

'Not a lot you don't already know. Cause of death was a single stab wound to the heart. Probably a serrated kitchen knife, about six inches long. No other wounds or abrasions. No fingernail marks so there didn't appear to be a struggle. It's not my job but if I was guessing, I'd say she opened the door and someone immediately plunged a knife into her.'

'What about time of death?' Bayford asked.

'Between 7-9pm on Wednesday evening.'

'Thanks Evelyn, anything else?' McIntosh said.

'We've got plenty of blood and fibres to analyse but I wouldn't raise my hopes. Apart from around the body, the crime scene was spotless which means the killer took care to cover their tracks. Why do that if you're gonnae casually leave DNA evidence behind. Just my thoughts.'

'Aye, thanks for cheering me up. Let us know when you've finished your report.'

'Aye, will do. I'll get Kareena to speed up the analysis.'

McIntosh was worried about the lack of evidence, Beswick's warning ringing in his ears.

Chapter 10

June 2021 - Greek island of Falkonos

The blue, cloudless skies, inviting turquoise shaded water and unspoilt sandy beaches made it an idyllic setting. Being a protected conservation area, few people were allowed to visit the island. It was situated halfway between the mainland and the largest island of Crete. Several weeks of persuasion and a couple of hefty brown envelopes eventually managed to seduce the Greeks into granting permission to film.

As a pair of speed boats loudly approached, two men stood on the beach wearing Hawaiian style shirts and aviator sunglasses. The boats stopped fifty metres from shore and eight nervous people jumped waist deep into the water, catching their breath. As they waded through the clear water and reached the golden sand, worried grimaces replaced the forced smiles from the boat. Soaking wet and numbingly cold, they looked at each other wondering what they'd gotten themselves into. The two men stifled grins.

'We've got a right bunch of misfits here Dave,' Peter Robson said.

'That would be your fault,' David Gill replied. Robson and Gill were the executive and assistant producers of Third Eye Productions.

The men watched as the presenter, Charlotte Parrish, made a grand entrance and stood in front of the eight people, now formed into two teams. She shimmered in a long flowery summer dress and sandals and suppressed a smile at the bedraggled group in front of her.

'Celebrities, welcome to Island Wars. In a week's time one team will win one million pounds to share between their chosen charities, the losing team will leave with nothing. Good Luck.'

'Bitch!' mumbled a contestant, under her breath.

Despite their spectacular surroundings the celebrities' initial enthusiasm soon dissipated as they understood what lay ahead. Within thirty minutes Sarah O'Neill's misery became palpable. 'Who the fuck does he think he is?' she said to Catherine Collins. 'This is meant to be fun and he's acting like a sergeant major.'

'We voted him team leader,' Catherine said.

'Yeah leader, not God-allfuckingmighty. He's strutting around barking orders and doing nothing. I doubt if he's done a fucking day's work in his life.'

The teams had to bolt thick timber struts and posts together to form the shell of the small structure which would act as their temporary home. Lightweight polycarbonate sheeting acted as a glass substitute. A simple construction, but designed to require input from the whole team. The set-up of the whole competition was designed with the premise of teamwork in mind.

'Magnus, stop strolling around and come and help. Electing you team leader did not give you a free hand to do fuck all,' Sarah shouted loudly.

'Don't speak to me like that.'

'Well, get your finger out, do some work and we'll get on fine.'

A TV and radio presenter, Sarah was used to getting her own way. With her superior attitude she'd perceived herself as the natural leader of this motley bunch but the rest of Team Alpha disagreed, imagining an MP would make a better captain.

However, Magnus Branch, disgraced former shadow Minister for Health, now reinvented as a darling of the TV panel show, was no ordinary MP.

Two hours later, temporary home built, they received basic ingredients to prepare their first meal. Catherine, a comedienne, assumed the role of chef, assisted by Sarah.

'If that fat little bastard says anything negative about this food I'll ram it down his throat till it comes out his arse,' Sarah said.

Catherine laughed. 'Scary thing is, I know you mean it. I wanted to ask. On the beach I heard you mutter 'bitch' when Charlotte was talking. What's that all about?'

Sarah looked embarrassed. 'Ah, you heard that? Just me being petty. She got the presenting job over me. This is a kind of second prize because they felt sorry for me. For years we've had an ongoing competition for presenting work and with me having taken a step back, lately she's been winning a lot.'

'But now you get to win a huge amount for charity.'

'Yeah, I suppose,' Sarah said, thinking about the fee Charlotte had negotiated for herself.

'How's the radio presenting business?'

'Yeah, it's ok. I prefer TV but I needed a break. Hopefully I'll get into it again soon. This would've been the first in a while. What about you? Stand up must be a tough gig?'

Catherine smiled inwardly. She'd heard Sarah could be a real cow that no-one wanted to work with and she was 'made' to take a break. 'It is tough. There's a lot of competition for little work but it's worth it. I'm getting more TV appearances and it's now about staying in the spotlight.'

Magnus and Guy Ekers chatted out of earshot as the girls prepared the food. They sat on a makeshift bench using spare polycarbonate placed between two rocks. 'That Sarah's a right pain in the arse isn't she?' Magnus said. 'She'd better stop speaking to me like that or she'll regret it.'

'But you could've done more work instead of strutting around trying to be the big man in charge,' Guy replied.

'Still, the way she spoke to me......' Magnus's face turned a shade of purple, 'the last person..........'

Guy raised his eyebrows

'........ doesn't matter. What about you, singer in a band I hear?'

'Used to be, recently done some solo stuff but mainly trying to earn a living doing shit like this.'

'Twenty grand for a week's work isn't too bad.'

'Drop in the ocean, the amount of money I owe.'

The wheels in Magnus's head started turning. 'I might be able to help you out.'

Guy raised his eyebrows. 'Doing something illegal?' he said, remembering Magnus's past indiscretions. 'Insider trading wasn't it?'

'Nothing was proven. I resigned to avoid further embarrassment to the party.'

'Sounds like a line you've trotted out a million times.'

'You're one to talk, if what I hear is true. Anyway, I might be able to help but this isn't the time or place. Once it's over we'll get together and have a proper chat.'

Chapter 11

Half a mile away, Team Bravo had also unwittingly elected an overbearing bully as leader. Television newsreader Andrew Harvey appeared cool, calm and collected behind a desk, but hid a ferocious temper, currently being tested to the limit.

'How difficult is it to hold the post straight?' he screamed at Natasha Cook, a twenty-four-year-old part time model and reality dating show contestant.

'I'm doing my best,' she uttered inadequately. 'If you stop screaming for one minute I'll get on better.'

'Andrew, you're out of order,' Ben Edwards said. 'If the rest of the week's going to be like this I'm off now.' The ex-footballer, now TV and radio pundit, dropped his timber post and walked away.

Emily Dean ran after him. Twenty-six years old, she appeared in daytime TV soap, The Tower. 'Ben, please come back. He's acting like a prick but if we sort it out now the rest of the week will be easier.'

'A quarter of a million for my charity is mind blowing, but it's not worth it if I want to kill myself before the week's over.'

'Play your cards right and we'll win, kill Andrew and take 333 grand each,' Emily said, smiling.

Ben laughed hard and agreed to give Andrew another chance.
'Andrew, Natasha, can you come over here please,' he shouted.

'We're busy,' Andrew said. 'If you've recovered from your little tantrum can you get a move on, we're losing daylight.'

Natasha let her post fall and walked over to Emily and Ben, making Andrew nearly fall off the ladder. He started to shout 'What the fu...'

'Get over here,' Ben yelled, 'NOW!'

Andrew slowly mooched over, evil in his eyes. 'Is this a mutiny?'

'Maybe. You need to start showing some respect, otherwise you might need to keep one eye open during the night.'

'Sounds like a threat.'

'No a joke, at the moment, but you need to reign it in. Big money is at stake here. A third of a million each for charity is huge.'

Andrew groaned. What did they say about thick footballers? 'It's a quarter of a million each, actually.'

Emily and Ben exchanged a smirk.

After dinner Andrew apologised to Natasha before seeking out Emily. 'I'm sorry about earlier. I get too competitive and easily lose my temper. I've said sorry to Natasha as well.'

'Being competitive is great but not if your own team wants to feed you to the sharks,' Emily said.

Andrew sighed. 'My temper's difficult to control. I've lost count of the times my wife's threatened to leave me.'

'Why's that?' Emily said, hesitantly.

'I scream and shout a lot. It upsets the kids. I've tried anger management but it didn't work. Neither has therapy. I've got to try and deal with it myself.'

'Well, hopefully we'll last the week without killing each other.'

Before bedtime, Emily and Natasha found a quiet spot for a chat. 'Saw you deep in convo with Andrew,' Natasha said. 'Were you listening to him complain about being unable to get laid in a men's toilet without being recognised?'

'What are you talking about?' Emily said.

'A reason for his anger issues.'

'He's married with kids.'

'NO WAY!'

'He told me, said he was forever screaming and shouting at his wife and kids. He's done anger management and therapy, all sorts.'

'Therapy for something else maybe. That man is as gay as the day is long.'

'I told you, he is married.'

'Maybe he's not out of the closet yet, but I'll bet my twenty grand fee Andrew Harvey's as bent as a nine-pound note.'

Chapter 12

October 2021

A shortish, chunky man with unwashed curly hair swaggered into the squad room like he owned the place, his creased suit, crumpled shirt and hanging tie at odds with the Adonis like image created in his own mind.

'So this is the high rollers hideout,' he said, loudly.

'You must be Stuart Strong,' Myers said. His mate at Notting Hill had filled him in.

'The very same, how did you know?' Strong said.

'Wild guess,' Myers replied. 'Sleep in your car did you?'

'Didn't manage home last night,' Strong said, winking. 'Heard you couldn't cope and needed expert reinforcements.'

'Cocky bastard,' Findlay mumbled under her breath.

'No, it's all under control but we do need someone for the menial tasks and heard you'd be perfect for the job,' Myers said.

Strong didn't bite. 'I'm game for anything me, just tell me where to start.'

DS Chris Dolan and DC Kelly Arnott also arrived and introduced themselves without fanfare. Heavy set with a worldly wise face, Dolan didn't look like someone you wanted to mess with while Arnott's piercing blue eyes darted between faces before the pretty blonde locked onto Joanne Findlay. She walked over.

'Watch yourself with him,' Arnott whispered, with a nod towards Strong. 'He's an arsehole. He won't stab you in the back, he'll come out and say it right to your face. He's dangerous and cuts corners. Don't be around when he fucks up or he'll take you with him. I lost count of the reprimands.'

'*When* he fucks up?'

'Hundred percent. Just don't be there when it happens.'

'Thanks for the warning,' Findlay said. 'Anything else?'

'He'll try it on with you, no doubt. He thinks he's God's gift.'

'He'll not get far with me.'

'Good, don't let him anywhere near you. I wanted to come here and be rid of him. Maybe make a fresh start. But that's not happening.'

Before Findlay could reply, McIntosh and Bayford entered.

'I trust everyone has been introduced. If not, do it later,' McIntosh said. 'As you know forensics have established a time of death between 7-9pm on Wednesday evening. They've estimated a probable height of the killer based on the entry angle of the knife. Somewhere between five foot seven and five foot ten inches tall. So, a fairly tall woman or an average man. Not much to go on but narrows it a bit. Forensics also found a mix of DNA from the house. Nothing directly relating to the killing but may be useful if we can match it. We need Sarah's movements on the day she died. Her driver, Trevor Broad usually drove her home after work. Was it a typical day or did he drop her somewhere on the way home. Check him out. Sarah's ex got in touch. David Blain claims he attended an all-night poker game in South London. Check his alibi, lets rule him out quickly, if we can.'

His eyes locked on to Stuart Strong. 'Laddie, if you want to be part of this team you cannae come to work looking like a dog's dinner. I'll no' let you conduct interviews smelling like a tramp in a doorway. You might get away wi' that at Notting Hill but here you'll be oot on your arse pronto. Understand?'

Strong nodded, his eyes meeting the floor. Arnott's smile was wide and beaming.

'Right, let's get to it'

Chapter 13

Glenn Myers met Peter Robson on the eighth floor of a Great Portland Street tower block. As he gave it the once over, Myers guessed the money spent on rent for the fancy Central London location left little for decent furnishings. The drab office space of Third Eye Productions consisted of a reception area with a curved white desk and grey metallic counter top. A small open plan space contained ten rectangular cantilever desks set face to face. Five employees tapped away at their computers, the other workspaces presumably used for employees returning from being on set. The men sat in Robson's office, at the head of a corridor, facing reception.

'Thanks for seeing me Mr Robson. If you don't mind me saying, you look young to be in charge of a TV production company.'

Robson shrugged. 'Right place, right time I suppose. It's a newish company. Doing well, at least we were,' he said, ruefully.

Myers studied the tall, blonde haired man, probably early thirties, his hard chiselled features suggesting a Scandinavian or Germanic origin, but speaking with an unmistakeably Essex accent. 'I assume you've heard about Sarah O'Neill?'

'Yes, tragic, she was a nice girl.'

'Really? We've heard differently.'

Robson hesitated, 'Well, no, not really, trying to be kind you know. She was difficult, needy, loud, annoying...you want me to go on?'

Myers smiled. 'Later, can you give me some background of the show?'

'The idea was to create a unique show. Celebrity teams in an unfamiliar setting, taking on challenges requiring total teamwork and physical and mental toughness.'

'I've seen these types of shows plenty of times.'

'True, but not for the cash on offer. One million pounds.'

'Wow! Why such a huge amount?'

'We wanted to make it more serious, not so celebrity, if you know what I mean. We hoped the money would keep them focussed and it wouldn't be all hugs and air kisses like other celebrity shows.'

'Did it work?'

Robson shook his head, 'Oh, there were no hugs and kisses all right but they were an absolute nightmare, every one of them. Constantly bickering, even some violence.'

'A lot of these celebrity shows are friends for life, swapping phone numbers and let's meet up when we get home. Do you think the money provoked their behaviour?'

'I wish I could say it did but I don't think so. It would have been the same, prize money or not. It became so bad we're not allowed to air the show.'

'How come?'

'Too many potential lawsuits from celebrities being shown in a bad light. Our lawyers didn't think it was worth the risk.'

'Did the prize money still get paid?'

Robson nodded glumly, 'Yes, we had to honour the contract and lost a fortune.'

'Did the cameras follow them twenty-four seven?'

Robson shook his head. 'Impossible, despite what other shows imply. Crews filmed during challenges but on a deserted Greek island we couldn't follow them everywhere. We didn't have enough resources.'

'Can we have a copy of the tapes please,' Myers asked.

'Of course, it'll be an eye-opener but I doubt you'll find anything relevant.'

'Thanks, can you tell me a little bit about the celebrities.'

'Magnus and Andrew were nasty people. So was Sarah but she seemed to turn it on and off. Magnus and Sarah detested each other. The others kept to themselves. Guy Ekers's drug and alcohol withdrawals left him struggling. In hindsight it was a mistake to sign him up. Ben Edwards wanted to leave on day one. Natasha, Catherine and Emily, probably the same. I imagine only the money kept them there. We had incidents of cheating, violence and serious injury.'

'Sounds like it would have been a cracking show.'

Robson smiled. 'You'll see for yourself but for all the wrong reasons.'

'Going back to the celebrities, what did you mean by Magnus and Andrew being nasty and Sarah turning it on?'

'I don't know, the two guys struck me as genuinely horrible people and behaved like they would any other day of the week. Sarah was more difficult to work out. At times she was a perfectly nice person but on other occasions she threw a tantrum if she didn't get her own way. A bit like Magnus and Andrew. I think all three are narcissists…were narcissists, oh you know what I mean.'

'You mentioned violence and injury?'

'Yes, someone clouted Sarah, knocking her unconscious. Andrew had a rock thrown at him, breaking his foot. We never caught the assailants.'

'Someone on the show?'

Robson nodded. 'It couldn't have been anyone else.'

'How did you feel when you heard about Andrew and Ben?'

'Shocked, obviously. Andrew didn't deserve that. An unpleasant, appalling man but still devastating. Ben must have been at the end of his tether. I only hope it had nothing to do with the show.'

'Did any of them meet up afterwards?'

'The after party. We re-united to celebrate,' he laughed sarcastically. 'They had to attend as part of their contract terms. It was held at Sarah's.'

Myers raised his eyebrows. 'Why?'

'Before the show started, Sarah offered and we thought it might be more cosy, plus it would save us paying for some fancy West End hotel. She certainly wouldn't have offered afterwards. Spooky, knowing it's where she got murdered.'

'How much did they get paid?'

'Twenty thousand each, flat fee. Small in comparison to other shows. The charity money was the main draw. We hoped for tough, fair competition which turned out to be wishful thinking.'

'You referred to cheating. What happened?'

'A map reading challenge. Magnus cheated by destroying a small bridge. It slowed the other team down and his team celebrated a win till we broke the news about the sabotage. It meant the other team came out on top. Magnus's team wanted to string him up, Sarah especially. Another time, he screamed at her and she pushed him from a raft, into the water,' Robson chuckled at the memory.

'You said Sarah was difficult and annoying. What did you mean?'

'As I said, she was narcissistic, continually craving attention, and she had no time for the others. Her and Magnus were a marriage made in hell. It should have made great telly but so much got cut and not enough remained to compile a show. Reputations were at stake so the show got shelved.'

'Had you worked with any of them before the show?'

'No, and I'll happily never see any of them again.'

'Anyone give you the impression they would be capable of murder?'

'All of them!' Robson smiled.

Chapter 14

The period of growth and regeneration being enjoyed by Brixton brought major capital investment to revitalise historic areas and buildings, new housing and community projects and improvements and upgrades to the retail sector.

Unfortunately, Dawson Avenue where Guy Ekers lived, did not benefit from any such progress. Resembling a Middle Eastern war zone, randomly abandoned cars smouldered amongst discarded mattresses and assorted furniture. The dirty, dilapidated rows of flats and terraced housing enjoyed many common features, likely omitted from the sales brochures, including peeling paint, loose guttering, stained walls and front gardens awash with broken white goods.

I like to do my homework. Guy's bleak, empty life guaranteed an undisturbed rendezvous as no sane person would ever dream of coming here to visit. If it wasn't the possibility of finding him in a drug addled state or alcohol stupor, the expectation of being caught in crossfire or subject to an arson attack might do it.

That didn't worry me.

Before killing Sarah, I'd contacted Guy about a dream investment proposal in which he didn't have to actually invest any money. He'd be the frontman of a construction development company's campaign with a tagline like.... *He turned his life around and so can you if you buy one of our ridiculously overpriced new houses.* He said it sounded too good to be true.

It was.

Dangling the prospect of a small percentage of sales for no investment, Guy would have been a fool to ignore it.

Except, of course, it was pure fiction.

His wife had disowned him and his bandmates sacked him after discovering he'd siphoned their cash to pay his drug debts. Now broke, living in a crummy Brixton flat, his alcoholism and drug habit out of control, I appealed to the thing closest to his heart.... cold hard cash.

I knocked and heard the shuffling of what sounded like an old man. A moment later Guy opened the door with a tentative forced smile. His scraggly brown hair matched his threadbare beard, and doleful hazel eyes depicted a man on a downer.

'Hi, it's good to see you,' he said miserably.

'You too.'

'Come in.'

I entered then politely avoided looking at the slum conditions all around. I stood aside to let him shuffle in front. The pungent aroma caught the back of my throat. I wasn't hanging around.

I whispered, 'Guy?' He turned and, without warning, I plunged a knife into his heart. For a second he looked at his chest, confused, then back at me, shock spreading across his face. He fell backwards, dead as he hit the floor.

The interior of the tiny pigsty matched the external look of the building so I refrained from a voyeuristic look through his personal effects, imagining the forthcoming forensic examination and what delights they may find.

Although the stench made my stomach heave, I couldn't rush, carefully executing the task at hand. After going through my change of clothes routine I took a brief moment to look at the state of what Guy's life had become.

It was difficult trying to picture Guy as a wealthy pop superstar, living a life beyond the ordinary person's comprehension. A couple of old photographs hung on the crumbling hallway wall and showed him in happier times. One with his arm around his wife, both smiling and the other on stage, with his band, at the height of their success. How did Guy feel when he looked at these?

Then I remembered he was dead and wondered how long it would take to find his body and if anyone would even notice the death smell amongst the constant reek of decay and acrid taste of smoke.

I strolled away, impossible to identify. Another early evening commuter, encased in warm clothes, face mask and headgear. On the way to Brixton tube station I saw another twenty people who looked just like me!

Chapter 15

June 2021

Magnus stood at the back of the inflatable raft, his face contorted in rage. 'Saraaaaaaah! What do you think you're doing?'

Sarah sat next to him and Guy and Catherine were seated at the other end of the boat. Sarah calmly turned to face him, her green eyes sparkling fiercely in the glare. 'The opposite to you, trying to win this task.'

'Stop questioning every instruction I give to you, do what you're told.'

Still calm, she said. 'You asked me to paddle twice as hard to compensate for you. I said, we're going round in circles because you're stood there doing fuck all.'

'I'm steering!'

'Steering us round in circles, you idiot.'

'Don't you dare call me that. I was a rower back in the day.'

Sarah laughed. 'Obviously a shit one.'

'Do what you're fucking told. I'M IN CHARGE.'

Now she cracked. She was only a couple of inches shorter than Magnus but rather than stand to confront him she grabbed her oar. With his left leg planted on the floor and the other perched on his seat, her gentle nudge saw him overbalance and fall backwards, creating an almighty splash. Catherine and Guy watched open-mouthed as Magnus floundered, gasping for breath, only his life jacket keeping him afloat.

Sarah and the others watched him thrash, trying to keep his head above water. No-one said a word. No-one jumped into the water to help. The crew boat sailing parallel, made no drastic rescue attempt, unhurriedly coasting towards the stricken MP.

Once he recovered from the initial panic and regulated his breathing, he screamed at the raft. 'Bitch, you're going to be sorry.'

The crew boat nonchalantly drifted alongside Magnus. 'Hurry up, get a fucking move on,' he said, gulping salty sea water.

The smiling four-man crew reluctantly hauled him aboard and laid him on his side. He wanted to shout at someone but his ragged breathing made it difficult. An oxygen mask was offered which he angrily swatted away.

After the fire in his lungs receded he said. 'I'll kill her.'

'No you won't,' Dave Gill said. 'She made you look like a prick and you're upset. Get yourself back on that raft and start playing nice or you'll lose every task and spoil everything.'

Magnus grudgingly re-joined Team Alpha's raft and sat in freezing silence, pulling his oar through the clear blue water with the rest of his teammates, avoiding eye contact with any of them. Ten minutes later, as a formality, they crossed the finish line to avoid receiving a penalty, a good fifteen minutes behind Team Bravo.

***

Despite the pledge to curb his behaviour, Andrew's tyrannical rule continued to unsettle Team Bravo and their winning celebrations didn't last long.

'I don't care about winning the money,' Natasha said. 'I'm not tolerating this any longer. If hiding in the closet is making him so obnoxious, I'm opening the door for him.'

'You can't walk away from this, you know you can't,' Emily said. 'Andrew's an arsehole but not just because he's gay and I'm not even sure I believe it.'

'Hold on a minute,' Ben said. 'Sounds like I'm late to the party. What's going on? Andrew's gay?'

'Natasha thinks he is, willing to bet her twenty grand fee on it,' Emily said.

'Look, it's a gift, one of my things. Gaydar or whatever they call it. Talking to someone for five minutes, I can tell if they're gay or not.'

'Wow, some gift. What University did you go to for that?' Ben said.

Natasha shrugged. 'No Uni, just natural ability. Andrew is gay. Unless he admits it and sorts out his behaviour, I'll do it for him.'

***

Next day, while his teammates slept, Andrew went for a quiet walk in the pleasant, early morning heat. Any later and it could get unbearable. Wearing just shorts and flip flops, the sun gleamed on his shiny, light brown head and slim toned torso. He headed inland to a lush, colourful landscape. The plentiful flowering plants and trees made him understand why the Greeks wanted this place to remain as an undisturbed conservation area. A great idea but not if no-one ever got to visit.

After a brisk ten minutes of solitude he sensed another presence behind him. He turned to find Natasha bearing down, no attempt to hide. She'd tied her long golden hair in a ponytail and wore a two-piece bikini which enhanced her ample cleavage. Andrew's obvious indifference didn't go unnoticed.

'You following me?' Andrew said.

'Wanted a quiet word, just you and me.' Natasha got uncomfortably close and he took a step back, his eyes at the perfect angle to look down her bikini top. He couldn't look less interested.

'About what?'

'Does your wife know?'

'Know what?'

'That you're gay.'

Andrew turned scarlet and spluttered, 'I don't know what you're talking about?'

'Don't deny it. I'm not listening to your tantrums anymore. Either being gay or hiding it is causing you to be a massive dick. If you don't acknowledge it, I will.'

'If you ever went public, I'd sue the arse off you.'

'You'd only win if it's not true and we both know it is.'

'You better watch your back.'

'Threats as well? Not a good idea. It's not just me, Ben and Emily also think you're a massive dickhead.'

'Do they know?'

'That you're gay? They know my suspicions and that sounded like an admission.'

Andrew went quiet and studied the grass for a long minute before whispering, 'I recognised the signs about ten years ago. My wife and I constantly argued and I always started it. We stopped sleeping together, drifted apart and led different lives.'

'Lots of couples drift apart, doesn't mean one of them is gay.'

'I started chatting to men on the internet and met a few of them. Coming out will ruin my career. You can't tell anyone.'

'I've no intention of telling a soul and I don't care if you're gay or straight but you're so fucking insufferable. It's affecting your life and, at the moment, ours.'

Andrew nodded, 'You're right, I promise I'll try. We better get back in case the other two think we're up to something.'

'That I doubt,' Natasha smiled.

***

The afternoon competition was a clash of individuals. Male v male and female v female. It didn't improve relationships.

During the climbing challenge, Ben's athleticism proved too much for Guy's addled state. Severe dehydration resulted in him requiring medical assistance. He was placed on a drip and Robson and Gill privately questioned if he would see out the week.

Magnus and Andrew's kayaking descended into farce, both intent on ramming each other with paddles, rather than race. With equal aggression on both sides, the producers left them to fight it out. A victorious Magnus reached the shore, hands aloft as a furious Andrew charged after him.

'You cheated again,' he raged.

'You hit me with your paddle first,' Magnus replied.

'You deliberately got too close, so you could interfere, otherwise I would've won by miles.'

'In your dreams pal, I rowed in the parliament team, I'd always kick your arse!'

Andrew's complaint to the producers fell on deaf ears. Still seething, he watched Sarah demolish Emily in the cross country running. Sarah won by a distance and Andrew blew a gasket. 'What the fuck……? You know this is a competition right, the idea is to beat your opponent?'

'I tried my best,' Emily said. *'But she's quicker than me.'*

'Quicker?' Andrew howled. *'Snails and tortoises overtook you.'*

Natasha stepped in. *'Andrew, remember?'* she said slyly.

He paused, mindful of Natasha's earlier veiled threat. He'd have to keep an eye on her. *'Well... I hate it when people don't try hard enough. It gets on my nerves.'*

'Emily did her best, it wasn't good enough, end of story,' Natasha said.

Andrew sneered. *'You're up next, let's see how you get on.'*

'Like Emily, I'll do my best but I'm not a great swimmer.'

True to her word, Natasha wasn't a great swimmer and Catherine won easily. Cold, wet and exhausted she squelched past Andrew, who'd watched with interest.

'Say one word and I'll break your fucking nose,' Natasha said.

Wisely, Andrew remained silent.

Team Alpha winning the challenge levelled the overall scores. Despite two of his teammates claiming victory in their individual battles, Magnus bathed in self-obsessed glory, recounting the tale of his triumph over Andrew to anyone within earshot. Sarah's disgust was evident.

'What's wrong with her?' Magnus said.

'You behaving like an arse again,' Guy replied. *'Everything revolves around you doesn't it.'*

'I beat Andrew which got us level. You weren't much help.'

'There you go again. I lost fair and square but Sarah and Catherine won and you've nothing to say about that. You won by borderline cheating again. You don't do anything fair or square do you?'

Magnus fumed. *'I didn't cheat. I defended myself. Andrew tried it on and I wasn't having it. If the rest of you listened to me this competition would be over by now.'*

'Give it a rest Magnus, we're all getting weary of you.'

'Remember Guy, stick with me and I'll see you all right.'

Without a word, Guy shook his head and slowly walked away. Magnus watched him go, thinking about the critical final day and the momentous weeks ahead.

Chapter 16

October 2021

McIntosh and Bayford chewed the fat over a Starbucks latte, bemoaning the lack of any tangible evidence, when the DCI's desk phone rang. He listened without speaking, before cupping the phone and whispering to Bayford, 'Simon, get everyone together - five minutes.'

He sat on an empty table, surrounded by his team. 'There's been another murder.' He resisted the temptation to growl that statement in typical Taggart fashion. 'A forty-year-old male named Guy Ekers, once a member of the band Foolish Ghost and latterly on the same Island show as Sarah O'Neill. Like Sarah, stabbed through the heart in his own Brixton flat. Body was found by a delivery driver as he put a 'sorry we missed you' card through his front door. Saw him lying on the floor. It's now our investigation.'

'Is that the Irish boyband from years ago?' Bayford said.

'Aye, so I believe.'

'I'd heard of the band but never knew any of their names.'

'Yeah, we believe you guv, bet you've got a secret stash of their albums,' Myers said, smiling.

Findlay raised her hand. 'Are we offering security to the remaining celebs?'

'Aye, possibly but let's try to find the connection. Look into the other deaths, Harvey and Edwards, in case something was missed. I want that show stripped bare. It's central to this case.'

'The big question is…. are we running a sweep on the next celeb to go?' Strong said.

Myers and Dolan laughed while Kelly Arnott said, 'That's disgusting.'

Strong spread his arms wide. 'It was a joke.'

'You're sick,' Arnott said.

McIntosh interrupted. 'That'll do.'

Strong shrugged but was pleased with himself. He'd worn a smarter suit, neatly knotted his tie and polished his shoes in the hope he could impress McIntosh and be more involved.

'Stuart and Glenn, get over to the murder scene, speak to the pathologist. Chris, Kelly, dig into Ekers life, see what he was up to before and after that show. Heather and Jo, arrange interviews with the remaining celebrities.'

'What about the Sarah investigation boss?' Walton asked.

'When we discover more about Ekers let's see how it ties to Sarah. We'll run them separately to start but I'd be amazed if it's not the same killer.'

At that moment Commander Beswick entered and everyone turned in his direction.

'Sorry, don't mind me,' Beswick said.

'We're just finished sir,' McIntosh replied. 'Do you want to say something?'

Beswick nodded, 'You all know how important this investigation is. Two celebrities murdered. These cases are precisely why this team exists. The media are all over it so we need a quick result. Failure means there's no point being here. I hope you all get my meaning.' Beswick kept calm and threatening at the same time. He nodded to McIntosh. 'A word in private.'

They disappeared into McIntosh's office. Beswick closed the door. 'Get your finger out, otherwise you'll be out of a job,' he said, without preamble.

'Aye, you'd love that, wouldn't you?'

Beswick smiled, 'It wouldn't be the worst but if you fuck up it reflects on me as well. What are you doing about Guy Ekers?'

'Interviews with the remaining contestants from the show, speaking to his family, friends and ex band mates.'

'What about security for the remaining celebrities?'

'A possibility but we want to establish a link between the murders.'

'Establish a link!' Beswick screamed. 'It's fucking obvious there's a link. Someone's killing celebrities.'

McIntosh heard Debbie's voice in his head and gave himself time. 'Aye, but how will it look if one of the celebrities is the killer and we've given them protection?'

'Don't be ridiculous, they're celebrities.'

McIntosh nearly choked. 'So, celebrities are incapable of murder? Are you for real?'

'Remember who you're speaking to, Chief Inspector,' Beswick spat out the last two words.

'It's my investigation sir. Get out and let me get on with it and, by the way, thanks for the words of support for the team.'

The sarcasm soared over Beswick's head. 'I swear, stop dithering or I'll have your head on a platter,' he said, storming out.

McIntosh closed his eyes. His family were a kidnapper's prey, some nutter was killing celebrities from a TV show and his boss would delight in disbanding his team and serving him up to the Commissioner and god knows who else. His eyes opened, hearing the sharp rap on his door.

'Beswick on your case again boss?' Bayford said.

'No more than usual Simon, how are the troops?' McIntosh said, nodding towards the squad room.

'A bit disheartened. Not much to get their teeth into. Hopefully this new one will throw us a nugget or two. You ok? You're looking tired. Still trying to sort out your other problem?'

'I'm not sleeping very well, too much going on but I'll be fine.'

Joanne Findlay knocked and burst in at the same time. 'Boss, we've had a call from the MP Magnus Branch. He's heard about Guy Ekers and thinks he might be in danger. Wondering what we're going to do about it.'

Chapter 17

Magnus Branch fidgeted uncontrollably in an interview room at Charing Cross station, sipping a cup of warm indeterminate liquid. His demand to be seen immediately fell on deaf ears before he went berserk, ended the call and jumped in a cab. The stumpy man bounced into reception and leant on the reception counter haranguing the duty Sergeant.

McIntosh didn't mind him coming in. Branch needed to be interviewed regardless. This way, he saved time and manpower. He'd heard about Branch's reputation and, without knowing much else about him, decided he didn't like him. He instructed the Sergeant to give him a cup of weak, horrible tea or coffee and an uncomfortable chair in the most oppressive interview room. A square, windowless space with no redeeming features. For no real reason, McIntosh then made him wait another twenty minutes.

McIntosh and Bayford breezed in, each carrying another Starbucks coffee, which looked and probably tasted a million times better than Branch's offering. His pock marked face and puffy eyes alluded to a man under stress. He continued to squirm, hands shaking as he held on to his tea.

'Hello Mr Branch, thanks for coming to see us. How can we help?' McIntosh said, brightly.

'You could have visited me or at least offered one of those rather than the piss you call tea,' Magnus said, immediately on the offensive.

'It was your choice to come here today. On the phone you mentioned being in danger? Tell us about that.'

'Yes, well it's obvious isn't it? First Sarah, now Guy and before that, Andrew and Ben. They're picking us off one by one.'

'Who is?' Bayford said.

'How should I know, that's your job.'

'Andrew Harvey had an accident and Ben Edwards killed himself,' McIntosh said. 'And, even if you are in danger, why would you be next?'

'No reason, I'm just scared and wondering what you're going to do about protection?'

'Can we talk about the show? It may help us find who is killing your friends.'

'No friends of mine,' Magnus snapped. 'Couldn't stand them. One or two were bearable, the rest were a nightmare.'

McIntosh smiled.

'How did you get on with Sarah?' Bayford asked.

'The bitch from hell, made my life a misery. She threw me in the water, you know.'

'How did you feel when you heard she'd been murdered?'

'I'll not lie, quite happy until I heard about Guy then realised I'm in danger too.'

'So, you were happy a young woman was murdered in her own home, just because she pushed you in the water?' Bayford said.

'You're twisting my words. I suppose not. I really hated her but getting murdered might be a step too far.'

'Very gracious of you. Why didn't you like Guy?' McIntosh said.

'I had nothing against Guy, he was the only one I actually conversed with.'

'What did you talk about?'

'General conversation, he'd been having a hard time, money and alcohol problems. I just listened and offered advice.'

McIntosh smiled. 'You gave him financial advice?'

'I know what you're thinking Chief Inspector but I can assure you I did nothing illegal. I resigned my shadow cabinet post to avoid embarrassment to the party, nothing else.'

'Before you got caught?' Bayford said.

'I don't like your attitude Inspector. I'm here of my own free will.'

'Mr Branch,' McIntosh said. 'Your previous financial dealings may be relevant if you gave Guy advice which resulted in his murder. Have you ever been to either Sarah's or Guy's home?'

Branch frowned, 'It sounds like I am being interviewed as a suspect. I take it I am free to leave?'

'Of course,' McIntosh said. 'One last thing, would you be willing to provide a DNA sample and fingerprints, purely for elimination purposes?'

Branch stood and glowered at McIntosh. 'Let me know when you will be providing police protection,' he said, storming out.

McIntosh and Bayford smiled at each other. 'I think Branch has just gotten more interesting Simon.'

'I don't like him boss. He hated Sarah, now she's dead. He maybe gave Guy dodgy financial advice, now he's dead. He's also an arrogant fucker. Guilty or not, I'd love to knock him off his high horse.'

McIntosh laughed. 'Aye, I gathered that.'

Chapter 18

Debbie munched on a piece of toast and locked eyes with her husband. He bristled, frown lines creasing his forehead, worry in his eyes. 'Where d'ye think you can go where he'll no' find ye?' he said.

'I'm not telling you. If someone asks, you can be truthful about not knowing,' Debbie replied.

Earlier on he'd sensed moves afoot. She'd risen sharply and got out of bed with a purpose. He'd given her space to tell him in her own time. After showering, dressing and brewing tea she'd made the surprise announcement that she and Amanda were leaving.

'Debbie, you don't get it. If no-one knows where you've gone, you've no way of staying safe. It'll be worse than staying here. Terry *will* follow you.'

'I'm not staying to look over my shoulder and worry about Amanda every five minutes. She's scared to go to college and doesn't want to leave the house. I trust you to sort this out and get us home as soon as possible.'

Her steely look was not unfamiliar and he wouldn't waste his time arguing. He had a reputation for toughness but his wife was on a different level.

McIntosh's upbringing on the rough Stirling streets could have landed him in prison, but with the guidance of a friendly local police Sergeant, he chose law and order. Still a teenager, London's bright lights beckoned and he signed up for Hendon's Police Training College. Despite being one of the youngest ever recruits to receive a commendation medal, his no nonsense approach and fiery Scottish temper threatened to stonewall his progress. He became known as a troublemaker, unable to back away from confrontation.

Then he met a pretty, gallus Glaswegian brunette, also far from home, studying at a London beauty college. Debbie didn't suffer fools gladly and couldn't tolerate McIntosh's firebrand approach to life and work. Over time her influence softened his attitude and inspired a spectacular shift in his personality. They married three years later, by which time his work had improved, attracting senior attention. He never lost his irascible nature but now knew when to switch it on and off.

He always appreciated Debbie's rocklike support for him but now she needed him and he didn't know what to do. 'I'll not be able to help if the worst happens and Terry comes after both of you?'

'When we get where we're going I'll contact you.'

Nodding reluctantly, he lugged a couple of suitcases into the hall. At the door he hugged Amanda. 'Don't tell any of your friends where you're going, especially your boyfriend.'

'He's NOT my boyfriend,' she said, defensively. 'Just a friend.'

'Aye, whatever, remember and stay off Facebook and all those other ones. Don't make it easy for anyone to track you. It's really important.'

'Don't worry dad, I'll be careful.'

'Taxi's here,' Debbie said. 'Let's go, I'll let you know when we get there.'

The taxi drove away and McIntosh felt a shiver up his back. He sat down with his cup of tea, thinking. Five minutes later his phone pinged - an incoming text. From Debbie or Amanda, he imagined.

The simple sentence sent a chill to his bones.

'So chief inspector theyre off bet they didn't even tell you where theyre going! Dont worry i'll give you a call when they get there'

Chapter 19

He sat, drumming his fingers on the edge of his armchair and decided against telling Debbie. It would only put her on edge. He closed his eyes, enjoying the peace, trying to blank his mind from killer celebrities and kidnapped wives and daughters. He succeeded, but a few minutes later sat bolt upright. He looked around. Had he fallen asleep? Rubbing his eyes and slugging some lukewarm tea, he stretched, reached for his phone and dialled a long forgotten number.

'Hello chief inspectorrr! Whit ken a do fir ye,' a voice said.

'Hello Sully, I'll let the annoying accent go this time coz I need your help.'

'What's happening guv? Been a long time,' Steve Sullivan said.

'I'm having some bother, dinna know who else to turn to. You got time tae meet?'

'Yeah, think I can sneak away for an hour, maybe about two-ish?'

'Aye perfect, the usual place?'

'Sounds good guv, see you then.'

The short conversation roused him and he felt better for actually doing something. He made himself more presentable before heading to the station.

As soon as he set foot in his office, Bayford appeared. 'Morning boss, everything ok?'

'Aye, well I'm no' really sure. Wife and daughter have gone into hiding. Personally I think it's the wrong move but she knows her own mind.'

'You know if there's anything I can do...'

'Thanks Simon, I appreciate it. Anything emerging?'

'Not a lot. Trevor Broad checked out. Ex-military with a sound record. Works for Private Transport. They drive a lot of famous people around. His work sheets tally with his account. He collected Sarah just after 12 noon from Electric FM, dropped her at Waitrose on the North End Road, waited twenty minutes then took her home. Approximately 12.45. Greenwood checks out as well. Collected his daughter, went home and never went back out.'

'What about the ex-husband?'

'David Blain? Another dead end. He attended a poker game in Chelsea where four people vouched for him and he's caught on CCTV outside the apartment block.'

'Ekers?'

'His wife left him a year ago, over his drinking. She thinks that's when the drugs started again. Hasn't heard from him since. No contact with his band either. He used to bypass rehearsals, and the times he did turn up, he'd be pissed or high. They binned him after a reunion tour five years ago. They discovered he screwed them for fifty grand. That was the last straw.'

'Fuck sakes, so we've nothing, absolutely zip?'

'Pretty much boss, some unknown fibres from Sarah's clothing, no match to anything she owns. Strong and Arnott have extended the CCTV search around where Guy lived.'

'Is that a two-man job?'

'Probably not, but we've nothing else so I'm trying to keep everyone busy. It's not easy.'

'Ok, I want everyone for a briefing at three thirty. Before that I've got a meeting at two o'clock.'

'About your family?' Bayford said.

'Aye, but it's still low key just now. Don't want to get you involved.'

Chapter 20

McIntosh sat in the alcove of the old Tea n Cake café, two minutes from Charing Cross station. He'd not been there since he'd last seen Sully. Now renamed Beans n Things and trying hard to be upmarket and trendy, it served various types of weird coffee and vegan food. Not McIntosh's thing. He settled for the basic house filter.

Detective Sergeant Steve 'Sully' Sullivan arrived looking flustered. As scruffy as McIntosh remembered, his diminutive frame was lost in an oversized grey suit. He topped the 'rolled out of bed look' with an ugly, spotted blue tie against an unbuttoned crumpled white shirt and brown suede shoes. McIntosh guessed Sully hadn't found love in the four years since his divorce. No woman of sound mind would allow their man out in public wearing such a fashion disaster. Sully was different to Stuart Strong. He simply didn't know any better.

An unconventional copper, for Sully the end justified the means. McIntosh had a lot of time for him. Plus, Sully owed him big time. Now in the Fraud Investigation unit of the Met, his adroit financial mind, advanced technological ability and unorthodox methods provided access to areas others couldn't reach. However, he missed the cut and thrust of chasing villains that didn't wear suits.

'Sorry guv, couldn't get away. Somebody squealed on their account manager for embezzling company funds and it just landed on my desk.'

'No worries Sully, I'm glad you're here, need someone to offload on.'

He sensed the mood and got his serious hat on. 'What's going on?'

McIntosh proceeded to tell his story, from the armed robbery to the current murder case, Terry Johnson, his family and stealing evidence, all summarised within five minutes.

Sully whistled through his teeth. 'Holy fuck guv, what a mess.'

'Aye, but I don't know what to do for the best. Hoped you'd provide a spark or two.'

'I'll try my best. What do you want to happen?'

'Above all else, keep my family safe.'

'I get that but giving Terry the evidence won't make your family safer? You'd be in his pocket forever. How about getting it in the open, telling the top brass?'

McIntosh shook his head. 'Not yet. If Terry senses police involvement, he'll act quicker. I want to buy time. Only my DI knows.'

'I know some people I can speak to on the QT. I'll call you later tonight but I better get back. Embezzlement doesn't solve itself.'

'Cheers Sully, I appreciate it.'

Chapter 21

June 2021

The sun dazzled a vibrant red and a lovely warm breeze wafted in the early evening twilight. But nightfall beckoned, meaning a cold, chilly nightmare ahead.

The teams stood apprehensively on the beach, each contestant miserable and ready to go home. Charlotte Parrish addressed them. 'Tonight you will compete as individuals. The aim of the final challenge is to reach a rendezvous point three miles from here. The scores are level which means the first person to reach the finish will win one million pounds for their team's charities. A word of caution though. A highly trained squad of marines and dogs will hunt and track your every move. You will need your wits to survive. You have ten minutes to confer with your team to talk tactics. Good luck.'

Both teams formulated similar plans. To individually fan out, hoping to spread the marines thin, leaving the stronger team members to prevail. Team Alpha waited nervously for the off.

'Catherine, you ok?' Guy said. 'You're very quiet.'

'Yes, just thinking. This is a big responsibility. It's not a game anymore. A million pounds is at stake. We have to win.'

'We'll win. I'm very confident,' Magnus said.

'No cheating though, we can't win then have it taken away,' Sarah said.

'Would you give it a rest for fucks sake. It was a one off, stop mentioning it every five minutes.'

Sarah turned and smiled. She liked getting under Magnus's skin.

***

By 7.30pm the hazy sunshine had given way to dusk. As spectacularly as it sparkled during the day, the island became a harsh, rugged landscape at night. Every stumble was energy sapping and, for some, energy was at a premium.

Without knowing the other was only fifty yards away, Emily and Natasha twice circled round on themselves and had no idea of the correct route. Guy fared no better, alien to this level of physical activity. He surrendered at the first glare of a flashlight, as his team knew he would.

An hour in, Sarah felt chipper. She'd have no trouble completing this task, if she could stay out of sight. From nowhere, she suddenly heard a noise and a faint glow in the distance. Shit, not already. Crawling under a bush, she held her breath, feeling smothered. When the light and noise finally disappeared, she waited another full minute before feeling confident enough to squirm from under the bush. She straightened, adjusting her eyes to the murk. The noise and light had gone.

She looked around at the sea of black. It was an eerie sensation. Like the end of the world. Deafening silence, unable to see her waving hand in front of her face. She collected her bearings and set off.

Ten steps in, she stopped, sensing a presence behind her.

Then a thud to the side of her head.

Then it went black.

Chapter 22

She stirred, realising her feet and hands were tied, trussed up like a chicken. Her ear-splitting screams only made her blinding headache worse. Where was the cameraman? Surely it couldn't have been him but why was no-one helping her?

In the distance a group of flashlights lit up the sombre scene, followed by the welcome sound of dogs barking. Cold, frightened and without a thought about winning, Sarah shrieked until her headache became unbearable. The marines arrived and cut the ties from her hands and feet, while a pair of Alsatians sniffed her inquisitively, aware that she posed no threat. Free from her shackles, a sobbing Sarah instinctively threw her arms round the first burly guy in front of her.

Ben had been ahead of the pack but disaster struck close to the finish. He misjudged the small leap over a stream, his left foot planting while his right foot slid away in the moist grass. He immediately felt a stabbing pain in his groin and collapsed in agony, hopes of glory gone.

Initially, Catherine had struggled, getting a stitch and having to take a break but having gotten her second wind she was doing well until she miscalculated the position of the road, walking straight into an ambush. The marines had another victim.

Despite setting off in different directions, and wandering around in circles Emily and Natasha finally managed to stumble over each other. After a quick confab they agreed. Cold, hungry and exhausted they traipsed onto the dirt road, waiting for the marines.

By the time Ben was transported to the rendezvous point, ice pack strapped to his groin and a crutch to help him walk, the other fugitives had congregated.

'Jesus, what happened to you?' Natasha said.

'Slipped, pulled a muscle in my groin and couldn't walk,' he said, noticing Sarah with an ice pack clamped to her head. 'What happened to her?'

'Got attacked. Someone knocked her out. When she came round she'd been trussed up like a chicken,' Natasha said.

'Yeah, right,' Ben laughed.

'No, seriously.'

'And when I find out who, I'll kill them,' Sarah said. 'Bastard left me for dead.'

'Jesus, any ideas?' Ben said.

'No, they hit me from behind.'

'Who's the most likely?' Emily asked.

'Probably Andrew. He's the only one left from Bravo. I must have been his main threat,' Sarah said.

'Surely a step too far, even for him?' Natasha said.

'Maybe,' Sarah replied. 'But I promise, when I find out, they'd better watch out.'

Peter Robson and Dave Gill stood in the corner of the room sipping coffee. Robson sidled beside Gill and whispered, 'Christ Dave, one attacked, one on crutches, two still out there, what the hell is going on?'

'Nothing I didn't expect. This is a result. I honestly thought we'd get one or two bodies,'

'It's not funny, our insurance will have a fit.'

'Ben had an accident, no-one's fault. We don't know who attacked Sarah so there's nothing we can do.'

'It's assault though. It should be reported to the police.'

'That's Sarah's decision but if she tells the police we'll be here for another week. I don't think I could take it. Maybe we should persuade her to let sleeping dogs lie.'

'I'll delegate that to you.'

'Gee, thanks. You're all heart.'

***

Close to the finish, Magnus saw the flash of a torch a hundred yards to his right. A single flashlight. Has to be a competitor. The marines would hunt in pairs, at least. He carefully strode towards it.

Now only twenty yards behind, he strained his eyes and saw a shape, but not a face. A twig snapped, creating an explosive sound among the deathly silence. He froze. The torchlight switched off and the other person went to ground. Magnus patiently waited until the light finally re-appeared. He watched it move away from him, further into the darkness. He wasn't going to chase. Didn't want a confrontation. He considered a different approach.

Get ahead and create mayhem from an advanced position.

Chapter 23

When Andrew heard the noise he'd hit the ground, switching off his torch. Might have been a small animal but he didn't want to take the chance. He'd barely breathed, lying still for five long minutes. Confident the danger had passed, he soldiered on, reaching a small incline with a little stream at the bottom. He waded through, and an uphill climb followed, after which, according to his map, the ground levelled off for the final three hundred yards.

As he slowly climbed he was aware of an object above him, on the incline. Another animal? A marine? He stopped, trying to make out a shape. Better safe than sorry, but before he could hit the ground, he heard a swishing sound, like a sniper's bullet.

The crack sounded a millisecond before his foot exploded in pain. He howled in agony before switching on his torch and seeing a huge rock beside his mangled foot.

***

Job done. He wasn't trying to kill Andrew, just disable him enough that he couldn't finish. Hearing the bones crack sounded painful. His maniacal screeching confirmed it. What a baby.

He turned around and jogged towards a glimmer in the distance. Must be the rendezvous point. Hero status within sight, he started a sprint, feeling triumphant, until five flashlights emerged from the blackness, blinding him.

'GET ON THE FLOOR!' a voice shouted.

Shit, did someone see him throw the rock at Andrew? Was this an arrest or a televisual performance? He dropped to his knees and put his hands behind his back. A couple of pairs of hands roughly lifted him onto his feet and marched him towards a small hut.

The first person he saw was Charlotte Parrish, who lifted his arm in salute. 'Magnus, despite being caught before reaching the rendezvous point, you are the last celebrity to evade capture and have won the task. Team Alpha have just won one million pounds for charity. Congratulations.' She hugged each member of the winning team, Sarah forcing a smile, despite the pain.

A beaming Magnus raised his hands in the air, unaware of the lack of riotous applause. Only after embracing Robson and Gill, did he notice the casualty ward.

'Jesus, what's happened here?' he said.

'Like you don't know?' Andrew replied.

Magnus shrugged. 'What are you talking about?'

'A mysterious flying rock broke my foot, Sarah got attacked and Ben pulled his groin.'

An incredulous Magnus laughed out loud. 'You're kidding right. How busy do you think I've been? And, Sarah's on my team!'

'A lot of strange things happened out there tonight and with your track record.......'

'I've seen a lot of bad losers in my time Andrew, but you take the biscuit.'

Chapter 24

October 2021

An animated Heather Walton was on the phone. 'Wait a minute, we were told suicide, now you're telling me he had a heart attack?'

She picked away at her nails, listening. Bayford silently mouthed, 'What is it?'

She raised a finger - wait a minute. 'Ok, thanks, I'll be in touch.'

'Listen to this,' she said. 'Ben Edwards committed suicide but suffered a heart attack at the same time. What are the chances?'

'Who was that?' Bayford asked.

'Oxfordshire police. I requested Edwards autopsy report and asked if there were any unusual circumstances. Edwards connected a hose to a car exhaust in his garage but suffered a heart attack while he waited to die.'

'Possible I suppose, stress of committing suicide might bring on a heart attack.'

'Unless someone's trying to kill you and make it look like suicide. There's more. Andrew Harvey's autopsy explains he drowned in a Majorcan swimming pool after suffering.... yip, a heart attack. So, two dead celebrities from the same show, one suicide, one accident, and both just happened to have a heart attack while dying of some other cause. I'm not buying it.'

'When you put it like that…I doubt we'd prove murder but, assuming it's the same killer, it's not a stretch to imagine they murdered Sarah and Guy. We might have a serial celebrity killer on our hands.'

***

While McIntosh had no time for Jonathan Beswick as a police officer, or a member of the human race for that matter, he recognised the menace Beswick could pose to him, and unwittingly his team, without more evidence to start building a case. The sparse whiteboard did not augur well for an investigation of this magnitude and McIntosh worried that top brass might call on the Murder Squad, effectively reducing his team to bystanders. They needed more.

Bayford took the lead while McIntosh remained seated. 'We've got a link between the Edwards and Harvey deaths. Both men suffered a heart attack at the exact moment they died, although official cause of death are drowning and suicide by suffocation. Although coincidental, in the context of everything else, it's worth reviewing the circumstances of their deaths.'

Strong raised his hand. 'I volunteer for the Spanish trip.'

Without missing a beat McIntosh said. 'You're staying here son. What else do we have?'

'Ekers death, confirmed between 4 and 6pm,' Dolan said. 'Nothing from CCTV so far. Face coverings are still common, making it impossible to identify anyone. We could widen the search but how far do you go?'

'I've watched the Island Wars tapes,' Myers said. 'It's like how Robson described. Arguing, swearing, confrontations and the occasional scrap but nothing we didn't already know. Pity it'll never be shown. Would've made a cracking TV show.'

'News from forensics,' Kelly Arnott said brightly. 'They found blood traces in Guy Ekers flat that are not Guy's but there's no match on the database.'

'Could've been anyone who visited Guy,' Bayford said. 'Maybe a cut finger.'

'Worth checking though,' Arnott said, hopefully.

'Of course,' Bayford continued, 'Stuart, arrange blood and fingerprint samples from the remaining cast members and crew. Chris, Joanne, you're going to Majorca. Talk to Harvey's friend and the local police then straight back to interview his wife. Heather, Glenn, get more details from Oxfordshire police about Ben and also talk to his wife.'

Kelly Arnott hesitantly raised her hand, 'What about me guv?'

'You're with me Kelly. We're going to see Magnus Branch.'

After the meeting dispersed, McIntosh took Bayford aside. 'Rattle that bastard's cage, Simon. He's hiding something.'

Chapter 25

Magnus Branch couldn't hide his displeasure at DI Bayford and some female DC turning up unannounced at his parliamentary office. His secretary lied about an important meeting and an unapologetic Branch fed them the same bullshit but Bayford advised they'd wait all day if necessary. Branch realised he'd be stuck there and admitted defeat, opening his office door and reluctantly inviting them in.

The small oval shaped office wasn't as fancy as Bayford expected. The worn wood wall panelling and bare oak floor had seen better days. Rotten floor to ceiling bookshelves housed a variety of books Bayford suspected had never been read. The tired room needed a serious upgrade, no doubt to be paid for by Mr and Mrs Taxpayer.

'Come to tell me how my protection is coming along Inspector?'

'Still waiting on official approval but we have been keeping tabs on you,' he lied.

'I haven't noticed,' Branch said, indignantly.

'Which is the point,' Bayford countered, 'We're here to request your cooperation. We need blood and fingerprints from every cast and crew member, for elimination purposes. Would you be willing to provide that?'

'Have you got something?' Branch asked.

'It's more of a procedural exercise but it will help quickly eliminate you if the situation arose.'

Branch looked sceptical. 'You're not a good liar Inspector. You treated me like a suspect before and it sounds like much the same again. Maybe I need my solicitor to ensure my civil rights aren't infringed. Also, why should I help you do your job?'

Branch noticed Kelly Arnott staring intently at him. In truth, he was a sucker for an attractive woman and the presence of the very pretty blonde haired detective with piercingly blue eyes was the main reason he caved so quickly and agreed to see them. However, those blue eyes, boring into his, started to unnerve the man. He turned to Bayford. 'Does she speak or just for decoration?'

Arnott ignored the jibe, shifting in her seat, 'I'm curious Mr Branch. Why would a man, with a lofty, responsible position such as yourself, go out of their way to hinder a murder investigation without doing everything in their power to help the police, assuming they've nothing to hide.'

Her bluntness and piercing stare put him off guard. 'Of course I've nothing to hide but…well…I'm not saying I won't help but I'm not sure I trust the Inspector. He clearly doesn't like me.'

Bayford sat back, enjoying the joust.

'Mr Branch, the Inspector doesn't need to like you and you don't need to trust him in order to co-operate. If you're innocent….

'I am.'

'…. then it's a simple procedure and we don't have to keep badgering you. Any refusal would simply raise our suspicion.'

Bayford smiled. Bringing Arnott was a smart move.

Branch pondered but didn't have another avenue to argue and resignedly shrugged his shoulders. 'Okay I suppose so, can't be today though,' he said, winning a small victory.

'Tomorrow at the station is fine.'

Branch nodded.

Bayford rose. 'One last thing Mr Branch, have you ever been to Sarah O'Neill's house?'

'You've asked me that before.'

'But you didn't give us an answer.'

Branch hesitated. 'Once, at the party after the show ended, why?'

'Just curious, what about Guy Ekers?'

'Never been to Guy's,' he said. 'You have found something haven't you?'

'Routine enquiries Mr Branch. We'll see you tomorrow.'

Chapter 26

Dave Gill tossed the keys to his Mercedes C Class estate to the Savoy Hotel's valet parking attendant. Aged thirty but looking ten years younger, Gill's short brown hair, round glasses and boyish good looks gave off Harry Potter vibes. The attendant looked at him, then his car and shook his head, wondering where he'd gone wrong in life.

Late and expecting a rebuke, Gill didn't get a chance to admire the famous hotel's ambience. He was escorted into the Savoy Grill to find Magnus Branch impatiently tapping his watch.

'You're late!' he barked.

'Nice to see you too. Traffic's a nightmare.'

Branch enjoyed a late breakfast and kept munching while Gill read the menu before ordering some coffee. It was a bit too fancy for Gill's liking but Magnus liked to be seen at the most stylish places. Then he felt the rumble in his stomach. What the hell. He beckoned the attentive waiter over and ordered the signature Arnold Bennett omelette, assuming Magnus would pick up the tab.

'We've got a problem,' Branch said. 'I went to the police to ask about protection, thinking it would be a friendly chat but they started asking questions, problems relating to the show and discussing my previous financial issues. Now they've come back asking for fingerprint and DNA samples and if I'd ever been to Sarah's or Guy's. They're sniffing around.'

'Idiot! Why bring attention to yourself?'

'I'm worried, I hoped they'd be more sympathetic. Have they asked for your fingerprints?'

Gill nodded. 'Yeah, I think it's just routine. Why are your old financial issues relevant?'

'They're not, but I mentioned Guy was having money problems and I'd talked to him, giving him advice. They jumped on the irony.'

'Fucking idiot. The account information is all stashed away right?'

'It's safe enough and encrypted, but if someone who knows what they're doing gets their hands on it, I'm done and you too.'

'Don't drag me into it.'

'I helped you make a fortune,' Branch growled.

'But who helped you get the money in the first place?'

'So you're in this as much as me.'

Gill sighed. 'Find a secure place to bury the account information until we're clear. Don't touch any money. When it all fizzles out, we can divvy it up and go our separate ways.'

Magnus hesitated. 'Guy knew, I wanted to help him so I invested some for him.'

'Jesus Christ, now he's dead as well. Did I mention you're a fucking idiot?'

'Do not talk to me like that,' Branch said in a calm yet threatening voice. In such an esteemed public place, causing a scene was not an option. 'Play it cool, let the police ask their questions. There are less people to give them answers.'

'I never pegged you as a good Samaritan Magnus. I really hope you've not fucked this up,' Gill said, storming off as Arnold Bennett hit the table.

***

Stuart Strong surveyed the expensive furniture in Natasha Cook's open plan living room and concluded life wasn't fair. He'd already noted the beautifully modern kitchen, large manicured rear garden plus a top of the range BMW in the driveway.

How could an airhead blonde, who's only claim to fame was crap reality TV, afford this? A secret sugar daddy? According to Google she was currently single but he couldn't imagine a knockout like her would be long without a man.

'There you go detective,' she said, handing him a mug of tea. 'Have a seat.'

'Thanks, call me Stuart.'

'Ok, how's the investigation going Stuart?'

'Early days. What did you think when you heard about Sarah and Guy?'

'Still can't believe it. With Andrew and Ben, it seems the show is cursed.'

'Are you worried?'

'I wasn't, but you being here makes me think I should be.'

'Sorry, this is just routine. There's no reason to believe you're in danger. I wanted your co-operation in providing fingerprint and blood samples, for elimination purposes. We're asking all the remaining cast and crew.'

'Sure, if it'll help.'

'Great, maybe sometime tomorrow, whatever suits you.'

'No problem.'

'I wanted to ask a bit about the show. Did you get embroiled in the clashes that occurred?'

Natasha laughed. 'I think we all did to some degree. None of us really got on.'

'Who were the biggest troublemakers?'

'Magnus and Andrew, god rest his soul, were two nasty, horrible men. Sarah was a bitch, living up to her reputation. The rest didn't bother me too much. I suppose Guy was a sap. I've no idea what he was doing there but he seemed harmless enough. Certainly didn't deserve to die.'

'I understand Magnus and Sarah had a real beef with each other?'

'Yeah, it was constant. Always screaming and butting heads. I wasn't on their team but still heard them go at it. It started off being quite amusing but later on I found it wearing. I think everyone did.'

'Did Magnus fall out with you?'

'Not really. On opposite teams, but I had plenty of issues with Andrew though. He couldn't control his behaviour. I told him to rein it in or I'd publicly out him.'

'How did he take that?'

'Not well. He scared Emily, and Ben threatened to leave on the first day.'

'Did Magnus have any friends on the show?'

'Not that I know of but I'm told he had a few conversations with Guy.'

'Were you ever at Sarah's house or Guy's?'

'Sarah's for the after party from hell. Never in Guy's.'

'What happened at the party?'

'Sarah got pissed and was itching for a fight, preferably with Magnus. Without a great deal of provocation, she punched him on the nose. Me and Dave Gill helped straightened him out and the party fizzled out soon after. Sarah was put to bed and the rest of us went home.'

'Why did you go to the party if you hated each other?'

She sighed, 'Attendance was mandatory or we'd forfeit our fee. I suspect if they'd known the show wouldn't get aired, the party would've been cancelled.'

Strong looked around. 'Must have been some fee,' he said, disparagingly.

'Twenty grand,' Natasha said, oblivious to his disrespect. 'Peanuts really, I signed up to get more exposure. I make a lot more from other stuff.'

'Obviously,' Strong said, standing. 'I should be going, I'll see you tomorrow and thanks for the tea.'

'You're welcome,' Natasha said, stroking his arm.

Walking to his car parked in her driveway, Strong wondered if he'd misjudged her. Not the dumb blonde he'd expected, and was the touch on his arm flirting?

She waved. He waved back.

He was out of her league but those little details had never held him back before.

Chapter 27

Between home life, interviewing suspects or witnesses, conversing with colleagues or fending off his Commander, McIntosh rarely enjoyed time to himself. He coveted solitude when it came.

However, struggling to enjoy a microwaved shepherd's pie, alone at his kitchen table, he missed the normality of family, not to mention Debbie's cooking. This stuff was no good. He gave up and made a mental note to complement her cooking more often.

His burner phone pinged. The one his clever clogs missus produced before she left, keeping another for herself.

'Hi, we're both fine, at your sisters, hope all ok at your end'

He text back. *'Good to hear, stay safe. All ok here. Speak soon'*

He had a funny feeling they would head north. Jean would take care of them and help them relax and he'd speak to Debbie about Terry once he had a plan. He threw the remnants of his microwave slop in the bin and heard his work phone ping in the living room.

Shite. He looked at a photograph of Debbie and Amanda getting into a car outside Jean's house, and felt a bead of sweat trickle gently down his neck.

Another ping.

'Time is ticking detective chief inspector' and a clock face emoji.

Fuuuck.

On cue, Sully phoned him. 'Guv, can I come over? Easier than meeting in a pub.'

'Aye, sooner the better. I've heard from Terry. It's not good.'

***

The painkillers weren't touching his pounding headache. He paced circuits around his living room coffee table imagining ringing Terry Johnson's neck, when the doorbell rang.

Sully breezed into the living room and sat without being invited. 'What's Terry done now?' he said, bluntly.

McIntosh showed Sully the photo and corresponding message.

'Where are they?'

'My sisters in Blackford, a wee village in Perthshire.'

'How did he find them so quickly?'

'I thought it might have been a bluff when he said he'd be watching and following them. Obviously not.'

'Even so, it's not easy to follow someone for ten hours straight.'

'Easier if they don't know they're being followed. I warned her but it didn't sink in. To be fair, I'm not sure I believed it either,' McIntosh said, defeated.

Sully took charge. 'Guv, it's no good telling your missus. It'll only put the fear into her. At least she can relax, go about her business, while we sort it here. I've spoken to some associates of mine who've unearthed a bit of intelligence on Terry's business. He's recently expanded his empire and recruited a lot more muscle. He's got a tie up with a hardcore OCG. They were involved in your armed robbery case.' He took a deep breath. 'And, word is Terry's got at least one, if not more, coppers on his payroll.'

'Who are the associates looking into Terry's business? Upstanding members of the community?'

Sully looked mildly offended. 'C'mon guv, you know me better than that. I'll admit they occasionally pop up on the wrong side of the law but I trust them a helluva lot more than most coppers. They owe me some favours so ask no questions.'

A smile crept across McIntosh's face. 'Just thought I'd ask. Can we find out who the rat coppers are?'

'Doubt it, they'll be pretty close to Terry's chest. Probably trapped them in the same way he's trying with you.'

'A DCI on his payroll seems extreme. It's usually PC's or DC's who get sucked into this sort of thing, isn't it?'

'You'd be surprised. The higher the rat, the more valuable the information. Means you can't trust anyone, even your own team.'

'Is that why Terry was able to keep tabs on Debs and Amanda?'

'Doubt it. Having coppers on his payroll is probably co-incidental to your situation. They could be in nicks all over London but they'll have friends and contacts everywhere, tapping them for bits and pieces so someone on your team may inadvertently be giving out information. Be extra careful what you say to people.'

'Simon Bayford knows. I trust him and need him onside to keep the investigation ticking over while I sort this out.'

'Ok, but from now on keep him at a distance as well.'

Chapter 28

July 2021

Ever the exhibitionist, Sarah's offer to host the after party gave her a chance to blow her own trumpet as well as showing off her beautiful flat. Unknown to anyone else, she'd wangled a bit extra on her fee. It all seemed like a good idea at the time. That was before. Tonight, she had to attempt being civil to people she hated.

Without being able to leave.

Despite it being Sarah's home, Peter Robson and Dave Gill were in charge of organisation. Music, drinks, the guest list and generally making sure the event ran smoothly. They arrived together.

'This could get interesting,' Robson said. 'I wish we'd spent more and held it somewhere else. I think this was a mistake.'

'If everyone leaves alive it'll be a success,' Gill replied. 'We're here now and might as well get pissed. Where's the bar?'

Natasha Cook, who'd already arrived, sashayed towards Robson, swaying on her high heels. 'Enjoying yourself Pete?' she said, snaking an arm around his neck.

'Just here, but you've obviously been here for hours?'

'No, not long but I guzzled a few earlier, no way was I arriving sober.'

'I hope everyone behaves.'

'You'll be lucky. What time have you booked the ambulances for?'

'Not funny! Stay out of trouble.'

'You too, try and enjoy yourself,' Natasha said, tottering away.

Gill came back with two beers. 'You and Natasha looked cosy. Something I should know about?'

'No, she's pissed. Do you think I should say a few words?'

'Good idea, open with...thanks for coming and thanks to Sarah for allowing us into her beautiful home. Enjoy yourselves and if you could avoid murdering each other that would be a bonus,' Gill giggled.

'I'm serious, I think I should say something.' Robson surveyed the tense scene, awkward conversations between cast, crew and others he didn't know. Must be uninvited plus ones. He didn't care. He clinked his glass. 'Evening everyone, I just wanted to say thanks for coming tonight.'

'We were contractually obliged!' a heckler shouted.

Robson continued, 'It's good to see you all and thanks to Sarah for opening her lovely home to us. Have a great time...' Gill waited for the punchline and sneered when Robson raised his glass. 'Cheers!'

A muted, 'Cheers,' from the crowd.

'Good effort but preferred my speech,' Gill laughed.

'I'm not drinking much. I want to nip any trouble in the bud,' Robson said.

By ten o'clock inhibitions were loosened and some dancing broke out. Natasha continued to slur her words, wobbling on her heels. Guy fell off the wagon and Emily and Catherine matched each other, cocktail for cocktail. Andrew and Magnus discovered the malt whisky while Ben's early start in the morning gave him a perfect excuse to leave after an hour. A drunk and agitated Sarah paced around like an angry tiger looking for a fight. Paul Greenwood guessed who was in her sights.

'You're tense Sarah, I think you should stop drinking. Maybe take a walk to clear your head.'

'Look at him, fat pompous little prick, thinking he owns the place. I'm going to tell him to get out of my fucking house because I own the place.'

'You're stuck, remember. You can't storm off if you cause a scene. You've nowhere to go. Go outside, get some air then try to have a good time.'

'I can't stand these other arseholes either. I could tell them all to fuck off.'

Greenwood sighed. 'Let me talk to Magnus, persuade him to leave early.'

Greenwood walked towards the two unlikeliest of best friends. 'What are we drinking guys?' he said.

Magnus turned first. 'Ah, it's Miss O'Neill's pet lapdog. Let you off the leash did she?'

'Watch, he might bite,' Andrew said, laughing hysterically.

Greenwood understood why Sarah hated these two. 'That's a good one, can we have a friendly chat, maybe clear the air.'

'Send you over did she, scared to come herself?' Magnus said.

'No, she'd rather put you in front of a firing squad. This is my idea,' Greenwood said, straight faced.

Magnus and Andrew paused before collapsing in a fit of giggles.

'I thought you two were sworn enemies?' Greenwood said.

'Well, he did break my foot,' Andrew said, lifting his moon boot, 'But I'm pissed, so I'll start hating him again tomorrow.'

'I told you it wasn't me,' Magnus replied.

'Can we have a private chat,' Greenwood said to Magnus, 'I've heard a lot about you and none of it complimentary. I'm sure it can't all be true.'

'Consider the source,' Magnus said.

'You talk to your new boyfriend,' Andrew said, 'I'm going to annoy someone else.'

They found a long sofa bed in Sarah's office, currently occupied by a dozing Natasha. 'The only thing I know about you is getting fired from the shadow cabinet,' Greenwood said.

'Allegations, nothing proved and I wasn't fired, I resigned.'

'Because they made you?' Greenwood said.

'Don't want to talk about it, water under the bridge. I'm still an MP and a legitimate businessman.'

'Sounds like a contradiction?'

Magnus smiled, 'I've a thriving printing business and chairman and trustee of Dream Givers, a children's cancer charity who, thanks to me, are 250 grand richer. So, not doing too bad, thanks very much.'

Natasha stirred on the couch and opened her eyes. 'Not another dodgy deal Magnus?' she said, between yawns.

'Back to sleep dear, grown-ups talking. About time you went home.'

Natasha stood. 'No chance, I'm getting another drink, want one?'

'If you insist. Whisky please. Don't drop them on the way back.'

'Cheeky bastard.'

Catherine and Emily appeared and sat on the edge of the couch. 'Right, we need to ask, did you assault Sarah?' Emily said.

'Yeah, Sarah said it had to be you. No one else would do something like that,' Catherine added.

Magnus reddened. 'That's outrageous. You can't go around making accusations like that.'

Natasha brought back two whiskies. As she handed them to Magnus and Greenwood, a livid Sarah marched into the office. She started to speak but Greenwood raised his hand, 'Sarah, I don't think....'

'Magnus, why don't you fuck off and crawl back under your stone,' Sarah slurred.

Magnus stood, 'Ah Sarah, nice to see you too.'

'I'm serious, I've seen enough of your annoying face.'

Magnus put his hand on Sarah's shoulder. *'Come on Sarah, you've drunk a bit too mu....'*

As Sarah's fist drove hard into Magnus's face, his nose burst in a crimson explosion. He dropped like a stone, his bloodstained hands checking to see if his nose was still attached to his face.

'Jesus Christ,' Greenwood said, pulling her away. *'Get outside and get some fresh air.'*

The altercation attracted the rest of the party. They watched a horizontal Magnus, groaning and covered in blood.

'She punched me,' Magnus whimpered, *'Someone call the police.'*

Dave Gill lifted Magnus off the floor and escorted him to the bathroom. Natasha followed and closed the door behind her.

'No-one's calling anyone,' Gill said. *'Let's have a look at your nose.'*

'I thought something like this might happen,' Natasha said. *'I said to Pete that things might kick off.'*

'It livened up the party,' Gill said, smiling.

'I'm glad my suffering amuses you. Is my nose broken?'

'I don't think so,' Gill said. *'Hard to tell with the swelling.'*

'I'm going to get her charged with assault.'

'No you're not,' Gill said. *'I'll get her to apologise but more bad publicity will kill the show.'*

Natasha rolled up some toilet paper and pushed it up Magnus's nose. *'It'll stop the bleeding and makes you look good.'*

'It's not funny,' Magnus protested. *'I'm the victim here.'* He washed blood from his face and hands before returning to a near empty living room. Bar a few, most of the guests had made an excuse and grabbed the opportunity to leave.

'I've put Sarah to bed,' Greenwood said.

'I want an apology from her or I'm reporting her for assault. I've got plenty witnesses.'

Maybe not many who'd be willing to back you up, thought Greenwood. 'Tomorrow maybe. She's sleeping.'

'Nice look Magnus, suits you,' Andrew said.

'Shut it, or I'll get someone to break your other foot.'

Natasha put on her coat to leave and winked at Peter Robson. 'Great party, let's do it again soon.'

Chapter 29

October 2021

Having discussed the plan at length, neither McIntosh nor Sully could think of anything better and McIntosh again headed downstairs towards the evidence room. Relieved to see PC Kevin Tait behind the desk, he said, 'Morning constable, I need access to the Johnson case evidence.'

Tait was in his early thirties with more time on the job than Carl Stanley but most of it was spent behind a desk. Known as the station busybody, street coppering wasn't his strength, his size and ever increasing weight rendering him useless in a chase. Despite his several phony declarations of lifestyle change, threats of dismissal hung over his head at his continued lack of action but he'd remarkably managed to create a niche for himself in the evidence room.

'More questions from the CPS sir?' Tait said. 'Carl said you popped in the other day.'

'Something like that Kevin, but I'm in a hurry, if you don't mind.'

'No problem, sir. You have to sign in and I need to accompany you?'

McIntosh sighed, 'Aye, PC Stanley insisted as well, god knows why.'

McIntosh signed the visitors book just as Tait's desk phone rang. 'Sorry sir, I'll have to answer that.'

'Kevin, I'll literally be no more than two minutes,' McIntosh said, walking into the evidence room, not giving Tait a chance to stop him. Tait's exasperation was evident as he tried to make sense of the call.

'Sir, I don't understand, what was your name again? ...But sir you're not making sense...I don't know what you're trying to say.'

Silence

'Yes…but…if you give me a chance to talk…No, I can't help you, I'm going to have to hang up now.'

The phone slammed followed by a couple of expletives. McIntosh heard footsteps and Tait appeared just as he closed the box, pocketing a small bag. 'Sounded interesting?' McIntosh said.

'What a nutter. Couldn't get a word in edgeways or understand what he was rabbiting on about. If I hadn't hung up, I'd have been there all day. Sorry sir, I should've escorted you.'

'No problem Kevin, literally had to check a signature on a form. I don't need my hand holding for that.'

'Fair enough but I'll have to record my absence, just to keep myself right.'

'Aye, whatever. I need to go, I'm in a hurry.'

He sauntered back upstairs, took a coffee to his desk and picked up the phone. Sully chuckled when he told him about the exasperation in Kevin Tait's voice.

'What a nutter. His words, not mine.'

'See, I can annoy people quite easily. A gift of mine,' Sully laughed.

'Don't I know it but it did the trick, gave me the minute I needed,' McIntosh added. 'Let's hope Terry plays ball.'

***

Stuart Strong handed Catherine Collins a cup of tea. They sat in a nondescript boxroom, off the main reception area at Charing Cross station. Probably a cupboard back in the day, just enough space for a table, two chairs and an overhanging spotlight. To Catherine it resembled a shady interrogation room she'd seen on spy TV programmes.

'Catherine, thanks for providing the samples we asked for. If I may I'd like to talk to you about Island Wars. What can you tell me about your fellow celebrities, four of whom are now dead?'

'Probably not much you don't already know. Sarah was the female version of Magnus, self-obsessed and attention seeking. Guy had ongoing issues with drugs and alcohol and always seemed in debt. I think it was a mistake to let him appear. He wasn't physically fit enough.'

'What about Ben and Andrew?'

'Ben was ok, I didn't have many dealings with him and Andrew struck me as a nasty piece of work but that's based on the other team's comments about him. One odious bastard per team seemed fair.'

'What can you tell me about Magnus?'

'Borderline sociopath. Hard to believe he's in Parliament. God help us if he ever got into power. A horrible man. He antagonised Sarah time after time and she always bit. She was no angel either mind. She shoved him in the water during a task, and punched him at the after party.'

'Do you think he's capable of murder?'

'Of Sarah? Definitely, although she'd have happily killed him too. Not so sure about Guy. He was the only one Magnus really spoke to.'

'What about Natasha and Emily?'

'Alike in many ways. Pretty girls, looked and acted very similarly. Like little dumb clones. I'm sorry for being rude and I know it's stereotypical. No dramas I'm aware of with them although I bet they got the sharp end of Andrew's tongue.'

'What did you think when you found out Andrew was gay?'

'Shocked of course, although it made more sense when we heard that the stress of hiding his sexuality made him such a rude, unpleasant man.'

'Anything else you can tell me?'

'Sarah and Charlotte Parrish had history. When Charlotte did her little speech at the beginning, Sarah muttered 'bitch,' under her breath. I heard and asked her about it. She apologised and gave me a story about their rivalry. Charlotte seemed to be winning the TV work that Sarah expected and I think she resented it.'

'Did Charlotte hear her say it?'

'I don't think so, too far away.'

'So, no reason to think Charlotte held a grudge and got revenge when they got home?'

Catherine laughed. 'By murdering her? I don't think so. In their business they'd need a thicker skin than that. I'm not even sure Charlotte was aware of any rivalry. It might have all been in Sarah's head.'

'Ok, any other grudges between the contestants?'

Catherine laughed. 'Apart from what I've just told you?' She pondered for a second. 'Well, there was the thing involving Magnus which got Sarah very excited.'

'What thing?'

'A few weeks after the show Guy told me Magnus's charity hadn't received the prize money. After mentioning it to Sarah she hired a private investigator who apparently found evidence of Magnus using the charity money to play the stock market. Sarah went mental, wanted to create a stink in the press but I assumed the allegation was false because it died a death....no pun intended.'

'Or she was killed before she got a chance?' Strong said, imagining the kudos of presenting the first real motive for murder.

Chapter 30

Strong marched into the humming squad room, a smug, satisfied grin on his chubby, red face. 'I've got a motive,' he said to no-one in particular. 'Catherine Collins heard there was something fishy about the charity money Magnus Branch received. Instead of handing it over right away he played the stock market with it. Sarah hired a P.I. and intended exposing him, not long before she died.'

'Thank you Stuart,' McIntosh said. 'You've corroborated the story Emily Dean just told Glenn.'

Strong looked disconsolate, his moment of glory ruined.

'Better luck next time,' Findlay said, smiling.

Strong shot her an evil glance.

'Would the charity not receive the money directly from the production company, rather than go through the celebrities?' Kelly Arnott asked.

Heather Walton smiled. 'It probably did but Branch is the chairman and trustee of the charity. It's likely the money landed on his desk first.'

Ten minutes later, Walton marched into McIntosh's office, an excited look on her face. 'Boss, forensics have matched some blood traces found at Guy Ekers flat. Belong to Magnus Branch.'

Bayford, who'd been talking to McIntosh said, 'That bastard said he'd never been to Ekers flat.'

McIntosh remained calm. 'Ok, let's no' dive in with the big stick just yet. Get him to come for another interview, with his solicitor. We'll give him ample opportunity to confirm or deny being to Ekers flat. If and when it's a definite no, we'll hit him with the blood.'

***

Magnus Branch was not used to being told what to do or where to go. Usually he was the one barking out orders. He seethed silently, making a mental note to kick Rupert Thornhill's arse. Imagine advising him to come of his own free will or he'd be arrested. He paid exorbitant solicitors fees to keep him away from these places. Given half a chance he'd sue for false arrest, then boot Thornhill into touch and get a new bootlicker.

Bayford and McIntosh strolled in and made themselves comfortable.

'Must be serious, if I've got the 'A' team,' Branch said.

'Thanks for coming, Mr Branch. Just a few additional questions. We'll try not to take up much of your very valuable time,' Bayford said.

'Like I had a choice,' Branch replied.

McIntosh ignored the comment. 'Mr Branch, please tell us, have you ever visited Sarah O'Neill's flat?'

'I've already told him,' Branch pointed at Bayford.

'Tell us again.'

Branch sighed. 'I've been to Sarah's once, the after show party.'

'Thank you, what about Guy Ekers?'

'Never been to Guy's.'

'You're sure? You've never been to his flat, not even to discuss the charity money?'

Rupert Thornhill jumped in. 'Chief Inspector, I must prot…'

Branch roared, 'I don't know what you're talking about? Christ, how many times do I have to say. I HAVE NEVER BEEN TO GUY EKERS FLAT.'

'No need to shout, we just need verification that you haven't forgotten about a visit,' McIntosh said, calmly.

Thornhill interjected again, 'Chief Inspector, this is unacceptable badgering of my client. He's told you multiple times he's never been to Guy Ekers home.'

Bayford produced a piece of paper from a folder. 'Mr Branch, please explain why traces of your blood were discovered at Guy Ekers flat. Forensics have confirmed a DNA match with the sample you provided.'

Branch slumped, wide eyed, confusion etched on his face. 'Thaat...caant...be…right!'

'Science doesn't lie, Mr Branch,' Bayford said, pushing the paper towards Branch and Thornhill.

'I've never been there, it must be a mistake,' Branch said.

'A mistake? Really? Isn't it more likely you murdered Guy and carelessly left blood traces behind thinking you'd sanitised like at Sarah's.'

'So I killed Sarah AS WELL?' Branch exploded.

'We know you hated each other and she threatened to expose you. It's a pretty good motive for murder,' Bayford said.

'Ridiculous, she hated me just as much as I hated her.'

'You're not dead, she is,' McIntosh said.

Branch didn't respond.

Thornhill interrupted. 'I think this is a good time for a break. I need to confer with my client.'

McIntosh stood. 'We'll resume in fifteen minutes.'

'What do you think?' McIntosh said to Bayford, upstairs.

'He looked shocked and angry but maybe at himself for making a mistake.'

'It's not a lot but at least something to get our teeth into. Let's see if he conveniently forgot about having tea and a chocolate biscuit with Guy.'

***

Upon resumption, Thornhill read a prepared statement

'My client insists he has never visited Guy Ekers property. Any DNA found at the scene must have been placed by others unknown or as a result of an error by the forensic lab. My client is innocent and will continue to maintain his innocence.'

'So, a big boy did it and ran away?' McIntosh said.

'No need to be frivolous Chief Inspector,' Thornhill said. 'At best the evidence is circumstantial and if you have nothing else I must insist Mr Branch is allowed to leave.'

'It would be circumstantial if Mr Branch confirmed visiting Guy Ekers flat but he's insisted, on several occasions, that he's never been there which means the evidence is more credible. Your client is lying. About what we don't know yet, but he's lying,' McIntosh said.

Branch perched on the edge of his seat, desperate to say his piece but Thornhill had demanded he leave the talking to him. 'Do you have anything else, Chief Inspector?'

McIntosh stood. 'Goodbye Mr Branch, until we need to speak to you again.'

Without another word Branch and Thornhill walked out.

Chapter 31

August 2021

In the weeks since the show ended, then the debacle of the after party, Sarah had sleepwalked her way through her morning radio shows, unable to think straight, her prevailing thoughts firmly fixed on one man. She busied herself unnecessarily re-washing already immaculately spotless floors, worktops and kitchen cabinets, nervously awaiting the arrival of the only people she thought might help.

'How's the head now, Sarah?' Catherine said.

'And the knuckles!' Emily added.

Sarah chuckled, 'Yeah, not too bad, I'll survive.'

Sarah poured some wine for Catherine and Emily while Natasha opted for a Diet Coke. The atmosphere awkwardly lingered as her guests waited for her.

'Honestly, I'm not even sure why I invited you here,' Sarah said. 'I know we're not friends but you're the only ones I can talk to about this. I'm overcome with rage towards Magnus. I can't think about anything else. It's taking over my life and my stress levels are through the roof. I'm positive he assaulted me, and possibly Andrew and I suspect he cheated to win the final challenge. We know he cheated on other tasks.' She paused, 'I know none of you are fans of his and wondered if you've any ideas or had any suspicions at the time?'

'Why didn't you invite the guys today?' Emily asked.

'I don't really know,' Sarah said. 'Thought they might be more empathetic towards him so I started with the girls first.'

'Tell us your suspicions,' Catherine said.

'Okay, he got to the end of the final hardly looking out of breath. He's the oldest, overweight and not particularly fit. How the hell did he do it? I bet you were all knackered when you got caught?'

'He managed reasonably well in the daily challenges, didn't he?' Natasha said.

'Something's not right. I think he may have gotten help from someone and I strongly suspect he's the one who assaulted me.'

'Doesn't make sense,' Natasha said. 'You were on the same team. It would have lessened his chances of winning.'

'Unless he knew he was going to win,' Sarah said.

'He was very confident at the start of the final task. Didn't look fazed at all,' Catherine said.

'There you go. Probably knew he would win so took the opportunity to give me a clout, just for the hell of it. To be fair, I might have done the same to him.' Sarah clocked their reaction. 'I know I'm as bad but you've no idea how much I hate him. Did you two notice anything suspicious going on?'

'Not really,' Natasha said. 'We didn't see him up that close and weren't looking for anything out of order. Remember, me and Emily suffered from our own overbearing bully.'

'Yeah,' Emily said. 'Andrew gave Magnus a run for his money in the arsehole stakes.'

'Wouldn't surprise me if Magnus threw the rock at Andrew,' Sarah said.

'Wait, there is something,' Catherine said, quietly.

All eyes turned towards her.

'From after the show. I called Guy the other day. Heard he'd been attending therapy sessions and wanted to see how he was doing and give him some support. He told me Magnus's charity hasn't received their money. Mine only took a few days, so did Guy's. What about yours, Sarah?'

'Not sure, certainly within a week,' Sarah said. 'What could be the delay?'

'Guy didn't say. I'm not sure he knew.'

'Interesting,' Sarah said. 'I'll do some investigating.'

'Why?' Natasha said.

'I can't prove he cheated, or assaulted me, but I'm going to ruin him one way or another.'

Chapter 32

October 2021

It was amazing what a little evidence and an actual suspect could do to a murder investigation. A renewed sense of purpose coursed through the busy EIU squad room. Furthermore, the imminent arrival of a forensic scientist, with new information, made the congregation fidget in anticipation, waiting on her arrival.

When Kareena Sidhu shyly walked through the door, the sea of faces turned as one. She balked and would happily have about turned. McIntosh clocked her reticence and quickly walked over to shake her hand.

'Hi Kareena, nice to see you. Thanks for coming over. Evelyn must have had a better offer?' McIntosh said, smiling.

'Not quite Chief Inspector, hello everyone,' Kareena said, regaining her composure. 'I'll get right to it. We've managed to obtain a decent fingerprint from the arm of the silk top worn by Sarah O'Neill on the night of her murder. It matches prints from a recently provided sample.'

You could hear a pin drop.

'It's Magnus Branch,' Kareena continued.

As they absorbed the news, low murmurs and isolated chatter broke out among the group. 'Bastard!' Findlay said loudly.

Glenn Myers tentatively raised his hand.

'You're no' at school son, ask your question,' McIntosh said.

'Kareena, I didn't think it was possible to obtain fingerprints from fabric?'

'That's a good question. It's a fairly recent innovation but there are advanced techniques with certain chemicals that allow us to extract fingerprints from fabric. It doesn't work on all fabrics and the success rate is still quite low but we got lucky this time. On its own it wouldn't be enough to convict, but alongside other evidence, it could prove useful in court.'

'We don't have much other evidence,' Strong said.

'Well, Branch really is the prime suspect now,' McIntosh said.

'Kareena, thanks for the good news.'

'You're welcome,' Kareena said, leaving.

'Ok, so we've Magnus's blood at Ekers flat, his fingerprints on Sarah's clothes from the night she died and an allegation he nicked charity money. Track his movements around Fulham and Brixton on the day of the murders, and the days before, just in case he planned his exit route.'

'We could get a warrant and search his house and office,' Bayford said.

'We've no' got enough for a warrant yet plus I don't want to tip him off. Let's do our homework first before we get him back in.'

***

With the murder investigation finally in full swing, McIntosh pondered his next bout with Terry. A common thug, but a clever, resourceful thug. Should he get some of Sully's dodgy acquaintances on his side? Maybe, or would that create as many problems as it would solve? No negative news from Debbie so far. They seemed to be ok, enjoying their time with Jean as best they could. At what point did he tell her Terry was close by?

Before he could answer his own question, his office door shuddered and two poker faced men entered. Their similar dark tanned skin, dark hair and strong jaw line suggested they could be brothers, although the age gap was around ten years. Wearing identical, sharp suits, crisp white shirts, perfectly knotted ties and gleaming black brogues, each carried a heavy briefcase.

McIntosh immediately knew who they were.

'Detective Chief Inspector McIntosh? I am Detective Sergeant Adam Skinner, this is Detective Constable Ryan Glass from Police Anti-Corruption. We would like a formal chat with you. Can we use one of your interview rooms?'

'What's this about?'

'A complaint has been made against you.'

'A complaint by who, about what?' McIntosh demanded.

'All in good time. We'll follow you to the interview room.'

McIntosh remained stoical. As they left his office to go downstairs, they bumped into a passing Simon Bayford. 'Everything ok boss?' Bayford said.

'Fine Simon, I'll come see you when I'm finished with these gentlemen.'

***

'So, who made the complaint?'

'I can't reveal our sources,' Skinner said. 'It relates to an allegation of evidence tampering. We've since discovered evidence of bribery.'

Glass pressed the record button. 'Interview with Detective Chief Inspector Angus McIntosh. Also present, Detective Sergeant Adam Skinner and Detective Constable Ryan Glass.'

Skinner started. 'Chief Inspector, I'll get straight to the point. We are investigating a complaint of evidence tampering and bribery. We have uncovered evidence which suggests that, without authorisation, you removed sealed evidence from an ongoing case file, passed it to an unknown third party and received a large cash deposit as payment for said theft. How do you respond?'

McIntosh hesitated, 'It's all true Sergeant….

Skinner and Glass's eyes widened. Easier than they thought.

'…. but not everything is as it seems.'

Chapter 33

Whilst not quite the BBC, Glenn Myers's first impressions of the Angel Glass Studios near Islington Green, were first-rate. Photographs adorning the walls confirmed some very famous people had visited the premises. A wall mounted TV displayed round-the-clock Sky News, above the eight foot, backlit, crystal glass reception desk and the map of London carpet. A continual stream of people kept the receptionist busy.

Charlotte Parrish silently glided up to Myers and placed a hand on the startled man's shoulder. 'Sorry, detective, ' she laughed. 'I didn't mean to make you jump.'

Myers smiled. 'Don't worry, I was daydreaming, checking out the photos. Can we talk somewhere quiet?'

'The canteen, we can get a coffee as well,' she said, leading the way.

Attractive without being beautiful, she must have been nearly six-foot tall with an impressive sereneness and self-confidence which he found appealing. 'Thanks for meeting me,' he said. 'I've watched the Island Wars tapes and, although your involvement is fairly minimal, I'd like to pick your brains.'

Myers had a way of making women feel at ease and, although Parrish was naturally self-assured amongst handsome men, his smooth caramel skin and dusky voice made her feel even more relaxed. 'Minimal on screen but lots happened behind the scenes. I watched the footage as it came in.'

'You must have an opinion on what made the show go off course?'

'Simple. Three people sucked the life from the show. Magnus, Andrew and Sarah. I didn't know much about Magnus or Andrew beforehand but they turned out to be real scumbags. I already knew Sarah could be a right cow and she lived up to it. Her many spats with Magnus made the rest uncomfortable. Waiting for the next verbal or, occasionally physical altercation. It is the worst show I've ever worked on.'

'Do you blame her more than Andrew or Magnus?'

'Not more but she was definitely no angel. Having said all that, I wouldn't wish any of them dead.'

'I assume you and Sarah crossed swords in the past?'

'Not really. I'd barely spoken to her but I've friends who couldn't stand her. She was a narcissist who rebelled when anybody got in her way.'

'She seemed to have an issue with you.'

'What do you mean?'

'On the beach, at the start of the competition, another celebrity overheard her call you a bitch.'

'Really? Who was that?'

'I'm afraid I can't say. They challenged Sarah about it and she intimated that the pair of you often competed for the same TV jobs and, more often than not, she was overlooked in favour of you, including Island Wars. She was offered a contestant spot as second prize.'

'God, I didn't know any of that. You often don't know who else is trying for these jobs. I never knew she felt that way.'

'So, from your point of view, nothing to constitute a feud between you?'

'Absolutely not,' Parrish said, emphatically. 'Don't get any ideas that I'm involved in her murder.'

Myers held a hand up. 'I'm not, but as you can understand, we need to tie lots of tiny pieces of information together and follow up on all of them.'

'Ok, sorry for sounding snappy,' she said, looking at her watch. 'Look, I really have to go. I'm due on camera in five minutes.'

'Ok, thanks for your time,' he said, not sure whether he'd closed one enquiry route, or opened another.

Chapter 34

McIntosh pressed send. '*got what you need, when do you want to meet'*.

He also texted his wife. '*everything ok?*'

He hated not being in control. Terry's unpredictability made him dangerous. Being headstrong made his wife susceptible to danger. He decided against mentioning the ACU. No need to worry her even more. After she replied he'd spill the beans about their stalkers. Maybe form a united front with a plan that suited everyone?

Debbie replied first. '*Yeah all good keeping a low profile*'

Thank God. He decided to make himself a coffee before giving her a quick phone. Nothing like hearing the other person's voice. He took a sip and settled into his chair. Before he got a chance to pick up his burner, his work phone pinged. '*hold your horses chief inspector change of plan*'

'Fuck, fuck, fuck!' he shouted. He grabbed his burner and called Debbie, a bad feeling surging through his body. Straight to voicemail. He rang again. Straight to voicemail. 'Fuck!' She must have switched it off after texting him back. He contemplated phoning his sister but didn't want to risk compromising her…at least not yet.

He called Sully who answered straight away. 'Guv?'

'Sully, Terry text to say something about a change of plan. I don't like it. Something's wrong. Debbie text me five minutes ago and I tried calling her back but her phone must be switched off. I'm worried in case Terry tries something.'

'Doesn't make sense. As far as he's concerned you've got what he wants.'

'Nah, something else is going on. I need to speak to Debbie. If only she'd answer her fucking phone. I'll call you back in five minutes.'

He tried Debbie again, then Amanda and finally Jean, but no joy. Running out of options, he called the Perthshire police and spent ten frustrating minutes on hold before finally hearing the click of a connection.

'Sergeant Jamieson, how can I help?' a voice said, in a comforting Scottish brogue.

'Sergeant, please listen, I don't have a lot of time. My name is Detective Chief Inspector Angus McIntosh of the Metropolitan police. My wife and daughter are staying at an address in Queen Street, Blackford, and I have reason to believe they are in imminent danger of kidnap…or worse. I need officers to visit the address and place them in protective police custody until I get there and decide what to do next. I'm sure you'd rather check me out first before engaging your officers, but this is urgent.'

In fairness to Jamieson he listened without interruption. When McIntosh finished, a couple of seconds passed before Jamieson spoke. 'Sir, I'm sure you can appreciate that before sending resources to fend off kidnappers, we need some verification to make sure you're not a random nutter…no offence.'

'None taken but we don't have time and no-one else can verify this. I can explain it all later and you can check out my credentials easily enough but my wife, daughter and possibly my sister are in immediate danger. The person following them sent me a photo to let me know he knows where they are. My wife text me a little while ago and I've tried calling back but no-one is answering, which isn't normal. Same for my daughter and sister. Please get officers to go and check the house.'

The panic in McIntosh's voice told Jamieson he wasn't a fruitcake. 'Okay sir, I'll check you out with the Met and, in the meantime, two PC's will call at your sister's. They're about ten minutes away.'

'Quick as they can please. It could be life and death.' Was he being over dramatic? Frankly, he didn't care.

'Give me your number and I'll call you back when we find out more,' Jamieson said.

For fifteen minutes McIntosh wore out his living room carpet. He kept trying Debbie, Amanda and Jean on a loop. No answer. Although anticipating a call and clutching his phone as he paced, he still jumped when it rang. The screen said **Commander Beswick.**

'Fuck off!' he shouted, declining the call.

Seconds later the phone rang again. 'You've gotta be kidding. That arsehole can fuck right……….'

The screen said **Perth Police**. He hurriedly pressed the green button. 'Hello.'

'Chief Inspector, Sergeant Jamieson here. Our officers attended your sister's house in Blackford and your wife and daughter were not there.' He hesitated. 'I'm afraid we've reason to believe they've been abducted.'

His throat tightened. 'Why?'

The man took a deep breath. 'A woman, who we assume is your sister, has been found unconscious with a head injury.'

Chapter 35

Eyes closed and gripping his phone, McIntosh's worst fears were coming true. 'Is she going to be ok?' he whispered.

'She's with the paramedics. They'll soon be off to hospital. I'm afraid I can't tell you anymore. A white van drove away at speed with, we assume, your wife and daughter. The van's been found abandoned and it seems they've transferred to a different vehicle. Unfortunately, we've no idea which vehicle or where they've gone. I'm very sorry.'

McIntosh resisted the urge to mention the ridiculous amount of time he'd been on hold. Recriminations could come later. He needed these people. 'I'm booking myself on the first available flight north. Could someone meet me at the airport?' he said.

'Let me know which airport and when and I'll arrange transport for you,' Jamieson said.

'Thanks, will be in touch.'

McIntosh immediately rang Sully

'Guv?'

'Trouble Sully, they've taken Debbie and Amanda and my sister's been injured.'

'Fucking hell, what happened?'

'I knew something wasn't right. They were put in a van, then transferred to another vehicle. Police have no clue where they are. Jean's unconscious, on her way to hospital.'

'Jesus, hope she's ok, what's the plan?'

'I'm going up there, first available flight. I can't wait here for that bastard to text or phone me.'

'I'm coming with you.'

'What about your case?'

'Fuck the case. It's embezzlement. It'll still be there when I get back.'

'Okay, I'll pick you up in twenty minutes. By then we can figure out which airport to go to.'

McIntosh called Bayford.

'Boss?'

'Simon, no time to fully explain. I'll be out of action for a bit so you're in charge. Don't believe everything you're going to hear about me. I'll be back soon.'

'Okay boss, hope everything works out.'

That's why McIntosh liked the guy. Direct. No unnecessary questions, just acceptance of what he'd been told. 'Thanks Simon, speak later.'

***

Chief Inspector McIntosh's absence, without explanation, continued to cause a stir. Some of the team had seen the men in his office and it didn't take a genius to work it out. Per his boss's instructions, Bayford continued to play dumb urging his junior officers to continue working the case.

Until the smug face of Commander Jonathan Beswick walked through the door, unable to conceal a smile of pompous satisfaction. Clicking his fingers like a school teacher trying to quieten a rebellious class, he eventually got everyone's attention.

'I know gossip and rumours have been tossed around so I'd like to confirm the facts as we know them. Detective Chief Inspector Angus McIntosh has been suspended from duty, pending an investigation into allegations of bribery and evidence tampering.' He waited for the disbelief to dispense before asking for calm. 'I know it's difficult to accept and I am as shocked as you but the facts speak for themselves. Until a replacement becomes available I will assume charge of the murder investigation.'

'Sir, you must know this is all bullshit. The DCI is as straight as you get,' Bayford said.

'I thought that as well Inspector but there must be real substance to the allegations if he's been suspended so quickly. I'm afraid he's fooled us all. It goes without saying that no contact is to be made with McIntosh, in any capacity, not least regarding the murder investigation.'

'Will you be stationed in the DCI's office sir?' Findlay said.

Beswick glanced towards McIntosh's tiny space. 'Em....no, I'll continue to operate from my own office but will be here every day and will obviously be contactable by phone. Keep me informed and run everything by me,' he said, exiting sharply.

'Well, this is a pile of shit!' Myers said, loudly. 'I don't believe for a second that the DCI is bent.'

'I've only known him a few days but he seemed a bit dodgy to me,' Stuart Strong said.

'Fuck off Stuart, you don't even know the man,' Myers said.

'Enough!' Bayford said. 'We'll just have to get on with it. Beswick will be no help but he'll be all over us like a rash, waiting to take any credit that's on offer or give us a kicking if it goes wrong.'

Once the dust had settled Myers and Findlay sought out Bayford for a word, gathering in McIntosh's empty office.

'Guv, something's not right,' Myers said. 'I don't believe any of this. I've never met a straighter copper in my life than the DCI.'

'Me neither,' Findlay added. 'What can we do to help?'

'Look, the boss has some serious personal stuff going on that I can't discuss with you. Not just the allegations against him. His words to me were, 'I'll be back soon,' and also, 'don't believe everything you hear about me,' so we've got to trust him. He'll get in touch when he can but it's more important than ever that we get our fingers out and catch this killer. If we don't, we'll all be out of a job.'

Chapter 36

September 2021

Sarah had attacked the last few weeks with vigour, on a mission to destroy the worst human being she'd ever encountered but no matter the circumstances, she couldn't curb her natural hostess compulsion, laying out refreshments on her dining table before anxiously glancing at her wall clock every few seconds.

Thirty minutes later, Andrew, Ben, Catherine, Emily and Natasha all sat in uncomfortable silence, avoiding the nibbles and drinks on offer.

Sarah wrung her hands together. 'Thanks for coming everyone. I know some of us have had our differences and I hope we can see past that. I'll get straight to it. Guy doesn't want to get involved. He got mixed up with Magnus and has enough on his plate.'

'What do you mean, mixed up?' Andrew said.

'He gave Magnus his twenty thousand fee to invest. Magnus more than doubled it for him in a couple of weeks but really wanted Guy's prize money. By then Guy's charity had already received it.'

'You're kidding,' Ben said. 'Isn't that illegal? Hold on, is that what Magnus did with his own prize money?'

Sarah nodded enthusiastically. 'He's a thieving bastard. I'm in the process of obtaining proof that Magnus defrauded his own charity to make millions for himself.'

'Wow,' Ben said. 'Where's the proof coming from?'

'I hired a private investigator. He's producing a detailed report but he's given me a few highlights. Magnus 'borrowed' the prize money and used it to play the stock market for a short period of time. Turned it into millions before giving the money back. Some of the P.I.'s information was obtained unlawfully so I can't take it to the police and it wouldn't be admissible in court. I can make a complaint or the alternative is to inform the press and splash his name over the front pages. The police would then investigate and, hopefully, find the same information.'

'How did he get his hands on the money?' Ben said.

'He set up the charity and is a trustee. Probably easy to pocket the money until he'd finished with it.'

'Risky though,' Natasha said. 'He could have lost it and been due the £250,000 from his own pocket.'

Sarah smiled, 'Not if you've got his insider knowledge and contacts. Remember, he's done this before. His stock market cronies are probably still around and the world's gone mad for PPE equipment, vaccines, that sort of thing. Plus, he's in Parliament so he'll know which companies are being given Government contracts. He'll have been tipped off about what to buy and when to sell. He's not daft. He wouldn't have risked it unless it was a sure thing.'

'Jesus, what a clever, devious bastard,' Andrew said, smiling. After noticing the sharp, disapproving looks, he added. 'I mean, it's reprehensible, obviously, but imagine having a mind to even think like that. He must have got help.'

'I've been thinking the same but the police can worry about that,' Sarah said. 'I'm only interested in Magnus.'

'Hold on a minute,' Ben said. 'This isn't just about stealing charity money. If he received help, and it seems likely, Team Bravo's charities have been defrauded out of £250,000 each. If he's guilty, I'll be chasing my share which might become a problem for you, Catherine and Guy.'

'We'll cross that bridge when we come to it,' Sarah said. 'I can't honestly see them asking for ours back. The bad publicity wouldn't be worth it.'

'How much did the P.I. cost?' Emily said.

'Just over eleven grand. Less than two grand each. I'm not asking Guy to contribute. He's potless. The fifty grand didn't make much of a mark on his debt.'

'I'm pretty potless too,' Ben said, unsmiling.

'I'm on holiday soon, not great timing for me either,' Andrew said.

'Look, if you can't afford it or don't want to contribute, it's fine. I don't care about the money. I'm only interested in seeing that bastard rot in hell.'

Chapter 37

October 2021

McIntosh and Sully flashed their badges through security and boarded the Gatwick to Edinburgh flight. They each carried a small rucksack with some clothes, just in case. On the way to the airport Jamieson provided some news that an attentive local jotted down the registration of a green van driving erratically, a few miles from the scene. Unfortunately, being slap bang in the centre of Scotland, the kidnappers could have gone anywhere.

While the rest of the flight boarded, McIntosh phoned the hospital to be told Jean had regained consciousness, had a mighty headache, but would suffer no long term ramifications. It didn't stop him berating himself for embroiling her in this mess.

'You ok guv?' Sully asked.

'Aye, I'm fucking raging, worried sick and annoyed with myself, all at the same time. That bastard will get what's coming.'

Sully had witnessed this stony look many times. 'No way Terry's in Scotland, he'll have muscle doing his dirty work. I've got guys trying to find him and his gang.'

'Getting Amanda and Debbie back safe is the only thing that matters. Terry can wait. His time will come.'

'Surprised he hasn't been in touch yet?'

'Probably waiting for the van to stop. At least we've got the reg number and he probably doesn't know that we know.'

He didn't want to chat anymore. As soon as they became airborne he closed his eyes and dozed off. When he woke an hour later, a blinding headache made him wish he'd stayed awake. He chugged paracetamol and water while the plane taxied to the gate. The cabin crew allowed them off first to meet a waiting black Vauxhall Insignia.

Ten minutes later the forty-five-mile journey to Blackford began with a quick tour of the Edinburgh outskirts before they hit the open road. Sully sat up front, chatting to the driver while McIntosh preferred to lounge in the back, hoping the painkillers would quickly take effect. As they drove through Fife, he studied the beautiful countryside of a place he knew so well.

Sully looked around. 'Wishing for a peaceful life in this neck of the woods guv?'

'Aye, at a time like this. Other times, not so much.'

'How long is it you've been away?'

'Over thirty years now. Still get a lump in my throat when I come back.'

Less than an hour after landing, they drove into Blackford and met Jamieson outside Jean's house. He was a stocky dark haired man, mid-thirties with a friendly face. He showed them the bloodstained front path which reminded McIntosh he'd forgotten to get another update on his sister. He quickly called the hospital. No change. He'd visit her soon but Jean would understand that finding his family remained the priority.

He'd been to more crime scenes than he could count but it felt surreal to visit a house, frequented by him on numerous occasions, but today an impersonal crime scene visited by evil. Presumably the car parked adjacent was Debbie's hire car. He had a look inside the vehicle as well as another walk around outside but there was not much else to see. While they retreated to an Audi Q7, parked out front, Jamieson took a call.

He got in the driver's seat. 'A glimmer of good news. The green van's been spotted heading west but it'll be tough trying to find it. There are hundreds of small farms and outbuildings on the A85.'

'But it's a start,' McIntosh said. 'Can we make a radio announcement asking for public help to look out for a green van.'

'We could but I doubt we'll have time to set it up. What's this all about?' Jamieson asked.

'A fair question Sarge but we don't have time to tell the whole story and you're probably better off not knowing. But the guy behind this will not hesitate to kill my family if he doesn't get what he wants.'

McIntosh's phone pinged. Dreading to look, he nervously glanced at the text. *'Tonight 8pm, I'll tell you where nearer the time'*

'Terry?' Sully asked.

Before he got a chance to answer, another ping.

'Oh, I forgot to say………', an attachment contained a photograph of a blindfolded Debbie and Amanda.

'Oh fuck!' McIntosh's heart sank.

Sully grabbed the phone. 'Shit,' He passed it to Jamieson, who studied the picture without comment.

'I'm no' meeting him,' McIntosh said. 'I'm gonnae tell him to fuck off.'

Sully put his hand on McIntosh's arm. 'Guv, he doesn't know you're here. We've got a few hours before he thinks he's meeting you. Don't reply at all.'

Chapter 38

After twenty plus years of marriage to a senior detective, Debbie McIntosh's sense of streetwise was finely tuned. Not much got past her. After leaving Shepherds Bush, the taxi had dropped her and Amanda at Stansted Airport but, instead of flying, they hired a car.

During the trip north, Mac's instinct that Terry would follow, bore fruit when she spotted the same white van at two different service stations. Foston, Grantham and again during a Scotch Corner toilet break. Knowing their car could easily outrun the van, she assumed they'd found a way to install a tracking device.

With no advantage in racing up the motorway, she let the situation play out.

***

Newcomers stood out in a small place and, whilst strolling through the village, Debbie noticed three men walking alone, two of whom she'd recognised from Scotch Corner. Now there was no doubt. She didn't let on to Jean or Amanda.

Despite the surveillance Debbie and Amanda enjoyed afternoon tea at a small café, drinks at the local pub and long walks through the village, chatting to the friendly locals. Debbie liked Jean a lot and when she'd asked if they could stay for a while Jean didn't hesitate. A retired head teacher, she quickly sussed it wasn't a marital domestic but didn't ask any follow up questions, curbing her natural busybody instinct.

Debbie could tell Jean was itching to ask and after telling Mac about the men and formulating a plan, it was only fair that she spill the beans.

That idea changed without warning.

Jean lived in the end terrace of a four house block, with a small driveway at the side where Debbie parked. A thirty foot slabbed path from the front door led to the pavement. As Jean locked her front door, Debbie and Amanda hurried towards the car, sheltering under an umbrella.

Two men appeared from nowhere and grabbed the two women, brandishing guns to scare them into silence. Jean ran to intervene but was brutally pistol whipped, falling heavily on the sodden grass. The men left her lying prone, not moving.

A devastated Debbie couldn't do a thing before their hands were cable tied, hoods roughly forced over their heads, and mother and daughter were bundled into a white van parked on the secluded street.

After five minutes, the van abruptly stopped and the women were crudely dumped into a different vehicle. Another van, Debbie thought. The box seating around the sides was a giveaway. The driver either wasn't very good or he didn't give a hoot about his hostages because the women careered against the walls of the van every time he took a slight bend. They decided it was safer to sit on the floor. Debbie comforted a sobbing Amanda, while trying to calmly count in her head.

After the turbulent journey ended, a bruised and battered Debbie and Amanda received scant relief, being roughly manhandled into a dank, musty barn smelling of rotten wood and damp grass. Their hoods were removed and a wrist each was cable tied to a rusty, wrought iron gate standing up against a stack of hay bales, amongst a collection of defunct farm machinery.

A damp, cold Scottish barn, in October, meant they'd never be wearing enough layers.

Amanda had stopped crying, quietly surveying their temporary prison wondering how anyone could get kidnapped twice in such a short space of time. Her mother's fidgeting caught her eye. She looked quizzically as Debbie fiddled with her coat and cardigan, unbuttoning them with her free hand.

'Mum, it's freezing. Keep your coat on.'

'Shh.'

Amanda watched incredulously as her mum produced a phone from underneath her clothes. Acutely aware of the ongoing surveillance, Debbie hid the small burner phone in her bra every time they left the house. It was worth the mild discomfort.

'Mum, why is there a phone in your bra?'

'Keep your voice down. I put it there as a precaution. If I switch it on the police might be able to find our location.'

'Phone dad and tell him where we are.'

Debbie stared at her daughter. 'Honey, we don't know where we are and your dad's hundreds of miles away. I'll text him but tell him not to respond in case the men come back and hear it. I'll keep it switched on as long as I can,' she said, quickly punching out a message.

'been kidnapped, in a barn an hour away from Blackford don't know which way. Jean injured. Don't text back, i'll text when I can. Get police to track phone I'll try and keep it switched on'

Chapter 39

Having declined Jamieson's offer to head back to HQ in Perth, McIntosh, Sully and Jamieson arrived at the local station in Blackford. Thankfully, Jean had started talking, physically unharmed apart from the nasty lump on her head and cuts and bruises from falling over.

Jamieson organised tea, coffee and biscuits and McIntosh couldn't remember when he'd last eaten. He quickly devoured four chocolate digestives before slumping back in his chair. Sully hadn't seen him look this defeated before.

'What's happening Sarge?' Sully said.

'Half a dozen cars are patrolling the A85 and surrounding area looking for a green van. Not much else to go on.'

A phone pinged. An incoming text. They looked at each other with an *is that you* look. It took McIntosh a few seconds to catch on. He looked at his screen, then the others and hesitantly said, 'It's Debbie's phone,' knowing it might not be from her. His heart started beating faster.

When she hadn't answered he'd assumed the kidnappers found her phone and switched it off.

'been kidnapped, in a barn an hour away from Blackford don't know which way. Jean injured. Don't text back, i'll text when I can. Get police to track phone i'll try and keep it switched on'

'YES! It's her, she kept the phone away from them. She's in a barn an hour away from Jean's. We have to quickly track her phone before she needs to switch it off again.'

'Give her a call,' Sully said. 'She's obviously able to use it.'

'No, she said not to and I trust her. Debs is clever, she'll know the situation. At least this narrows the search.'

Jamieson called in the new information and called Perth for them to triangulate Debbie's phone. 'We should get something soon if she keeps her phone on.'

'Can I borrow a car or have someone drive me? I want to head in their direction,' McIntosh said.

'I'll drive you myself,' Jamieson said. 'Let's get going.'

***

She'd intended waiting fifteen minutes but an argument outside changed her thinking. Debbie switched off the phone and stuck it back in her bra. Just then the barn door opened and the youngest kidnapper entered with a plastic bag which he tipped onto the damp floor. 'Something to eat and drink,' he said, as water, crisps and a cheese and cracker snack fell out.

'How long are you keeping us for?' Debbie asked.

'Until your husband plays ball. Now shut up and eat your food,' he sneered, slamming the barn shut behind him. Although neither felt hungry, Debbie insisted they eat.

'They're not hiding their faces,' Amanda said quietly. 'That's not good, right?'

***

The road conditions didn't suit a fast drive but the blue flashing lights encouraged other motorists to move out of their way. The inside of the car pulsed with tension until Jamieson received a call. 'Sergeant Jamieson, you're on speaker with DCI McIntosh and DS Sullivan,' he said.

'Sarge, it's PC Haggart. No signal, the phone must be off.'

'Fuck!' McIntosh said. 'She must have got spooked.'

'Okay, call if it comes back on,' Jamieson said.

Sully said, 'Look guv, we've got a rough idea where they've gone. There's half a dozen patrol cars out there searching. We'll find them, don't worry.'

'It's a massive area. We've only got an hour before Terry thinks he's meeting me and its pitch dark. Excuse me if I don't get all optimistic on you.'

***

The previous bickering could have been discord about their next course of action. It didn't appear to be the most thought out plan in the world which worried Debbie. More chance of doing something reckless. She quickly switched the phone on and sent a text.

'It's going to kick off soon, they're getting edgy. We're ok just now. Get someone here asap'

Debbie left the phone in silent mode, buried beneath hay and mouldy grass to deaden noise or vibration. Risky, but a chance she had to take.

***

McIntosh's burner pinged again. *'It's going to kick off soon, they're getting edgy. We're ok just now. Get someone here asap'*

'It's her, thank god.'

At the same time, Jamieson's phone rang. 'Yes?'

'Sarge, phone's back on. I'll let you know when we have something,' Haggart said.

'Thanks.'

'How long before they get a location,' McIntosh asked.

'If the phone stays on, shouldn't be more than fifteen, twenty minutes. Remember, this isnae the Big Smoke where things happen instantly. The wheels run slower in rural Perthshire.'

McIntosh bit his tongue. 'My signal's getting worse the further west we go. Will that be a problem?'

'Not as long as she's still got a signal. Might be more difficult if they're moved.'

Twelve minutes later Jamieson's phone rang again. 'Yes?'

'Sarge, we've got a location. Half a mile radius from the centre of Tyndrum. That's as exact as we're going to get. The patrol cars are on their way.'

'Ok, we're heading there as well,' Jamieson said.

'How long will it take us to get there?' McIntosh said.

'Ten minutes or so.'

Chapter 40

Mounting evidence against Branch should have provided the catalyst for the EIU to close in on their man, but it didn't. McIntosh's suspension had sucked the energy from the previously eager detectives. Those who hadn't gone home worked away in silence, without enthusiasm.

Commander Beswick breezed in with an arrogant self-importance. Sensing the mood, he gathered the team. 'You better get a grip and buck up your ideas. Get out of this malaise. McIntosh's failings allowed this investigation to slip but I'm not going to tolerate that on my watch. What do you have on Branch?'

Findlay stood, 'Sir, I've trawled the cameras surrounding Sarah's flat. Nothing directly on her street but Branch's car was spotted a mile away, at 5.30pm on the night she died. I've looked at every other camera in the area but don't see his car again.'

Arnott spoke next. 'Sir, one of Sarah's neighbours remembers shouting and arguing from Sarah's flat on the night of the murder.'

'What time was that?' Beswick said. 'And why wasn't it mentioned at the first canvass?'

'Happened around 5.30-6pm. She left for a casino night shift and hadn't returned when the neighbours were first questioned.'

'Earlier than the time of death,' Beswick said. 'Myers, what about you?'

'Like Joanne, there are no cameras directly on Guy's street but Magnus's car was in Brixton on the day of his murder. One of Guy's neighbours remembered a maroon Bentley driving along his street about 3pm. He'd never seen a fancier car in the neighbourhood so it stuck in his memory. He never checked the number plate but it's surely got to be Magnus.'

'So, we've an argument at Sarah's around the time his car is spotted and not long before her death plus his fingerprint on her clothing. A car like his in Guy's street around the time of his death and traces of his blood in Guy's house. A helluva lot of circumstantial evidence. Good work, despite all the moping around. Think what you'll be capable of when you really get your teeth into it.'

'Are we bringing him in, sir?' Bayford asked, changing the subject.

'Yes, tomorrow. Early, before he gets a chance to contact his lawyer.'

'What about a search warrant?' Findlay said.

'Interview him first and we'll arrange a search warrant afterwards.'

'That doesn't make sense,' Bayford said. 'Arresting him without searching his home and workplace might give someone a chance to destroy evidence.'

'Do it my way Inspector,' Beswick said, abruptly about turning. 'I'm in charge now.'

'Arsehole,' Bayford muttered under his breath.

Chapter 41

A worried Terry took another sip of his malt whisky, the alcohol not helping the complexion on his flush round face and large red nose. He'd instructed McIntosh to meet him at the same Boots in Clapham but hadn't heard back. He clutched his phone. 'Rollo, how secure is that barn?'

'Secure enough boss, it's dark and abandoned. Think we're safe enough here.'

'Something's wrong. I haven't heard back from McIntosh. He's buying time for some reason. What if you were spotted when you were scouting that place. Maybe McIntosh has contacted the local plod and they're on their way.'

'All these farms look the same boss. It's dark, they'd never be sure of the right one, even if they were coming.'

'Move them now, Rollo.'

'Where to boss? It's dark, we've nowhere else to go.'

'Fuck sake Rollo, you're in the middle of nowhere. There's bound to be another farm somewhere or keep them in the van somewhere till I let you know if he turns up. If he doesn't, you know what to do.'

'Ok boss.'

Although not the brightest soldier on Terry's payroll, the fiercely loyal Rollo could be relied upon to carry out his explicit instructions. Stevo and Donny, not so much. They were relatively new and Terry didn't fully trust them yet. In his world, a little brain power in the wrong hands could be a dangerous thing which is why they answered to Rollo.

'We've got to move them,' Rollo said to the other two.

'Whaat. Where to? This is ridiculous,' Stevo said.

'Terry's orders, let's get moving.'

'Terry's not here though. More dangerous to keep moving. No-one knows we're here so it's better to stay.'

'I'll call Terry back and tell him your thoughts,' Rollo said, punching numbers.

Stevo's shoulders sagged. 'Fuck! Ok, let's get on with it,' he said, defeated.

The three men entered the barn while the two women sat quietly. Debbie stared straight ahead avoiding eye contact with the mound of mouldy grass.

'Right, let's get moving,' Rollo said, handing a hood to each of his colleagues.

Debbie protested, 'You can't keep throwing us in the back of your van, tied and blindfolded.'

Stevo drew his hand back and slapped Debbie's face, hard. 'Shut up,' he growled. She screamed more in shock than pain. Amanda also screamed and Donny drew his hand back.

'Do you want the same?' he said.

Amanda stopped screaming and instantly felt ashamed.

'Good,' Rollo said. 'It'll be easier if you do what we say.'

The hooded, tied women were again bundled into the back of the van. Debbie wished she'd managed to put the phone back in her bra but it was too late. All she could do was pray.

Stevo put the van into gear and turned to Rollo. 'Right Einstein, where to?'

'Just drive, keep heading west and we'll wing it,' Rollo said.

Stevo shrugged and manoeuvred the van slowly through the dirt track puddles until they reached the farm entrance. He veered right onto the main road and immediately started driving too fast for the slippery conditions.

'Slow down, you'll get us all killed,' Rollo said.

Stevo eased off but still pushed over 60mph on the winding single carriageway. 'Right, what's the plan?'

Rollo pored over a map using the inside light. They passed through a tiny hamlet called Arrivain. 'Keep heading west towards Oban. It's about an hour away. We may have to go off road a few times to keep out of sight.'

'Aw fuck, too late,' Stevo shouted, as a police car passed on the opposite side. In the rear view mirror he saw brake lights illuminate. 'Fuckity fuck.'

Rollo, the calming influence in this weird kidnapper trio said, 'Get a grip and concentrate on keeping the van upright. Look for a turn off. If we can go off road we can leg it.'

Stevo tightly gripped the wheel as he slammed his foot down, a brooding expression on his face.

Chapter 42

Jamieson drove at a snail's pace, with Sully and McIntosh scouring every opening, hoping a green van would magically appear. At just after 7.30pm a breathless voice crackled on the radio.

'The van's heading west, just after Arrivain village. In pursuit.'

'Tell them not to engage,' McIntosh said. 'We don't want to spook them. We don't even know if Debs and Amanda are in the van.'

Jamieson gave the command.

McIntosh sent a text to Terry. *'see you there'*

***

'They're not getting closer,' Stevo said.

'Keeping their distance until backup arrives. Not good,' Rollo said. He grabbed his phone.

'What's happening?' Terry said.

'Cops on our tail boss. They must have been right on us before we moved. We can't shake them off. There's nowhere to go,' Rollo said.

'Don't let them catch you until I've met McIntosh. He's just text me. Once I've got the evidence you can surrender or try to escape, I don't really care,' Terry said.

Rollo sighed. 'Gee, thanks boss.'

'What's the plan?' Stevo said.

'Keep driving until Terry's met McIntosh, then every man for himself.'

'Fuck that. I'm not hanging around to get caught.'

'Do what he says, Terry's not a man to cross.'

Stevo's face darkened again.

Debbie knew the driver was out of control. With the amount of rainfall, the road would be treacherous. Amanda screamed as the van skidded round a bend on two wheels.

***

'The patrol car's up ahead,' Jamieson said.

It had to happen now. Sully's idea to text Terry, agreeing to meet, might reduce the risk of him doing something stupid. 'We need to stop the van,' McIntosh said, 'I'd normally suggest a road block but not if there's a chance my wife and daughter are in the back.'

Jamieson accelerated past the patrol car and tailgated the van, flashing his lights. A long shot but worth a try. The van accelerated again, skidding.

'Shite, try and get ahead of him,' McIntosh said.

As Jamieson overtook, the van veered into his path forcing him to brake and swing back on the correct side of the carriageway. A black BMW driver, traumatised by headlights mixed with blue strobe, swerved to avoid the van which dived back into the proper lane. With a free pathway ahead Jamieson hammered the accelerator to the floor and flew past, until the van jerked violently, catching his rear passenger door.

Jamieson spun out of control, his car hit a fence post and flipped twice, landing on its roof. It skated fifty yards along the wrong side of the road, eventually spinning to a halt.

Stevo could have removed his hands from the wheel for all the good they did. He tried to correct his steering but couldn't stop the van toppling onto its side and sliding down a steep bank, ramming into a tree with a hideously loud crunch.

Dust and smoke emanated from the van, while an eerie silence hung over the blistering mass of fused metal.

Until a crackle of flame began to glow from the mangled wreckage.

Chapter 43

A born trier, Stuart Strong didn't stand still for long if he sniffed half a chance. He nervously waited for her in Bella Cucina, a posh Italian restaurant in Chelsea. Dating witnesses was verboten but Strong never played by the rules, especially when it involved sizzling hot blondes.

Natasha Cook had been dumbstruck when Strong asked her to dinner. Yes, he had a certain boyish charm but his cocky, lairy personality was a turn off. But what did she have to lose? She'd wing it for a while and have a little fun. When the maître d ushered her to their table, an acceptable ten minutes late, ever the gentleman Stuart Strong remained seated.

'Evening Detective Constable, how are you tonight?'

'Fine thanks, what about you, and remember it's Stuart.'

'Good thanks, I didn't expect to hear from you. Is this the protection policy? Do I have to move you into my house?' she giggled.

I wish, Strong thought. 'Well, it depends on what happens tonight,' he said with a leering grin.

'I didn't think the police allowed personal contact with witnesses?'

'They don't, but we can call this a follow up interview which just happened to take place in a restaurant.'

The waiter came over and Natasha ordered a Mojito and the House Special Lasagne. Strong settled on Moretti beer, Chicken Parmigiana and garlic bread. They received their drinks and relaxed, waiting on the food.

'Tell me about your family, are you close with them?' Strong said, faking sincerity.

'No, I have no family left. My mum and sister both died and I never knew my father.'

'Oh God, I'm really sorry. How long ago?'

'Long time ago, when I was a teenager, I don't really like to talk about it.'

'I understand, so what led to you being on the telly?'

'I was modelling around the time reality shows really took off and I received an offer to appear on a dating show. You know what it's like, get noticed, it leads to something else and so on. Except I didn't enjoy it. I didn't find love, still looking in fact. I still do modelling from time to time.'

Strong nodded and thought about sugar daddies. 'What about this Island thing?'

'I heard about it from a friend and really fancied it. Lucky really, as I was the least known out of the group but they wanted an airhead blonde with fake nails and lashes and I fitted the bill.'

'You talked before about the animosity amongst the group. I thought celebrities were all nicey, nice to each other on these shows, at least when the cameras were rolling?'

Natasha laughed, 'Not this one. There isn't a single person from that show I would meet socially. Probably only two or three I wouldn't walk past in the street. The producers bunched eight flawed people together hoping to create friction. Unfortunately, they got more fireworks than they bargained for and a show they couldn't edit into six hour long episodes. Serves them right.'

'Doesn't help you if no one sees the show?'

'Maybe, but there's plenty exposure now. What do they say? No such thing as bad publicity.'

'Surely can't do your career any good being associated with the show?'

'Maybe, but I don't plan on doing this forever.'

Strong nodded, 'Last time we spoke you said Sarah punched Magnus. We've since heard she had it in for him about a dodgy deal with the charity money. Did you know?'

'Yeah, Sarah contacted us about irregularities with Magnus's prize money. She went to a private investigator and got excited about the prospect of giving Magnus a kicking.'

'What happened?'

'Nothing. She said she'd contact the police or press but I heard nothing more. I assumed the PI's information didn't stand up.'

'Sarah never got in touch about it?'

'Not after the first time, and she died not long after.'

'He got sacked didn't he, for insider trading?'

'Magnus? So I believe, something along those lines. Do we really need to talk about this?'

'I don't want to but if someone finds out, at least I can keep up the pretence of an interview.'

The waiter brought their food and Natasha spent an educational ten minutes staring at Strong shovel Chicken Parmigiana into his mouth like he'd fasted for a week. He barely looked up. She didn't know humans could eat like that.

Natasha politely continued the conversation, hoping to avoid flying debris. 'What about you, what's your story?' she said, chewing slowly.

'Not much to tell. Born in Brighton but moved to London for my dad's job. Got into a few scrapes as a teenager and my parents thought joining the police would keep me out of trouble.'

'And?'

'What do you think?' he said, winking. 'Started as a PC and became detective at twenty-five. Based at Notting Hill and on secondment to the EIU, as you know.'

'Oh, you're not permanently on that team?'

'No, when a specialist team needs extra support they ask for the best detectives from other stations.'

'Wow, impressive,' Natasha said with a twinkle, 'Aren't you a bit old to still be a DC? You must be what, thirty-eight?'

He frowned and gave her a dirty look. 'Just turned thirty-three actually and no, not really, some guys in their forties and fifties are still DC's.'

'But surely they're the least talented or they've fallen foul of their bosses. I'm not going to be responsible for an old, grey DC Strong am I?' she said, smiling.

'Not me,' he said bluntly, 'I know what I'm doing. My career is mapped out.'

'Dating witnesses wouldn't help would it?'

'It's an interview, not a date,' he snapped, 'And no one's going to know unless you plan on telling someone?'

'Not me Stuart, my lips are sealed,' she said, exaggerating a zipping motion.

'I think it's time we got the bill, I've an early start in the morning.'

'Wow, ten o'clock, you know how to show a girl a good time.'

Before the date Strong envisioned a meal and drinks before doing the business at her place, escaping sharpish then bragging to his mates he'd shagged a telly star. His deluded plan was disintegrating. 'Some of us have important stuff to do, not TV bullshit,' he snarled, waving his hand at the waiter.

'You've gone all weird Stuart. I'm hurt,' she mocked.

'Not me but I think you're taking the piss now and I need to get going anyway.'

'I didn't mean to upset you,' she lied. 'But, if you're trying to catch a killer you probably need all the rest you can get.'

When the waiter laid the bill on the table, Strong angrily threw some notes at it. 'I'll be in touch.'

An amused Natasha remained, sipping her drink. She'd been on the wind up and wondered when he'd click. Quite quickly, to be fair.

Chapter 44

McIntosh stirred slowly. He must have blacked out for a few seconds. Groans came from his fellow passengers but his main concern was the van's whereabouts. 'Is everyone ok?' he said.

'I think so,' Jamieson said.

'Leg's busted but yeah,' Sully added.

Gripping the armrests and overhead grab handles, they carefully released their seatbelts. McIntosh and Jamieson crunched the battered doors open and gingerly crawled from the wreckage. Blood trickled down McIntosh's leg and his cheek was wet, presumably from a gash while Jamieson's eye leaked from a cut on the lid.

Sully wasn't so fortunate. Other police officers gently dragged him away from the wrecked car, a badly broken ankle leaving him howling in pain. McIntosh saw smoke nestling among the trees. Hobbling towards it, panic set in when he spotted the first glint of fire.

A smattering of flame emanated from the engine area. He didn't have long. With the van on its side he had to dodge flames to peer through the broken side window. Two blood spattered men lay broken, heads at weird angles, clearly dead.

He staggered round the back and wrestled with the door before finally wrenching it open. He saw nothing but blackness. Not caring about his pain, he blindly inched his way into the back of the ruined van, on his knees, feeling with his hands. He silently prayed that the kidnappers had done a runner and Debs and Amanda were tied up in a barn, freezing cold on some manky old farm.

He suddenly became aware of the intensifying heat and quickened his search. He brushed against a rough carpet or blanket and felt a leg, a hip and the rest of a body. Frantically, he pulled the cover off and, as his eyes adjusted, saw his daughter's bruised and battered face. When he found the rhythmic beat of a pulse, he cheered inwardly. Then he heard a voice.

'Hurry sir, the van's really on fire. It'll blow soon,' Jamieson said.

'Shite, gimme a hand.'

He gently lifted his daughter and passed her to the waiting Jamieson.

'Is she……?' Jamieson asked.

'Unconscious,' McIntosh replied. 'Phone for an ambulance.'

'They're already on their way, what about your missus?'

'No sign yet.'

'Get a move on, you've no' got much time.'

Ignoring the overpowering heat, he crawled back into the smoky van and roughly prodded and poked into the corners of the van until he touched a shape covered by a dirty overall. He threw the overall off and pressed the shape hard until Debbie involuntarily winced at his heavy handedness. 'Thank fuck,' he muttered.

By now, coughing and spluttering uncontrollably, he coarsely dragged the semi-conscious Debbie to the van door, then lifted her and passed her to Jamieson.

'Sir, get away from here, NOW.'

Jamieson carried Debbie up the steep bank and placed her by the roadside, next to Amanda and Sully. Ascending the incline slowly on his hands and knees, McIntosh had not quite reached the sanctuary of the road when the van exploded in a fury of fire and hot metal. The blast propelled him face down into the wet scrub as he tried to protect his head from flying debris.

Jamieson and a young PC dived down the bank and ruthlessly dragged McIntosh to safety.

Paramedics arrived and took control. They concluded Sully was most in need of treatment and once they had his pain under control, he was whisked to hospital. McIntosh needed several blasts of oxygen for the smoke inhalation and he and Jamieson were also treated for minor lacerations. Amanda and Debbie suffered non serious head injuries but were covered in bumps and bruises from being tossed around the back of the van. They continued to drift in and out of consciousness.

When she came to, Debbie wondered if she was dreaming, unable to comprehend why McIntosh was there, never mind holding her hand. She also recognised the man with a busted leg but couldn't remember his name. She was too exhausted to quiz her husband, more concerned about Amanda who was being treated for a cut on the back of her head. She hadn't said a word.

In the midst of the chaos McIntosh located Jamieson. 'Thanks for everything Sarge, I owe you a pint. We wouldn't have found them without you.'

'No problem sir, I'll hold you to that. One day you'll need to tell me all about it.'

McIntosh laughed, 'Aye, will do.'

The ambulances left for Perth. Despite showing no signs of serious injury the paramedics insisted Debbie and Amanda be checked over in hospital and would likely be admitted overnight.

Like Jamieson, McIntosh refused to go to hospital, his breathing having returned to some degree of normality. His mind now drifted towards Terry, who would be raging.

Chapter 45

A furious Terry waited half an hour before calling it quits and going home. He got no answer from Rollo but as he aimed his phone at the wall, he received an incoming call.

'Yes,' he said abruptly. He listened intently without a word. Eventually he said, 'Are you fucking kidding me? And you waited till now to tell me. It's too fucking late, idiot. What am I paying you for?' Terry's normally red face turned a shade of purple. 'I'll deal with you later,' he shouted.

***

Miraculously, apart from a banging headache, Rollo survived without a scratch. Seeing his obviously dead colleagues, he patted himself on the back for wearing a seatbelt. He'd climbed over his stricken accomplices and kicked the door open. Heading deeper into the woods he heard the violent explosion and turned to witness the mix of smoke, blue lights and raging fire. His relief turned to frustration at the lack of battery on his phone and no signal.

***

Lying in her hospital bed, a more composed Debbie told her husband the story of their abduction, her horror at the violence inflicted on Jean and the events leading to the crash. She explained there were three kidnappers and a manhunt was now underway but she was still perplexed about why he was there in the first place.

'So, you knew we'd been followed and didn't tell me?' she said, annoyed.

McIntosh smiled. 'I'm guessing you already knew.'

She ignored him. 'How's Amanda?' she asked.

'Aye, she'll be all right. Concussion and some cuts and bruises but otherwise ok. She got knocked out as well when the van overturned. She'll be fine by tomorrow. Do you think you'll be able to fly?'

'Hopefully, if we've got plenty of painkillers. I just want to get home. How's Jean?'

'On the mend and getting out in the next couple of days. I'll go and see her before I leave. I'll collect you both tomorrow, then we'll head to the airport.'

Debbie shrugged. 'You realise Jean would have avoided all this if we'd gone somewhere else.'

McIntosh nodded uncomfortably but he was confident Jean's only concern would be everyone's safety. 'Aye, but now she's a village celebrity with a story to tell. She'll be in her element.'

Debbie smiled and closed her eyes. He left her to rest, walked into the men's ward and spotted Sully, his plastered left leg raised on a mountain of pillows. 'You've never changed. Always with your feet up.'

'That's hilarious!' Sully said. 'I should be charging you for this.'

'Your treatment's free and your time isn't worth much either,' McIntosh laughed. 'Seriously though, I couldn't have done it on my own. Thanks for everything. I think that's us even now. When are you getting out?'

'Tomorrow, all being well. I'll need to get a train home.'

'Let me know when you arrive at Kings Cross or Euston and I'll get someone to pick you up. Least I can do.'

Sully suddenly got serious and dug out his phone. 'Remember I arranged for some guys to keep an eye on Terry and his goons.'

'Aye.'

'They sent me some photos. Do you recognise anyone?' Sully said, handing his phone over.

McIntosh nodded, his face like thunder.

***

The small hotel, arranged quickly by Jamieson, was basic but comfortable and had everything he needed. A bed, shower and coffee making facilities. McIntosh stood under the steaming, cascading water and felt the tension release from his body. He lay on his bed, coffee by his side and relaxed for the first time in a while. He closed his eyes and felt sleep was close until he heard his phone ping.

'Congrats chief inspector, you've won the battle but who's going to win the war'

Chapter 46

McIntosh walked through the front door, threw his jacket onto the newel post at the bottom of the stairs and collapsed into his favourite armchair. The last few days had taken their toll and, while knackered, he couldn't afford to relax.

He'd seen Debbie and Amanda off on holiday. No time limit. They needed to recover with sun, sea and R&R, especially Amanda. She'd been traumatised by the events of the last couple of weeks.

He'd booked it personally through an independent travel agent he knew on South Africa Road and paid cash. He told the owner, Benny Bowden to let him know when he needed more cash, if Debbie decided to stay on. Benny was an old acquaintance and discretion was part of his armour.

He'd collected Sully from Kings Cross and taken him home. Able to work remotely, Sully would soon be back on the fraudsters trail. McIntosh promised to update him on any Terry related business and progress of the murder investigation.

McIntosh put his feet on the coffee table and closed his eyes, blocking it all from his mind. He managed twenty minutes before thoughts of murder entered his head.

It was time to set the cat among the pigeons.

***

The EIU had been kicking their heels, unable to arrest Branch and going round in circles re-checking CCTV, forensic reports and witness statements to ensure they hadn't missed anything and what they did have stood up to scrutiny. Nothing else of interest emerged. The boring humdrum grind did nothing for morale but the one upside was Beswick's lack of visibility. Without a chance to bang his own drum he steered clear and left Bayford in charge. Morale remained low and in the absence of any chatter, the squad room thrummed only with the tapping of computer keys.

Arnott burst through the door breaking the inertia. 'I saw the DCI's car driving into the car park. Is he coming back?'

'I haven't heard anything,' Bayford said. 'Must be another ACU interview.'

Ten minutes later all eyes followed Angus McIntosh as he entered his own office. He silently surveyed the scene, satisfied no interlopers had taken over his domain. He settled into his bespoke chair and switched on his laptop. Only then did he look through his Perspex window, clocking every head turn away. He smiled.

He logged in before slowly wandering into the open plan squad room, air thick with unease. Nobody dared speak. He stood in a position where he could see the whole team.

'Hello everyone. Good to see you all. I trust the temporary SIO gave you his full support during my absence but as you can see I'm back and again in charge of this investigation. I want a briefing in ten minutes, at which time I'll answer any of your questions. Simon, can I see you in my office?'

When McIntosh left, the previously subdued squad room was awash with smiles, crackling chatter and decibel levels above anything heard in days. Glenn Myers punched the air.

'What's going on boss?' Bayford said, closing the door. 'I know you said everything would turn out all right but I genuinely didn't think you'd be back.'

'I've been reinstated. All charges dropped. Beswick went apoplectic but I got the Federation got involved and he didn't have a choice.'

'What happened? Beswick mentioned bribery and evidence tampering.'

'All true,' McIntosh smiled, 'But, as I said to Anti-Corruption, not everything was as it seemed.'

'Meaning?'

'You know Johnson told me to steal evidence or he'd come after my family. Well he followed them to Scotland and sent me a photo of them, as a warning. To buy some time I pretended to steal evidence. Nothing's secret in this place and I knew the blabbermouths would get the information to the right people. I got suspended but when AC checked the case evidence, it hadn't been touched. By then Johnson abducted Debs and Amanda so I flew to Scotland and, long story short, there was a car chase, then a crash which resulted in two of Terry's men dead and Debs and Amanda unconscious.'

'Jesus Christ, I wish you'd said so I could've helped. How's the family doing?'

'There's bugger all you could've done and you did help by keeping things going here. I knew I'd be back, just didn't know when. Debs is strong but Amanda's going to need more time. She's been through a lot. I've sent them on holiday for a bit to get some rest. It'll give me a chance to get stuck into this shitshow.'

'What about the bribery allegation?'

'Unknown to me, £25,000 mysteriously arrived in my account. I told the AC officers and showed the video of Amanda and the laddie, tied and blind folded. Gave them the texts as well. They agreed it was intimidation to make me complicit but they wouldn't reinstate me until they traced the money.'

'Where did it lead?'

'Nae idea, they wouldn't say but they were content letting me return to work. It's still a sensitive subject so be careful what you say.'

'Who shopped you to the ACU?'

'They wouldn't tell me that either, even after the allegation proved false.'

Before Bayford could reply, the door nearly burst from its hinges.

'DI Bayford, could you leave us please,' Beswick said. He closed the door and sat. 'I don't know what stunt you're pulling?'

'Stunt? I've been cleared of any wrongdoing.'

'How did you explain the money?'

'I'm not at liberty to say,' McIntosh said calmly.

'NOT AT LIBERTY?' Beswick exploded, red faced and bulging eyes.

'It's confidential and ACU are still investigating. Bottom line, I've been reinstated and back in charge of the investigation.'

'I noted you sneakily got the Fed involved and made it political.'

'Not sneaky at all. I assumed you'd do your best to keep me away so I used whatever means I could.'

'You threatened to go public.'

'I can't comment. It's with the Fed lawyers.'

'Your card's marked Chief Inspector. You better get results otherwise you'll be out on your ear and no union's going to save you. I've done a better job than you and managed to get a prime suspect. You'd better finish that off,' Beswick said, marching away.

Bayford waited thirty seconds before knocking and entering. 'Taking it well?'

McIntosh smiled, 'Exactly as I thought he would. He's an angry man but a very dangerous man. When is Branch being arrested?'

'Later today.'

'Why wasn't he arrested before now?'

'Beswick bottled it. Branch was due at a conference in Manchester. Beswick thought it would be inappropriate to do it before then. He arrived home last night.'

'Inappropriate? He's a fucking murder suspect.'

Bayford shrugged.

McIntosh shook his head in disbelief. 'Get everyone together while I get a coffee.'

Chapter 47

They gathered in the meeting room. Less chance of any interruptions. The team sat agog, desperate to hear the real story, to put these canteen rumours to bed. You could hear a pin drop.

McIntosh decided to be frank. 'What I'm about to tell you doesnae leave this room. It is still an active investigation and I dinna want more gossip spread about me, even if it happens to be the truth. Understood?'

Every single head nodded in agreement.

'To coerce me into destroying evidence from a recent case, my daughter and her friend were abducted. Released unharmed the next day but it was to show me the kidnappers meant business. To get out of harm's way, my wife and daughter went to Scotland but were followed and abducted again. I couldn't make it official or jeopardise any of your careers by asking for help so I pursued matters on my own. I went with an old friend to Scotland to get them back. We succeeded, but only after a high speed car crash which left two of the kidnappers dead and my family injured. Not seriously, thankfully.'

He watched eyes nearly pop out of heads and one or two jaws get wider.

He continued. 'In between times the ACU suspended me pending an investigation into evidence tampering and bribery, all of which proved to be unfounded. The charges have been dropped and I've been reinstated. My family is safe and well. Any questions?'

The collective exhaling of breath coincided with the movement of limbs. No-one had moved a muscle for the two minutes it took McIntosh to tell his story. The room relaxed but remained silent until Myers raised his hand.

'Boss, it's brilliant to have you back. Wasn't the same being scolded in a plummy English accent.'

McIntosh smiled at last. 'Thanks Glenn.'

Myers continued. 'I need to ask. Did you steal or destroy any evidence?'

'Aye, but just the fake kind. I needed to make it look real and get the gossipmongers talking but I didn't bet on someone snitching to ACU.'

'Who were the kidnappers?' Findlay asked.

'I don't know who they were but I know who they worked for. One escaped uninjured, now in custody in Scotland. Their boss is still at large but his time is coming.'

'Who is it?' Dolan asked.

'I'm not naming names but it relates to a previous case so you can probably work it out.'

'How are your family?' Arnott said.

'Aye, they're good. Suffered some minor injuries but nothing serious. They're away on a well-earned holiday. Anything else?' A few heads shook. 'Remember, if I hear that someone is telling tales I'll no' be happy. Right, let's move on to the happier subject of murder. Give me some good news.'

Bayford spoke first. 'Branch is being arrested later today. He's in the House of Commons just now but he's got a meeting in his parliamentary office at 5pm so we'll do it then.'

'Can we no' just drag his arse out in front of the whole House?' McIntosh said.

'Beswick bottled that as well. We've got Branch's blood at Guy's, his fingerprint on Sarah's clothing and his car in the area of both murders around the right times. All circumstantial.'

'Anything else?'

Dolan spoke next, 'There's a link between the Harvey and Edwards deaths. Both suffered heart attacks but neither were the cause of death. The Spanish police confirmed Harvey collapsed, fell in the pool and drowned. No suspicious circumstances and they'd no interest in disclosing any more information. Harvey shared the villa with a young Spaniard, Juan Pablo. In his words Harvey was a controlling bully and the guy only stayed due to his generosity.'

Strong butted in, 'Natasha Cook figured out right away Harvey was gay and threatened to expose him.'

'Doesn't make sense,' McIntosh said. 'If he felt threatened, why is he the one who's dead?'

'Maybe being blackmailed and a row got out of hand,' Arnott added.

'No, if Harvey was murdered, someone went there to induce a heart attack. Falling in the pool was maybe coincidental,' Bayford said.

'Anything else from Spain?' McIntosh said.

'Juan Pablo didn't know much. Went to the market half an hour away and when he came back Harvey was floating in the pool. It's a remote location and a stranger would have stood out but no-one from the surrounding villas saw anything,' Dolan said.

'Any indication of involvement by this Juan Pablo?'

'No, the Spanish police ruled him out. Harvey treated him badly but looked after him financially. Now he's a waiter, living in a dingy apartment. Can't see him wanting to kill Harvey, never mind being able to source a heart attack inducing drug.'

'Did Harvey's wife know he was gay?' McIntosh said.

'No, they separated before the TV show. She only found out when she heard that a hunky Spaniard discovered his body.'

'You didn't mention he was a hunk, Sarge?' Arnott said, smiling.

'Not a hunk you'd be interested in.'

'Ok, what about Edwards?' McIntosh said.

Myers jumped in. 'Similar to Spain. Edwards sustained a heart attack, probably knocking him unconscious while he suffocated in his car. His wife confirmed a gambling addiction back when he played football. He'd been to counselling and she thought he'd kicked it but since he began radio and TV punditry, he'd more money in his pocket than when he played. She suspected he was still gambling but never got a straight answer from him.'

'A loan shark?' McIntosh asked.

Myers nodded. 'Maybe into someone for a lot of money and decided to end it all.'

'I don't like coincidences,' McIntosh said. 'These deaths feel significant to the O'Neill and Ekers murders.'

Chapter 48

Magnus Branch was not the most patient of men. Where the fuck was Rupert Thornhill, he thought, stewing away in cell 5 at Charing Cross. He paid that smarmy bastard exorbitant fees to ensure his needs were first and foremost in Thornhill's mind. Snapping his fingers should be enough to have him come running.

Despite a mountain of preparation work he needed to complete for a different case, Thornhill dropped everything. He had to keep Branch sweet. The MP never missed a chance to tell his solicitor how fortunate he was to have him as a client. To be fair, the money did help. Escorted by a PC, Thornhill appeared at the door of cell 5.

'About fucking time!' Branch said.

'Magnus, you only called an hour ago. I got here as quickly as I could,' Thornhill said.

'These bastards dragged me from my own office in handcuffs, in front of the party chairman, and left me hanging around like a criminal. I need you to get me out.'

'They've obviously got something or they wouldn't have arrested you, but please stay quiet unless I tell you to speak.'

***

The custody Sergeant escorted Branch and Thornhill to the same interview room as before, minus the refreshments. McIntosh and Bayford entered and Bayford pressed the record button. Despite feeling a weight lifted from his shoulders, McIntosh was in no mood to chit chat.

'Interview commencing. I am Detective Chief Inspector McIntosh, alongside me is Detective Inspector Bayford. Also present are ....'

'Magnus Branch, MP.'

'Rupert Thornhill, Mr Branch's solicitor.'

'...thank you. I'll get right to it Mr Branch. You previously stated in interview that you've never been to Guy Ekers flat. Do you still maintain that position?' McIntosh said.

'No comment.'

'We found your blood in Mr Ekers' flat, how did it get there?'

'No comment.'

'Mr Branch, your car was in Brixton around the time Guy Ekers was murdered. Why were you there?'

'No comment'

'A witness placed your very distinctive, maroon Bentley in Guy Ekers' street. He remembers it clearly because he'd never seen a car like it in Brixton before. Why were you there Mr Branch?'

Thornhill interjected. 'Chief Inspector, did the registration plate match my client's car?'

'The witness wasn't able to take note of the plate?'

'So, there's nothing to suggest this was my client's car. It could have been anyone?'

'Anyone? Aye, two different maroon Bentleys were trawling the streets of Brixton at the same time? What were you doing there Mr Branch?'

Magnus glanced at his solicitor, sweat forming on his forehead. 'No comment.'

'Mr Branch, you have clearly being advised to answer no comment and that is your right of course. But, remember, it's you who's been arrested for double murder, not your solicitor. If you think a no comment interview will get you released, you're mistaken.'

'Mr Branch, how many times have you been to Sarah O'Neill's house?' Bayford said.

'No comment.'

'You previously stated once, for the after show party. Do you maintain this?' Bayford continued.

'No comment.'

'We can place your car in Fulham on the night Sarah O'Neill was murdered. Can you explain what you were doing there?'

'No comment.'

A frustrated McIntosh wasn't expecting this from the man who could talk for England. 'Mr Branch, we can hold you for twenty-four hours, then apply for a further twelve. If you continue to remain uncooperative you'll be held for the maximum time allowed. I assume Mr Thornhill explained this?'

The sweat dripped onto his clasped hands. 'No comment.'

McIntosh continued, 'Mr Branch, we have evidence placing you inside Sarah O'Neill's flat around the time she was murdered. Why were you there?'

Branch's eyes widened and he stared at Thornhill.

'What evidence?' Thornhill said.

'Mr Branch, please answer the question.'

Magnus glared at a stone-faced Thornhill. 'No comment.'

'Mr Branch, you left a fingerprint on the clothing Sarah O'Neill wore that night and she had bruising on her upper arm where someone grabbed her. Did you have an argument with Sarah, lose control and stab her to death?'

Hands shaking, Branch used a tissue to wipe the sweat from his cheeks and chin.

'I would like a moment to confer with my client,' Thornhill said.

'Absolutely, then please stop wasting our time,' McIntosh said.

In the quiet corridor, Bayford said. 'What do you think, boss?'

'He's hiding something. He's desperate to talk but his solicitor is calling the shots.'

'We don't have enough.'

'Exactly what Thornhill is hanging his hat on. He's hoping we kick him.'

***

'Mr Branch, before the break I asked you to explain the bruising on Sarah O'Neill's arm and your fingerprint on her clothing. Do you have an explanation?' McIntosh said.

Branch hesitantly looked at Thornhill, 'No comment.'

'Here's what I think happened,' Bayford said. 'You hated Sarah O'Neill. That's a fact, you said it yourself. She discovered you stole the charity prize money from the TV show and you found out she intended exposing you. You brutally killed her before she got the chance. Guy was the whistleblower who told the others, so you killed him before he could say anymore,' Bayford sensed an unnaturally quiet Magnus needed to speak, 'How am I doing so far?'

'No comment.' Branch said, with gritted teeth.

McIntosh rose, 'It's 7.02pm. Mr Branch, you will be taken back to your cell, pending further enquiries.'

Thornhill quickly interrupted. 'Chief Inspector, may I suggest Mr Branch is bailed, pending these further enquiries. There's no need to detain him. He's a Member of Parliament, you know where he'll be.'

McIntosh pretended to deliberate, before gathering his paperwork. 'Not a chance, he's had his opportunity to talk, now he's going back to his cell. Uncooperative suspects are usually hiding something. Maybe he'll come to his senses over the next twenty hours.'

Magnus finally exploded. 'This is fucking ridiculous. I haven't done anything wrong. I'll sue you for false arrest and Thornhill, you're fucking useless as well.'

'Mr Branch, you've wasted enough of our time. At the appropriate juncture you'll be re-interviewed, released or charged,' McIntosh said, walking away.

'Thornhill, sort this out, I need out of here,' Branch said, being led away.

Chapter 49

A mountain of evidence boxes lay strewn across the squad room floor. The search of Branch's house, office and car took longer than anticipated. Branch's Chelsea townhouse was a warren of passageways with small cupboards and drawer cabinets everywhere, filled with photographs, knick knacks and other trinkets. His wife was less than co-operative which was not unexpected, her parting shot reminding them that she wanted everything back intact.

'What did we get?' McIntosh asked, impatience getting the better of him.

'Nothing incriminating yet,' Dolan said. 'His clothes are off to forensics. We've got his laptop, phones, and some financial documents. They'll take time to process.'

McIntosh looked disappointed. 'Ok, I'll sweet talk Evelyn Marsh, make sure her team are on the ball. We could do with a wee nugget to nail his arse.'

Twenty minutes later Bayford rapped on McIntosh's door. 'Boss, Joanne's got Branch's laptop but something's not right. It's too clean.'

'Clean?'

'I mean purged. Literally nothing. No Parliamentary stuff, meetings, speeches, nasty emails. No personal letters or information. Nothing financial. It's like it came out of the box.'

'Maybe it's never been used?' McIntosh said.

'Meaning?'

'It's for show. He's got another one, somewhere we haven't looked.'

'Would make sense,' Bayford said. 'Even if he isn't the killer, the charity theft would come to light unless he hid the evidence. Maybe he's smarter than he looks?'

'But maybe not as much as he thinks he is.'

'Boss,' Kelly Arnott said, knocking and entering at the same time. 'We found a key, among a box of random junk. It's distinctive, looks like a security deposit box key.'

McIntosh looked at Bayford. 'His laptop?'

'Does it tell us the name of the bank?' Bayford said.

'No, nothing at all,' Arnott said.

***

After a very late night, and a few hours rest, the EIU detectives arrived unenthusiastically to resume the drudgery of sifting through Magnus Branch's crap. The prickly mood didn't last long, changed by the glimmer of a smile creeping across their boss's face.

He held court in the middle of the room. 'Some very good news from forensics. Jacket fibres taken from Magnus's house, match fibres from Sarah's clothing. If we can confirm Sarah wore different clothes to the party, then we can place that bastard at her flat, on the night she was murdered.'

'I'm on it, I'll ask her agent,' Findlay said.

Thirty minutes later she finally tracked down Paul Greenwood and he confirmed Sarah wore a glamorous dress to the party.

'The evidence gets stronger and stronger but it's all still circumstantial,' McIntosh said, 'No evidence directly connects him to the murders. Only a few hours before we charge or release him. Let's have another chat.'

Chapter 50

Branch looked ready to drop. He hadn't slept, his hair flew in different directions and his normally ruddy complexion was borderline scarlet. McIntosh had zero sympathy for the man although something nagged away at him. He didn't seem like a master criminal and it wasn't easy to commit two murders, four if you count Harvey and Edwards, without leaving a shred of hard evidence. There was no suggestion of Branch being in Majorca when Andrew Harvey died but also no cast iron alibi ruling him out. McIntosh couldn't be swayed by that. His only interest was O'Neill and Ekers, and Branch was the only person who could rule himself out…if he started talking.

'Mr Branch, I'm not going to waste any time. Do you have anything to add relating to our previous interview?'

'No comment.'

'Forensics have confirmed that a fibre from one of your jackets is a match for fibres taken from Sarah's clothes, the night she died, which indisputably places you at her flat that night. What happened?'

'No comment.'

'To summarise the evidence against you so far, your car was in Fulham the night Sarah died, your fingerprint was on her clothing and a fibre from your jacket matches fibres from Sarah's clothes. Her imminent exposure of you suggests a motive for her murder. Your car was at the scene of Guy's murder, traces of your blood were found in his flat, despite your claim of never having been there and he grassed you up about your charity money theft, suggesting a motive for his murder. Have I left anything out?'

'No comment.'

'Mr Branch, a search of your home uncovered a safety deposit box key. Which bank does it belong to?'

'No comment.'

'We could bring your wife in for questioning, if you'd prefer.'

'Leave her out of it,' Magnus spat, receiving a sharp glance from Thornhill. 'No comment.'

'Mr Branch, we'll find the box. It would be so much easier if you co-operated, unless that's where you've hidden the murder weapon?'

McIntosh watched Branch bubble away before he erupted. 'NO COMMENT!'

'Only two explanations make sense. You were at Sarah's flat the night she was killed. That's a fact. Which means you murdered her or went for another reason and left before she died. These are the only reasonable options. In the absence of a sensible explanation from you, or any explanation really, we have to conclude that you murdered her and hope there is insufficient evidence to convict.'

Magnus looked at Thornhill and stared back at the two detectives. His lips twitched and his eyes bulged. 'No comment,' he said, reluctantly.

McIntosh stood. 'Have it your way Mr Branch. I trust Mr Thornhill advised you how a jury is allowed to draw its own conclusions from a no comment answer?'

'Jury? What jury? What are you talking about?' Branch spluttered.

Bayford almost laughed, 'At your trial!'

Branch turned to Thornhill, 'What trial? You said there would be no trial,' he screamed.

'They're bluffing Magnus, trying to scare you. Chief Inspector, you have less than two hours to hold my client. If you have finished your questioning, I must insist he be allowed to leave.'

'Your client is suspected of two murders. On what planet would you think he's leaving?' McIntosh said.

'You've insufficient evidence to charge him with murder,' Thornhill said.

'That's for the CPS to decide.'

Chapter 51

While they walked upstairs, McIntosh and Bayford listened to Magnus continually berate his solicitor. His profanity amid threats to sack Thornhill, or worse, reverberated around the station. Clearly the game plan hadn't worked.

Commander Beswick had watched the interview unfold. 'You should have pushed him harder,' he said.

'I don't think so sir. We put everything to him and he was desperate to talk but his solicitor obviously believes we haven't enough evidence to put to the CPS,' McIntosh said.

'He'll go straight to the safe deposit box and move or destroy its contents.'

'He can't sir,' Bayford said. 'We've got the key and the bank won't have issued another.'

'Unless he's working with someone else?' McIntosh said.

'Maybe,' Beswick said. 'The CPS are not keen to charge him. They'd prefer to have a murder weapon or stronger evidence linking Branch to the killings.'

'I'd probably agree,' McIntosh said.

'I don't want to let him go. I'm sure he killed them. I say charge him and try like hell to find the box. We might even find evidence relating to the charity theft.'

'But he's not going to be charged with that offence,' Bayford said. 'Not yet anyway.'

'I'm aware, Inspector. But he's guilty, I'm sure of it. I'll talk to the CPS again. How long have we got?'

'Less than an hour sir,' Bayford said.

Without another word Beswick turned and walked out.

'I've got a bad feeling, boss?' Bayford said.

'Aye, me too. I'm not convinced Branch is the killer. He wanted to talk but Thornhill said no. They obviously had some sort of plan to ride it out and it backfired.'

Myers joined the conversation. 'But if he didn't do it, who did? Everything indicates Branch. We've nothing on anyone else.'

'Fair point Glenn, but if I had to guess, I'd say Magnus is more worried about the charity theft allegation. He's being naïve. I don't think he understands how much trouble he's in for murder which might be because he knows he didn't do it. He's definitely guilty of something but god knows what.'

'If we assume his solicitor knows what actually happened, why wouldn't he tell us, to eliminate him from the enquiry?' Findlay said.

'Another good question. If he knows about the theft he probably advised Magnus to say nothing, hoping we don't charge him with murder due to lack of evidence, or we catch the real killer first. Otherwise, the focus would be on the charity theft and Magnus would have different questions to answers. He's tried to muddy the waters.'

'Whatever's happening needs to happen quickly. We've only got twenty minutes,' Bayford said.

On cue, Beswick appeared and nodded to McIntosh and Bayford. 'A word please,' he said, making his way to McIntosh's office.

A heated debate between the three men ensued, overheard by the rest of the team, before they made their way down to the cells. An exhausted Magnus didn't seem to comprehend the double murder charge coming from the custody Sergeant's mouth. His mouth opened and closed several times before he eventually shouted at his solicitor. 'YOU IDIOT!'

Thornhill protested. 'You're making a mistake. You don't have enough evidence to charge him.'

'CPS thinks we do,' McIntosh said.

Thornhill protested again but McIntosh held up his hand. 'Mr Thornhill, your client has had nearly twenty-four hours to speak to us but chose to waste our time. If Mr Branch is innocent of murder, then you have given him very bad advice. Do not put this on us. He'll get his chance to speak in court,' McIntosh said, walking away.

'I'm not sure about this boss,' Bayford said.

'Aye, me neither, Simon.'

Chapter 52

Next morning the box of assorted cakes and cookies, provided by Commander Beswick, were being demolished. Stuart Strong was on his third custard tart before anyone else had finished their first. Kelly Arnott looked at him in disgust, silently shaking her head. Not much work was being done but the chat was cheerful and the mood upbeat, which usually came from getting a suspect charged with murder.

McIntosh and Bayford strolled in and the DCI picked up a doughnut and took a bite, careful to avoid a jam spillage on his shirt.

'What happened boss?' Glenn Myers said.

'Remanded in custody to Belmarsh. Thornhill pleaded for bail but the magistrate was having none of it. He looked awful, obviously hadn't slept and blotches covered his face. He shuffled into court, rather than walked.'

'It's a double murder charge. Why would he think he could get bail?' Dolan said.

'Oh, he's a respected MP and an upstanding member of the community, don't you know. The evidence is all circumstantial and he's no' a flight risk, blah blah. The judge considered it for aboot a second before telling him to get on his bike!'

'Magnus blew his top,' Bayford said. 'Shouted at his brief and the judge. Very entertaining.'

'Aye, if we've got the right guy,' McIntosh said. 'And I'm no' sure we have.'

'Am I hearing some dissent, Detective Chief Inspector?'

All heads turned to see Commander Beswick standing in the doorway.

'In a word, yes. I've got doubts sir, as I explained yesterday. I'd have liked more robust evidence before charging him.'

'I think we've enough and the CPS agree. It's your job to get the hard evidence that'll put him away for life.'

'Aye, ok sir,' McIntosh said wearily.

'Good work everyone, can I see you for a minute?' Beswick nodded to McIntosh.

He walked into McIntosh's office and sat, uninvited. 'How's the family, all recovered?' he said.

McIntosh's brow furrowed. Beswick never engaged in small talk. 'Yes sir, they're fine. Recuperating, you know.'

'You'll be glad to get them home?'

'Thought it best if they stayed out of sight for a bit. They're in a hotel in town.'

'Good idea, any more leads on the kidnappers?'

'Not heard any more but I'm not really in the loop to be honest. SCD7 and Police Scotland are liaising with each other. I don't think they need interference from me.'

'You're probably right. Ok Angus, let me know if I can be of any help.'

McIntosh stared at the back of Beswick's head. Angus? What the fuck was that about?

Chapter 53

Born into a petty criminal's family, Richie Barker's career path was never in doubt. Dad Tommy was always abroad, making the odd fleeting appearance before vanishing again. Growing up, Richie realised what abroad meant and Tommy's death in prison, from a drug overdose, had an air of inevitability.

Richie's mother Stella continued to care for him and his wheelchair bound brother Jason, a downs syndrome boy, paralysed from birth with limited speech. Home was a grotty, two-bedroom ground floor flat adjacent to Finsbury Park, but as Jason developed and grew, the flat became woefully inadequate.

Aged seventeen and smothered by his mother and brother, Richie earnestly began running errands for a local gang boss. Over time, as he climbed up the career ladder, prison became an occupational hazard and his only regular home.

In 2017, with Richie halfway through a two stretch in HMP Brixton, Stella begged her local MP for help to move to suitably adapted accommodation, designed to provide Jason free movement and give her much needed respite from his constant mental and physical demands.

The sympathetic MP vowed to help, but after six months and three further visits, no progress had been forthcoming. On her fourth and final visit, despite Stella's tearful pleadings, the MP yelled in her face. 'Fuck off and leave me alone! You people always want something for nothing.'

While Jason blankly stared at his broken mother, Stella sobbed uncontrollably.

Two days later, after Stella and Jason failed to arrive for a pre-arranged cup of tea with a neighbour, the police found a suffocated Jason in the living room and Stella sprawled on her bed, pill bottles on the floor. After discovering Stella's note, and finding no conflicting evidence, the coroner's verdict was murder/suicide.

Upon his release, and now alone in the world, Richie fell in with a tougher crowd, enjoying the intimidation and violence of armed robberies and protection rackets, somehow evading the law for two brutal, bloody years.

His luck couldn't last and, acting on a tip off, the police intercepted the hijack of a security van, but not before Richie viciously clubbed a guard over the head. The man survived, but with life changing injuries and for the next fourteen long years, Richie's new home became HMP Belmarsh.

He grew to enjoy prison life, quickly establishing himself as top man on his wing and craved the frequent, usually unpunished violence. The guards, under threat to either themselves or their families, turned a blind eye to his transgressions, permitting him a freedom not enjoyed by other lags.

Whilst enjoying an in-cell shave and haircut from Dapper Dan, who once ran a barber shop on Barnet High Street, Richie's runner, an ageing bald man with an eye patch, came knocking to tell him a celebrity had been remanded to Belmarsh on a double murder charge.

Richie froze when he heard his name.

Chapter 54

Although a near neighbour to the police station, the Duke's Head on Charing Cross Road wasn't a typical copper pub, The Prince of Wales being the hostelry of choice for most of Charing Cross nick. DC's Arnott and Findlay could enjoy a glass of wine without being interrupted every five minutes. Still lacking self-confidence, Arnott had sought out Findlay and invited her for a drink to get to know her better.

'It's really busy,' Arnott said. 'Is it always like this?'

'Pretty much, this time of the day, people getting food and drink on their way home. I'm not in here that often though. Are you hungry?'

'I'm fine, I'll eat later, you have something if you want.'

'No, later for me too.'

'Thanks for agreeing to come. I still feel like an outsider and wanted a general feel for the team. You seem the friendliest,' Arnott said, smiling.

'I don't know about that. They're all pretty ok, at least the permanent members. If you're doing your job properly you shouldn't have any worries.'

'I can't figure out the DCI. He flies off the handle, then he's very measured. I'm not sure how to take him.'

Findlay smiled. 'That's just his style. He knows how to switch it on and off. Takes a bit of getting used to but after working under him for a while, you'd run through a brick wall for him.'

'He's obviously got personal issues. He looks a bit stressed. Do you think he can cope?'

'He's a great copper and unless you piss him off, he's very supportive. Will always have your back. He only gets stressed when the Commander's around. They don't get on at all but you've seen Beswick. It must be hard to bite your tongue. What's Notting Hill like?'

'Ever seen the TV series Ashes to Ashes where the women cops only get to make the tea? Like that, a throwback to the seventies. Doesn't matter how good I am, I'll never have a future there.'

'What about Stuart Strong?'

'He's the worst. He's keeping a low profile just now, but trust me, it'll surface. I wouldn't like to repeat the stories I've heard about him. I don't know if they're true or not.'

'If the boss hears about any scandals he'll kick his arse off the team.'

'Whatever you do, don't trust him. He's a wrong un. What's Glenn Myers like?'

'A lovely guy, good copper, sometimes thinks he's better than he is but that's just over confidence. The DCI keeps him in check though. Glenn will give you any help you need.'

'You know he fancies you right?' Arnott said.

Findlay sighed. 'Yeah, I've known for a while. I give him zero encouragement though, hoping he gets the message.'

'You're kidding? Handsome, clearly works out and you know what they say about coloured men,' she said, grinning. 'You could do a lot worse.'

'He's not really my type, if you know what I mean.'

Arnott stared curiously, before the penny dropped. 'Ah ok sorry, I didn't realise.'

'And you're not my type either,' Findlay quickly added, laughing.

Kelly Arnott wiped her brow, 'Phew, thanks for clearing that up.'

'No one at the station knows and I'd like to keep it that way. At least till I'm ready.'

'They won't hear it from me. Why'd you tell me? We've not long met and you don't really know me very well.'

'I don't know, it's not a huge secret. I'd just rather let people know when it suits me, not them.'

'Thanks for trusting me. Another wine?' she said, lifting their glasses and heading to the bar.

Arnott returned with their drinks but her good mood only lasted sixty seconds. Stuart Strong walked in and stood at their table. 'Hello ladies, lesbian night out is it?' he said.

'That's right Stuart, don't think you could handle two women though, not with the size of your equipment,' Findlay said.

Although momentarily taken aback, Strong recovered quickly, 'You've obviously been speaking to the wrong people. I've had no problems before, right Kelly?'

Arnott blushed, 'Fuck off Stuart,' she said angrily. 'Why can't you have a proper conversation without pissing someone off.'

Strong retreated to the bar and conversed with the barman, while waiting for his pint.

While Strong was away Findlay turned to Arnott. 'You and him, really?'

Arnott shrugged. 'Biggest regret of my life. A one-off drunken mistake that he never lets me forget, even if I can't remember what happened.'

'Is that why you can't stand him?'

'Not really. He's an obnoxious guy and drunkenly sleeping with him three years ago, and him never letting it go, just reinforces that.'

Strong returned with his half full lager and sat without acknowledging the unwelcome atmosphere. 'So, what are we talking about?'

'Nothing we want to share,' Findlay said.

'What's your plan when the EIU goes tits up?' Strong said.

'You'd love that, wouldn't you?' Arnott replied.

Strong grinned. 'The guvnor hasn't a clue. I don't buy all this kidnap crap. Smells like bullshit to me.'

'His family got abducted and you say it's bullshit?' Findlay said.

'Nah, he's shifty. I'm keeping an eye on him.'

'I'm sure he'll be really concerned about your analysis of him,' Arnott said.

'He should be. If he's up to something, I'll catch him out.'

'It's more likely you that's up to something,' Findlay butted in.

'What do you mean?' Strong asked suspiciously.

'You look like you've got a few secrets.'

'Careful what you say Joanne,' Strong said menacingly. 'Don't spread any rumours, could get you in trouble.'

'What the fuck are you talking about?'

'Never mind, I better go,' Strong rose, took a slug and left abruptly.

'What's his problem?' Findlay asked.

'God knows,' Arnott said. 'I hardly notice it anymore. He's a weirdo but watch your back. He won't hesitate to drop you in it, now you've got under his skin.'

Chapter 55

The Parliamentary clout Magnus Branch currently enjoyed would only be eclipsed if his party ever gained the Governmental rule he craved, enabling him to equip himself with the knowledge and tools to satisfy his drive towards huge personal wealth. In fairness, he hadn't done badly so far.

Firstly, he needed out of this hell hole. He doubted pleading his innocence would cut much ice with the other inmates which meant biding his time and keeping out of trouble till that idiot Thornhill got him out. Once the murder charge was thrown out he'd bulldoze his way through the inevitable allegation of financial impropriety. That was his field of expertise.

The Governor of Belmarsh advised, that as a notoriously unpopular figure, he'd be a target for the worst scumbags. Probably in Pentonville too, where he was headed in a couple of days. For now, a locked single cell was his friend, except for exercise hour, during which, prison officer Holdstock escorted him on his daily stroll.

Branch doubted Holdstock's suitability for this type of employment, looking too fragile to cope with the hooligan element of the prison population. An amiable fellow, he chatted to Branch about his family, complaining about the expense involved in raising his two young daughters. Naturally unsympathetic to any pleas of hardship, but unable to shy away from an opportunity, Branch offered the young man a chance to make some extra money in exchange for being his personal Belmarsh bodyguard. Holdstock nodded his agreement and unenthusiastically never left Branch's side for the next twenty-four hours.

In the course of afternoon exercise hour, during Holdstock's last shift before days off, Branch couldn't help but hear the threats and cat calls from other prisoners. Empty threats, but he got a snapshot of the contempt in which he was held. During the trudge back to his cell and trying to drown out the intimidation, he chatted aimlessly to Holdstock, asking about his daughter's schooling and his wife's career, not that he was remotely interested but he was trying to keep the man's focus on him. As they climbed the stairs to the first floor landing, he sensed, rather than observed, the man leave his side. Branch looked around and Holdstock was gone. Undeterred, he sped towards the safety of his cell and almost made it, when he felt a tap on his shoulder.

***

Despite feeling less safe in London than her hometown Bristol, Joanne Findlay walked the half hour home to Lambeth. Whilst the pleasant stroll home cleared her head, she still felt relief at arriving unmolested at her front door. She shoved a mac 'n cheese in the microwave, poured another glass of wine and after eating, fell asleep on the couch.

A short distance away, a man wearing a face mask slunk behind a tree, his jacket hood over his head. Staring. Shadowing her was unplanned but when the opportunity arose he couldn't help himself.

Now he knew where she lived and she'd soon get what she deserved.

Chapter 56

When Richie first heard, he knew he couldn't wait long. The bastard might get relocated or placed into twenty-four-hour solitary. He bribed a guard with cash and threats of intimidation to get him a remand wing pass. Holdstock did the rest by letting Branch believe he was safe.

Imagine the arrogant fucker, who was complicit in the deaths of his mother and brother, turning up on his doorstep having killed two celebrities. Couldn't make it up. Richie quite liked Sarah O'Neill in the mornings.

In prison, fashioning a shiv was easy but Richie had lackeys to do his dirty work. Weapons could be created from a multitude of humble materials. Glass shards, broken tiles, even pens. An inmate who owed him a favour used a broken piece of terracotta floor tile, shaping it to a point where it became a deadly tool.

Branch's deal with Holdstock became redundant after Richie showed the young prison officer photographs of his daughters in a playpark. With the promise of his kid's safety and a few hundred quid, Holdstock decided what was most important. Branch almost reached the sanctuary of his cell when Richie tapped his shoulder and bundled him into his bland, white, blockwork home.

They sat on the floor, side by side, with Richie's makeshift blade never more than four inches from Branch's side. Although terrified, the master bullshitter relaxed when Richie started talking. Branch could normally talk his way out of any situation.

That was until Richie began to calmly speak of his mother Stella and wheelchair bound brother Jason. Magnus recalled the woman and her son and when Richie described their deaths and Stella's suicide note, panic washed over Magnus. When Richie stopped talking, tears rolled down his face, the man silently lost in his own thoughts.

The men sat quietly for a couple of minutes, Magnus fearful of opening his mouth. He thought he'd ridden out the storm until Richie abruptly leapt to his feet, hauled Magnus up by his shoulders and plunged his weapon into Magnus's armpit, twisting violently.

Magnus slumped to the floor, blood pumping from the wound. As his life ebbed away he thought of Sarah and Guy. Life wasn't fair sometimes. A blood soaked Richie slid down beside him while Magnus fought for breath.

He finally succumbed and died on his prison cell floor.

Richie had no escape plan, no change of clothes, gloves or face coverings. He braced himself for the inevitable kicking from the screws and knew he'd never leave prison again.

He didn't care. He liked it there.

Chapter 57

Rather than inhibiting the investigation, Branch being locked up intensified the search for the evidence that would negate any doubt about his guilt. Finding the bank that issued the security box key was crucial. McIntosh's theory, which he kept to himself, was that Branch had secreted some form of evidence in that box. Maybe not relating to murder but if they could prove his connection to the charity fraud allegation it may get Branch to realise his predicament and provide a checkable alibi for the murders. He still had serious doubts. He looked through his window and smiled at his team, heads down, hard at work. He liked these people, well most of them, and if they didn't like him back he hoped they respected him at least. His desk phone rang.

McIntosh listened for a minute, face turning ashen white, eyes closed. 'Ok, thank you,' he said, clicking off. 'FUCK, FUCK, FUCK!'

It wasn't particularly unusual for the team to hear their boss swear at the top of his voice, but they still turned expectantly as he entered the squad room.

His sombre look was matched by a quiet whisper. 'I've just been informed that Magnus Branch has been stabbed to death in Belmarsh prison. Bled out before help arrived.'

'Jesus Christ, what happened?' Findlay said.

'We don't have all the details but it seems Branch entered an area he shouldn't have been in, or his attacker wormed his way into the remand section and used some glass as a shiv.'

'Do we know why?' Chris Dolan said.

'No idea Chris, it'll come out but it's safe to say Branch wasn't the most popular of people. In prison some inmates will do anything for their fifteen minutes of fame, without worrying about the consequences.'

'What does this do to the investigation?' Myers said.

'Business as usual. Find evidence to strengthen the case against him or rule him out. If he didn't do it, we need to find out who did.'

'I can't believe it,' Bayford said. 'This totally fucks things up.'

'Unfortunately, knowing Beswick, he'll want to close the case and put it to bed.'

***

McIntosh's prophecy came true.

'Chief Inspector, we charged our only suspect, with strong evidence against him. It's not our fault some lunatic stabbed him to death. That's the prison authorities' concern. They're the ones who've failed,' Beswick said.

'I don't disagree about the evidence sir, but it was all circumstantial and, at trial, he'd have probably walked. I want to continue the investigation whether it exonerates Branch, or confirms he's the murderer.'

'Sounds like you'd relish the chance to prove me wrong?'

McIntosh almost smiled. More like the Commander he knew. 'Not at all sir, I only care about getting the right man. If we've charged an innocent, serving Member of Parliament who was then stabbed to death while on remand, we'll get crucified.'

'You mean I'll get crucified. No, forget about investigating further. The case is closed. The killer's been killed, end of story.'

Beswick about turned, military fashion, and stomped out.

McIntosh beckoned Bayford to his office, 'I take it you called it right?' Bayford said.

'Aye, he wants us to wrap it up.'

'In case he got it wrong?'

'Exactly. He couldn't wait to charge Branch to get the DAC off his back and he's not worried if it turns out to be the wrong guy.'

'Perfect for him. Suspect dies, case closed. No one knows if he did it or not.'

'Aye, except the real killer who may or may not kill again. I'm not sure Beswick thought about that. Anyway, I'm not shutting this down. If he finds out, I'll deal with him. Gather the troops.'

***

'As per Commander Beswick's directive, the case is officially closed, meaning we're not to look at other suspects, which is easy because we don't have other suspects. But I want to keep digging to establish Magnus's guilt to prove we had the right man all along. During that process, if we uncover new evidence pointing at someone else, so be it.'

'What about the security deposit key?' Myers said.

'That's a priority. Find out which bank issued that key and dig into all of the celebrities' background, even the dead ones.'

'What are we looking for?' Findlay said.

'Any previous associations with Branch, financial irregularities, that sort of thing. I want to show we couldn't have done any more to prove or disprove Branch as the killer. The press will have a field day. Probably paint Magnus as some sort of modern saint. Short memories, the lot of them.'

'What if we find evidence proving his innocence?' Dolan said.

'Beswick will have to deal with the fallout. The shit will hit the fan but he stood in front of the TV cameras proudly telling the world we're not looking for anyone else in connection with the murders.'

Strong answered a phone call. 'Boss, front desk saying someone here to see you, a Rupert Thornhill.'

McIntosh looked at Bayford. 'Come on, let's see what that slimy weasel's got to say.'

***

An awkward Thornhill nervously explained this was an off the record chat so Bayford ushered him into an unoccupied family liaison room, clearing toys from a couch onto a larger pile on the floor.

'Excuse the mess Mr Thornhill, what can we do for you?' McIntosh said.

'This is a very delicate situation because it falls within client confidentiality and I probably shouldn't tell you at all but obviously Magnus is dead and it may be relevant to your investigation.'

'Go on,' McIntosh said.

Thornhill cleared his throat. 'He told me he visited Sarah O'Neill on the night she died, to warn her off after hearing about her allegation concerning his charity's prize money. An altercation ensued and he grabbed her. There was shouting and swearing from both sides before he left. Sarah was very much alive. He also went to see Guy Ekers on the same day he died, but he wasn't home. It's why your cameras caught his car in Fulham and Brixton on the relevant nights.'

'And you advised him to withhold that information and say no comment to every question?' Bayford said.

Thornhill nodded sheepishly.

'For fucks sake man, why?' McIntosh said, angrily.

'Strategy. I didn't think for a minute you'd enough to charge him and if he'd confessed to being at Sarah's you might have charged him anyway.'

'You lawyers and your fucking games,' a frustrated McIntosh said. 'And you believed him?'

'Absolutely. Magnus was no angel. His financial dealings were often dubious and I'm sure you'll investigate the charity thing further but I'm convinced he didn't kill anyone.'

'I could tell he wanted to talk,' McIntosh said. 'I didn't want to charge him. If you'd let him speak I could've made a case to the Commander to release him on police bail but without his co-operation there was no chance.'

Thornhill looked defeated. 'I know, I'm sorry. I can't do anything about it now. Don't make this public or I could get into trouble. I wanted you to know because there is still a killer out there.'

'Did Magnus talk about a safety deposit box?' Bayford said.

'No, you mentioned a key but how is it relevant?'

'We don't know for definite but the search of his house revealed very little. We think the box contains significant information.'

'Sorry, he never discussed it with me,' Thornhill said.

'Thanks for coming in, even if it is too late,' McIntosh said.

Bayford followed Thornhill to his car, reminding him not to utter a word about their conversation. When he returned, McIntosh was deep in thought. 'Does his story sound plausible?'

'Unfortunately it does. Branch's whole demeanour screamed of concealing something but probably financial rather than murder.'

'I'm leaning that way as well. We need to find that security box, pronto.'

Chapter 58

October 2021

After calling him on the off chance he might want to increase his investment, Guy let slip that Catherine knew about Magnus's charity having to wait for their money. Magnus also learned she'd told the others and Sarah had a plan to discredit him, or worse. He went ballistic and gave Guy an ear bashing.

He knew he'd have to confront that bitch.

Mindful of the blanket CCTV camera coverage in London he did a bit of advance research and found a suitable street to park before walking the rest of the way. When she opened the door Sarah's jaw dropped. 'What the fuck do you want?'

Magnus barged past in a blur.

'Get the fuck out of my house.'

'No, I hear you've got some half-baked idea I stole the charity money. I want to know what you're up to.'

'You did steal it you thieving scumbag and I'll see you rot in prison where you belong.'

'You don't want to do that,' he said, menacingly. 'I have friends everywhere and a very long memory. It would end very badly for you.'

'I'm not scared of you and I see you're not denying it.'

Magnus tightly gripped the top of her left arm and her right wrist. 'Sarah, this is a fair warning. Back off or you'll regret it.'

'Oww, you're hurting me. Get off or I'll call the police.'

Magnus released his grip. 'I should have finished you off when I had the chance. Back off or you'll be sorry.'

'You bastard, I knew it was you. Get out now,' Sarah screamed.

Magnus exited sharply and Sarah ran behind him, double locking and bolting her door, sobbing uncontrollably.

A breathless, red faced Magnus hurried back to his car, contemplating his next move. That bitch would have to be taken care of.

Chapter 59

A widow for four years, Evelyn Marsh's husband succumbed to a weak heart passed down by generations of hard drinking, tobacco smoking Glaswegians. Now in her late fifties her soft spot for Angus McIntosh was partly a Scottish thing and partly because she harboured a secret crush on him. Despite that, Evelyn would never embarrass herself by making a move, knowing he was happily married.

Usually, after him asking for yet another favour, she'd put him through the mill, explaining how busy she was, how many other cases her team were dealing with before agreeing to his request with a smile

McIntosh was fond of her too, in a different way, but he milked the Scottish connection for his own ends. He knew she was top notch at her job and if he could worm his way to the head of her queue it was worth keeping her onside. When he advised that a low key, slightly off the books investigation was continuing into the O'Neill and Ekers murders, Marsh was very enthusiastic. She enjoyed breaking rules, as long as it didn't come back to bite her.

McIntosh knew, if evidence existed, she'd find it.

When she called, saying she'd be at his office in twenty minutes, he knew it must be important. His impatience matched his anticipation until she marched into his office, folder in hand. She sat, uninvited.

'You look like you're on a mission,' he said.

'Aye well, as you know, I'm a busy woman and I've no' got time to muck around. You asked for my help and I'm here to save the day,' she said, with a wink. 'My team re-analysed everything, including cross checking the cast and crew DNA samples.'

'When you say cross checking, you mean…'

'Against each other, and…guess what…we have a match,' Marsh stared at McIntosh.

'Well?' he said, aware he was dangling on the edge of his seat.

'Magnus Branch's DNA hit a 99% match with one of the other celebrities.'

He couldn't contain himself any longer. 'For fuck's sake Evelyn, who?'

'Natasha Cook. Natasha is Magnus's daughter.'

'Jesus Christ,' he said, slumping back, mouth open.

'I thought that information might be of interest.'

'I can't believe it. Does she know, did he?'

'That's for you to discover Chief Inspector, I only deal the cards,' Marsh smiled as she stood, leaving the folder on his desk. 'Good luck.'

'Thanks Evelyn,' he shouted after her. McIntosh studied the folder, trying to process the words. He walked into the squad room and bumped into Bayford.

'Did I see Evelyn Marsh downstairs?' Bayford said.

'Aye, she's discovered something very interesting.'

He saw other detectives looking their way. 'Please stop what you're doing. Evelyn Marsh has provided some very intriguing information. Forensics cross matched the cast and crew's DNA samples and Magnus Branch's DNA matched another celebrity on the show.'

He sensed the same tension he'd experienced and milked the moment. 'Magnus Branch is Natasha Cook's father.'

No-one spoke as they tried to take it in until Kelly Arnott innocently asked, 'What does it all mean?'

McIntosh stared at her. 'Kelly, at the moment I have no fucking idea.'

'Did either of them know?' Arnott continued.

'Not a clue but, for a start, let's get her in for a chat. Maybe she's completely innocent or maybe she and Magnus were in cahoots?'

'What about Beswick?' Bayford said.

'Keep it quiet. Let's make some headway before involving him. I don't see how he could ignore this information but he might try.'

Stuart Strong desperately struggled to recall if he'd spilled any state secrets when he tried, and failed with Natasha but he didn't open his mouth. Coming clean wasn't his style.

Chapter 60

Bayford, Myers and Findlay congregated in McIntosh's office, patiently waiting for the DCI to finish his conversation. He replaced the handset slowly, pondering before speaking. 'Natasha Cook has reluctantly agreed to come to the station this morning. I want Glenn and Joanne to interview her.'

'You sure?' Bayford said.

'Aye, we don't know if this lassie is involved in any way and I don't want to scare her off if she's another innocent victim of Branch. Joanne can offer the feminine touch and Glenn can use his charm. She might clam up talking to a couple of old fogeys like us rather than two DC's. She might not realise how important it is, no offence guys.'

'None taken, boss. How do you want us to play it?' Myers said.

'Softly at first, speak about her family, when they died and the aftermath. Ask if she already knew Magnus, see her reaction then hit her with the news.'

'What are we trying to achieve?' Findlay asked.

'Honestly? I don't know. It's a fishing expedition. If she's part of this, we need her to make a mistake. Alternatively, we need to satisfy ourselves that she's innocent and maybe his next victim.'

***

When Myers went to meet her at the front desk he tried not to gawp. He hadn't seen her this close before. Natasha looked stunning. Perfect makeup, not a blonde hair out of place and dressed in tight skinny blue jeans, a white tee shirt and black leather jacket. He put his tongue back in his mouth.

'Thanks for coming Miss Cook. I'll show you to the interview room, would you like tea or coffee?'

'Call me Natasha. Just some water please?'

Myers led the way to the slightly more pleasant interview room. Same uninspiring décor but a more comfortable chair and less battle scarred table.

'Sit yourself down and I'll get your water.'

Findlay and Myers entered and formally introduced themselves. Myers handed Natasha a bottle of water.

Findlay began, 'Natasha, thanks for coming today. We're exploring the background and lifestyles of the celebrities on the show. Can I ask how Island Wars came about for you?'

'I thought Magnus being killed closed the case?'

'Not quite, we need to understand his motives and what drove him to commit murder, and so far it points to the show. So Island Wars, what can you tell us?'

'Simple really, the producers called, asked if I fancied it. They wanted a dumb blonde type and I fitted the bill.'

'They said that?'

'Not in so many words, but I could tell.'

'No agent involved?'

'I don't have an agent, not yet anyway. I'm not keen to give my money away.'

'How many celebrities signed up before you and did you know any of them before the show?'

'I think I was the last. I'd heard of most of them without knowing much about them, apart from Andrew and Ben. Watching football or the news isn't my thing.

'What did your family think about you appearing on the show?'

'I don't have any family left. It was just my mum and twin sister but mum died of cancer when I was fourteen and Naomi, a year later. I went to live with an aunt but I'm on my own now.'

'I'm so sorry, how did your sister die, if you don't mind me asking?'

'She drowned, walked into the sea and no one ever saw her again.'

'Suicide?'

'Apparently.'

'Oh my god, how awful. Where did it happen?'

'Off the coast, on a day trip to Southend. Naomi struggled after mum died but none of us saw the signs. While we were on the beach she went missing and we later found out someone had watched her walk into the sea and go under. They raised the alarm but it was too late.'

Myers butted in, 'Could she swim?'

'Yes, she was a very good swimmer but there are strong currents around there and she had nowhere to swim to even if she wasn't trying to kill herself.'

'And her body's never been found?' Findlay asked.

'Not to my knowledge.'

'I'm so sorry. Can I ask about your father?'

'I never knew him. He abandoned us when I was a baby.'

'That's tough, and you lived with your aunt after your mother died?'

'Yes, until I reached seventeen, then I went to college and flat shared with a group of girls.'

'Which college did you go to?'

'East London Beauty Academy. I lived near Romford at the time.'

'Did your mother ever tell you about your father?'

'She said they had a fling, nothing too serious, but when we arrived he didn't want to know. In her words, he was a total waste of space.'

'Did you ever contact him?'

Natasha got defensive. 'No. If he didn't want to know us, why would I be interested in him. Look, would you please stop faffing around and get to the point of these questions? I know it's leading somewhere.'

'How was your relationship with Magnus Branch?' Myers said.

'I didn't have one. I'd never met him until the show and I've only seen him a couple of times since. Now he's dead.'

'How did you get on with him?'

'Like most people, I didn't. He never gave a shit about anyone except himself.'

'How did that make you feel?'

'I didn't care. He's not the first arsehole I've ever come across and he won't be the last. Why are you asking me all this?'

Findlay steeled herself. 'As you know our forensic team obtained samples from yourself and others involved in the show. Tests have since concluded that two of the celebrities are related to each other.' She paused. 'Yourself and Magnus.'

Natasha frowned, trying to understand. 'Meaning what exactly?'

'It is a 99% certainty that you are Magnus Branch's daughter.'

Natasha stared open mouthed before laughing out loud. 'You have got to be fucking kidding me.'

Chapter 61

Myers and Findlay sat stone faced watching Natasha's laughter become a nervous snicker. 'Science doesn't lie. You are Magnus's daughter,' Myers said.

'I can't believe it,' Natasha said, anxiously.

'It's true, your mother definitely didn't say anything?'

'She never told me his name, just that he was a loser. I can't believe that bastard abandoned us as babies.'

'Could your sister have known and his desertion tipped her over the edge?'

'I don't see how. She would have told me. What does this mean?'

'We really don't know but we have to consider you in a different light. Did Magnus line you up as his next victim or were you collaborating?' Myers said.

'You seriously think I was involved with Magnus?' Natasha snorted.

Findlay sighed, 'Natasha, we don't know, but we have to discount lines of enquiry, as well as consider them. If Magnus acted alone, we need to understand his motive to commit these murders.'

'Magnus hadn't seen me since I was a baby. Did he know I was his daughter?'

'We'll probably never know,' Myers said. 'But it's an unbelievable coincidence that father and daughter, who've never met, appeared on the same celebrity TV show. Father begins murdering his fellow celebs, possibly his daughter being next in line, but is himself killed before being brought to justice. Film companies would reject the story for being too far-fetched.'

'I don't know what to tell you, detectives.'

'Did you have suspicions that someone else may have been in league with Magnus?' Findlay said.

'Not during the show but later we suspected someone helped him. He shouldn't have been able to win the final challenge but we never found anything to support that theory.'

'So, probably not a celebrity, maybe a crew member?'

'Possibly but I need to try to process this, she said, standing. 'Is there anything else?'

'One last thing. Can you provide us with your movements on the nights Sarah and Guy were killed?' Findlay said.

'Off hand, I don't know,' she said. 'My diary's at home. I'll check when I get back and let you know.'

'Ok, as soon as possible please. It is important we quickly discount you from our investigation.'

***

Findlay and Myers joined McIntosh and Bayford for a quick debrief. They'd watched the interview unfold.

'How do you think it went?' Findlay asked.

'Personally, I thought she lied through her teeth,' McIntosh said. 'Far too smooth for me. She's no' a bad wee actress. The DI isn't so sure.'

'For me it was inconclusive,' Bayford said. 'She did look shocked about Magnus but, if she already knew, that could have been an act.'

'Everyone we've interviewed said she acted like an airhead,' Findlay said. 'I thought she seemed smarter than that. Maybe she was playing at being the dumb blonde.'

Myers added, 'She's a bit too smooth for me too boss. If I'd found out I'd appeared on the same show as the father I'd never met, he was charged with murder then stabbed to death in prison, I'd have been a blubbering wreck. I didn't buy it.'

'Aye, there's something about her that I don't trust,' McIntosh said. 'Get her movements on the nights of the murders and go through them with a fine tooth comb.'

***

Natasha breathed deeply before pummelling her steering wheel three times. 'Fuck, fuck, fuck!' How long would it take for them to realise she'd screwed up?

Chapter 62

Upset women were not Chris Dolan's forte. Kelly Arnott was on hand to offer the softer touch, if required, but appeasing the grieving widow was his responsibility.

Alison Branch surprised him. Younger and much more attractive than he'd imagined. What on earth could she have seen in Magnus? Dolan surmised that her casual sweater, joggers, and unwashed hair tied back in a ponytail was not representative of her usual image. The sagging puffy eyes matched her unwelcoming body language.

'Mrs Branch, my name is Detective Sergeant Dolan and this is Detective Constable Arnott. I spoke to you earlier. I wonder if we may have a word.'

'Of course Sergeant but you're too late. You managed to get my husband killed. What more do you want?' Alison showed them into the living room and invited them to sit. She continued to stand.

'Mrs Branch, I'm very sorry for your loss. We won't take up much of your time. We are still investigating the O'Neill and Ekers murders and the circumstances of Magnus's death but I have something very specific to ask.'

'Sounds cryptic Sergeant but go on.'

'Did Magnus ever discuss if he had children from a previous relationship?'

Alison sat, not expecting that question. 'Well, yes he did, not long after we first got together. What does this have to do with anything?'

'At the moment we're not sure. We've received information that is under consideration. What did he say about this relationship?'

'Not much, he'd been involved with a woman and she got pregnant. Nothing serious and it fizzled out before she gave birth to twin girls. As far as I know, he never saw them or her again.'

'Did the mother stop him from seeing the twins or did Magnus walk away?' Arnott asked.

Alison looked embarrassed. 'Magnus left them. I couldn't believe it when he told me but he said he wasn't ready and it would have complicated his career path into politics.'

'He's had no contact with the mother or children since then?'

'Not that I'm aware of. Look, what's this about? I have a right to know.'

'Mrs Branch, I am really sorry but it's part of the ongoing investigation and I really can't say,' Dolan said. 'One more thing. Did Magnus ever mention having a bank security box?'

'Not to me but it wouldn't surprise me if he did. Why?'

'We found a key during the search of the house. You've no idea which bank it might belong to?'

'Sorry Sergeant, can't help you. Magnus never discussed anything financial with me.'

Dolan got up to leave, followed by Arnott. 'Thank you for your time Mrs Branch.'

'Sergeant, promise me one thing. Find out what really happened. Magnus had a fierce temper and a terrible reputation and I wouldn't have wanted on his wrong side in Parliament or across the negotiating table, but he wouldn't kill anyone.'

'Mrs Branch, I promise if we find evidence to exonerate Magnus, we will.'

Chapter 63

Desperate to inject life into her stagnant career, Kelly Arnott badly wanted to make an impact at the EIU. The sexist jibes and innuendos had gotten out of hand at Notting Hill and it was a pleasure to work in a place where, even as a newbie, her endeavours were appreciated and she could leave at the end of a shift without having been ogled or subjected to a vulgar comment or two.

And, not that it was the most serious aspect of her life right now, her love life had stalled as well, although Glenn Myers seemed like a nice guy. Handsome and athletic as well. If he knew about Joanne, she might be in with a shout. She dreamily stirred a cup of tea when someone sidled up behind her.

'What do you want Stuart?' she said.

'How did you know it was me?'

'The stale smell,' she said, without humour.

'Rude! I need to talk to you. Can we go somewhere private?'

'I'm not going anywhere private with you. If you've got something to say, say it here.'

'OK, but lower your voice. I may have screwed up.'

'Wow, there's a shock!'

'I'm going to need your help. You know that Natasha is now under investigation. Well, I interviewed her a week ago. It kind of turned into a date. I'm worried I may have let sensitive information slip out.'

A stunned Arnott couldn't comprehend what she was hearing. 'You fucking idiot. Thinking with your dick again. What do you want me to do?'

'To cover for me if it ever came to light. If she's involved in this and mentions our date, I'm history.'

'Why on earth would I help you? You've made my life a misery for three years.'

'Come on, it's just guys having a laugh, you shouldn't take it to heart. I don't know anyone else well enough to ask.'

'Stuart, I'll make this as clear as I can. I wouldn't piss on you if you were on fire,' she said, striding back to her desk.

Strong gave Kelly Arnott daggers. Another one just made his list.

Arnott sipped her tea, trembling. She needed to confide in someone. When she got a chance she'd speak to Joanne Findlay.

***

Arnott was no snitch but, after entrusting Findlay with Strong's confession, they nervously stood outside DCI McIntosh's door, tapping softly.

'Come in.'

'Can we have a word boss,' Findlay said, closing the door.

'Aye, but there's only one chair, one of you will have to stand.'

'We'll both stand, Kelly's got something she needs to tell you.'

McIntosh folded his arms impatiently. 'Well?'

'I'm not a tell-tale and I'm not trying to get anyone into trouble. It may not even be important but…'

'For God's sake lass, spit it oot.'

'Stuart spoke to me and told me he'd been on a date with Natasha Cook. Asked me to cover for him if it came out. I said no, of course, but started thinking. What if Natasha divulged something important? Maybe he didn't realise at the time and his main concern now is someone finding out.'

McIntosh unfolded his arms, face like a bubbling volcano. 'Fuck!' he said, louder than intended. 'Stay there.' He knocked on his window, pointed at Strong and gestured for him to shift his arse.

'Boss?' Strong said.

'What's this I'm hearing about a date with Natasha Cook.'

Strong turned to Arnott. 'Bitch!'

'Hey, that's enough. Dinna forget laddie, you're the one who's fucked up. Dating witnesses or suspects is off limits. DC Arnott correctly suggested you may have some information about Natasha that you don't realise or would rather bury. We need to hear it. We'll deal with the dating thing later. Did you sleep with her?'

'No, we ate dinner and I left about 10pm. There's nothing to tell. It's wasting your time, bothering you with this,' he said, glaring at Arnott.

'I'll be the judge of that. I want a report on everything discussed on this date, down to the smallest detail. Get on to it now. You've got half an hour.'

Strong left, tail between his legs.

'Kelly, why didn't you come straight to me after Strong collared you?'

'I didn't want the guys thinking I wasn't a team player but I knew it would eat away at me so I told Joanne. She suggested I come to you and that Stuart might have valuable information. Sorry.'

'Aye ok, off you go. Joanne, wait there.'

McIntosh waited for Arnott to leave. 'What do you think of her?'

'She's a decent officer boss, just lacking a bit of confidence. She told me Notting Hill is full of male chauvinist pigs, Strong included, and she can't stay there so she's keen to make an impression.'

'Ok, keep an eye on her and watch out for Strong. He'll be looking for some tit for tat on both of you.'

***

Strong had been giving her the evil eye which made Arnott more anxious to prove her worth. She couldn't wait to share the information she'd discovered.

'Boss! Natasha's real name is Ashley Ward. Mother Margaret died from cancer when she was fourteen. The girls were taken in by an aunt and about a year later her twin sister Naomi committed suicide. When Ashley turned seventeen she went off to college to do a beauty therapy course and later got signed by a modelling agency. The TV stuff started at twenty-one.'

'Aye, she told us about the mother and sister but said she didn't have an agent unless she ditched them when she became well known. We need to find the aunt. If Magnus's abandonment caused the mother's ill health and the sister to kill herself, maybe Natasha's harboured a grudge all this time.'

Myers said. 'Maybe Magnus knew Natasha was his daughter and offered her a deal to help him steal the money.'

'Aye, let's not discount anything yet. Did she provide her movements on the days of the murders?'

'Yes,' Findlay said. 'Nothing checkable though. She lives alone so no-one can corroborate her story. Stayed home both nights watching TV and listening to music.'

During these exchanges Chris Dolan was sitting down, looking at his screen while on the phone. When he dramatically stood, everyone turned. 'Boss, I've back checked flight manifests. Ashley Ward booked a flight from Luton to Palma on the 7th September. She arrived in Majorca six days before Andrew Harvey died.'

'Do we know for definite she was on that flight?' McIntosh said.

'Yip, her passport got stamped on arrival.'

'When did Ben Edwards commit suicide?'

'A week after Harvey died.'

'Well, well. Proves nothing but the coincidences keep on coming,' McIntosh said. 'So, she's got a passport in Ashley Ward's name. Find out if Natasha Cook has a passport. Maybe she's using her old name to avoid detection.'

'I'm on it,' Dolan said.

***

Stuart Strong's punishment for having dinner with Natasha was the mind numbing task of checking CCTV for someone who probably wasn't there. Having seen Natasha up close and personal, McIntosh reasoned Strong was the perfect man for the job. Bullshit! His scant reporting of the date with Natasha, offering no useful information, annoyed the DCI. Truth was, he couldn't remember much. He'd been focused on what might happen later.

Bored out of his skull and continually yawning, his eyelids drooped and his mind wandered, until something made him sit bolt upright. A girl. She'd appeared on another camera but he hadn't thought much of it. But now, the timing matched, ten minutes from Sarah's. A face mask and baseball cap made her unrecognisable but…. the way she walked. He'd seen that walk not long before. Same height, build and posture. He couldn't swear but instinct told him it was her. 'Think I've got something,' he said to himself, hoping someone was listening.

Dolan and Findlay didn't move. 'What is it?' Dolan said, uninterested.

'Look at her,' Strong said, pointing to the image on screen. 'I'm positive it's Natasha.'

Dolan and Findlay reluctantly forced themselves to look. 'How the hell can you tell from that?' Findlay said.

'I know it's not clear but that's her walk and the way she holds herself. Like a model. Same height and build. It's her. That's why I'm on this Sarge, right?'

Dolan sighed. 'Absolutely. Better get the boss,' he said to Findlay.

Strong walked the DCI through his hypothesis but a sceptical McIntosh said, 'I appreciate the theory but it's still just a hunch and I don't want to waste time following a ghost.'

'But I can track her with the cameras. You never know and I'm not doing anything else.'

Penalising Strong and keeping him away from the guts of the investigation had been McIntosh's prime intention but could it do any harm? 'Aye, ok, follow her and if there's anything to pursue, do it. If not, put it to bed and keep looking.'

'Will do boss, thanks,' an energised Strong said.

Chapter 64

Dave Gill didn't know whether to laugh or cry. Against all odds, the plan worked just as Magnus said it would. Not just that, it was easy, despite Magnus's best efforts to fuck it up by cheating and fighting with all and sundry. A few messages sent to the tiny secreted device to let Magnus know where his competition was and that was Gill's job done. The gratuitous violence was all Magnus.

Now all the money was his but he had zero experience dealing with ten million quid. He functioned better with a partner, even an egomaniac like Magnus with his shady devious brain. Why did the loathsome prick have to go and get himself killed?

Picking up his mail he noticed a heavy, hand delivered envelope. Inside he found a burner phone and a typed, unsigned note.

David Gill

You've defrauded one charity out of £250,000 and another four out of £1M. Magnus is dead so you'll be the fall guy. Hope you enjoy prison, Dave!

To keep your freedom, avoid the police and retain most of your ill-gotten gains, transfer £2.5M to an account of my choosing. Once the money is transferred, destroy the phone. The account details will be texted and you will have one hour to complete the transaction. Failure will result in a visit from the police.

Gill closed his eyes, trying to block the pain in his head. Magnus could be a real bastard but he excelled in this type of situation. Gill, not so much.

Guessing the blackmailer wouldn't hang around, Gill needed immediate access to his offshore account information.

Chapter 65

McIntosh sat at his desk, sipping a black McDonalds coffee, looking longingly at the sausage and egg McMuffin. His wife wouldn't approve. But she wasn't here. Might as well enjoy it while it lasted.

Simon Bayford passed his open door and peeked his head in. 'While the cat's away?' he said, smiling.

McIntosh finished his food and took his coffee through to the squad room. 'There's gotta be some perks about being on your own.'

Bayford laughed, 'I know, I'm just jealous. Speaking about living by yourself, how's the family?'

'Aye, they're fine, back from holiday but not home just yet. Staying in a Holiday Inn north of the river, just for a wee bit. Safer. We meet up from time to time.'

'Makes sense, but you can't live like that forever.'

'Aye, but it'll not be much longer. Come through to the office, there's something I want to tell you.'

***

The recently returned Heather Walton received a quick resume of the case from Joanne Findlay, her closest confidante on the team. She'd taken a short leave of absence, on the DCI's orders, to deal with her ongoing personal issues. Findlay didn't pry or ask for details. She knew what was going on.

While the rest of the squad room hummed with whispered conversations, phone calls and tapping keys, an animated Strong stood suddenly and shouted. 'Got her.'

Strong's carefree attitude towards rules and regulations dissolved once he became engrossed in an assignment, no matter how tedious. Without a care about his position in the EIU unpopularity league table, he eagerly knocked on the DCI's door.

'All right, let's hear it, what have you got?' McIntosh said, trying to feign interest.

'Ok, so I tracked the girl from the area around Sarah's flat until Worlds End where she jumped on a number eleven bus. The bus company provided the camera footage and I tracked her to Westminster, where she got off.'

'Do you ever see her face?'

'No, she always keeps her cap on and her mask over her nose. I switched to Westminster CCTV and I clocked her getting into a black cab. I tracked down the driver and he confirmed dropping her off in Sandford Road, two streets from Natasha's house.'

'Did the taxi driver give you a description?'

'Only what we already know. She never lowers her mask or takes her cap off. Paid cash.'

'Any CCTV after she got out of the taxi?'

'Nah, nothing. There's not much around there but what there is, she's not on. Probably sussed it out well in advance. What do you think?' Strong said, hopefully.

'Still inconclusive but adds to the suspicion that the lassie is involved. There's not much more we can do until some hard evidence drops in our lap.'

'What will I do now?'

'Compile a comprehensive report of everything you've just told me, including CCTV screenshots. If we only ever have circumstantial evidence, I want it all properly laid out.'

***

Terry Johnson had scrapped the notion that McIntosh could get Matthew's charges dropped. This was now a revenge mission. He lounged casually on his large, black leather sofa, coffee in one hand, cigarette in the other, mulling his next move. That bastard thought he'd outsmarted him but Terry knew his family were holed up somewhere in North London. Billy Mason, his trusty lieutenant, sat opposite, watching the wheels turn over in his boss's head.

After half an hour they'd checked a dozen Holiday Inns between them but fell at the first hurdle. No McIntosh's at any of them.

'Shit,' Terry said. 'What a pain in the arse this is going to be. Must be using a false name. Any ideas, Q?'

If Billy Mason ever caught the lads calling him Q, they were dead meat but Terry was Terry, and he'd once drunkenly told Billy his bald head reminded him of a cue ball.

'We could keep an eye on every hotel for a glimpse but that means a lot of bodies,' Mason said.

'We're running out of manpower. Wait a minute, he's a Jock right. He's probably given them a fake Jock name.'

'Boss, we can't phone every hotel and ask for a list of Scottish residents. There'll be hundreds and they wouldn't tell us anyway. What about the wife's maiden name? She's maybe used that.'

'Could be, but how the fuck do we find out.'

'Not too hard, a bit of trawling through public records.'

'Ok, do it'

Chapter 66

Within an hour they had a name. Deborah McAlister. 'If this doesn't work, we're going to have to try Presidents or fucking Prime Ministers,' Terry said.

Thirty minutes later Terry clicked off his phone. 'Q, you're a fucking genius. Twin room for McAlister at the Holiday Inn, Oxford Circus, room 322. Booked under the daughter's name. Clever, but not clever enough. Let's get over there and suss it out.'

'I'll get a couple of bodies to do a recce of the hotel. Make sure we get eyes on them. Then you can let us know how you want to do it.'

'Ok, easier outside than in but we might not get a choice.'

Terry's plan failed to materialise. During a patrol of the third floor, one of his men twice received suspicious glances by the same person, so abandoned his surveillance. The other spotter drank an imaginary coffee in the lounge for two hours, in full view of the lobby area, the hotel staff too busy to notice or care.

Neither woman surfaced.

'Must be ordering food to the room,' Terry said. 'Can we check if 322 have had room service delivered.'

'I'm sure we can persuade one of the staff to cooperate.'

'Don't go heavy handed. Offer them a ton.'

'That's what I meant,' Mason said, a little offended.

***

An hour and one hundred pounds later, Terry possessed the room service order for 322. One double cheeseburger with fries, a macaroni cheese with garlic bread, a diet coke and a banana milkshake. It irked him that they hadn't set eyes on the women. They were going in blind so he had to use his four best men.

Along with Billy Mason's nickname, Oddball's Asian appearance and Jaws' crooked teeth, convinced the rest of the gang that Terry was a James Bond freak. The two Bond villains were to engage the women in their room. Olly positioned himself in the corridor, to clear a safe passage from the hotel, via the service lift. Freddie waited in a battered unmarked brown van, illegally parked at the rear of the hotel. Billy Mason stationed himself in a pristine white van at the transfer site, just off the Edgware Road.

The distance from the passenger lift to room 322 was almost forty yards. Olly's job was to remain inconspicuous until Oddball and Jaws restrained the women, at which time he would navigate to the much closer service lift, which stopped at the rear exit.

Neither Bond villain was a poster boy for the hotel industry. Oddball's flattened nose, broken during a bar brawl, never got fixed. A razor slashing during a gang fight left Jaws scarred for life, with permanently busted teeth. Both over six foot three inches and weighing over 250 pounds, Terry was willing to sacrifice style for substance. Their intimidating presence should have been sufficient but both carried firearms, to be produced, only if absolutely necessary. Jaws stood to the side, out of peephole sight while Oddball knocked on the door of 322.

'Room Maintenance.'

A woman's voice, from inside. 'What is it? We didn't call anyone.'

'Faulty smoke detector miss, our computer flagged an issue with this room. We have to double check or the hotel insurance becomes invalid.'

'Okay, just a minute.'

In the poor light a woman, who didn't look like Debbie McIntosh, stood in the doorway. Oddball pushed her back into the room, quickly followed by Jaws who scoured the small room for the daughter. Oddball's huge hand covered the woman's mouth but she had no compulsion to scream and she let her body go slack. A second later the bathroom door flew open.

'ARMED POLICE, GET ON THE FLOOR.'

Chapter 67

Two armed policemen rushed from the bathroom and trained their Glock 17's on the stunned thugs who immediately dropped to their knees, hands interlocked behind their heads. The woman, who'd thrown herself sideways, rose and safely extracted the assailants' guns and the four inch hunting knives tucked in their socks. She made a call.

'We've got two, arrest the others.'

A voice replied. 'One outside the service lift and another in the van, both in custody.'

Turning to the two armed officers, Heather Walton said. 'Good work guys,' as she dialled another number.

***

Heather Walton's anxiety over the separation issues with her ex had prompted her leave of absence request. A sympathetic McIntosh told her to stay away until she was ready. He knew not to pry. Her ex was a DI at Kennington and coming between two police officer's marriage was not recommended. McIntosh had a lot of respect for Walton and knew he could rely on her when it mattered. When she asked to return to work, and hoping to give her a surge of belief, he invited her into his confidence and she'd eagerly accepted the role of his wife in the sting operation.

He'd kept the details about his family's fictitious whereabouts deliberately vague, otherwise Terry would suss it was bogus, but he knew canteen gossip would spread and the rats would get wind and do their thing. Sully's associates had constant eyes on Terry's gang and when the call came, McIntosh knew they were in business. When the receptionist confirmed he'd received a hundred pounds for 322's room service order, armed support started mobilising.

After Walton called, a quietly satisfied McIntosh knew it wasn't quite over. Terry remained free and dangerous but his family were safe and he knew exactly where they were. That's all that mattered.

Mason called each man but when no-one answered, he knew. After telling Terry the news he threw his phone into the river.

Terry's depleting numbers were a concern. Three in Scotland, another four tonight. Some of his best, most trusted guys. He'd plenty of bully boys but needed blokes to think as well as intimidate. Time to take stock, regroup and back off McIntosh for a while. Matthew would have to do his time.

However, he still had unfinished business to take care of.

Chapter 68

An eminent Mayfair bank since 1851, the typically Victorian home of Byers and Son was enriched with small stained glass windows, ornate cornices, and an open interior accommodating high, sculpted ceilings and a huge oak reception desk, currently occupied by three smartly dressed clerks in company uniform.

Having finally tracked down the home of the safe deposit key, Myers and Findlay sat frustrated in the Manager's office, their earlier attempt to gain access to the box rebutted by Richard Barnaby. A tall, thin man with a small handlebar moustache and wearing penny round glasses, he could have been a movie extra from the 1940s.

'Your warrant Mr Barnaby,' Myers said, slamming the document on the table. 'Can we see the box please?'

'Absolutely detective, I do understand your frustration but you must understand our procedures.'

'And you realise you're hindering a murder investigation?'

'I can't bend the rules without proper paperwork. Let's go downstairs.'

The vault containing the bank's reserves held less cash than the general public imagined. In the digital age, holding the bare minimum discouraged theft and Barnaby prided himself on the fact Byers hadn't witnessed a robbery in 170 years. The vault also contained seven hundred and fifty safe deposit boxes, each rental at least £1500 per year. Expensive, but with extra cost comes extra discretion and security.

Findlay inserted the key into the lock of box 517. Although normally an underling's role, Barnaby felt compelled to attend and inserted the other key in the adjacent slot. He took a step back. 'Please take your time. I will be outside if you need me,' he said, solemnly.

'That nosy bastard gives me the creeps,' Myers said. 'Like a fucking funeral director.'

'Shh, he might hear.'

As if a bomb was inside, they delicately opened the rectangular metal box, 18 x 12 x 6 inches high before turning to each other in amazement.

It was empty.

They exited the vault and Barnaby hovered, expectantly. 'Did you get what you needed detectives?'

'In a manner of speaking,' Findlay said. 'Was Magnus Branch the only keyholder?'

'I can't divulge such information, sorry,' Barnaby said.

'Do any of these boxes have more than one keyholder?' Myers said.

'Yes, a maximum of two keyholders per box. However, in such cases, both parties must be present. One keyholder cannot gain access independently of the other.'

'Can you tell us when someone last accessed this box?' Myers said.

Barnaby tried to look apologetic and failed. 'Again, I'm sorry. You're going to think I'm a frightful stickler but our clients insist on privacy. I'd need another warrant, I'm afraid.'

'For fucks sake, you're enjoying this. We'll be back,' Myers said.

Myers and Findlay sat in their car, frustrated at a promising lead going nowhere. 'That bastard got on my nerves,' Myers said.

'Forget him, we've more important things to worry about. Either Branch's stash is somewhere else or someone got there first and took everything.'

'How could they? You heard creeping Jesus, two of them needed to open the box.'

'Maybe before Magnus was arrested or after he died and someone made the case that he was never coming back.'

'Natasha?'

'We've nothing on her so I can't imagine her drawing attention to herself. If we found her with Magnus's goodies, she's put a target on her back. Whoever it was, we need another warrant for Barnaby to release the records. Better tell them the news.'

Chapter 69

After receiving the blackmail note a panicking Dave Gill went straight to Byers and practically begged that prick Barnaby to open the box, reasoning that Branch could hardly attend as well. For his own amusement, Barnaby made the case that rules were rules and he unnecessarily made Gill squirm, squeezing every ounce of enjoyment he could from the man's discomfort, before abruptly relenting and escorting a sweating Gill downstairs.

Gill retrieved the contents of the box and returned home. He needed the account information at hand when the text came through. An hour wasn't long if you didn't really know what to do. It never crossed his mind not to pay. If pushed, he'd have parted with the full ten million.

He wished it was all over, but knew it was just beginning. At the outset, Magnus's scheme sounded too good to be true but now Gill found himself rich beyond his wildest dreams. The police couldn't be far behind though, so the money had to be moved again, before he destroyed everything.

His phone rang. Unrecognised number. 'Hello.'

'Is that David Gill?'

'Yes'

'Mr Gill, this is Detective Inspector Bayford of the EIU. Sorry to bother you but I'd like to meet to ask you some questions regarding Magnus Branch. Your office or your home, whatever suits best.'

'Em, it's not a great time at the moment detective but I could see you later this afternoon.'

'Sorry to insist Mr Gill but I need to do this now. Are you at your office?'

'Yes, but I'm about to leave for a meeting. I'll be back in an hour.'

'Fine Mr Gill. I'll see you in an hour.'

Fuck! It sounded routine but he couldn't take the chance. He needed to take everything and disappear, at least till he figured out how to leave the country. He placed the laptop and Magnus's phone in a small suitcase along with clothes, photographs and personal items. He took a last look round, figuring he'd never see his flat again.

He unlatched the door to find Simon Bayford and Chris Dolan staring at him.

'Hello Mr Gill. Going somewhere?' Bayford said.

Chapter 70

Richard Barnaby's work kicks came from spouting regulations, client's rights, privacy procedures and generally being as annoying and obstructive as possible. However, he'd never come across someone like DCI Angus McIntosh who threatened to, 'knock down his fucking door and sift through every safe deposit box with a fine tooth comb,' inviting the media to film it as it happened. Bluff of course and Barnaby probably knew, but he'd enjoyed his fun while it lasted. Without fuss he released access records for Box 517 and suddenly the empty box made sense.

***

Gill initially denied any wrongdoing and refused Bayford's polite request to see in his case but on the threat of arrest, a defeated Gill capitulated. The detectives clocked the laptop, phone and various financial documents and arrested Gill regardless. He walked to their car in handcuffs, head bowed, looking ready to cry.

They sweated him in a cell until his solicitor arrived and McIntosh and Bayford chewed the fat over a cup of weak tea and a digestive biscuit. 'First impressions, Simon?'

'Gill and Branch were in it up to their necks for stealing the charity money. Not sure about the murders though. Gill's a pushover. I don't think he's capable.'

'Pushovers can be murderers too. Maybe Branch lined him up as an easy scapegoat. A ready-made fall guy?'

'Sounds more like it. The man can't lie to save his life. He'll tell us whatever we want to know.'

'Famous last words.'

***

Bayford's assessment proved spot on. A crestfallen Gill confessed everything. Magnus approached him about the TV show and said they could make a lot of money. Gill provided general support on the daily challenges, without making it obvious, but his main assistance came on the final task, keeping Branch appraised with the position of the marines and his fellow celebrities. Branch's only job was to ensure he crossed the line first.

As charity founder and trustee, Branch held his winning share until ready to invest. Despite cross party discord, he had many friends in powerful Government positions and contracts were being issued willy-nilly to newly hatched companies, for vaccines, testing kits, PPE equipment and face coverings.

Branch's stock market cohorts guided him on which companies and how much to invest. Within a fortnight, his share of the prize money turned into ten million. He couldn't risk more without suspicions being raised.

Strangely, Branch's improbable benevolence contributed to his downfall. Guy Ekers jumped at the chance to invest his own fee - he felt he had nothing to lose - but rejected investing his charity money. That was a step too far. Guy told Catherine, who told the others and Sarah became a dog with a bone. Gill denied all knowledge of the murders, claiming a cast iron alibi for Sarah's.

'Good work Simon,' McIntosh said. 'Do you believe him about the murders?'

'Yes boss, he's a terrible liar. If he was bullshitting, it would be obvious.'

'Problem now is we've now got a fantastic motive for murder but only if Magnus did it, and we're not convinced he did. I cannae get my head around what Natasha's motive could be.'

'When I mentioned Natasha, Gill drew a blank. Didn't know what I was talking about. Couldn't understand why I even mentioned her name in the conversation. If she's involved, I don't think it's with him.'

'Which puts us back to square one.'

'Not necessarily. Interestingly, Gill paid someone two and a half million, the day after receiving a blackmail note. Not long after Magnus died. He's no idea who.' Bayford handed the note to McIntosh.

'Someone who knew about the charity theft and the profit margin, if they could ask for two point five mil just like that.'

'The cast knew, what's left of them. Natasha, Emily and Catherine, which keeps Natasha in the frame.'

'Unless we can trace any money back to her we've got nothing,' McIntosh said gloomily.

'Gill could talk to Natasha, draw her out, maybe get her to incriminate herself.'

McIntosh looked sceptical. 'He'd need to be wired up. You said he's a shite liar. He'd probably piss himself plus we'd have to trust him with our suspicions about her.'

'Yeah, you're probably right. What about a phone call? Tap his phone and give him a script to follow. Less likely to crumble on the phone.'

McIntosh sighed. They were running out of options. 'Aye ok, set it up.'

Chapter 71

Having finished another tasteless microwave meal, he switched on the television. Another quiz show, full of eager contestants who seemed desperate to prove how stupid they were. Then he imagined which of the four was the murderer. Was that the pre-requisite for a TV show these days? Not his problem. He had his own worries. Some of his team were at loggerheads with each other, a murderer was possibly, even probably, still free, his boss hated him and he still didn't feel quite ready to bring his wife and daughter home.

Despite all of the above, he felt good. Beer in hand, settled in his comfy armchair, Angus McIntosh finally relaxed, until his phone pinged.

'Evening chief inspector, guess who? You probably thought you heard the last of me but here I am. I have something for you but I'd rather discuss it in person. Meet me tomorrow at 9pm. I'll text you where nearer the time, come alone'

McIntosh immediately dialled a number.

'Hey, how are you?' Debbie McIntosh said.

'Aye, I'm fine, how are you two? I wanted to hear your voice, make sure you're both ok.'

'Yeah we're good, relaxed and tanned. Can't wait to get home though. How much longer do you think?'

'Not long, a week, maybe less. You could probably come back now but I'd rather be safe than sorry.'

'Ok, I suppose we could slum it for another week.'

'How's Amanda?'

'She's fine, out for a drink with a pal she met. She's recovering well, or so she says.'

'You don't believe her?'

'I do, but who knows what's going on in her head. She doesn't tell me much.'

'Who's the pal, do you know them?'

'A girl her age. Here with her mum and dad. Don't go all private investigator.'

McIntosh smiled. 'Aye ok, better go, be in touch soon. Tell Amanda I said hi,' McIntosh clicked off and dialled another number.

'Guv, it's really sweet of you to check on my welfare,' Sully said.

'Aye right, that would be a first. Guess who sent me a text.'

'The Queen. You're getting an MBE for services in butchering the English language.'

McIntosh smiled. 'Close. Terry Johnson. Wants to meet me alone. Says he's got something for me.'

'Shit, when?'

'Tomorrow night, he's texting me the place nearer the time. I phoned Debs and they're ok so God knows what he wants. What d'ye think?'

'Personally, I'd tell him to fuck off but if you're set on meeting him, you tell him where and when. Don't let him dictate to you.'

'He's smart though. He'll know I'm curious. Also, he often only texts once and loses the phone so if tomorrow's text is a different burner there'll be no time to react. It's either meet him or don't.'

'I wouldn't guv. It's not worth the risk. You might be alone but he definitely won't be.'

'Aye ok, Sully, I'll sleep on it. Go back to relaxing wi' yer feet up.'

Chapter 72

Promises of wealth had twisted Dave Gill's mind, but those promises came with a price especially dealing with a master manipulator like Magnus. Accompanied by Bayford and Dolan, he surveyed the state of his shithole flat. Floorboards gone, sanitary ware removed, cupboards stripped and replaced without much care or attention. He hardly cared. He was going to prison.

Bayford prepared the recording equipment. For some weird reason they thought Natasha had colluded with Magnus and if he called her to nose around they promised to put in a good word at his sentencing. Why not? What did he have to lose?

He made the call

'Hello!'

'Natasha, it's Dave Gill, how are you?'

'Hi Dave. I'm ok, what's going on? We haven't spoken in a while.'

'Quite a lot really. I've been arrested for conspiracy to commit fraud.'

'Jesus Christ Dave, what have you done?'

'Magnus cheated to win the charity money. I helped him and got in way over my head. I think I'm going to prison.'

'Dave, I'm so sorry. But wait, if you cheated, that cost me a quarter of a million as well. I'm not happy about that. Why are you telling me this?'

'While the police interviewed me, they often mentioned your name and after Magnus died I was blackmailed for a lot of money. Was it you?'

'Fucking hell Dave, don't be daft. What did they say about me?'

'Didn't go into detail but they implied you were in cahoots with Magnus and possibly involved with the murders.'

'They actually said that?'

'Not in so many words but they quizzed me more about you than Magnus. Were both of you in it together?'

'How could you and me both conspire separately with Magnus without knowing about the other?'

'Yeah, that's a good point. I never thought of that.'

'Dave, you've enough on your plate without worrying about me.'

'You can tell me. Magnus is dead so he doesn't care and I'm going to prison anyway.'

'Unless you're using me to get a reduced sentence?'

Gill laughed nervously. 'Don't be daft. I like you. We always got on well didn't we?'

'Dave, in my experience, people will do just about anything to get themselves out of a tricky situation.'

'Not me.'

'Why don't we meet and talk properly? Be good to get a catch up. God knows, there's a lot to talk about. I'll text you tomorrow, okay?'

'Okay, look forward to seeing you.'

Gill clicked off and breathed deeply. 'What did you think?' he said.

'She didn't give much away,' Bayford said.

'I think she sussed you out,' Dolan said. 'Do not meet her alone. When she texts, arrange somewhere public. Under no circumstances does she come here or you go to her house.'

'You really think she's dangerous?'

'Let's not take any chances,' Bayford said. 'If she's a murderer, and a blackmailer, she won't think twice about killing you to hide her secret.'

Bayford watched Gill turn a paler shade of white. 'You'll be fine. When you come to post bail, ask for me and we'll talk more. 'If you haven't heard from her by then, call her and arrange something.'

'Ok, Inspector,' Gill said, shivering.

After realising they'd gone six hours without eating, Dolan and Bayford stopped at McDonalds on the Edgeware Road. Bayford paid and they took a seat on a brightly coloured bench. Dolan hungrily inhaled his Big Mac before stopping for breath. He took a sip of Sprite.

'Guv, do you honestly think Natasha is clever enough to get in league with Magnus and/or Gill, steal the charity money, murder anyone who found out about it, then blackmail Gill for another two million plus. Really?'

Simon Bayford slowly finished chewing before taking a deep breath. 'I do Chris, I really do.'

Chapter 73

His flat was in darkness. Gill lay on the bed, depressed, thinking about suicide but deep down, he knew he didn't have the guts. How long would he go to prison for? A couple of years if the judge took pity and the police put in a word. After all, he was just the assistant. Two years, carry on with his life, still relatively young. He could do that. He needed to give himself a shake, keep a positive outlook.

He got up, splashed water on his face and studied his busted kitchen. He was pretty sure the police had a duty to reinstate any damage arising from a search of someone's property. Maybe they'd send over a tradesman to carry out repairs but he wasn't sure he had the energy to pursue it if they didn't.

In a crisis, reassuring comfort food always helped so he decided to make a lasagne for dinner. He browned mince and chopped onions, lost in thought.

Was that a knock on his front door. Sounded like it but his buzzer didn't go off. Maybe someone at the wrong flat.

He peered through the spyhole. It wasn't the wrong flat.

With confusion etched on his face, he opened his door.

Chapter 74

McIntosh was torn between studying his computer screen and glancing at the phone on his desk, waiting for a ping. The words on his screen may have been Swahili for all the attention he was paying. He got up and paced around his office, like an expectant father. When it came, the buzz of the incoming text still made him flinch. A different number, as he suspected. Unrecognised, when he called it back.

'Alleyway at side of Hungry Horse pub - 9pm alone'

Aye right. Down a dark alley on his own. Terry must think his head zipped up the back. However, his thorny curiosity got the better of him. He phoned Sully.

'Evening guv.'

'Sully, Terry wants to meet at 9 pm, alleyway beside the Hungry Horse.'

Sully started to laugh, 'Please tell me you're not considering it.'

'Not directly but I'll be nearby. If I don't show he's bound to call, then I can tell him where to meet.'

'I don't like it, guv. I'd help but I'll not be much use if there's any running involved.'

'No worries Sully, I'll let you know when I hear from Terry. I'm keeping you posted, for you to send reinforcements if it goes tits up.'

'Ok guv, did I tell you I didn't like it.'

McIntosh laughed, 'Aye, once or twice,' he said, disconnecting.

***

He parked a few streets from the Hungry Horse, wondering if he should have brought Bayford as back up. His phone rang at 9.05. Unknown number.

'Aye.'

'You disappoint me Chief Inspector. I thought you'd have been fascinated to see what I have for you.'

'You disappoint me Johnson. You honestly thought I'd meet you in a dark alley to let you and your gorillas kick the living shite out of me?'

'Give me some credit, Chief Inspector. I know where you live, and work. If I wanted the living shit kicked out of you, do you think I'd be out here on a cold dark night rather than waiting in my cosy living room for the call to tell me you're in hospital.'

'What d'ye want?'

'Like I said before, to meet. I've something for you.'

'In ten minutes come to the Co-Op car park at the back of Parker Street. Stand by the trolley bay and if I see anyone come within fifty yards of you, I'm gone.'

'You're getting better at this. See you in ten.'

McIntosh could see the whole car park and it would take Terry five minutes to get there. He called Sully who warned him the cavalry would be there in twenty. He watched Terry's Mercedes turn into the car park and stop. Terry exited and stood by the trolley bay. McIntosh waited for any goons to show themselves, remaining hidden for two long minutes. When he was satisfied, he emerged from the shadows.

'Evening Chief Inspector,' Terry said, his voice echoing in the silence. 'All a bit clandestine isn't it?'

'No more than meeting in a dark alley.'

'Touché. Thanks for coming. I wanted to apologise and hope there are no hard feelings. Just did what I felt had to be done.'

243

'No hard feelings?' McIntosh spluttered. 'You kidnapped my family, you fucking arsehole. They could have died, then you tried again. What do you want me to do? Shake your fucking hand and say its ok?'

Terry casually nodded. 'I thought you might take it personally so I want to offer you an olive branch.'

'Eh, whit are ye talking about?'

Terry reached into his jacket pocket, produced a flash drive and handed it over. 'You may find it interesting. Listen to it on your own. Again, no hard feelings.' He walked back to his car and drove off.

A stunned McIntosh watched him leave before heading to his own car. He took his phone out. 'Sully, call off the dogs. Terry gave me a flash drive and left. I'm heading home.'

'What's on the drive?'

'I haven't opened it yet. I'll wait till I get home.'

Chapter 75

The flash drive was Terry's next chess move. Despite being a common criminal, Terry prided himself on his strategy and business acumen. Everything was done for a reason.

His heart racing, McIntosh plugged in the drive and clicked on the only folder. Three audio files appeared. He opened the first, heard voices and crackling sounds but poor quality and interference made it impossible to comprehend. The second was clearer, but not much. He hit paydirt on the third. As clear as a bell.

'Got a hit on the family. They're in a Travelodge, North London.'

'You took your time.'

'That's as quick as I could. I've got to be careful.'

'Remember how much I pay you. I expect instant answers.'

An audible sigh, *'That's as much info as I could get. You'll have to do the rest.'*

The audio ended. McIntosh shrunk into his armchair, digesting what he'd heard. Although he recognised both voices, one might not withstand scrutiny in court. The other was indisputable.

He whispered. 'You bastard.'

***

He buzzed the intercom and smiled, picturing Sully hobbling across his living room.

'Come up, doors open.'

McIntosh pushed the flat entrance door and walked into the living room to find Sully sprawled across his couch, moon boot perched on a stool.

'Lazy bastard. Feet up again, that's all you ever seem to do.'

'Piss off, if I realised the effort needed to answer the door, I'd have given you a key.'

'How's the leg?'

'Not bad, just a mobility issue now. Not easy lugging this around. I can work easily enough from the couch. No pain, which is good.'

An open laptop lay on the arm of the couch beside Sully. 'Ready?' McIntosh said.

Sully nodded. 'Go for it.'

They listened and, although Sully already knew who said what, he whistled through his teeth. 'Still can't believe it.'

'It's not enough though,' McIntosh said. 'A decent lawyer would argue it's not clear.'

'What about Terry?'

McIntosh laughed. 'You think Terry's going to take the stand and admit he's got the Met in his pocket.'

'Yeah, fair enough, what's your other options?'

'Confront him and get him to admit it.'

'As likely as putting Terry in the witness box,' Sully said. 'What about Anti-Corruption?'

'I'll think about it. He tried to have my family killed. I need to get it right.'

'Don't do anything daft like a revenge hit, nothing to get you in trouble as well.'

'How much do you think Terry would charge?'

'Fuck sake guv, you've got to be kidding.'

McIntosh laughed out loud. 'Relax, I wouldnae waste any money on that bastard. No, I want to see him in jail, afraid for his life every single day.'

'Actually guv, I've thought of a very simple plan.'

Chapter 76

At 10.15am Bayford impatiently tapped his watch. The office wall clock verified the correct time. A call to the desk sergeant confirmed Gill hadn't arrived.

'Boss, no sign of Gill. He should have been here at ten to post bail and to update me on Natasha.'

'Keep trying his mobile and if you've not heard by eleven, go round to his place. Hopefully he's not topped himself,' McIntosh said.

At 11.20am, Bayford and Dolan drove to Gill's Paddington flat and parked in a reserved space knowing someone would be upset enough to send a strongly worded email to the resident's association. Gill's car was parked in bay 3C.

After pressing the service button enough times for a resident to get fed up, they entered unchallenged. Bayford knocked on 3C and shouted Gill's name through the letterbox, loud enough for 3B to investigate. At the word police, the young woman quickly closed her door, her eye no doubt jammed against the spyhole. With no response, Bayford phoned the station in case Gill showed up late.

He hadn't appeared so Bayford went to the car while Dolan rapped loudly on 3B. The woman opened the door tentatively but quickly, probably only standing six inches behind it.

'Sorry to bother you Miss, have you seen Mr Gill today?'

'No, not for a few days. He comes and goes, at odd hours.'

'Did he give you a spare key, you know, for emergencies?'

She shook her head. 'I doubt he knows anyone well enough to trust them with a key. He must have had visitors last night though. I heard knocking and muffled voices.'

'At what time?'

'Around 7ish, I think.'

'Did you see anyone going in or out?'

'No, I heard voices and looked through the spyhole but they had already gone inside.'

'Could they have gone back downstairs, maybe an Amazon driver or pizza delivery?'

'Maybe but they often wait for a signature or a photograph or a tip, but they were only outside a few seconds.'

'Did it sound like he knew them?'

'I'd say yes. Nobody invites a stranger in after only a couple of seconds. Also, they left a bag outside.'

'What do you mean a bag? Plastic bag, suitcase, handbag or what?'

'Just a bag, like a small holdall, the type people use for the gym or sports.'

'And it sat outside while his visitor was inside? Did you see anyone lift it?'

'Sorry no, I lost interest and forgot. I looked half an hour later but it had gone.'

'Anything else you can tell me, Miss….?'

'Walker…Hannah Walker. Not really. I didn't think much about it at the time.'

'Ok, thanks for your help. Here's my card. I'm DS Dolan. My colleague DI Bayford will be back soon. We'll need a formal statement from you but can you go inside for the moment while we smash the door down.'

'What the hell is going on? Is Dave in trouble?'

'Maybe, but please wait inside, we'll knock if we need you again.'

Whilst Dolan engaged with Hannah Walker, Bayford obtained McIntosh's permission to use an Enforcer to break down Gill's door. He retrieved it from the boot of the car and wedged the communal door open. He suspected there would be soon be significant comings and goings.

Bayford handed the Enforcer to Dolan and smiled. 'Benefit of rank Chris. Why get dirty when someone can do the work for you.'

'Thanks guv, you're all heart.'

While Dolan brutally battered the door above the lock mechanism, the first couple of smashes saw the 16kg of hardened steel merely bounce off. Dolan looked at Bayford. Reinforced in some way.

The third and fourth efforts saw small gouges emerge but Dolan started to tire after the fifth attempt. Bayford took over and three massive hits later, the battered door succumbed and the gouges grew larger allowing Bayford to force his hand inside and twist the lock.

'If you have trouble getting lids off jars at home, give me a shout. Happy to help,' Bayford said.

'You're a laugh a minute guv, I did most of the damage but let you get the glory,' Dolan retorted.

They took a side of the hallway each and opened every connecting door, one at a time. Two bedrooms, a bathroom and a boiler cupboard. Nothing, except the chaos left by their own officers. One door remained meaning an open plan kitchen/living room or a separate door from the living room leading to the kitchen.

Dolan entered slowly and immediately saw Dave Gill sprawled across the living room floor.

Bayford followed, 'Shit. Fucking shit,' he said.

Gill's blood had spilled from the open chest wound and massed in a blob on the floor. Already knowing the outcome, Bayford knelt carefully beside the body and checked for a pulse. He nodded to Dolan. 'Get the troops.'

Chapter 77

McIntosh had trouble believing even Beswick could overlook this turn of events but that man made decisions based on nothing but self-interest. Branch's inevitable innocence would lead to the finger of blame pointed at McIntosh and no amount of Beswick's strutting for the TV cameras or pleading to the CPS would change that. McIntosh needed a result, and quick.

But, every person of interest was dead, apart from Natasha. Difficult to imagine, but could she be responsible for all of it?

A bunch of dejected detectives gathered in the Incident Room for a meeting. For every step forward there seemed to be two back.

'What've we got, Simon?' McIntosh said.

'I think Natasha figured out what Gill was up to, possibly sussed we were listening. She said they would arrange to meet. What if she just barged in? Telling her to get lost would've made him look guilty so he played along and she killed him. Exactly the same as Sarah and Guy. One stab wound to the heart.'

Dolan added. 'The neighbour heard voices and looked through her spyhole. She spotted a holdall by Gill's door. Maybe containing cleaning products and new clothes?'

Myers said, 'No cameras directly face Gill's flat, but at 7.38pm a figure is seen in South Hill Drive, a fifteen-minute walk from his building. Wearing a baseball cap, thick scarf and the obligatory face mask but they're holding a bag. A slim person, average height, no distinctive clothing. Similar to the previous CCTV likeness that could've been Natasha.'

On the rare occasions Kelly Arnott publicly spoke, people tended to listen. She hated being the centre of attention, but if she was sure of herself, what she said was usually worth listening to. She put her hand up. 'Can I say something,' she said, softly.

Every head swivelled to meet Arnott's gaze. 'Knock yourself out Kelly,' McIntosh said.

'I've just Googled Natasha Cook. Plenty of stories and pictures, but one in particular from last night. She attended a PETA event in the west end. Lots of photos, the whole works. So, unless she murdered Gill and was still in the area at 7.40pm, then scuttled home to get glammed up and photographed dozens of times by 8 o'clock, I don't think she could have done it.'

The room fell silent.

'What the fuck is going on?' McIntosh said, rhetorically. No one offered an answer anyway. 'Kelly, I want to know exactly when she arrived and the time of every photograph. There must be a digital record. When did she leave and was anyone with her? We've no time of death yet so we're only going by Gill's neighbour. Maybe we're miles off. Maybe she killed him at midnight. Nail these facts down first and we'll see what the pathologist says. Have we found her aunt yet?'

'Not yet boss,' Findlay said. 'Margaret Ward didn't have a sister so it wasn't a blood relation. Must have been a family friend?'

'Ok, find her. We need to fill in the blanks in this lassie's life.'

'Are we still keeping this under the radar?' Dolan said.

'Fuck that,' McIntosh said. 'I don't care if she knows we're snooping around. Hopefully it'll make her make a mistake. Same for last night. If a photographer asks why you want to know, say it's part of an ongoing enquiry. Don't give them more but don't hide it either. I want this lassie on the back foot. Let's meet later so get what you can as quickly as you can.'

Chapter 78

His strict Stirling upbringing was fostered more from respect than outward demonstrations of love. McIntosh had no doubt his parents loved him, they just had trouble showing it. He and his big sister were taught to speak out if they viewed injustice or bad behaviour and both had carried that mantle into adult life. A philosophy which had generally served McIntosh well except for the occasion when he went nose-to-nose with his boss and called him a self-serving prick to his face. Unfortunately, it was in a very public arena, full of senior police officers.

That incident happened not long before his father passed away from colon cancer but he never discussed it with him before he died. Looking back, the stress of his personal situation probably contributed to his actions but he never used it as an excuse. Although he received a severe censure, a warning about his future conduct and demotion back to Detective Inspector, he never once regretted saying it. He also knew, beyond doubt, that his old man would have approved.

As luck would have it, the same self-serving prick was on his way to see him right now. On cue, his door lightly rapped, and Commander Jonathan Beswick walked in.

'Chief Inspector, I'm a very busy man. I don't appreciate a summons from a lower ranking officer. You should have called my PA and made an appointment. I've also been made aware you're still investigating these bloody TV murders despite my explicit instruction to stop. You better have a damn good explanation.'

'I apologise sir. What I need to show you must be here. Otherwise I would've, naturally, come to see you.'

Lie number one.

'Also, we've connected another murder to the show and it obviously couldn't have been Magnus Branch. I suspect when we find Dave Gill's killer we'll discover they killed the others.'

Hopefully, not lie number two.

Beswick suspiciously eyed McIntosh, before snapping out of it. 'Careful Chief Inspector, you're on a sticky wicket. I don't like my authority undermined. Get on with it.'

'Sir, I need to run this by you. It's a very sensitive audio recording, related to the attempted kidnap of my family.'

Beswick's eyes widened. 'How did you come by it?'

'Posted through my letterbox, hand delivered of course.'

'Ok, go ahead and play it.'

McIntosh clicked his mouse and the audio started.

'Got a hit on the family. They're in a Travelodge, North London.'

'You took your time.'

'That's as quick as I could. I've got to be careful.'

'Remember how much I pay you. I expect instant answers.'

An audible sigh, 'That's as much info as I could get. You'll have to do the rest.'

'Is that it?' Beswick said. 'Could be anyone. Play it again.'

Second time around Beswick still remained dubious. 'I don't recognise any voices. Who do you think it is?'

McIntosh jerked his head towards the squad room. 'My DI, Simon Bayford.'

Chapter 79

Beswick's lips were pursed and he scratched his nose. He didn't look convinced. 'Why do you think it's him?'

'I know his voice plus he's been fishing for information and I was daft enough to trust him. I can barely believe it myself. Bastard!'

'Go on play it again,' Beswick said.

After the third time Beswick said. 'I still don't think it's clear but it could be.'

'I disagree sir, I think it's very clear. I'm confronting him and I wanted you to be present.' Before Beswick replied, McIntosh knocked on his window and signalled to Bayford.

'You should have waited till you're sure,' Beswick said.

'Oh, I'm a hundred percent sure, sir.'

Bayford entered. 'Yes boss, sir,' acknowledging Beswick.

The three men stood and McIntosh was inches from the slightly taller Bayford. 'Simon, I always considered you a loyal and trusted officer, maybe even a friend, someone I could absolutely rely on. Would you agree?'

'Yes boss,' Bayford said doubtfully.

'Listen to this.' McIntosh played the ten second recording. 'Simon, I believe one of those voices is you and you conspired, with Terry Johnson, to attempt to kidnap, and possibly murder my family.'

Bayford frowned, 'Boss, I don't know what you're talking about. I'm not on that tape,' he said, calmly.

Before anyone spoke again, the door rattled and two men entered, carrying official looking briefcases. Smart suits, double knotted ties, highly polished shoes. They'd been here before.

'What are you doing here?' Beswick said. 'Who asked you?'

Detective Sergeant Adam Skinner of the Police Anti-Corruption Unit said. 'We've received an allegation of conspiracy to kidnap. Myself and DC Glass have been made aware of a recording containing evidence against a serving officer.'

'You're wasting your time, it's not me,' Bayford said.

'All in good time sir,' Skinner said.

'Chief Inspector, can you give me the flash drive. I'll use my laptop if you don't mind,' Glass said.

Glass placed his laptop on McIntosh's desk and plugged in the drive. He whizzed through the first two unintelligible audio recordings before clicking on the third.

'Got a hit on the family. They're in a Travelodge, North London.'

'You took your time.'

'That's as quick as I could. I've got to be careful.'

'Remember how much I pay you. I expect instant answers.'

An audible sigh, 'That's as much info as I could get. You'll have to do the rest.'

Glass played the recording three more times. He and Skinner looked at each other.

'I'm satisfied one of those two people is in this room,' Skinner said.

Glass nodded, 'I agree.'

McIntosh said, 'You know I agree. Sir?'

'Yes I think so,' Beswick said, reluctantly.

All heads turned to Bayford. 'I also agree,' he said.

Beswick did a double take. 'You admit that's you on the tape?'

'No sir, I agree one of those voices is in this room.'

'What do you mean?'

'It's you on the tape sir.'

Beswick laughed nervously. 'That won't work Inspector, the rest of us agree it's you.'

'I agree with Simon,' McIntosh said. 'It's you, you piece of shit!'

'I agree,' Skinner said.

Glass nodded, 'Me too.'

Beswick opened his mouth but couldn't form any words.

Skinner spoke next. 'Commander Jonathan Beswick, I am arresting you on suspicion of conspiracy to kidnap and murder. You do not have to say anything but it may harm your defence if you do not mention, when questioned, something which you later rely on in court. Please come with us.'

Beswick protested. 'I'm going nowhere Sergeant, have you forgotten who I am.'

'Sir, you are a serving police officer under suspicion of committing a crime and you are under arrest. You'll be placed in a cell until interview. I assume you want your solicitor informed?'

'This is fucking outrageous,' Beswick yelled. He turned to McIntosh. 'You arranged this. You'll be sorry. Your career is over.'

'My career? It's your career that's over you piece of low-life scum. Enjoy prison, once it gets around who you are. You're the one who'll be sorry…. sir.' McIntosh balled his fists and took two steps towards Beswick, fury in his eyes.

Bayford caught his arm in time. 'He's not worth it boss. His shitty life is finished. Let him go.'

Skinner and Glass marched Beswick away, protests still ringing loudly. McIntosh could have drawn his blinds but decided to let everyone see their

Commander in his true light. The rest of the EIU unashamedly watched the whole performance. Once Skinner, Glass and Beswick had gone, he turned to Bayford.

'Well played Simon, nice work.'

'Thanks boss, would you really have smacked him?'

'Aye, probably. Just as well you were there. Nice when a plan comes together.'

Bayford laughed, 'Even Beswick looked perplexed at you, convinced it was me on the tape when he clearly heard himself.'

'I know, I wanted him confused until ACU arrived. Make him think the target was someone else. I'd already given ACU the flash drive, so they knew it was him.'

'Is it enough? A semi decent QC will argue it's inconclusive.'

McIntosh nodded. 'They've already looked at Beswick's bank accounts. The arrogant prick didnae even bother hiding the money Johnson's paid him. Over £300,000 in total. The bastard is going down.'

'I still can't believe he helped Johnson try to kidnap your family again.'

'Takes all sorts Simon. Unfortunately, he's not the only one.'

'You think others are involved?'

McIntosh nodded. 'I know they are.'

Chapter 80

Despite witnessing the excitement, the EIU detectives were oblivious to the narrative behind Beswick's arrest. On McIntosh's instruction, Bayford refused to say a word, not wishing to add any fuel to the rumour fire. But the squad room continued to crackle with tittle tattle and McIntosh knew his team deserved the truth. After keeping his fragile spirits to himself for so long he hankered to tell his story. He stood in front of an expectant group, their eyes burning a hole through him.

'Firstly, I want to say thanks for all your hard work. It's been a long, tiring day and I appreciate you're still here. I'm hearing rumours and speculation about the events of earlier so I want to be straight with you. Bear in mind it's still an active investigation and, like any case, evidence needs to be gathered. Therefore, discretion and professionalism are called for. Do not jeopardise the case by shouting your mouths off or you'll have me to answer to. Understood?'

No one spoke but plenty of nodding heads.

'Earlier today Anti-Corruption officers arrested Commander Jonathan Beswick on suspicion of conspiracy to kidnap and murder. Evidence suggests he co-operated, with others, in the attempted abduction of my family. The abduction was foiled and my family are safe. Any questions?'

Every hand went up. Chris Dolan was first. 'Was he involved in the previous kidnapping, in Scotland?'

'They're looking into that but I'd say it was extremely likely.'

'What was this attempted abduction meant to achieve?' Myers said. 'You were exonerated before. What were they trying to get from you this time?'

McIntosh sighed, 'Nothing Glenn, it seems like it was payback for the previous episode going awry. Sounds like a revenge mission. I think they planned to kill my wife and daughter.'

Joanne Findlay turned pale. 'Do you think Beswick knew?'

'Who knows Joanne, I wouldnae want to speculate. It's over now and as I said, it's an active case so I'll no' go into any more detail. Essentially, you know what I know. But we've our own case to worry about. Who's got some good news? Kelly?'

Kelly Arnott looked grim-faced. 'Afraid not, boss. The PETA photographer confirms he took photos of Natasha arriving at 7.30pm. Some social media photos were uploaded between 8 and 9.30 and the event organisers remember her still there after 11pm. Doesn't sound possible for her to have done it.'

'Shite,' McIntosh said. 'Do we have a time of death?'

'Pathologist reckons between 7 and 8pm,' Dolan said.

'So, if Natasha is innocent, we're looking for someone else and we're right back at the start. The Natasha and Magnus connection means nothing.'

Stuart Strong cleared his throat. 'Boss, the person I tracked from Sarah's on CCTV looks like the same person with the bag from the Gill murder. Similar height, model-like posture. Baseball cap, scarf, face mask, jacket, leggings and trainers. If it's the same killer, it can't be Natasha. It's maybe a guy.'

'Your taxi driver confirmed it was a woman,' Myers said.

Strong shrugged and nodded.

'What about two people working together?' Findlay said.

'Who look and walk like each other. C'mon Joanne, get real,' Myers said.

'I don't hear any bright ideas from you,' Findlay said, defensively.

'Enough,' McIntosh intervened. 'Let's concentrate on what we do have. Three murders, five deaths if we include Harvey and Edwards. A dead prime suspect who couldn't have committed the last one. The suspect committed fraud and his associate is the latest murder victim. The suspect was the long lost father of another celebrity on the show who became a particular person of interest after our suspect, her father, died. Images resembling her can be traced from close to Sarah O'Neill's crime scene all the way to her home address. She flew to Majorca at the time of Andrew Harvey's death but, to date, we have zero hard evidence against her. She has a solid alibi for Gill's murder, leaving several possibilities...

...One - Natasha killed the first four. We'll call Harvey and Edwards murders for the time being. A.N. Other killed number five. Why did someone else get involved?

... Two - Natasha is completely innocent and A.N. Other killed them all. Who are they and what is their motive?

... Three - Magnus, Natasha and A.N. Other conspired together. What is their motive and the end game?

... Four - Someone blackmailed Dave Gill for two and a half million pounds. Who are they and how does it connect to the murders?

... Five - Natasha is Magnus's daughter. She says she'd no idea. Was it coincidental they appeared on the show together or part of a larger plot? Does anyone have anything else?'

'Can we definitely rule Magnus out as the murderer?' Dolan said.

'We're not ruling anything out but need to be realistic. Gill's death is the same M.O. as the others. We know Magnus didn't do it. I believe his solicitor's story about being present at Sarah and Guy's. Thornhill has no axe to grind but his advice to keep quiet got Magnus killed. I'd have released Magnus on bail but Beswick overruled me. Only three remaining Island Wars celebrities are still alive and we need to know everything about them, including Natasha. She might be out the frame for Gill but she's not off the hook yet.'

Findlay said, 'Glenn and I are interviewing Natasha's aunt tomorrow, although she's not really her aunt. She was Margaret Ward's best friend and they swore to look after each other's kids if anything happened. She took the twins in when Margaret died. She hasn't seen or heard from Natasha in years but seemed happy to talk.'

'Good, find the gaps in that lassie's life. We're missing something important and I want to know what it is.'

Chapter 81

McIntosh patiently waited for the kettle to boil. Again. Already his third of the day. He'd arrived early, so he could leave sharp to collect Debs and Amanda from the airport. It had been a while and he craved the return to normality at home. While he poured, he overheard a muffled conversation between Joanne Findlay and Kelly Arnott.

'Did you hear who got attacked last night, outside the Drunken Dog in Peckham?' Findlay said.

'No.'

'Kevin Tait, a PC who only ever works in the evidence room.'

'Jesus, what happened, is he ok?'

'In a bad way, apparently. Two broken legs, broken arm, face beaten to a pulp. In intensive care.'

'Holy shit, do they know who did it?'

'Not yet. Sounds like something beyond your average bar fight though.'

'Poor guy. Do you know him?'

'Yeah, to say hello to, don't think we've ever had a proper conversation.'

'Local CID will be all over it like a rash.'

'No doubt.'

McIntosh stirred his coffee. He knew about Tait and knew the culprits. Payback for duff intelligence he gave Terry. Tait told Beswick about the evidence theft, unaware he'd been duped. Beswick then compounded the error by failing to tell Terry about the ACU clearing McIntosh, until after his family survived in Scotland.

The bogus hotel tip sealed their fate. Tait lapped up the fake canteen gossip and told Beswick, who fed Terry the dodgy information. They'd both become surplus to Terry's requirements. In Scotland, when Sully showed McIntosh the photograph of Tait with Terry's gang, the pieces of the puzzle started falling into place.

He had zero sympathy for either of them.

Chapter 82

The twenty-three-mile journey to Essex took an hour. Myers hated driving through London for work during the day, the frustration and stress build up rendering him tetchy and bad tempered. Findlay knew the signs. They stopped for a drive-thru coffee to let Myers calm down before parking directly outside the modest three-bedroom terraced house in Riverside Lane, Grays.

'How do we play this?' Findlay said.

'Slowly to start but if we think she's holding back we have to go for it. You heard the boss. The gloves are off.'

They strode along a communal path to the front garden, a rectangular green space with paved offshoots to each front door. No privacy fencing or a chance to hide your business. They rang the bell, waited and rang again. Thirty seconds later they heard scuttling in the hallway.

'I'm sorry, I was out the back,' a small, chunky woman said, breathlessly. Although no expert in assessing older women's ages, Myers considered her between fifty and sixty years old, and probably very attractive in her youth.

They showed their warrant cards. 'Detectives Findlay and Myers, we spoke on the phone,' Findlay said.

The woman gave a cursory glance at the ID and invited them in. 'I'm Andrea Dunn,' she said, formally offering a seat. 'You were a little vague on the phone, can you tell me what this is about?'

'Natasha Cook,' Myers said.

'I know her as Ashley and I guessed as much, but what exactly?'

Findlay took the lead. 'Mrs Dunn, I'm sure you're aware of a recent series of murders connected to a TV show Natasha appeared in just a few months ago. Only three of the eight celebrities remain alive, including Natasha. We need to know as much about their background as we can. It may help save their lives.'

'You think Ashley's in danger?'

'We really don't know but we can't rule it out.'

'But I haven't spoken to her in years. Why not ask her yourself?'

'We have but she's been vague about the period she lived with you. We assumed she can't remember or has blocked it out, coming after the trauma of her mum and her sister. What was your relationship with Natasha's mum?'

'Best friends, but like sisters in so many ways. Our kids called the other mum auntie and it stuck. We made a pact that if anything happened to either of us, the other would look after their kids. People say these things and it never happens. Well, for us it did.'

'What actually happened to Natasha's mum?' Myers said.

'Margaret was diagnosed with stomach cancer. I think she knew she was ill but by the time she visited a doctor, it was too late. Quite quickly she became housebound, then had to be transferred to a hospice, where she died soon after. By then, I'd already become mum to Ashley and Naomi.'

'Natasha's twin sister?'

'Yes, they lived with me. I fed them, clothed them and took them to school. The twins and my daughter Emma were like cousins growing up, then became more like sisters. When Margaret died, the girls fell apart, especially Naomi. She never got over her mother's death. There was a lot going on in the poor girl's head. She killed herself a year later. Ashley had just about come to terms with her mother, when her sister died. She became inconsolable, as you'd expect.'

'Naomi drowned didn't she?'

'Yes, disappeared on a day trip to Southend. Someone claimed they saw her walk into the sea. We never saw her again and her body's never been found.'

'How old were the twins at that time?' Findlay said.

'They would've been fifteen. Natasha stayed with me until she was seventeen, then went off to college. She got a part-time job and stayed with friends. I haven't heard from her since.'

'How come? Did you fall out?'

'Not really, I tried keeping in touch but she never answered any calls or texts. I eventually stopped trying.'

'Couldn't have been easy?'

'No, but I needed to remind myself she wasn't my daughter.'

'Did you get resistance from the authorities when you took them in?'

'Not at first, then social services came round. I think a neighbour tipped them off. Of course I didn't have any official paperwork but they seemed satisfied after speaking to the twins. I assumed they didn't want the hassle and the girls were happy. Obviously, Naomi had demons in her head but the three girls got along well enough.'

'Did the girls ever mention their father? Talk about trying to contact him?' Myers said.

'Not to my knowledge. When they were quite young Margaret told them how he'd abandoned them as babies and she made no secret of her contempt for him. She asked them never to try to contact him. I doubt they'd have gone against their mother's wishes.'

'Even when Natasha became an adult?'

Andrea Dunn shrugged. 'You can never tell but I'd like to think her respect for her mother counted for something.'

'When Natasha left at seventeen you've no idea where she went or what she was doing?'

'I knew she went to a local college and I heard she popped up on a crap TV dating show. She changed her name but I didn't want to annoy her.'

'What about your daughter Emma? Would she know where Natasha's been the last few years?' Myers added.

'I doubt it. I know she hasn't heard from her either. Ashley fell off the face of the earth, until she appeared on that dating show. You'll probably find out as much from the internet than from Emma or myself.'

'Can we talk to Emma?'

'No, she doesn't live here anymore. I don't know where she is at the moment. She gets in touch from time to time but otherwise, I hardly hear from her.'

'What does she do?'

'An actress, she's never in the same place very long.'

'Sounds like they've all deserted you Mrs Dunn,' Myers said, more sharply than he'd intended.

She looked keenly at him, smiled and said, 'They've got to live their own lives, detective. As long as they're happy.'

Findlay sensed they were wasting time. Andrea Dunn had filled a few gaps, without being overly helpful. She stood and considered the coffee she'd drank and the drive back. 'Thanks for your time, Mrs Dunn. Do you mind if I use your bathroom before we get going?'

Chapter 83

Although she genuinely needed the toilet, on a whim Findlay decided to snoop a little, peeking in each upstairs room. Three bedrooms and a bathroom. Although immaculately clean, two of the bedrooms clearly hadn't been used in a while, probably receiving a dust and vacuum every few weeks. One was likely Emma's room and the twins probably shared the other.

Findlay ignored Andrea Dunn's room, guessing nothing would be gained by rummaging in her drawers, and entered the twins room. She didn't have much time – she still needed to pee - so concentrated on what she could see. Andrea was clearly very house proud. The two perfectly made beds were covered with a fresh smelling duvet. The free standing wardrobe and chest of drawers were empty and apart from a large poster of Robbie Williams on one wall, the rest of the immaculately kept room was bare.

Findlay moved into Emma's room. She hoped to find a diary or journal but the sparsely garnished room offered little more than the twins. Thinking of her old room in her parent's house in Bristol, full of clothes, photographs and knick knacks, Findlay thought it unusual for an offspring to remove all signs of existence from the family home, but Emma had evidently emptied her whole life when she'd moved out.

Posters of Eminem and Jay Z remained stuck to the walls, not making the cut in the move, or Emma had grown out of them. Findlay smiled at a little picture of Take That, cut from a teen magazine, apologetically tucked away in the corner beside the bed. Something caught her eye.

A small photo of three girls, pinned to Gary Barlow's head. Dressed identically and at first glance, Findlay thought they were triplets. She unpinned the photo for a better look as a shout came from downstairs.

'Everything ok up there?' Andrea Dunn said.

'Just coming.'

She couldn't push her luck any further. She quickly snapped a photo with her phone before re-pinning it to Gary Barlow. She left the room, closed each bedroom door and flushed the toilet before heading downstairs, legs crossed.

'Thank you Mrs Dunn, we'll be in touch if there's anything else. If you think of anything helpful, give us a call,' she said, handing over her card and hurrying out.

Myers looked quizzically at Findlay shuffling back to the car. 'You were a bit abrupt there.'

'Glenn, shut up and drive, I'm bursting for a pee,' she said, in no state to chat.

Chapter 84

Myers frowned in confusion, before driving away at speed. He parked on double yellows outside Grays Shopping Centre while Findlay dashed in to a Burger King. Five minutes later she re-appeared and relaxed into the passenger seat.

'Want to tell me what's going on,' Myers said.

'When I went upstairs I really did have to pee but I took the chance to have a quick look around and ran out of time. I didn't want her getting suspicious. There are two unused bedrooms, probably Emma in one and the twins in another. Both clean and tidy but unused for some time. Next to nothing in both rooms apart from a photograph of three girls. I only had time to take a quick photo on my phone. I checked it out in the loo.'

'Let's see it then.'

Findlay touched the photo and maximised it as wide as she could.

'Triplets?' Myers said.

'I thought that at first but now I think it's twins plus one. The middle one and the one on the left look like Natasha so must be her and Naomi. The right one's mouth is slightly different plus she has a narrower face.'

'I'm not sure any of them look like Natasha,' Myers said.

'Remember, we've never seen her without full make-up plus I'm sure she's had plastic surgery.'

'I don't think her boobs count,' Myers said, smiling.

'Trust you! I'm sure one of those two is Natasha, which makes the third girl Emma Dunn. I'm sure I recognise her from somewhere.'

'Doesn't ring any bells with me. The photo must be ten years old. Girls change a lot between early teens and mid-twenties.'

'Depends what you're looking at,' Findlay said, smiling. 'Just drive and I'll keep looking.'

Thirty minutes later Findlay yawned loudly. She put her phone away and her head on the backrest. 'I'm going to shut my eyes to see if it comes to me.'

Myers smiled. He knew what that meant. He spent the next twenty minutes increasing the radio volume bit by bit before giving her a nudge as they neared the station. Findlay stirred, opened her eyes and realised they were only two minutes away. She dug out her phone and found the photo.

'Enjoy your kip?' Myers said, smiling.

'Resting my eyes.'

'I didn't think people snored, resting their eyes.'

'I don't sn....' she said, glancing at the photo. Her mouth opened wide as Myers eased into a parking space and switched off the engine.

'What!'

'Holy fuck! I know who the other girl is.'

Chapter 85

Findlay bee-lined upstairs to find the DCI's office empty. The only person in the squad room was Stuart Strong, still persona non grata.

'Where is everyone?' she said.

'All out,' Strong said.

'Shit, I think I've got something.'

'Yeah?' Strong said, uninterested.

'Wait till I print this off.'

'What's she talking about?' Strong said to Myers.

'A link to Natasha's past, she wanted to tell the whole team.'

Strong looked around the room, 'Well this is it.'

Findlay came back with several sheets of paper and gave one each to Strong and Myers. 'This is a photo I found in Andrea Dunn's house. Natasha, her twin sister plus one other. Andrea's daughter I assume. Do you recognise her?'

Myers shook his head. 'No, I'm not even sure I recognise Natasha.'

Strong studied the photo hard.

'What about you, Stuart?'

'One of them is Natasha. I've seen her up close, remember,' he said winking. 'I know the other girl too, can't think from where.'

'It's Emily Dean from Island Wars. She must be Andrea's daughter. What was her name, Emma Dunn……now changed to Emily Dean!'

'Yeah, I think you're right, now you've said it,' Strong said.

'Glenn, this means Andrea Dunn lied through her teeth.'

'How?'

'She said she hadn't seen her daughter for a while but they regularly spoke so she must know Emily appears on a daytime soap and that she signed up for Island Wars, meaning it's inconceivable Emily didn't tell her mum that Natasha signed up too. They were basically sisters.'

'She didn't say Emily hadn't told her, only Natasha hadn't spoken to her.'

'But why wouldn't she mention it in conversation, unless she's hiding something. She maybe didn't lie but she deliberately withheld information. If we hadn't found the photo we'd be none the wiser.'

'You think Emily and Natasha hatched a plan and the mum knows?' Myers said.

'That's exactly what I think. I mentioned three celebrities were still alive from the show and she asked if Ashley was in any danger. Never mentioned her daughter. Why not? Because she knew they weren't in any real danger.'

'There's still no evidence, even if they did it together,' Strong added.

'Maybe not, but we're not starting from scratch after all,' Findlay said, sending a text.

Chapter 86

McIntosh laid two steaming cups of coffee on Sully's living room table. 'So, it worked like a charm?' Sully said.

'Aye, it did. I suppose I have you to thank for the idea.'

'Hey, don't go overboard with the praise guv,' Sully laughed. 'I'd have paid money to see his face when they read him his rights.'

'His jaw dropped and he couldnae speak. It was beautiful. He honestly thought we heard Simon Bayford's voice. When I singled out the wrong man I saw his confusion, then amazement. He'd have gone along with it too, slimy bastard. Simon had to hold me back. I was ready to smack him in the puss.'

'Would you really have hit him?'

McIntosh shrugged, 'I'd like to think I'd restrain myself at the last minute but who knows. I'm glad I didn't. The arrest and probable dismissal wouldn't have been worth the two seconds of joy watching his teeth fly from his mouth.'

Sully laughed, 'Is it a slam dunk?'

'It never is, but the money helps. Terry pointed us in the right direction. The arrogant prick thought he'd get away with it forever.'

'Why was Terry so keen to nail him?'

'Cost finally outweighed his usefulness?'

'He's lucky Terry never put a bullet in his brain.'

'Terry's no' daft though. Do that and the whole of the Met are after him. This way, Beswick's the bad guy and he gets rid of him without lifting a finger.'

'Any investigation into Terry's involvement?'

'Probably not. Beswick won't say a word and none of his guys will talk. There's nothing to implicate him.'

'So, he's free to carry on?'

'Aye, for the moment, but he'll fuck up at some point and we'll be waiting. The main thing is, he's not a threat to me anymore. There's even a grudging respect.'

'With the man who kidnapped your family and intended to murder them?' Sully said, eyebrows raised.

'Aye, weird right. Don't get me wrong, he's still a scumbag and I'll delight in sending him away for life, hopefully soon. But at the moment, we've both got what we want. Small victories, Sully.'

McIntosh's phone pinged. *'Caught a break, need to discuss asap'*

'The good news keeps on coming. Joanne Findlay's got something. I'll have to get going.'

'No worries guv, maybe when I'm back on my feet we can put the team back together?'

'Angling for a job, Sully? Fraud and embezzlement not enough anymore?'

'Just a thought, I miss the excitement. You dragging me all over Scotland whetted the appetite. Bear it in mind?'

'Aye, will do Sully, gotta go.'

Chapter 87

While he made himself yet another coffee McIntosh listened to Findlay's interpretation of the Andrea Dunn interview and the photograph. Impressed by her intuition, he was keen to let her take the lead. When the pair entered the meeting room, the rest of the team waited, aware of a new development.

'Quiet everyone. We have a new line of enquiry due to some quick thinking on Joanne's part. I'll let her talk you through it.'

Findlay blushed slightly and stood. 'Glenn and I interviewed Margaret Ward's best friend, Andrea Dunn. After Margaret died of cancer, she took Natasha and her sister Naomi to live with her. Naomi committed suicide a year later. Natasha continued to live with Andrea until she left for college, aged seventeen. Andrea claims she's not seen or heard from Natasha since. However, before we left, I managed to have a quick look upstairs. In a bedroom I found a photo of three girls, which I've printed off for everyone.'

The whole team, as one, cast their eyes over the photo.

Findlay continued, 'At first I thought they might be triplets but, if you look closer, two are identical and the other looks a little older with a slightly different appearance. The identical twins are Natasha and Naomi. I believe the other girl is Emily Dean, from the Island Wars show. Andrea said her daughter's name was Emma. It doesn't seem a huge leap to go from Emma Dunn to Emily Dean. Glenn isn't so sure that Natasha and Emily are in the photo. What does everyone else think?'

Two minutes later, after much chatting and pointing, the whole team, excluding Myers, agreed the two Island Wars girls were looking at the camera.

'I'm sure,' McIntosh said. 'We'll confirm it later, but for now, we work on that assumption. Carry on Joanne.'

'Thanks boss, it suggests Andrea Dunn lied to us or knows more than she let on. She hears regularly from her daughter but doesn't know where she is because of her job. It's beyond belief she's unaware her daughter is a soap actress and implausible that Emily didn't tell her mum about her and Natasha appearing on Island Wars. Either Andrea didn't know about the photo or didn't bank on us finding it. Either way, she didn't want us making the connection. There's no DNA cross match between the pair because they're not blood relations. Maybe Andrea knew about Magnus being Natasha's father and they devised the whole plot to frame him for murder and take some of his money. Andrea asked if Natasha was in danger but never mentioned Emily which suggests she knew neither of them were in any real danger.' Findlay sat and took a deep breath.

'Thanks Joanne. That all makes a lot of sense but let's proceed with caution. We can worry about Andrea's involvement later but let's concentrate on Natasha and Emily. Where was Natasha between college and appearing on the dating show. Was she in contact with Emily? Boyfriends? We still need more background info. Natasha's aware of our suspicions of her but we need to keep the Emily thing under wraps for now.'

'What about additional interviews with Natasha, Emily and Catherine Collins?' Dolan said.

'For what purpose?' McIntosh said.

'Dave Gill's just been murdered. Wouldn't they think it odd if we didn't speak to them?'

'Good point Chris, let's have informal chats with those three. We'll go to each of them, unthreatening. Natasha didn't do it so she'll be cocky and full of herself. Grill Emily without getting her suspicious and Catherine…. well, Christ knows, maybe she's also involved just to fuck everything up.

Stuart, you and Heather talk to Natasha. You'll be the last person she expects so she'll try to get under your skin. Rise above it. Glenn and Joanne, you take Emily. Softly, softly though. Keep the conversation to Dave Gill.'

'I'll take Kelly and speak to Catherine Collins,' Bayford said.

McIntosh nodded, 'We're getting closer and I don't want to lose momentum.'

Chapter 88

Walton rang the doorbell while Strong remained two steps back, a scowl on his face. Despite being the guilty party, he was still annoyed at Natasha for becoming a suspect. Yet, even the semblance of a shot at her would encourage him to happily cut off his right arm.

'You're awfully quiet Stuart.'

'Trying to get into friendly mode.'

'Do it, there's a lot at stake.'

The heavy door opened and a vision appeared. She wore a simple white blouse, tight denim jeans and cowboy boots up to her knees. Her immaculate blonde hair cascaded over her shoulders and her flawless make-up completed the catwalk model look. Strong's eyes popped and he struggled to keep his tongue in his mouth.

'STUART, if I'd known it was you coming I would've made an effort.'

Strong leered at her from top to toe, absorbing none of her words.

'I'm DS Heather Walton and I believe you know DC Strong?'

'Of course, we're old friends, right Stuart?'

Strong mumbled incoherently as they trooped into the living room.

They sat and without prelude, Walton said. 'Thanks for agreeing to meet us, Miss Cook. We'll not waste much of your time. You'll have heard about David Gill being stabbed to death?'

'Yes, it's tragic. Dave was a nice guy and didn't deserve to die. Hope you don't think I'm involved? You asked me questions about the other murders.'

'Do you mind telling us where you were four nights ago, from around 6pm to 10pm.

'That's Friday night? I attended an event in central London with a couple of friends. I think we arrived around 7pm. Before that I'd got myself ready and called a taxi for 6.30pm. Should be easy enough to check.'

'Were you friends with Mr Gill?'

'Not really, we were friendly towards each other but not socially.'

'What kind of a person was he?'

'A lovely guy, easy to get on with. I can't believe anyone would want to kill him.'

'What would you say if I told you he participated in the charity fraud with Magnus Branch?'

'Yeah, Dave told me he'd been arrested. He called a day or two before he died.'

'What did you say to him?'

'I gave him a hard time because he'd cheated my charity out of the money but afterwards I started feeling sorry for him. I presumed Magnus coerced him into it.'

'Why would he call you, if you weren't really friends?'

'He warned me that you'd asked a lot of questions about me, more than you quizzed him about the money. His words.'

'Questions about what?'

'I wasn't there Sergeant. You lot were asking the questions. I'd never have imagined Dave getting involved in something like that.'

'Well he did. Helped Magnus win the money, invested it and made millions. Didn't you ever suspect him?'

'Not really, Magnus winning the last event seemed dodgy. I can't explain why, but I never suspected Dave.'

'What about Andrew, Ben and Emily? Did you ever speak to them about your suspicions?'

'No. When the show finished, we couldn't wait to get the hell away from the place.'

'How did you feel when you learned Magnus was your father?'

Natasha tensed and her mouth got tighter. 'What do you think? Even though I never knew him, I always hated my father for abandoning us. Then it transpires, he's this overbearing bully, loathed by everyone, and ten times worse than I ever imagined.'

'How did you react when you heard he'd been murdered.'

'Shocked of course, but not because of any feelings towards him. I didn't know he was my father at that point. Just the never ending fallout from the show.'

'Can we go back to Dave Gill?' Strong said. 'How did he behave at the after party?'

'Ah Stuart, you're awake,' Natasha said, the glint in her eye returning. 'I think he enjoyed himself. He said at the start there would be a fight and he was bang on.'

'Sarah and Magnus?' Walton said.

'Yeah, Sarah broke Magnus's nose. It was hilarious. She'd been gagging for a pop at him all night. Me and Dave went to help him. When we returned most people had left and Sarah had been bedded. Magnus wanted to call the police but Dave and Pete pacified him. Said the show had suffered enough bad publicity.'

'When you and Gill cleaned up Magnus, did you notice anything suspicious between them?'

'Nothing at all. Magnus didn't kill Dave so I don't understand the relevance.'

Strong interjected, 'We're trying to understand how Gill's murder may be connected to his relationship with Magnus.'

'If you say so Stuart.'

'Miss Cook,' Walton said. 'Only three of the original cast remain alive. Have you contacted the other two, to discuss what's been going on?'

'No, haven't talked to them in a while. Why? Do you think I should? Are we in danger?'

'We don't think so but please be vigilant and if anyone raises your suspicions, let us know.'

'Like Stuart?' Natasha said, belly laughing. 'Sorry Stuart, couldn't resist.'

Walton stood, trying not to laugh, and motioned to the stony faced Strong. 'Thank you Miss Cook, we'll be in touch.'

'Thank you detectives.' As Natasha watched them walk away, Strong turned. Natasha put her thumb to her ear, pinkie to her mouth and mouthed the words *'call me'*

Chapter 89

McIntosh was looking forward to getting home. He loved eating proper food again and couldn't help wonder how tonight's menu was shaping up. Debbie had taken a couple of days before resuming lecturing duties at West London College while Amanda forced herself back to Westminster College, needing a routine and some degree of normality.

The humdrum chore of poring over interview transcripts and witness statements was more of a morning task with a sharper brain, but he rarely got a chance. He often tried to schedule time in the early evening when it was quieter, but tonight he was making little headway. His mind was on mince and tatties, hopefully. Debbie's call came as welcome relief.

'I was just thinking about you,' he said.

'I'll not ask. How are you?'

'Aye, not bad. You're saving me from going cross eyed.'

'Again, I'll not ask! I wanted to speak to you about something. You need to call Lucas's parents and tell them what happened.'

His shoulders slumped. He'd been dreading this. 'Has the laddie said something?'

'Lucas.'

'Aye, whatever his name is. What's he been saying?'

'He told Amanda you'd promised to tell his parents once it was all over and she was safe. Guess what?'

'Aye, but what's the point in resurrecting it. It's done now and the last thing I need is a complaint, if they decide to take it further.'

'You promised. He kept his side of the deal. Didn't say a word to anyone. If he told his parents now it would be worse than coming from you.'

McIntosh sighed. 'I'm starting to dislike this laddie.'

'Starting?' she laughed. 'You can't even say his name.'

'Course I can. Luke, or something. Maybe I should have another word, set him straight.'

'Don't you dare. After everything Amanda's been through, do you really want to upset her? If you don't speak to them, I will.'

'Fuck,' he said, knowing Debbie would do exactly that. 'Aye ok, tell Amanda to get me a phone number. I better go, these witness statements have suddenly become more appealing.'

As he clicked off, someone rapped loudly on his door, waiting for permission to enter. 'Fuck sakes, what now?' he muttered, quietly. 'Aye, come in.'

Chapter 90

PC Carl Stanley stood at the door, nervously interlocking his fingers. 'Hello sir, I wondered if I could have a few minutes of your time.'

He was strongly tempted to tell Stanley he was too busy but curiosity got the better of him. McIntosh invited him to sit. Stanley struggled to open the conversation, studying his knitted fingers.

'C'mon son, spit it oot, I've no' got all night.'

'Sorry sir. Em..., I wanted to explain that it was me who reported you to Anti-Corruption.'

McIntosh sank into his chair. With a thousand guesses he'd never have predicted those words from Carl Stanley's mouth. He stared at him, eyebrows raised, waiting.

'I... em just thought you should know. I could've remained anonymous but I'd rather be upfront and after I heard about your family, I felt guilty. I hope I didn't make things worse?'

'Why did you report me?'

'I hate bent coppers, sir. Kevin Tait said you looked shifty. Thought you took evidence from the Johnson case but couldn't be sure, so didn't want to mention it. I knew you'd been there with me,' he smiled. 'I assume that was a trial run. I couldn't overlook what Tait said, as well as our interaction, so I got in touch with ACU. Now I know why Tait didn't want to report it. He's under investigation. They believe he was working for Johnson.'

Stanley stood to leave.

'Aye, I heard but he's got other things to worry about just now. Sit down for a minute, son.'

Stanley reluctantly took his seat.

'It took guts to report a senior officer Carl, especially with such flimsy information. The rank and file would vilify you. They don't like that sort of thing. I'd keep it quiet if I was you and no-one's going to hear it from me either.'

'Thank you, sir, turning a blind eye wouldn't sit right with me. I just wanted you to know.'

McIntosh stood, offering his hand which Stanley eagerly accepted. 'I appreciate your honesty son, and for the record, you did the right thing.'

Stanley left, the weight melting from his shoulders.

McIntosh ticked another thing off his list. For the life of him he hadn't been able to work out who tipped off the ACU.

Chapter 91

After fruitless phone calls and showing up on the set of her workplace, Myers and Findlay discovered Emily Dean had travelled to Brighton for a short break. Not ideal to spend four precious hours driving, but this couldn't wait. They parked just off the promenade and waited for Emily in the back booth of a Starbucks, as agreed.

Arriving fifteen minutes late, she stopped to place her order before joining them. She wore double denim, jeans and a jacket. Blonde hair tied back in a ponytail, looking windswept, as if she'd jumped off a motorbike. He hadn't noticed before but Myers could see the Natasha likeness. Emily was an inch or two shorter but just as stunning.

'Miss Dean, thanks for meeting us on your day off,' Findlay said. 'A trip with your boyfriend?'

'Yes, we don't often get time together but I don't know what the rush is. I could have easily seen you in London. Save you the trip.'

'Sorry, it couldn't wait. We're investigating a murder. You're aware David Gill is dead, the assistant producer of Island Wars?'

'Yes, I couldn't believe it. Dave was one of the good guys.'

'Can you describe your relationship with him?'

'What relationship? I never had a relationship with him.'

Myers butted in, 'Just generally, not in a romantic way,' although something in her voice....

'Oh, we got on pretty well. Dave could be quite funny really.'

'But definitely nothing more between you?' Findlay said.

Emily hesitated, a fraction too long, allowing Myers to jump in. 'Emily, if there is something, tell us now. We'll find out anyway and the situation might get worse.'

Emily took a big gulp. 'Ian knows nothing about this?'

'Your boyfriend?' Findlay said. 'If it's not relevant he won't find out from us. Go on.'

'I slept with Dave before the show. A one-off thing. I'm not proud of it and, to be fair, he didn't make a big deal. As far as I know he kept quiet about it.'

'How did it come about?' Myers asked.

'I heard about this celebrity reality show. A couple of the soap actors I work with turned it down. I'd never been considered for those type of shows so I thought it was my time. My agent approached Dave but he said no. I went to see him, asked him to dinner and made it clear there was more on the table. Back at his flat we had sex and the rest is history. He signed me up.'

'Emily, we're not here to judge, we just want the truth. Gill didn't expect more from you afterwards?' Findlay said.

'No, for someone in his position, I suspect it wasn't his first time but he stayed cool and, like I said, didn't make a big deal.'

Myers said, 'How would you describe Gill's relationship with Magnus Branch?'

'Non-existent? I don't think Magnus got on with anyone.'

'You're aware Magnus stole his charity's prize money. We discovered Gill helped him along the way?'

'You're kidding? Dave? I don't believe it.'

'It's true, he'd been arrested and released on bail just before his murder.'

'Jesus! I thought it was a random killing. Is this connected to the others? Does that mean I'm at risk?'

'There's nothing to suggest that. However, we may need to contact you urgently. Can you give us a mobile number?'

'You'll already have it in your records.'

'I know but it'll save me looking it up. I can put it in my phone right now.'

Emily hesitated but couldn't think of a good reason not to share her number. She read it out while Findlay made a new contact entry. Findlay then rang the number to make sure.

'Thanks Miss Dean, we'll be in touch, enjoy your days off,' Myers said.

Despite being a restless passenger, Myers deferred to Findlay's request to drive. At least he wouldn't have to listen to her snoring.

'She frantically thought of an excuse not to give us her mobile number. I'm going to double check it's the same number we already have,' Findlay said.

'Maybe sleeping with Gill was a calculated move to find out about his liaison with Magnus and the overall plan?'

'Maybe. I think we handled it ok. Don't think she questioned our motives.'

Chapter 92

Catherine Collins was in central London on business and arrived at Charing Cross station of her own volition. In her words, it made sense to get it over with.

'Catherine, thank you for coming,' Bayford said. 'You're aware of David Gill's murder?'

'Yes I heard. Don't tell me it's linked to the others?'

'We don't know but we want to rule you out of our enquiry. Can you give us your movements last Friday night?'

She thought hard but said nothing. 'My mind's gone blank I'm afraid.' She produced her phone and pressed the screen a few times. 'Nothing specific for Friday. I had a gig on Thursday night so it would have been a rest day. I think I slept late and, yes I remember, met a friend for afternoon coffee and a chat. We went our separate ways around 4.30pm. I went home, made dinner and spent a quiet night with my husband.'

'If you provide contact details for your friend and husband, we'll corroborate your alibi before you leave. It'll help if we can clear you right away,' Bayford said.

'If it's really necessary, but I can't believe you think I might be involved,' she said, scribbling on a piece of paper. Bayford handed the paper to Arnott, who went outside and passed it to the desk Sergeant.

'We don't but only three of you are left. Either, one of you is involved or you're all at risk.'

Catherine Collins nodded.

Kelly Arnott sat down again, 'Catherine, tell us about Dave Gill's relationship with Magnus Branch.'

'Why would you think they had a relationship?'

'You're aware Magnus stole his charity's money. Dave Gill helped him and shared the profits from investing in the stock market.'

'Christ! I thought Dave was one of the few decent people I met on that show.'

'Did anything make you suspicious about the two of them, on the show or afterwards?'

'Not really, I only remember seeing them together once, at the party when Sarah whacked him. Magnus's nose looked broken and they tried to stop the bleeding.'

'Just those two?' Bayford said.

'And Natasha, who'd been drinking all night so god knows what help she'd have been. That was my cue to leave so I don't know what happened afterwards.'

'Anything else?'

'Sorry, nothing I can think of.'

'Thanks Catherine,' Bayford glanced at his phone. 'Our colleagues have confirmed your alibi so you're free to leave.'

Arnott escorted Catherine to the exit before returning to the interview room.

'She's not involved but she did say something very interesting,' Bayford said.

Chapter 93

Joanne Findlay did not scare easily which many villains….and coppers, had already discovered to their cost. Her petite frame belied a mental steeliness and she rarely retreated from a challenge. Tonight though, she felt vulnerable. Alone in her two bedroom Lambeth semi.

From her upstairs bedroom window, she glimpsed movement from inside a car, one hundred yards away. Her copper's nose told her this was the same car from the other night. Then, she'd spied it for a few seconds before it switched on its headlights and drove off. Unable to identify the model or registration, she'd dismissed it as unimportant.

Although probably nothing, an agitated Findlay couldn't settle. Challenging the driver might provoke an unnecessary confrontation and lead to embarrassment, or worse. Instead, she made a phone call.

'Hello,' Kelly Arnott said, wearily.

'Kelly it's me,' Findlay said. 'You still up?'

'Yeah, just going away to bed. What's on your mind?'

'I need a favour.'

Findlay quickly explained the situation and Arnott didn't hesitate to drive the twenty minutes from Bermondsey. She was to approach from behind, note the car make, model and registration, then keep driving. No heroics.

As Arnott neared Lambeth she called Findlay to provide a running commentary. 'I've turned into your street from the south end. I'm still a few hundred yards away. There are a lot of parked cars. Which one am I looking for?'

'I see your lights. The car's parked just before the second tree. There's a bit of a gap between it and the car ahead. When you go past, keep your eyes straight. Don't look at the driver.'

'Ok, I see it. It's a Volkswagen, maybe a Passat. Yeah definitely a Passat, maybe dark blue or black, hard to tell. Going by it now.'

'I saw them cower as you went past. Didn't want to be seen.'

'I didn't look,' Arnott confirmed the plate number. 'Will I keep going or wait somewhere?'

'Keep going Kelly, thanks and I'll see you in the morning.'

'No worries, I'll call for an update when I get home.'

Findlay swept the house, re-checking window and door locks. By the time she looked again, the car had driven off. She text Arnott.

'Car gone, all quiet, see you tomorrow, thanks again'

***

She stared at the screen, drumming her fingers. Took a sip of tea and munched her pen. Still staring. Trying to pluck up courage. The information was a few keyboard strokes away. She thought of Stuart Strong and the trouble he found himself in. She didn't want to be pigeon holed with that idiot. After procrastinating to the point she couldn't do it, Findlay put on her sensible head and knocked on the DCI's door.

'Aye, come in.'

'Morning boss, have you got a minute.'

'Aye, sit down, what's on your mind?'

'I'm hoping you can help with a personal matter. I've noticed someone outside my house, sitting in a car, just watching me. The last couple of days. It's creepy.'

'What makes you think they're watching you? There's bound to be other houses on your street?'

She nodded, 'I don't know, call it a coppers instinct. They're not waiting on anyone. The other night I looked out, and when they saw me they upped and left. The same car was parked again last night around 11pm, the driver just sitting, doing nothing. So, I phoned Kelly and she did a drive-by. Got the number plate and the driver ducked as she drove past.'

'And you want to run the plate?'

'I won't lie. I came in early to do just that but I couldn't.'

'Wise move, but there are other ways. Call it in. A concerned citizen who's noticed a suspicious car and you're worried they're casing houses for robbery, some shite like that. When the plate's in the system we'll call in a favour, get a name and you haven't compromised yourself.'

'Sounds like a good idea boss, thanks.'

'No worries, how did you get on with the background info on Natasha?'

'Waiting on a couple of call backs but she must have kept herself to herself. It's been difficult to find someone who actually knew her.'

'Ok, let me know when you've got something.'

Chapter 94

Despite his brain being in the correct place, Stuart Strong wasn't the sharpest tool in the box, doing most of his thinking below the waist. Undeterred by the mass of trouble he was already in, Natasha's sexy pose, mouthing *call me,* got him fantasising.

On a whim he called her, and could barely believe it when she invited him over……at night. He purposely parked a couple of streets from Natasha's but his blurred mind could hardly remember the drive over. Composing himself for a minute, he took deep breaths before exiting the car. Hopefully, the walk back in the morning would be with a spring in his step.

As he rang her doorbell, the naturally cocky detective's racing heartbeat was unrelated to meeting the prime suspect in a multiple murder case.

Natasha opened the door, smiled sweetly and said, 'Stuart, I'm so glad you could come.'

Strong inadvertently blurted, 'Wow!' A pink T shirt barely covered her midriff and denim shorts displayed her glistening model legs. Her blonde hair swirled haphazardly over her shoulders. She wouldn't have won any fashion contests but she looked exactly as intended.

'You look nice Stuart, sorry I'm not dressier. I went informal.'

'You look amazing,' he said, licking his lips. His respectable jacket and casual slacks looked out of place but he didn't care. He couldn't take his eyes off her.

'Thanks, I cheated a bit. Couldn't be bothered to cook so I've already ordered Chinese. We can reheat it when we're ready. Do you want some wine?'

Strong thought about his car, then about Natasha. Fuck it. Worst case and she kicked him out, he'd get a taxi or maybe drive home if he wasn't too bad. 'Yes please,' he said, politely.

Play it cool, don't be lairy. While Natasha fetched the wine, Strong switched his phone off. He definitely didn't want to be disturbed.

After placing the wine on coasters she drew her legs up on the single armchair, leaning sexily on the rest. On the couch opposite, Strong's eyes locked onto her legs. Natasha smiled inwardly.

'We got off on the wrong foot and I'm sorry I got you into trouble although, I suppose, this will get you into more trouble,' she giggled.

'If anyone finds out.'

'They won't find out from me. I know your boss thinks I did these murders but I can't understand why. Do you think I did it?'

'I shouldn't really talk about the case.'

'Come on Stuart, you're visiting a murder suspect, drinking her wine, will soon be eating her Chinese food and we may see more of each other later. Formality's out of the window, don't you think? I don't want chapter and verse, just trying to understand why someone would think I could do this.'

'We only have circumstantial evidence. There's no way we'd get a conviction.'

'But I didn't kill poor Dave. Surely that puts me out of the frame for the rest?'

'There's a theory you're working with someone else.'

Natasha coughed into her wine. 'Jesus, sounds like you're trying to fit me up. Who am I supposed to be working with?'

Strong's eye was firmly on the prize but he wasn't completely dumb. He didn't mind talking about it but knew he couldn't tell her everything. 'We don't know, it's still a theory. We think someone planned to frame Magnus but he went and got himself killed. When we found out you're his daughter you jumped to the top of the list.'

'I didn't kill anyone Stuart,' Natasha said, getting serious.

'Then you've nothing to worry about. Do you have an idea who might have held a grudge against him?'

'Thousands of people,' she laughed, 'But if I think of anyone specific, I'll let you know first. Might put you back in the good books. I'm getting hungry, let's eat.'

No matter how polite he tried to be, Stuart Strong ate like a pig and Chinese food, in foil containers, was right up his street. More than once, Natasha asked if he wanted a plate but he shook his head, rifling noodles into his mouth. He tried and failed to contain a large belch, while she rolled her eyes, hoping it would be worth it.

When they finished, the containers went straight in the bin, before they grabbed their wine and headed back to the living room. Natasha sidled up to him on the couch and sat, cross legged.

'So, how much trouble did you get into the last time?'

'Not much, I'll probably get another reprimand, when the case is over.'

'Another reprimand! You bad boy.'

'And I spent two days tracking you on CCTV, not the most exciting few hours I've ever spent.'

'You wouldn't have found me, I wasn't there.'

'I saw someone who looked like you.'

'Tall, blonde and female? Not many of them in London.'

'Look I know, but with you being Magnus's daughter, my gaffer put you in the frame. I never said I agreed with him.'

'Thanks Stuart, I'm glad someone's looking out for me.'

'I'd love to show them you're innocent but I'd need someone to point the finger at.'

'I'll keep it in mind. I'm going to bed now. Do you want to join me?'

Strong nipped himself in case he'd fallen asleep and was dreaming. 'Em…ok…yeah, are you sure?'

'Don't sound too keen. If you don't want to, it's fine.'

'I do,' he said quickly. 'I want to be sure you're ok with it.'

Natasha took him by the hand and led him upstairs.

***

Half an hour later Strong thought he'd died and gone to heaven. He lay on his back, hands behind his head, a smug smile on his face. Wait till the lads at Notting Hill hear about this.

A few minutes later he was zonked and a few minutes after that she got out of bed, put on a robe and went downstairs, unable to cope with his hellish snoring. She'd been with some dodgy guys in her time but Strong topped the charts. She poured a glass of water, contemplating a whole night dealing with that insane noise. She might have to wake him up and kick him out. A more attractive prospect than waking next to him in the morning. He might want to do it again, God forbid.

As she rinsed her glass, she heard a light knock on her front door.

Chapter 95

It had been a long few weeks and, despite reaching the business end of the case, McIntosh sensed his team's receding energy levels. Only a few stragglers remained tonight. When the toner light appeared, Chris Dolan thumped the printer, looking lost, wondering what to do next. Heather Walton scribbled away on a notepad, head down, alone in her thoughts, nails bitten to the quick. He ambled towards Joanne Findlay's desk. 'Joanne, any info on Natasha's previous life?'

'Yes and no, boss. A girl called Melissa appeared alongside Natasha on a show called Love Match. The idea was to find love but really about finding fame. In Natasha's case it worked. Anyway, Melissa said Natasha hardly interacted with anyone, didn't find love and no-one knew a damn thing more about her than when she arrived.'

'How did she find fame on the back of that?'

'Not sure, apparently she got close to some guy called Pierre, a Frenchman who worked behind the scenes.'

'So, she found love in the wrong place? What's this Pierre's story?'

'The production company who made the show went bust so it's been difficult tracing him.'

McIntosh sighed and rubbed his eyes. 'Jo, time you went home. Pierre can wait till tomorrow.'

Findlay hesitated, 'Can I have a word in private, boss.'

McIntosh motioned her to his office.

'I wondered, did you find out more about my stalker?'

'Shite, I forgot. Let's do it now.' McIntosh looked up a number from a little notebook in his drawer and dialled. 'Hello, this is DCI Angus

McIntosh, Elite Investigations Unit. I wonder if you can assist me with something. One of my officers reported a suspicious car, parked for long periods, outside her house in Lambeth. Her initial concern was burglary but, after bringing it to my attention, I concluded it may relate to an ongoing case of ours. I'm interested in finding the owner.'

McIntosh provided the car details before stony silence. He hoped someone was tapping away on the other end.

'Yes I'm still here.'

More silence.

'No problem. Correct, a dark blue Volkswagen Passat. Do you have the owner's name?'

Findlay knew he'd heard a name when she saw the emerging frown on McIntosh's brow. 'Can you double check please.'

When the check came back, McIntosh turned pale. 'Ok, thanks, yes it's definitely related to our case. We'll be in touch. Findlay was desperate to ask but his hands covered his head so she sat tight until he finally looked at her, his face fizzing.

Findlay said, 'Boss?'

'The person parked outside your house was Stuart Strong. What the hell is going on?'

Findlay looked amazed. 'Stuart! I've no idea. What was he playing at?'

'Are you two………?'

Findlay laughed involuntarily. 'Em, no boss, absolutely not. Me and Kelly had a drink a while back and Stuart showed up, all full of himself, trying to be the big man. We put him in his place and he left, tail between his legs. Plus, Kelly told you about his date with Natasha. No other issues I'm aware of.'

'Well, those things have obviously festered away at him,' he said, punching buttons on his phone.

'Fucking voicemail, 'Stuart, phone me as soon as you get this. It's urgent.' Jo, go home. If you see Strong anywhere near your house, phone me. Do not approach him.'

'Ok boss, see you tomorrow.'

McIntosh leant back and looked at his office ceiling. Jesus Christ, as if he didn't have enough on his plate without an inter-office revenge mission.

A hunch told him that Joanne Findlay wouldn't look at Stuart Strong if he was the last bloke on earth, but that hunch might not sway Strong if he was hell bent on doing something stupid.

Chapter 96

Strong woke with a start. Something caused him to stir and he nudged Natasha, finding an empty space. He strained his ears. Movement downstairs…and voices. More than one. He slid out of bed naked and padded quietly across the dark bedroom. He switched on the light and poked his head through the gap of the slightly open door. Female voices but he couldn't distinguish any conversation. He quickly put on his shirt and boxers and tiptoed out to the landing, leaning over the timber balustrade to hear the whispered exchange.

'I told you………..here'

'……know……to do'

'We shouldn't……together'

'I think……to me'

'Sh………. upstairs'

Strong observed the back of a blonde haired female. Similar, but not Natasha. As the penny dropped, he darted back to get fully dressed. From being in dreamland, he now saw an opportunity. He threw on his socks and slacks and checked his pockets. Where the fuck did he leave his phone? He finished tying his shoelaces as Natasha entered the bedroom.

'Aw, you're off already Stuart. You were out for the count so I got myself a drink. Hope it wasn't something I said?'

'Er... no it's fine but I have to be somewhere early in the morning. Too far to drive from here so better get home first. Have you seen my phone?'

'No, I hope you didn't use it to video us in bed,' she smiled, raising her eyebrows.

Strong hesitated for a second. 'No, don't be daft. I need to find it though,' he said, urgently.

'Calm down. Maybe you left it downstairs. Go have a look and I'll check up here.'

Strong hesitated again. 'Ok, give me a shout if you find it.'

He walked out of the bedroom, across the carpeted landing to the top of the stairs and saw Emily Dean at the bottom, looking up, clutching his phone.

Chapter 97

Strong froze, mouth open, turning to look at Natasha who'd followed him, then back to Emily. How could he play this for maximum glory? He took a step.

'Evening,' Emily said.

Strong stared at her before stuttering. 'Emily Dean, I am arresting you on suspicion of the murder of David Gill. You do not have to say anything but anything you do say may be given in evidence.' He took another step.

Emily stared back. Neither spoke for several seconds.

Natasha broke the silence. 'STUART!'

As Strong half turned, Natasha forcefully nudged him, leading to a flailing whirl of twisted arms and legs as he propelled down the top flight onto the half landing, around the crooked bottom flight, landing on the hall floor at Emily's feet.

His left leg had bones sticking out, his head and face leaked blood and his neck was unnaturally bent. His blank staring eyes had nothing behind them.

'Fuck sake Ash, you've killed him.'

'I didn't have a choice. It's your fault for coming here. I told you to keep a low profile.'

'I'm sorry. What are you going to do now?'

Natasha descended slowly and elaborately stepped over Strong's body. 'Something else I'll probably regret but, like killing Strong, I don't have a choice.'

A small table at the foot of the stairs was home to a thin glass vase, full of chrysanthemums. Natasha lifted the vase, threw the flowers and water on the floor and, before Emily could react, viciously clubbed her over the head, twice. The soap actress slammed against the wooden floor, little pieces of bone mixing with the brain and blood oozing from her head.

'If you want something done right, do it yourself,' Natasha muttered.

Chapter 98

She emotionlessly studied the bodies at the foot of her stairs, neither part of the agenda. Have some fun with Stuart, learn more about the police's strategy and action plan, then kick him out. That was the aim. In truth it hadn't been much fun and she'd learned very little before Emma blundered in.

Although a spur of the moment decision to push Strong down the stairs, him putting two and two together made up her mind and it made tactical sense to get rid of Emma. As her adopted sister she knew everything and it broke her heart, but she'd become a liability.

Now to disappear never to return, which was high on the agenda, but needing implemented sooner than anticipated. She doubted if Strong blabbed of his whereabouts so she figured it would be mid-morning before the police showed any concern. His phone was off and by the time they pieced together his last known location, she planned to be a long way away.

She stared at poor Emma lying on the floor with her head caved in. Lovely girl but a nervous, unstable one. It wouldn't have been long before she cracked and told the police everything.

Before the current course of events had taken seed, Natasha's fanciful ambition was to become an interior designer, the first project being her own property. She'd purchased several heavy duty cotton dust sheets for floor and furniture protection. Perfect to wrap bodies in.

Easy one first. She snapped on a pair of nitrile gloves. The abundance of her fingerprints and DNA would be explainable but she didn't want to make it easy for them. She rolled out a dust sheet on the hallway floor and wrapped Emma like a burrito. It had been tough having to remember to call her Emily. She dragged the bundle to the tall kitchen cupboard, removed several boxed appliances that had never seen the light of day, and unceremoniously stuffed Emma in the void.

Natasha pinpointed the hall cupboard for Strong, not least because it was closer. His broken bones formed an awkward shape and her wrapping wouldn't win any Mexican cuisine awards. The vacuum cleaner, ironing board and linen basket were removed from the cupboard and she roughly dragged Strong ten feet, squeezing him in, ensuring the door would close.

She spent an hour cleaning blood and brain smears from the walls and hallway floor but ignored the bloodstained stair carpet. The specks weren't too obvious and she was running out of time. She packed a minimal amount. She'd have plenty of money to buy anything she needed.

Natasha locked her front door, put her case in the car and drove away, punching a number into her car phone system.

Chapter 99

The Strong and Findlay thing had played on his mind all night. He yawned and closed his eyes. McIntosh hated dealing with internal personal squabbles amongst his team. He was aware of the rumours about Strong as well as the true stories. Strong wasn't EIU material and wouldn't last much longer.

A head appeared at his door. 'Something on your mind boss?' Bayford said.

McIntosh yawned again. 'Aye, sit down. Is Strong in yet?'

'Haven't seen him, should be in soon,' Bayford said, looking at his watch.

'Tell him to see me before his arse hits a chair.'

'What's he done now?' Bayford said, before McIntosh filled him in.

'Shit, what's this got to do with anything?'

'God knows,' McIntosh shrugged. 'Maybe he was just pissed off about getting humiliated and hoped to scare her. Anything else doesn't bear thinking about. I might have to kick him off the team today.'

'I take it you've called him?'

'Aye umpteen times, straight to voicemail. No answer at his house and his car's no' there so god knows where he is.'

'When I see him, I'll send him your way.'

'Aye, but don't tell him what it's about.'

***

An internet search told Glenn Myers that Nicholas Forgan had been the person in charge of Treehouse Productions, makers of the dating show Love Match. According to Wikipedia, Treehouse was an aberration Forgan preferred to forget and he had since returned to theatre, his first love. He now headed Format, a London Theatre company.

Myers rang Format, experiencing the frustration of the automated answer system, until he heard the purr of a ringtone.

'Yes?'

'Can I speak to Nicholas Forgan please?'

'Speaking, who are you and what do you want?' he said abruptly.

Myers sighed. Forgan sounded difficult so he'd need to turn on the charm. It sometimes worked on men. 'Mr Forgan, my name is Detective Constable Glenn Myers from the Elite Investigation Unit of the Metropolitan Police.' Myers spoke slowly and clearly, avoiding acronyms. Over the phone people sometimes couldn't fathom out what they meant. 'Sorry to call out of the blue but I'd like to ask you a question about your previous production company, Treehouse, and the TV show Love Match.'

Myers heard the sigh and sensed Forgan's attitude softening. 'If you must detective. Not my finest hour and I'd hoped to consign that period of my life to the bin. Ask away and I'll answer if I can.'

'Simple question sir. Did Treehouse have a French employee who worked on Love Match, by the name of Pierre?'

In the silence that followed Myers could picture the churning in Forgan's head.

Eventually he said. 'Well, yes but he's not French. Well, in a way he is. He's British born and bred, with a French mother.'

'Did Pierre have a relationship with one of the contestants, Natasha Cook?'

'Ah, Natasha,' Forgan said, wistfully. 'Much too reserved for that show. I don't know about a relationship but he was one of the chosen few she actually talked to. What's this about?'

'Routine enquiries. His name's cropped up in an investigation. You wouldn't have a number or address for him? He's not in trouble. We'd just like to talk to him.'

'I really don't know. My old contact details are in a box in the house but they're probably not up to date.'

'Could you at least have a look and call me later today please. It's very important.' Myers gave Forgan his mobile number and nearly hung up before barking. 'Oh, wait, I nearly forgot. What's Pierre's surname?'

'Robson, Pierre Robson.'

Chapter 100

The incident room was packed, except for Stuart Strong. With a whiteboard full of information, McIntosh couldn't understand how any of it aligned but at least they had leads to chase down. Where they would steer the investigation, God only knew. He addressed Myers first, who was sitting closest.

'Peter Robson, are you sure?' he said.

'Hundred percent boss,' Myers said. 'Forgan sent me a photo and it's definitely him.'

'What's the theory? Robson and Natasha in it together, recruited Emily for a go at Dave Gill. Branch and Gill were expendable and the rest lived happily ever after?'

'Doesn't sound so far-fetched,' Bayford said. 'Think about it. Natasha resented Magnus for years so she hatches a plan to humiliate him. Robson signs her up to the show. They discover Magnus and Gill's plan and use it as leverage to blackmail him.'

'Where do the murders fit in? I don't see the need for Sarah, Guy, Andrew and Ben to be killed.'

'Me neither, but something must have happened to trigger the killing spree,' Bayford said.

'We know the other celebrities found out that Magnus stole the charity money and Sarah planned to ruin him. Maybe Natasha wanted the glory of his humiliation to herself?' Findlay said.

'Maybe,' McIntosh said. 'This presupposes Natasha is still our prime suspect but there's zero evidence against her.'

Chris Dolan, listening while tapping away at his computer, suddenly shouted. 'Boss, Stuart Strong's phone. Last location is an address in Holland Park. House belongs to Natasha Cook.'

'For fuck sake, you've gotta be kidding me.'

Findlay muttered, 'Probably following his dick.'

'Simon, Chris, go and haul his arse back here, in cuffs if necessary. Rest of you, find Peter Robson. I want to know how he's mixed up in this shitshow.'

Chapter 101

A furious Bayford kicked the glove box in Dolan's car. 'Stupid prick. I can't believe him.'

Dolan frowned, looking at the footprint. 'The guy's a liability. It's one thing interfering with a witness but the prime suspect in multiple murders? Jeez, that's something else.'

'I think the boss will kick him off the team today regardless, which might be his best scenario. Worst will be tampering with a witness/suspect. He'd get kicked off the force, maybe even face charges.'

They drove past the Royal Albert Hall, into Kensington. 'What was going through his mind? Does he just not care?'

'Turn down here, it's a bit quicker. It's not his mind that's the problem,' Bayford said, before recounting the story of Strong outside Joanne Findlay's house.

'Jesus Christ, who is this guy?' Dolan took a right into Addison Road. 'Hold on, did you see that?'

'What?'

'I think that was Strong's car back there.'

'Turn around.'

'I can't, it's one-way.'

'Well, go back round, he might be sleeping in it.'

Dolan spent seven minutes fighting traffic lights and congestion before approaching the dark blue Volkswagen Passat again. 'Yip, definitely his car, I recognise the plate.' He parked illegally, ignoring the hollering from other drivers. The detectives circled the car with an element of caution.

Locked, without Strong conveniently curled up on the back seat. They looked at each other, then headed back to their car.

'Why would he park there? It's a ten-minute walk to Natasha's house,' Dolan said.

'Maybe didn't want his car seen in her driveway. Right here it is, let's see what he's got to say for himself.'

Dolan parked on the street outside Natasha's empty driveway. 'Where's her car?'

Bayford shrugged. 'Let's check it out.'

They knocked several times. No answer. The closed window curtains prevented a proper look inside but the exposed stair windows allowed a cursory view. Bayford was left with a dilemma. He had no good reason to bludgeon the door. Nothing was amiss, but his gut told him a different story. They went round back and knocked on the door, expecting the same response.

Oh, well. Better to ask forgiveness than permission. 'Take off your jacket,' Bayford said.

Chapter 102

Dolan protectively wrapped his jacket a little tighter. 'What for?' he said, suspiciously.

'I'm going to wrap it round that fence post and break the glass. Should be able to unlatch the door from the outside.'

'Shit guv, you sure? That's unlawful entry, shouldn't we get a warrant? More importantly, why don't you use your jacket?'

'It's new, I don't want to ruin it,' Bayford smiled.

Dolan reluctantly handed over his jacket while Bayford lifted the four-inch square post, lying on the back garden lawn. The movies portray the hero nonchalantly elbowing or punching a pane of glass, whereupon it shatters. No injuries, or lasting effects. Bayford might have been tempted, if he'd wanted to break his arm or slash it to ribbons.

After further assessment, wrapping the post risked flying glass, so Dolan held the coat across the small panel above the lock. Easier to unlock from above than manoeuvre the latch from below.

Bayford jabbed the glass, and jabbed and jabbed. On the fourth attempt, it shattered enough to allow him to carefully break through, clearing loose shards away from the opening. He reached inside, found a key in the lock and delicately turned, feeling the mechanism relax.

The deceptively spacious downstairs area looked hastily vacated. Unwashed dishes were set on the draining board, an empty linen basket lay on the kitchen floor, while equipment to mix bread and soup occupied the worktop.

In the living room, Bayford found an upstanding ironing board. No signs of life downstairs. 'POLICE, IS ANYONE HOME?'

Silence.

'You keep looking down here and I'll go upstairs,' Bayford said.

Dolan nodded. They snapped on gloves and disposable overshoes. Less than ten seconds later Bayford shouted.

'CHRIS!'

Dolan raced from the living room and found Bayford looking at the stair carpet. He pointed. 'That's blood and there's a bit more. Let's both go upstairs.'

They slowly and methodically checked each room. Nothing untoward. The main bedroom duvet was in disarray while clothes from an open wardrobe and drawers were strewn across the floor.

'I think she's done a runner,' Dolan said.

'Yeah, with Strong in tow.'

They returned downstairs, carefully avoiding the stair carpet bloodstains.

'Carry on in the living room and I'll do the kitchen,' Bayford said.

He opened each kitchen cabinet and drawer. Nothing significant. When he reached for the handle of the tall boiler cupboard and yanked the door open, he jumped.

'Jesus fucking Christ. CHRIS!'

Chapter 103

Dolan couldn't see what his Inspector was staring at. Bayford nodded towards the cupboard, stepping back to allow Dolan in. They saw a dust sheet, shaped like a body, with its knees squashed underneath its chin.

'Bloody hell, who is it?' Dolan said.

'No idea, give me a hand to get it out of there.'

Dolan grabbed the legs and Bayford the head to ensure no further damage. Not wanting to compromise evidence by cutting the sheet, they gently carried the body shape to the roomier hallway floor, gingerly unwrapped the bundle and stared open mouthed at the lifeless form of Emily Dean.

Despite blood and brain having leaked from the huge gash on her crown and the fact she'd been shrouded in a cupboard for an indeterminate time, Bayford went through the motions of a pulse check before stepping back and staring at Dolan.

'What the fuck is going on? What was she doing here?' Dolan said.

'Maybe confronted Natasha and got her head caved in?'

'So, where is Strong?'

'Christ knows, keep looking.'

The living room offered no clues leaving the empty hallway and it's only closed door. Bayford apprehensively nodded to Dolan.

Your turn.

Dolan slowly pulled the handle, finding the same tableau as the kitchen cupboard. He put his hand to his mouth. 'Jesus,' he said, before stepping back for Bayford to look.

They knew instantly.

The size and shape confirmed this was no slim female. In silence, they cautiously manoeuvred the body from the cupboard and laid it beside Emily, painstakingly unravelling the cotton sheet.

Stuart Strong's dead eyes looked back, neck broken and a leg at a ninety-degree angle. Trying to keep his emotions in check and maintain professionalism, Bayford called McIntosh and was told to sit tight until a small army descended on Holland Park.

It mattered not whether he was a bent copper, a potential rapist or an imbecile. As a police officer, murdered in the line of duty, Stuart Strong deserved the same respect as any serving officer.

At Charing Cross, McIntosh gathered the team and solemnly relayed the news. None seemed particularly grief stricken. Notably, Findlay maintained a steely glare.

'A separate enquiry will be launched but I think we can assume these murders relate to our investigation. Our first priority is still to find Natasha Cook and Peter Robson. Robson didn't arrive for work today and his phone's switched off. Check all trains, airports, ports, ferries, dockyards, anything with transport across land or sea. Car hire companies. I don't care how you do it but I want them found. We cannae allow them to disappear into the sunset.'

Chapter 104

Myers dragged a chair alongside Findlay's desk. 'You all right?' he asked.

She nodded. 'Can't get my head around it. Can't decide whether I'm sad because a fellow copper is dead or happy because a potentially dangerous guy is out of the way. I'll never know what his intentions were.'

'Stuart was all talk and no action. He'd have kept it going, scare you for a bit before getting bored. I think that would've been enough for him.'

'I don't know. Kelly lost count of his reprimands at Notting Hill and he was on his way to the same here, if not worse. He didn't care about getting in bother, his murder location being a prime example. Why go to her house if he gave a shit about this investigation?'

'He was a weird bugger but you don't need to worry anymore. Fancy a drink later to talk about it?'

Findlay rolled her eyes. 'Glenn, c'mon. We've been over this a million times. It won't work.'

Myers held his hands up in surrender. 'Honestly, just to talk. I know nothing will ever happen between us,' he said, with a wink.

Findlay's eyes narrowed. 'What do you know? What did Kelly say?' she demanded.

'Whoa! What's Kelly got to do with anything? I finally sussed why you wouldn't be interested in this,' he said, extravagantly puffing out his chest. 'I don't understand why you never told me.'

'It's nobody's business but mine. I wanted to tell you but it never felt right. Maybe I should have. Would've put a halt to you asking me on a date every two weeks,' she laughed.

'I'd still like to go for that drink….as friends.'

Findlay relaxed. 'Ok, but not till the case is over.'
'Deal.'

Chapter 105

Well, that all turned to shit didn't it?

I just wanted some fun with Stuart, get the scoop on the police investigation, then kick him out. No harm, no foul. I certainly didn't plan to kill him.

Then Emma breezed in.

She'd known about the plan from the start. After shagging Dave to get signed up, her directive was to keep alert but under the radar. We'd maintained a cautious distance on the show but, after I delicately explained I needed her to kill Dave, rather than be horrified, she became positively excited.

In that instant I knew she'd be a millstone round my neck. Like when we lived together, she couldn't keep her nose out and has somehow managed to fuck things up.

The public perception of celebrity reality shows is hugs, air kisses and 'wow, you're one of my idols, so nice to meet you.' What a crock of shit. I knew all there was to know about each one of the famous faces on that island. Why else would I have been so keen? For a poxy quarter of a million for charity?

Murder was never on my radar until Sarah fucking O'Neill waged war against Magnus. A bitter and twisted cow, always had been, although I grudgingly admired her hatred of him.

The glory of Magnus's public disgrace was my gig, but Sarah firing up the others meant I needed to slam the door in Andrew and Ben's face. They'd positively salivated at the prospect of Magnus's downfall.

I'd nothing against either of them. Ok, Andrew was an obnoxious prick but he didn't deserve to die the way he did and I felt bad for Ben. Nice enough guy but I saw the spark in his eyes after Sarah lit the fuse. I then needed to pinch the P.I.'s report and Sarah's supremely organised filing system made it easy.

I felt the most guilt over Guy but he was so down and depressed, it felt like I did him a favour. Then, rather than expose Magnus, I realised I could frame him for murder. Even he might have difficulty bullshitting his way out of that one. It might have worked if some prison low life hadn't stabbed him to death.

I can still hardly believe Magnus was my father. The police were always going to figure it out but it was easy to fake the shock. I've been practising for a while.

So, here I am in the arse end of nowhere. Waiting on Pea, wishing he'd get a fucking move on.

Chapter 106

McIntosh perused Strong's police record, gathering ammunition for the shitstorm that would surely land in his lap. As his superior officer, he would not come out smelling of roses.

Several reprimands for tardiness, one for smelling of alcohol during interviews and a couple for disappearing without being contactable. More seriously, Strong had been subject to two allegations of sexual misconduct, one with a witness in her home, the other a fellow officer. Both dropped due to lack of evidence. Ultimately Strong's word against the complainer.

He'd call Kelly Arnott in for a chat to get her opinion, although he was pretty sure how that conversation would go. While Strong's dalliance with Natasha Cook added fuel to the fire, it might work in McIntosh's favour. If the hierarchy were disinterested in trashing a dead officer's reputation, they could hardly censure him for not controlling said officer.

The best way to mitigate incoming flak would be getting a result. Frustrated, his eyes turned to the evidence board, as he patrolled up and down like a hungry bear at the zoo.

'BOSS.' Arnott said. 'Natasha Cook is booked on a flight later today. The 6.50pm from Stansted to Barcelona.'

'Hold on a second,' Walton said. 'I've got her tomorrow at 9.30am, Heathrow to Rio de Janeiro.'

Findlay jumped in, 'No, she's on the 11.40am, Gatwick to Bangkok, tomorrow morning.'

McIntosh rolled his eyes. 'Ok, I see a pattern emerging. Keep digging, let me know what else you find.'

Two hours later the situation became clearer, or not. Natasha was booked on five flights, departing within the next two days, from London airports to destinations in Europe, South America and Asia.

To add to the confusion, Ashley Ward had also booked herself on five flights from different UK airports to Europe and North America. A car hire agreement, in Ashley's name, also flagged on their system.

'I don't get it, boss. What's she trying to achieve,' Glenn Myers said.

'Misdirection Glenn. She's hoping we spread ourselves thinly, to let her squeeze through a gap. We've underestimated this lassie.'

'If she intended getting on a flight, she'd never make it past the airport police,' Findlay added.

'I doubt flying's part of her plan. Something else is in play. But, just to be on the safe side get her names and photograph at every UK airport.'

'Must have cost her a few bob though,' Myers said.

'Drop in the ocean. She's got millions squirreled away somewhere. We need to address her collusion with Peter Robson.'

'He's dropped off the face of the earth boss. No-one's seen him for twenty-four hours,' Arnott said.

'You and Joanne, get over to his office. They must have an emergency contact number for him. Tell them you're not leaving until you've spoken to him. If we find Robson, we find Natasha. If we lose them both we'll all be down the Jobcentre.'

Chapter 107

From the off, Findlay and Arnott were frustrated by security at the Great Portland Street office block. Thirty minutes of flashing their badges and demanding access to Third Eye Productions had no effect. At the mention of Robson's name, the company closed ranks. In no mood to be fobbed off, Findlay wanted to wallop someone. The head security guard had to calm her down in case she did something she might regret.

After an intervention by their furious DCI, and recognising the detectives were going nowhere, security persuaded Third Eye to give them access to the lift. A pissed off Findlay and Arnott seethed in silence as they rode to the eighth floor. When the lift stopped, Findlay marched emphatically towards reception, in no mood for niceties. 'Where is Peter Robson?' she demanded of the woman staring at her.

'As I told your colleagues, Peter hasn't been seen since yesterday. I'm sorry I can't help you.'

'You've interfered with a police investigation by instructing your security to refuse access. Only the threat of arrest made you see sense. Stop wasting our time. Let me see his office.'

'That would be completely inappropriate,' the woman said. 'You can't just come and go as you please. You'll have to get a warrant.'

An exasperated Findlay said, 'I don't want to search his fucking office, just make sure he's not in there. This is life or death. Let me see his office now or your arrest for obstruction will become real.'

'Is he in danger?'

'Yes, very much so,' she lied.

'Well, why didn't you say so? You managed to get David killed so I'd rather you saved another of our colleagues. Come with me.'

Findlay bit her tongue and followed through a short corridor with two offices on the left and a kitchen and a bathroom on the right. Robson's office faced them like the head of the table. The woman unlocked the door and stood aside. 'One minute, no more.'

It didn't even take a minute. The office offered no space to hide an average sized man. A cursory glance told them Robson wasn't there. 'We need to check the other rooms,' Findlay said. The woman made a pronounced sigh but didn't resist. Findlay took the offices and Arnott the kitchen and bathroom. Empty. They nosed around the open plan area to the right of reception where a few employees were more interested in their screens than the two women poking around.

'Satisfied?' The woman said.

'Not really,' Findlay said. 'Who makes decisions when Peter Robson isn't here?'

The woman gave Findlay a funny look. 'No one, Peter's the boss here but he's not in charge of the company. He doesn't make decisions.'

Findlay rubbed her eyes. Her head throbbed with the cryptic information. 'I thought Robson owned the company?'

The woman shook her head like this was the stupidest thing she ever heard. 'No, no, no, Peter is executive producer but the owner lives in America. He makes company decisions.'

'How can he run the company from America?'

'He visits once a month, but otherwise lets us get on with it. It worked well until the Island show nearly ruined us.'

'What's his name and number?'

'Max Chesterman, but before you ask, I'd get fired if I gave you his number.'

With Findlay hovering at the edge of the precipice, Arnott chipped in. 'You could call him for us. It's very important.'

***

The woman couldn't think of a reason to refuse so beckoned them to an empty office where she dialled a number from memory. It took a few moments but someone finally answered. The woman picked up to talk privately. 'Hi, Alisha, this is Grace in London……. yeah, I'm good thanks. Listen, I've got two police officers here looking for Peter. No-one's seen him and they want to talk to Mr Chesterman. They say it's urgent………. I know but they won't leave. They're threatening to arrest us all. Peter may be in trouble……. Ok, thanks, quick as you can.' She replaced the phone in its cradle.

'He's on another call. You can stay in here and I'll put him through when he's free.'

Findlay nodded and sat, mentally exhausted. She couldn't get the Strong thing out of her head. A couple of days ago he was camped outside her house, planning god knows what, and now he'd been brutally murdered.

Arnott read her mind. 'Thinking about Strong?'

She nodded. 'Yeah, doesn't seem real. I'll never know what he planned.'

'Probably nothing, maybe scare you a bit. He was all mouth, no action.'

'Glenn said the same but he got action with you, if I remember correctly.' Findlay saw Arnott's expression and realised she'd gone too far. 'I'm sorry Kelly, I didn't mean that. My head's scrambled. I don't know what day of the week it is.'

Arnott softened. 'Forget it, I was drunk, remember.'

'You seem to be taking it well,' Findlay said.

'I'm not a hypocrite Joanne. I hated the guy. Did I want him dead? No, but he made my life hell and I'm not shedding crocodile tears. And I don't like to say I told you so but remember my first day? I said it was inevitable Strong would fuck up.'

Findlay nodded. 'You certainly warned me about him, that's for sure. By the way, Glenn sussed out why I'm not interested in him. Seemed quite pleased with himself. Still wants to meet for a drink to talk.'

Arnott hesitated before speaking. 'How do you feel about him knowing?'

'A bit relieved, to be honest. At least I don't have to think of excuses not to go on a date.'

'And it gives the rest of us a chance,' Arnott laughed. Before Findlay replied, the phone rang.

'Detective, this is Grace. I have Mr Chesterman on the line,' she said, abruptly hanging up.

'Hello Mr Chesterman, my name is Detective Constable Findlay and my colleague, Detective Constable Arnott is also here. I'm going to put you on speaker so we can both hear the conversation.'

'Hello detectives, I'm Max Chesterman, I understand you're trying to locate Peter Robson?' Chesterman's accent sounded unmistakably southern, Findlay thought. Georgia or Louisiana. Arnott leant towards Texas. 'I hope it's nothing to do with that damn TV show?'

'I'm afraid it is Mr Chesterman. Peter Robson's life may be in danger and we urgently need to find him,' Findlay said, ignoring the fact Robson had become a suspect. 'How do you normally contact him?'

'Just his cell phone. I've never not been able to get in touch with him. Have you used GPS from his phone?'

'Of course, its last location was here at the office yesterday, then nothing. It must be switched off. You haven't contacted him in the last twenty-four hours?'

'No, it must be three days since we last spoke. I'm busy here, before next week's trip to the UK. Peter gets my house ready for me.'

'What do you mean, gets your house ready?'

'He keeps it clean and tidy. He kinda babysits it, when I'm in the U.S. He uses it as a weekend cottage whenever he wants.'

Findlay felt her heart beat a little faster. 'Do you mind telling me where your cottage is?'

'Sure, a quiet little place called Portmellon, in Cornwall.'

'A long way from London sir, if you don't mind me saying.'

'I stay in London when I've got meetings, but it's so peaceful at the cottage, I'm able to get much more work done when I'm there. The beach is close-by and I like the water sports.'

'Sounds amazing. Hopefully Peter's gone to get it ready for you. Can you send me the cottage address please?' Findlay read out her email.

'You think he's in trouble don't you?'

'We are worried so if you could send it through right away, I would appreciate it.'

'That's it sent detectives. Let me know what happens.'

Arnott checked Findlay's phone. 'Got it.'

'Thank you, sir,' Findlay said, slamming the phone down.

They looked at each other, exploded from their chairs and exited Third Eye without glancing in Grace's direction, Findlay already punching the DCI's number.

Chapter 108

Before Findlay and Arnott arrived back at the station, McIntosh had already contacted the Cornish police and Googled the small village of Portmellon. Six miles south of St. Austell, which he'd heard of. Tiny population, plenty of holiday cottages for rent, probably overrun by tourists in the summer. The perfect anonymous location. Robson had been there before so no busybodies poking their nose in or cameras recording every move.

Getting eyes on Robson and Cook was paramount and a covert surveillance was being organised. In the name of the big man, he hoped this pair weren't holed up somewhere in London but he couldn't just sit back and let it play out. His gut told him to get to Cornwall.

'Listen, our eggs are all in one basket but it's the only strong lead we've got. They won't know that we know about the cottage. Chris, Kelly, I want you to stay in London. I know you'd rather be in amongst it but, if I've misjudged the situation, we need a Plan B. It's no reflection on you.'

Before anyone had a chance to move, Arnott's desk phone rang. She shouted over the background noise. 'BOSS, call for you. Inspector Hatcher of Cornish Police.'

McIntosh took the phone and listened intently. 'Ok Inspector, thanks. I'll call you back.'

'Fuck,' he said loudly. 'The cottage is empty. A local copper posed as a delivery driver but no one answered. Once they were sure it was unoccupied, they gained entry and found a warm kettle and fresh mud on the front door mat and steps, so they'd recently been there. Christ knows where they've gone now. Hatcher's maintaining surveillance in case they return.'

'What now boss?' Findlay asked.

'God knows, but we can't let these bastards get away.'

***

Peter Robson guessed they'd have found the bodies by now, and the police couldn't be too far behind. Max probably spilled about the cottage as well. It was wise to move on. He'd arrived in Cornwall eight hours after Natasha. Although relieved, she furiously chastised him for leaving her so long. She could be so fiery, even when she was in the wrong. He sensibly neglected to remind her why they were suddenly on the run.

Chapter 109

With no bright ideas emanating, McIntosh called Third Eye and politely asked Grace if Max Chesterman could call him. Thankfully, she was still at the office. After a long thirty minutes, his phone finally rang.

'Hello, Mr Chesterman, thanks for calling. I'm Chief Inspector McIntosh, in charge of the investigation. We've hit a brick wall, I'm afraid. The Cornish police have advised your cottage is empty but someone's definitely been there today. We can only assume it was Peter. It's vital we speak to him. Can you think where else he might have gone?'

'Nothing springs to mind Chief Inspector, maybe back to London?'

'No, that wouldn't make sense. We're pretty certain he just left London for Cornwall. Does he frequent other places in Cornwall, or further afield?'

'I'm sorry, I don't know. I've never really asked what he does on his weekend trips. What about the airport?'

'He's not booked on any flight from a UK airport. Which one do you mean?'

'Newquay. It's only forty-five minutes away. After staying at the cottage, he often flew to France to see his parents. He preferred Newquay to the busy London airports.'

'Ok sir, thanks for your help. We'll check it out,' McIntosh clicked off. 'Robson's been known to fly to France from Newquay.'

'We've checked. They're not booked on any flight,' Myers said.

'This has been planned for a long time. They're maybe using fake passports. Can't be many flights leaving Newquay tonight. Check them all again. Get their photos to the airport police.' McIntosh pushed some buttons on his phone. 'There's a 7 o'clock flight from Gatwick to Newquay. We might need them to hold it for us but we'll be on it.'

Ten minutes later McIntosh, Myers, Walton and Findlay squeezed into Bayford's car, blues flashing and two's booming.

***

At 6pm, the West car park of Newquay airport was half empty. They'd declined PH&F's offer of their small waiting area, preferring the relative anonymity of a public car park. The 8.15pm departure time felt like an eternity but Robson's instinct told him it was smart to leave the cottage early. They hoped for an earlier time slot but the company refused, advising taxiing could only commence after the last incoming flight had landed and reached its allotted gate.

They nervously hunkered down in the car, on alert for any heightened police activity.

Chapter 110

Bayford drove as fast as his car and the city traffic would allow. Reaching the motorway, the speed limit was inconsequential. McIntosh called the airport police, told them the story and they agreed to escort the EIU car from Junction 9 on the M23, into Gatwick, then directly to the aircraft.

His weariness and lack of energy filtered down to the other passengers. Silence in the back, no chat or small talk. Maybe managing to sleep, although at the speed of the Audi A4, that was unlikely.

His phone buzzed.

Chris Dolan. He listened for a minute before hanging up, mind immediately switched on. 'Ya beauty! A private charter is leaving Newquay for Nice at 8.15pm. Two passengers, Pierre Robson and Ashley Ward. Real names as well. We've got them.'

'But we only land at 8.10,' Walton said. 'We'll have no time to stop them.'

'Local police could arrest them before they get on,' Findlay said.

'I don't want them blundering in mob handed. Robson and Cook will disappear if anything's out of the ordinary. I'll think of something. Faster Simon, put your foot down.'

Bayford looked at his speedometer and didn't think that was possible.

***

At 7.30pm a man driving a black Range Rover drew alongside the Volvo and signalled to Robson to lower his window.

'Mr Robson?'

'Yes.'

'Follow me please. I'll take you to the waiting area and car park.'

Private Hire and Fly's fee included a parking space as close to the aircraft as possible, but it cost a fortune and only lasted for three days. Thereafter, Robson would have to have the car picked up or incur further costs.

He'd agreed. He'd no intention of coming back for it. He didn't care about the cost or what they did with the car.

Chapter 111

The Gatwick police met Bayford's Audi a few minutes before Junction 9 and escorted the car to a guarded side entrance. After being waved through, Bayford parked and the Met detectives boarded a small mini-bus which brought them airside to the waiting aircraft. It was 6.45pm.

McIntosh called Inspector Hatcher asking for assistance in delaying the departure of the private jet. Whilst Hatcher's authority didn't extend to amending aircraft flight plans, he promised to do his best. The frazzled EIU team took their seats at the front of the plane, unaware what awaited at the other end.

Before they were airborne, a weary McIntosh slumped, ready to catch a few winks. Until his phone rang.

Debbie. He thought hard about rejecting the call but she would just keep ringing. 'Hello,' he said.

'Have you phoned Lucas's parents yet?' she demanded.

'Not yet, I can't really talk. I'm on a flight to Cornwall.'

'Cornwall! What the bloody hell are you going to Cornwall for? When will you be back?'

He moved the phone a few inches from his ear. 'It's the murder case. Hopefully only a few hours but I cannae say for certain.'

'Promise you'll phone them when you get back.'

'Aye ok, mibbee better face to face. I'll arrange a meet.'

'Do that and don't forget. Got to go, see you tomorrow,' she said, hanging up.

'As if you'd let me forget,' he mumbled to himself. Bayford eyed him with a smirk on his face. 'Simon, you dinna want tae know,' he said, switching off his phone.

***

Robson followed the Range Rover to a small facility emblazoned with PH & F signage and was directed towards a security barrier. A man approached, wearing a yellow hi-viz jacket and carrying a clipboard.

'Mr Robson?'

'Yes'

'Glad you made it. A bit of bad news I'm afraid. Your flight has been delayed by approximately thirty minutes. French air traffic control warned of a slight weather warning across Northern France. It's causing a little concern and the pilot wants to hold off, as a precaution. After parking, feel free to use our small refreshment area. Coffee, tea, toilet facilities.'

'Thanks but I think we'd prefer to wait in the car.'

'Not a problem. When it's ready, a buggy will take you and your luggage to the plane.'

'Thank you.'

Clipboard man disengaged the barrier and Robson drove into the empty, five space car park. He repeatedly clasped and unclasped his hands, while Natasha relaxed and closed her eyes. 'Calm down, it's only an extra half hour,' she said.

'I hate when things don't go to plan. It cost enough money so we should be in control, not a damn air traffic controller, or pilot. I won't settle till we're on that plane.'

'I think the pilot knows more about flying conditions than we do and we can afford it,' she said, calmly.

Robson rubbed his forehead. 'My head is killing me.'

Natasha grabbed two bottles of water from her bag and opened both. She handed one to Robson and took a slug from the other. 'You must be dehydrated. Have a drink.'

Chapter 112

At 8.40pm, clipboard man knocked on the driver's side window. 'We're ready for you,' he said, pointing at a buggy, which looked suspiciously like it belonged on a golf course.

Robson finally smiled and helped load their luggage on to the golf cart. Natasha and he slid into seats behind the driver. The cart was open to the elements and Natasha's teeth chattered. She snuggled into Robson. 'Not long now, Pea.'

The buggy moved at a leisurely 10mph towards Hangar 10, half a mile from the car park. 'Is it normally this quiet?' Natasha said.

Clipboard man nodded. 'At this time of night, yes. Flights are finished for the day so often it's just a handful of people doing nightshift work.'

The hangars were lined up in a row. A floodlight illuminated the exterior of No.10, the only brightness among the evening gloom. The hangar door was open, as was the door to No.11. They'd dawdled halfway when Natasha screamed, 'STOP!'

Clipboard man nearly jumped out of his skin before slamming on the brake. He swivelled to see Robson staring at Natasha, confused.

'Did you see that?' she said.

'What?'

'That blue light coming from Hangar 11. Just a flash, a fraction of a second. I definitely saw it.'

'I never saw a thing. You're imagining things,' Robson replied.

'Am I?' she said, grabbing clipboard man by the shoulder. 'Are the police up ahead?'

He shrugged, but his expression betrayed him. 'Fuck!' she shouted, unceremoniously grabbing the man's hi-viz collar and yanking him onto the cold asphalt. 'Drive back to the car,' she yelled at Robson.

***

McIntosh also witnessed the blue flash on the security feed and watched Natasha violently haul a man to the ground. 'Shite, we're blown,' he shouted into the radio. 'Get in the cars and pick us up outside Hangar 9.' Someone was going to get their arse kicked.

Two police cars pulled up outside the hangar, lights flashing. No need for cagey now. McIntosh clambered into the back of the first, while the second car picked up Bayford.

Myers, Findlay and Walton continued monitoring the live camera feed.

Chapter 113

Robson got the buggy up to around 18mph. That bastard with the clipboard was milking it, Natasha thought. They reached their car, forgot about luggage and dived into the front, Robson at the wheel.

'Drive!' Natasha instructed.

'Where to?'

'Anywhere, away from here.'

'Shit,' he said, seeing the two sets of headlights hurtling their way. 'I can't see a way out.'

'Drive straight at them. They'll move.'

Robson did what she said, despite thinking she might be insane. Something he had considered over the last few weeks. He accelerated to 60mph, on a collision course with the lights ahead. As Natasha predicted, a second before impact, the two cars swerved either side of Robson's Volvo S60 before executing textbook handbrake turns, now giving chase from the rear.

'It's completely fenced in, there's no way out,' Robson said.

'Drive up the taxiway.'

'Onto the runway?'

'You heard the man. Flights in and out are finished for the night.'

Robson careered along a taxiway, before finding himself on the main runway, reaching speeds of 100mph. 'We'll soon run out of runway,' he said, glancing in his mirror to find two sets of blue flashing lights hurtling after them.

'Shit, we'll have to turn around and drive through the security barrier.'

'Are you nuts? You want me to turn around and drive at them again?'

'What other choice do we have?'

Robson sighed and shook his head. He slowed and steered the car in a wide arc and found himself roaring down the main Newquay airport runway towards two police cars.

***

'Move out of their way, turn and follow. They're going to exit the same road they came in,' McIntosh said.

'There's a security barrier sir,' the driver said.

'Aye, but something tells me they're no' stopping to put in a ticket.'

Both police cars averted a collision and turned the same arc as Robson, maintaining pursuit. Robson veered off the runway and bombed down the taxiway towards the PH&F entrance. The seven occupants of the two police cars watched helplessly as the Volvo effortlessly smashed the steel barrier like it didn't exist.

***

With all exits blocked the police seemed happy to follow at a distance knowing there was no way out, content to let the fugitives run out of fuel or energy, whichever came first.

The more calculating of the two, Natasha recognised the need to escape from the labyrinth of the airport network and onto the open road but they'd driven aimlessly for a few minutes without any egress opportunity. Until she remembered the Aerohub Business Unit at the South end of the airport. It led to the A3059. Almost certainly no direct access to the airport grounds but maybe a flimsy gate or fence?

'Head towards the south end of the airport Pea, towards the Business Hub. I doubt the police have covered that position. There must be a gate or fence we can get through.'

'One security gate not enough for you?'

'You just want to give up?'

Robson sighed and put his foot down, past the taxiway, onto a scruffy road that seemed to lead nowhere.

'Keep going, it must end somewhere,' she said.

His speed crept up. He needed a semblance of momentum to knock down a fence but it was risky to go this fast.

'Stop!' she said, 'Look, up ahead.'

His headlights illuminated a strip of overgrown scrub and bush entwined with a ten-foot high wire mesh fence, topped with barbed wire. She looked behind. Clear, for the moment.

'Reverse and get up some speed, aim for right between the concrete post. Put your full beam on and de-activate the airbags.'

***

The driver of McIntosh's car blurted out, 'Shit, they're heading into no-man's land. We've no cover at that end, we expected them to head for the B3276 to Newquay.'

'What's out there?' McIntosh said.

'A Business Unit and an RAF base, then the A3059.'

'Can they escape?'

'I don't know sir. I mean there's a secure fence but...?'

'Fuck, get after them, quick as you can.'

***

Robson hit the accelerator and, at 70mph, crashed through the centre of a fence panel covered in creeping bush. The couple closed their eyes on impact. The Volvo teetered but somehow remained on four wheels. De-activating the airbags had been a real gamble. All sorts of injuries could have occurred but the airbags deploying would have meant game over. Minor bumps and bruises were a small price to pay.

'Go Pea go,' Natasha shouted. 'They're not far behind.'

Robson put his foot down and headed towards the junction with the A3059. It loomed much quicker than he anticipated.

'Pete, slow down.'

'I'm trying,' he said. 'Nothing's happening. Oh fuck.'

The brakes failed. The Volvo overshot the junction, collided with a van heading west, and rocketed into a roadside ditch, landing on its roof.

***

Despite the abundance of police resources, McIntosh and Bayford's cars were first on the scene. From a distance, McIntosh watched the Volvo soar, like an aircraft from the neighbouring field, and he winced at the jarring contact with the ground. The flurry of assembling blue lights slowed the steady traffic and kept everyone inside their vehicles. Myers, Findlay and Walton got out of a different vehicle to join the party.

McIntosh was first to reach the Volvo and saw Robson struggling to move. 'Get him out,' he said, moving to the passenger side. The empty seat threw him for a second. In the twilight he spotted Natasha crawling towards a line of trees, twenty yards away. He ran over to lift her up but, as he gripped her round the waist, he instinctively jerked back on his rear end, feeling the initial rush of pain and wetness through his fingers.

Fuelled by a rush of furious adrenaline, he pushed himself up and charged after her. Without a hint of delicacy, he knee dropped her into the dirt, his full weight crushing the wind from her body. He probably cracked some of her ribs.

He didn't care.

'Time to give it up lass, you've had a good run,' he said, letting his driver apply the handcuffs.

They lifted her up, resistance broken. McIntosh watched Bayford manhandle Robson towards a waiting police van while Myers joined his boss, seeing pain etched across his face.

'Boss, what happened? You're covered in blood.' McIntosh removed his hands from his side to let Myers see the damage. 'Fuck sakes boss, you've been stabbed.'

McIntosh was on the verge of passing out, so Myers grabbed his arms from behind and lowered him gently to the ground.

'I need an ambulance, quickly!' he shouted.

Chapter 114

Robson and Cook were arrested and placed in holding cells at Newquay police station. Natasha's ribs survived McIntosh's mauling but she'd have some lovely bruising as a memento.

McIntosh remained conscious but an ambulance rushed him to hospital where his deep gash was cleaned and twelve stitches inserted. Luckily the blade avoided any major organs. In the waiting room, Bayford breathed a sigh of relief when the doctor relayed the news.

At Newquay police station, the rest of the EIU filled up on coffee and biscuits, soberly waiting on information, any buzz at capturing the pair put to one side. The small station was busier than usual but Myers, Findlay and Walton munched away in silence. The subdued mood was forgotten when Bayford and McIntosh walked in.

The female detectives embraced the DCI. 'Christ boss, what are you doing here? Walton said, smiling. 'Thought you were on your deathbed?'

An embarrassed McIntosh said, 'Nah, I'm all right. No real damage. Stitched up and told to get on my way.'

'That's not strictly true, is it?' Bayford said. 'The doctors recommended you stay in for observation. In case of infection.'

'Aye well, you know what doctors are like. Always playing it safe. Stay so we can observe you. Fuck that. I'm no' hangin about, twiddling my thumbs with some wee nurse watching me.'

'I don't think they literally observe you boss,' Myers said.

'Aye, whatever. They're no' gettin the chance.'

Bayford laughed. 'He turned into Braveheart and the doctor's decided it wasn't worth it. At one point I thought he was going to shout, FREEDOM!' The others convulsed into laughter.

'Aye, very funny. Are ye all just going to sit there or is somebody going to make me a coffee?' McIntosh said, before Myers stood and started to pour. 'What's going on with the gruesome twosome?'

'We were waiting to hear about you first,' Walton said. 'Then deciding whether to keep them here overnight or ship them back to London right away?'

'I'd rather go back now. I know it's a five-hour drive but there won't be much traffic and we can get a few hours in our own beds before having a crack at them tomorrow.'

***

Formalities complete, the prisoners were placed in separate police vans, each with a driver and two PC's, who rubbed their hands at the thought of overtime. A car was provided to the EIU, who travelled at the rear of the convoy. Being the most alert, Myers was assigned driver duties.

McIntosh took the opportunity to phone home. 'Hi, it's me.'

'Jesus, what time is it? I was sleeping.'

'Just after 1am. We're on our way back. It'll probably be around 6ish before I get home. I'll crash on the couch to save waking you.'

'Did everything go ok?'

He hesitated, couldn't help it. 'Em…yeah, I'll tell you tomorrow, or later today I suppose.'

'What happened?' she demanded.

'Ach, nothing much. I got injured a wee bit, had to go to hospital.'

'Bloody hell. What did you do?'

'I got stabbed, nothing to get excited about, a few stitches and I'm right as rain.'

'Stabbed!' she bellowed. 'And you mention the time you'll get home and sleeping on the couch before telling me you got stabbed? Fucking hell, Mac.'

'Honestly, it's nothing to worry about, just thought you should know. I'm absolutely fine.'

'You'll do anything to get out of meeting Lucas's parents, won't you,' she laughed.

'Ach, that's no' fair. Look I better get going, I'll see you later on.'

'Aye ok, good night,' she said.

He turned to see a big grin on Myers face and stifled giggles came from the back. 'Everything ok, boss?' Walton said.

'You lot can wrap up. I'm away to try and get a kip.'

Chapter 115

After a scheduled toilet break near Bristol, the police van drivers changed and the convoy continued on its way. Myers was happy to carry on which pleased his passengers, none of whom were excited about taking over driving duties. Content after a stretch of legs and use of the facilities, they got comfortable, hoping to drift off back to sleep.

Until McIntosh's phone buzzed

He listened intently, a worried frown on his face. He ended the call. 'Robson's ill. Vomiting, coughing up blood. They're diverting to Bristol Royal Infirmary. He seems to be in a bad way,' he said, dialling at the same time.

A voice answered. 'Yes?'

'This is McIntosh. The other prisoner's been taken ill. Going back to hospital in Bristol. When they turn off, keep going but don't let her know.'

***

At 5.58am the convoy, or what was left of it, arrived exhausted at Charing Cross. Details on Robson remained sketchy. He'd drifted in and out of consciousness and remained attached to a drip, critical but stable. Despite being handcuffed to a rail, two officers guarded his bedside.

Natasha was processed, put in a cell and advised to get some rest before her interview.

Still on overtime, the Cornish officers had some breakfast then turned around for the trek back to Newquay, happy to divvy up driving duties.

McIntosh instructed his team to go home, get some rest and be back by 11am.

His phone rang as he pulled into his driveway. He listened and closed his eyes. 'Ok, thank you,' he said, before throwing his phone onto his front lawn.

'FUCK!' he shouted, not caring if he woke his neighbours.

Chapter 116

By 11.15am the EIU tucked into an array of breakfast rolls, sweet pastries, coffee and tea. Dolan and Arnott looked alert, the benefit of a decent night's sleep. Myers couldn't stop yawning and would have loved to curl up in a quiet corner. The rest, including McIntosh, needed the energy boost from the sugar and caffeine.

'As we know Peter Robson died at 5.30 this morning. He suffered major organ failure and his body shut down. We don't have an official cause of death. He seemed fine during arrest and detention but possibly suffered undetected internal injuries during the crash.'

'Do we tell Natasha?' Bayford asked.

'In due course, but not right away. If she thinks we're interviewing him as well, she may slip up.'

'They were an item. Don't you think she has a right to know?' Myers said.

McIntosh stared keenly at Myers. 'Glenn, in other circumstances I might agree but this wee lassie stabbed me so her rights are oot the window. My gut tells me she's mixed up in Robson's death. I've no idea how, but if she's innocent, her reaction will be genuine. For now, let's use every advantage we have.'

A chastised Myers brightened considerably when he and Bayford were chosen to conduct Natasha's interview.

***

A dishevelled Natasha Cook hunched in her chair, wild haired and sleep deprived. She looked nothing like the statuesque catwalk model who'd previously sat opposite Myers in the same room. In fairness, he probably looked as ropey to her.

Surprisingly, she waived her right to counsel despite Bayford's strenuous attempts to change her mind. In her words, she'd done nothing wrong.

'Natasha, you've been arrested on four counts of murder. Do you understand?' Bayford said.

'Not really, the man at the desk mentioned four, including Emma and Stuart Strong. I can't believe Emma's gone. She was my sister. What happened?' she sobbed.

'The bodies of Emily Dean and Detective Stuart Strong were found in your house, wrapped in dust sheets and stuffed into two separate cupboards. Can you tell us about that?'

Her hand flew to her mouth. 'Oh my God, I don't believe it but it wasn't me. I wasn't home the night before last.'

'I didn't say when it happened.'

'I'm guessing. Last night you chased me all over Cornwall and I wasn't home the previous evening.'

'So you're denying all knowledge of the murders of Emily Dean and Stuart Strong....in your house?'

'Absolutely.'

'Who could have done it?'

'Peter, I suspect.'

'Peter Robson?'

'Yes.'

'Why would you think it was Peter Robson?'

'He killed Sarah and Guy.'

'Wait a minute. You're accusing Peter Robson of murdering Sarah O'Neill and Guy Ekers, as well as Emily Dean and Stuart Strong?'

'Well, I know he killed Sarah and Guy. I only suspect he killed Emma and Stuart.'

'What was Stuart Strong doing at your house?'

'I've no idea. I told you I wasn't there.'

'He must've visited for a reason. When we receive the forensic report on Strong's body what are the chances of finding your DNA?'

Natasha appeared sheepish. 'Probably quite high. We slept together. A few weeks ago, when he first asked me to dinner. One thing led to another.'

'He said you had dinner and he left early.'

'That was the official line. I didn't want him getting into trouble so I kept quiet but I suppose it doesn't matter now.'

'Why are you so sure Robson killed Sarah and Guy?'

She sighed heavily, a secret ready to be unlocked. 'It was Peter's plan. He knew about the hook up between Magnus and Dave, to defraud the charity. He saw an opportunity to make some real money. Unfortunately, Sarah had the hots for destroying Magnus. That would've spoiled it so he killed Sarah to stop her and Guy because he knew too much.'

As Bayford put his pen down, Myers jumped in. 'That's a nice story Natasha but where do you and Emily fit in to the plan?'

'Our goal was not to win the money, without making it too obvious.'

'Who killed David Gill?'

'Pete never said, but I presume it must have been him.'

'Is it possible Emily Dean stabbed Gill to death? We found her DNA in his flat.'

Natasha shook her head. 'I know she had been there. She slept with Dave to get on the show but she couldn't murder anyone.'

Bayford interjected. 'You've neatly wrapped it up Natasha, but is it likely Peter Robson is telling my colleagues the same story, with you as the protagonist?'

'I hope not, because it would be a lie.'

'Why did you stab DCI McIntosh last night?'

'I don't know what you're talking about.'

'You crawled away from the wreckage and he grabbed you and got stabbed.'

'Not me, he must have cut himself on something. Did you find a knife? Ah, is that why he flattened me like a pancake?'

'So, you deny stabbing him?'

'Of course.'

Bayford felt a buzz from the phone in his pocket. A text from the DCI.

'Interview suspended at 12.06pm. We'll resume again at 1pm,' he said.

Chapter 117

The core of the interview had pretty much gone as McIntosh expected. 'She's an intelligent lassie and she's bloody good. She knows we suspect she killed nearly all of these people but she's merely an innocent bystander. It was all Robson's idea, the money and the murders. But, does she know he's dead?'

'If she killed him it would make sense to shift the blame. He can't defend himself. Muddy the waters enough for reasonable doubt,' Bayford said.

Findlay chipped in. 'Yeah, if Robson was still alive and they blamed each other, a jury would likely convict them both. Now, she can deflect it all.'

'But if she slipped him something it must have been before we reached Newquay. If we hadn't shown up he'd still have taken unwell, most likely on the flight to France,' Myers said.

'Probably part of her plan,' McIntosh said. 'Sucker him to get her out of the country, then he becomes dispensable. Time to tell her about Robson and see how she reacts.'

***

In a twist to proceedings Natasha had requested counsel. While they waited for Robert Cox QC to arrive, McIntosh and Bayford enjoyed a coffee while debating this latest development.

'What do you make of this boss? Running scared?'

'Hard to say. Maybe needs someone to buy into all her crap and set it out in a format a jury might believe, if it gets that far.'

'You really think she can blind people to the two bodies found in her cupboards?'

McIntosh shrugged. 'Blame it on the dead guy. Wouldn't be the first time, or the last. You were right before. Create enough uncertainty and reasonable doubt comes into play. I'm guessing that's the reason for the solicitor.'

A knock and Myers entered, holding a folder. 'He's here.'

Chapter 118

Natasha and her solicitor whispered as Bayford and Myers re-entered the interview room. Her smile remained intact but carried a little less self-assurance.

Robert Cox formally introduced himself before Bayford jumped straight in. 'Natasha, you've blamed Peter Robson for each murder, the blackmail of David Gill and conspiracy to defraud several charities. Despite your knowledge of the plan, you maintain you're innocent of any offence. Correct?'

'Correct'

'I'm afraid I have some bad news to tell you. Peter Robson died in hospital this morning.'

Natasha cupped her hands either side of her nose and mouth, eyes darting between Bayford and Myers. 'Oh my God, what happened? What did you do to him?'

'We'd like to know what you did to him,' Bayford said, calmly.

'What do you mean? I don't understand.'

'He died of multi organ failure, cause unknown at the moment. He appeared in good health prior to transportation back to London so, whatever he ingested, or whatever caused his deterioration, occurred before we arrested you both. Care to tell us what happened?'

Robert Cox interjected. 'Inspector, I appreciate that the interview has only just resumed but can I ask for a few minutes for my client to compose herself. You have given her some terrible news and I think it would be unfair to continue.'

Bayford nodded, 'Ten minutes,' as he and Myers left the room.

***

Upon resumption, Bayford sensed the return of Natasha's natural self-confidence. Because her plan to divert the blame was very much in play?

'Ok Natasha, hopefully you've managed to collect yourself at this very difficult time. I'll ask my question again. Can you provide any information why Peter Robson could have become so unwell?'

'Sorry, I've no idea. He met me at a cottage and we drove to Newquay. I didn't see him eat or drink anything.'

That was the response they'd anticipated and Myers altered the interview dynamic with a pre-arranged shift of perspective.

'Natasha, can you fill in some blanks for me please. During a previous interview, I advised you Magnus Branch was your father and asked about your relationship with him. You replied that you didn't have a relationship with him and……..,' Myers glanced down at his notes, '.... you'd only seen him a couple of times since the show. We know you both attended the after show party. On what other occasion did you see Magnus?'

Natasha's smirk disappeared and she looked into Myers deep brown eyes. 'I'm not sure. I must have been mistaken. I only remember seeing him once.'

Bayford smiled and shook his head. 'I don't think so. If you'd seen him ten times but only remembered nine, I could accept you made a mistake. Nobody says, I saw him a couple of times when it was only once. Tell us about the other time?'

'I must have been flustered. You'd just told me Magnus was my father. I think it's an excusable mistake in the circumstances.'

Myers chipped in. 'You told us how many times you'd met Magnus, before you were told he was your father.'

Natasha shrugged. 'I made a mistake, I don't know what else to say.'

Cox interjected. 'Detectives, you've asked your question and my client has answered. Can we move on please?'

'Natasha, explain to us why you booked multiple flights, from different airports, in different names, some of which were on the same day? Bayford said.

'I wasn't sure where to go, so I gave myself a choice.'

'Come into a lot of money have you?' Bayford said, smiling.

Natasha glared ahead.

'Okay,' Bayford continued. 'Why were you in Fulham on the evening of Sarah O'Neill's murder?'

'I wasn't in Fulham that night.'

'I'll reword the question. Why would your car have been in Fulham on the evening of Sarah O'Neill's murder?'

Natasha's eyes widened, for a split second. 'Who says it was?'

Bayford sensed Myers staring at him. 'If it wasn't you, who could have been driving?'

'I…I'm not sure. Maybe Pete borrowed it?'

'Did he ask to borrow it?'

'Erm, I don't remember. He occasionally borrowed it but I can't recall that particular night.'

'So, you really want us to believe you're home alone, car in the driveway, and you don't recall Peter Robson borrowing or returning it. You didn't report it stolen and this, coincidentally, is on the same night as Sarah O'Neill's murder.'

'Believe what you like,' Natasha said, before Cox jumped in.

'I'd like a moment in private with my client.'

'Five minutes, no more,' Bayford said.

Myers couldn't wait. As soon as they left the room he said, 'Guv, what was the car thing about?'

Chapter 119

Bayford took Myers aside, out of earshot. 'I took a punt. I discussed it beforehand with the boss. She blundered about how often she'd seen Magnus. I think she followed him and saw him confront Sarah. When he left, Natasha knew Sarah would have to go or Magnus's face would have been plastered over the front pages the next day.'

Myers whistled through his teeth. 'Risky. What if she denied it point blank?'

'Well she didn't and it got her flustered. We better find her car though. Go upstairs and get them to start looking. At least three hours before Sarah's murder.'

Five minutes later, Myers returned with a bottle of water for Natasha, who smiled her thanks.

'I'll ask the question again,' Bayford said. 'On the night of Sarah's murder who could have been driving your car?'

'I honestly don't know. It must have been Pete but I don't remember him asking to borrow it. It wasn't me.'

'I believe you were following Magnus, and saw him at Sarah's?'

'I don't know what you're talking about, Inspector.'

'Magnus had never been to Guy Ekers flat but we found traces of his blood there. How could that have happened?'

'How the hell would I know?'

'Because you put it there.'

Natasha laughed. 'I hope you can prove that.'

'When Sarah punched Magnus at the party, blood spurted everywhere and you cleaned him up. You could've kept some and planted it at Guy's.'

'Dave helped as well, and maybe Magnus did kill Guy?'

'We know for a fact, neither Magnus nor Dave Gill killed Guy Ekers. You planting it is the only reasonable explanation for discovering Branch's blood in a place he'd never been.'

'It's a nice story, Inspector.'

'Let's get to the murders of Emily Dean and Stuart Strong. Can you remind us where we found their bodies?'

Natasha stared at Bayford, face like thunder.

'Why did you kill Emily and DC Strong?' Myers said.

'Who says I did?'

'I say you did, but why?'

'I was home till 7.30pm, then left to drive to Cornwall. Emily and Stuart must have arrived later than that.'

'Why did DC Strong come to your house at all?'

'I've no idea. I didn't ask him over.'

'He made a one-minute call to you two days ago. What was that about?'

'Oh yeah. After him and the other detective had visited me about Dave. He called to say he enjoyed seeing me again.'

'And he took that as an invitation to your home, unannounced?'

'Stuart could be a little strange, couldn't he?'

Bayford's face belied his agreement. 'You're trying to have us believe that you left your house for Cornwall at 7.30pm. A short time later, Peter Robson arrived and let himself in before Stuart Strong turned up, no later than 8.42, from his phone's GPS. Either before or after Strong arrived, Emily Dean put in an appearance and for no obvious reason, Robson killed them both before following you to Cornwall. Can you see how nonsensical that sounds?'

'Not if it's the truth.'

'Stop wasting our time. We'll check traffic cameras, your car will show up and your story will unravel. I understand your anger towards Branch but why did the others need to die. If Sarah exposed Magnus you'd still have the blackmail money. Branch would have been disgraced and in prison. You didn't have to kill anyone…….. unless you started to enjoy it.'

Natasha's steely eyes bored into Bayford. 'Nice theory Inspector but Peter's the one you want.'

'And he's conveniently dead,' Myers said.

Bayford felt a buzz from his phone. 'We'll stop for a break. Interview suspended at 2.45pm.'

***

McIntosh instigated the interruption. 'She's canny, manipulative and she's right, we've no real evidence against her. If she continues to point the finger at Robson, nothing we've got disproves that theory.'

'We've a mountain of circumstantial though,' Walton said. 'And I can't see how she can get away with the Dean and Strong murders?'

'Imagine her telling her story in front of a jury? They'd lap it up. Even if we found twenty bodies in her house we'd be the bad guys for even considering her as a suspect. We've no murder weapons and even if we find one, her fingerprints and DNA will be all over it. Same as her DNA on Strong's body. She's got a lie for that too. We need one piece of hard evidence to drive a bus through her fantasy story. Her car's not at the cottage so where did she leave it? Start checking CCTV and ANPR cameras en-route to Cornwall. It's a mammoth task and we need to get lucky.'

Chapter 120

McIntosh had successfully applied for a twelve-hour extension to Natasha Cook's custody, but they were now into the last six of those hours and he predicted they might need every minute.

His prediction proved wrong.

The unappealing grind of locating a single car on congested London streets, and the open road to the far west of the country, was slightly softened when McIntosh announced he was buying everyone's lunch, as a thank you for their hard work.

The next headache was agreeing on a cuisine. Myers and Walton wanted a dirty burger with fries. Findlay preferred a Pret or something less greasy while Bayford and Arnott were happy to go with the flow.

McIntosh couldn't care less but didn't want to argue about it. 'Somebody please order something on their phone and I'll reimburse them,' he said, loudly.

After several minutes of back and forth with no result, McIntosh held up his hand. 'What about Lombardy's in Garrick Street. They do pizza or pasta.'

The team looked at each other as if they hadn't considered something from a proper restaurant. 'Sounds good to me boss,' Walton said.

'Me too,' Findlay said.

The others nodded in agreement. 'Thank Christ for that,' McIntosh said. 'Order me a pepperoni pizza. Somebody will probably have to go for it. You can take my card.'

Chris Dolan, who had been peripheral to the conversation, suddenly jumped to his feet and did a complete 360 turn, commanding everyone's attention. 'CHINESE!'

Arnott shook her head. 'No, that's more of an evening meal for me, don't fancy Chinese for lunch. Anyway, we've agreed on Italian. Were you not listening?'

Dolan shouted, 'No! Natasha had Chinese food containers in her kitchen rubbish bin. There were remnants of food in the containers.'

'So?' Arnott asked.

'She must have ordered a Chinese meal, the night Strong and Dean died. If we can find out the delivery time it might prove she was there at the same time as Stuart.'

'Brilliant Chris,' McIntosh said. 'She'll have used one of those phone apps and that'll leave a trail. Get on to that, rest of you keep looking for her car and somebody order my bloody pizza.'

Chapter 121

Twenty minutes later Dolan announced that Natasha placed an order with the Oriental Express, Notting Hill, at 7pm on the night of the Dean and Strong murders. 'Doesn't sound like she was planning to leave for Cornwall at 7.30 but I don't have a specific delivery time.'

'Good, but it's not definitive. We need to know if and when she took the food. Give the takeaway a call, see if they have a record of delivery. Better still, speak to the driver.'

When he came off the phone Dolan had a beaming smile. 'Bingo! Delivered to Natasha Cook at 8.02pm. The driver's been to her house umpteen times, remembers it well. Said she looked stunning, like a model. Sounds like she had quite the night planned for Stuart.'

'Aye, but he got a lot more than he bargained for. Ok, so she got Chinese food delivered forty minutes before we can prove Strong was there. It blows her 7.30pm escape out the water but it doesn't categorically prove she was still there when he died,' McIntosh said, before gazing into space.

'Boss?' Dolan said.

Dolan and Bayford looked at each other, then at the DCI who was now staring intently at the floor. 'Boss, you ok?' Bayford asked.

'Aye, never better. You said the driver knew her, been to the house a few times, yeah?'

'That's right,' Dolan said.

'Phone him back. Ask if her car was in the driveway.'

Chapter 122

'You sure you're up to this?' Bayford asked, concern all over his face.

'Dinna be daft, course I am.'

'But you look absolutely knackered and every time you move, you grimace in pain. Sit back and relax. Let me and Glenn carry on.'

'No, I want to look in her eyes and see the realisation in her face. A wee bit of pain will be worth it. I can relax afterwards.'

McIntosh and Dolan entered the interview room and Natasha raised her eyebrows. The big dog had joined the party. The break hadn't helped her appearance. The last forty-eight energy sapping hours had left her exhausted, her make-up free face and bedraggled hair mocking her model image.

Dolan switched on the recording device. 'Interview with Natasha Cook recommenced. DCI McIntosh and DS Dolan replacing DI Bayford and DC Myers. Natasha, I hope you managed to get some rest and something to eat and drink?'

She nodded.

McIntosh looked at a piece of paper in his hand. 'Chicken Chow Mein, Salt and Pepper squid, Fried Rice, Chips, Curry sauce and Prawn crackers......

Natasha studied him, blankly.

'........your order from the Oriental Express on the night Emily Dean and Stuart Strong were murdered. Delivered to your front door and accepted by you at 8.02pm. You told us you left for Cornwall at 7.30pm.'

Natasha shrugged. 'I must have mixed up the time. Must have been later than I thought.'

'So, your Chinese arrived at 8.02pm and Strong was in your house at 8.42pm. You said you didn't see him, correct?'

'Correct.'

'So did you take the Chinese, eat it and leave before Strong arrived or did you leave right after the Chinese was delivered?'

'Must have left just after the Chinese came, I wasn't really paying attention to the time.'

'Why?'

'Why what?'

'Why order a Chinese, leave it untouched, then drive five hours to Cornwall?'

'I'd arranged to meet Peter so I had to go.'

'Natasha, in our line of work we get told all sorts of lies and fantasy stories. Day in, day out. Desperate people trying to cover their tracks. The one recurring theme in those lies is that when a far-fetched story makes absolutely no sense, it's because it's not true. You said Robson carried out the murders after you left the house. In what universe would you drive five hours to meet someone who's not even at the destination, because he's just arrived at your house to murder random people. People you claim shouldn't have been there? See how that just doesn't make sense.'

'He must have wanted me out of the way.'

'Why didn't you take the Chinese with you? You could've re-heated it when you got to Cornwall.'

'I never thought of that.'

'How did you drive to Cornwall?'

'What do you mean?'

'Did you drive your own car?'

'Of course.'

'Where did you leave it?'

'You can't park right beside the cottage so I think it was a street or two away.'

'It's just, we can't find any trace of your car in Portmellon village. How do you explain that?'

'Must have been stolen.'

'Aye, Portmellon is well known for its car crime.'

'No need for frivolity, Chief Inspector,' Robert Cox chirped.

McIntosh raised his hand in apology. 'Natasha, you say your BMW must have been stolen in Portmellon, but we discovered a BMW 1 series, registration WC10 ANT, parked in the adjacent street to the cottage.'

'What's that got to do with me?'

Dolan butted in, 'It's registered to White City Motors, located on the Westway in London. We contacted them and spoke to a really helpful man called Tony. Do you know him?'

Natasha glared at Dolan.

'Anyway, Tony told us your BMW was in for a service and they'd given you a courtesy car to use. A……' he said, dramatically checking his notes, '........BMW 1 series, WC10 ANT. Does that ring any bells? In case you're still not sure, your Chinese delivery man confirmed the 1 series was parked in your drive when he delivered the food.'

Natasha continued to glare

'Guess what? Your courtesy car is spotted on the ANPR cameras, heading out of London, westbound at….' another melodramatic note check, '…12.30am, five hours after you claim to have left. Plenty of time to eat Chinese, because someone ate the food, do whatever you were doing with Stuart and kill him and Emily Dean.'

'It wasn't me,' she said, weakly.

'Lass, you'll have to do better than that,' McIntosh said. 'Give it up before you tie yourself in more knots.'

'Fuck you!' Natasha snarled, 'It must've been Peter. I've been cooperative but you're twisting everything. I'm not saying another word.'

McIntosh stood. 'Interview terminated. You'll be returned to your cell and a charging decision will be taken in due course.'

In the reception area, McIntosh took Robert Cox aside. 'Hang around, this won't take long.'

Chapter 123

The CPS were happy to charge Natasha with the Dean and Strong murders but, despite the stack of circumstantial evidence, they remained hesitant regarding the O'Neill and Ekers killings, requesting more robust proof.

Privately, McIntosh had no doubts that Natasha also killed Andrew and Ben but prosecution couldn't be considered with the meagre information available and lack of witnesses. In Andrew's case, trying to cut through the red tape would be counter-productive. An investigation into Peter Robson's death would follow after the pathologist and toxicologist reports had been fully submitted.

***

A collective satisfaction radiated through the EIU when DC Arnott identified Natasha's BMW in Fulham, on the night of Sarah's death. Whilst solely inconclusive, it supported their version of events.

The blackmail pay-off remained the missing jigsaw piece. The brightest IT brains in the Met couldn't trace its final resting place. Proving Natasha solicited the money would tie everything together. McIntosh needed an unorthodox approach and knew the very man.

***

Natasha's trial was provisionally set for the summer of 2022. She pled not guilty and a half-hearted bail application was denied.

The prosecution's case was built on a revenge plot gone wrong. They theorised that Natasha resented Magnus for abandoning her and her family and blamed him for her mother, then her sister's death. She watched him rise, fall, then rise again before hatching her plan.

Her deep seated hatred and need for personal vengeance rendered Sarah O'Neill's contempt for Branch insignificant. However, Sarah's persistence and determination to expose Magnus, sealed her death sentence, launching a series of events Natasha couldn't control.

McIntosh and Bayford relaxed in the DCI's office. Bayford sensed the shift in his boss's demeanour. 'I haven't seen you this chilled out in weeks,' he said.

McIntosh laughed. 'Have you forgotten what's happened the last few weeks?'

'I know but at least it's over. No way she's talking her way out of this.'

Before replying, McIntosh heard a ping and studied his laptop screen. 'Wow, it gets better. Peter Robson's toxicology report. He ingested bipyridinium dichloride.'

Bayford looked blank, shrugging his shoulders.

'Paraquat to you and me,' McIntosh said. 'She fucking poisoned him. Her own boyfriend.'

'Jesus Christ, how did she manage that?'

'Two bottles of water were found in their bags, one riddled with the stuff. You don't pick that stuff up in B&Q. She must have been planning this for years.'

'Is paraquat not illegal in the UK?'

'Aye, but the internet's an incredible thing. You can buy anything if you know where to look. I can just about understand the other killings if revenge was her motive, but Robson might be the worst one of the lot. She murdered him purely to get him out of her way. There's got to be a digital trace of the purchase. Let's nail it down and make sure she never gets out.'

Chapter 124

This place isn't so bad, or so I keep telling myself. HMP Bronzefield they call it. I expected a public toilet with the horrible rectangular white tiled walls but it's quite modern really. I suppose I'll stay here until my trial, then after that, who knows!

Have I any regrets? Just one……well maybe two. If Emma hadn't appeared at my house that night she'd still be alive. Her weird enthusiasm about killing Dave got her excited about her next assignment and she became a liability. What could I do?

And Pea. A lovely guy who even changed his name after I explained his was too memorable. He protected me when I had no-one, understood what I'd gone through and got me on the Island to do something about it. I regret making Pea suffer. I wish I'd thought of a less painful way for him to die.

I've always been a lone wolf and it would have worked but for Sarah fucking O'Neill. That bitch is the reason I'm in here. She couldn't let it go. When I saw Magnus's shouting match with her I knew she had to die.

This cell is not the exotic lifestyle I pictured, but all is not yet lost. As far as I know, they've not found the money and if all else fails, I'll play the diminished responsibility card.

After all, I think I've proved my worth as an actress.

Chapter 125

In the three weeks since Natasha's plea hearing, the EIU returned to normal business. Investigations into a daring robbery at a Premier league footballer's house, while he was playing, and an alleged sexual assault by a wealthy Russian businessman were currently on the docket.

Kelly Arnott's request for a permanent transfer to the EIU was in the system and she remained on secondment, pending a final decision. Chris Dolan returned to his Hammersmith day job.

Robert Ellison had been installed as the new Specialist Crime Commander. A new name to McIntosh but after asking around, the general consensus was a solid, no-nonsense operator who cared about his officers and didn't suffer fools gladly. The polar opposite to Jonathan Beswick.

Sully came up trumps. His ability to sneak through back doors undetected, paid dividends. An offshore account in the name of Naomi Ward, originating in the Cayman Islands, received a deposit of two and a half million pounds which then bounced around the world, before resting in an account in a less than upstanding Belize bank.

Immense wealth, tantalisingly out of Natasha's grasp, and now in the process of being seized by the police. Having viewed the documentation required to open the Belize account, in the name of Tatyana Malewski, Sully was seriously impressed at Natasha's knowledge and expertise, not to mention her underworld connections.

Definitely no dumb blonde.

***

Being stabbed, the car crash, as well as his poor diet and lack of sleep had contributed to a general deterioration in Angus McIntosh's health, not to mention the stress of his family's ordeal. The slightly gentler pace of the current workload suited him.

Much to Debbie's amusement he enrolled in a local gym and now welcomed his early morning workouts. To his amazement, he actually enjoyed it. He'd failed to coax Debbie along, her bed calling out to her, and she continued to chib him about meeting Lucas's parents. He didn't know how much longer he'd be able to bat away her unsubtle hints.

He'd worked up a sweat and felt good. His rowing machine performance continued to improve and the condescending looks from his fellow morning enthusiasts had diminished. The searing heat from the shower relaxed his muscles and he felt tension drain away. He was tying his shoes when the call came in.

A sudden death in Kensington, not far from Natasha Cook's house.

He jumped in his car and arrived at the address at 7.15am, surprised at the lack of police vehicles. Simon Bayford was waiting.

'What've we got Simon?'

'Not sure boss, it's all a bit hush hush.'

A man wearing a long brown overcoat and a silk scarf, walked from the townhouse steps to greet the pair. 'DCI McIntosh?'

'Aye, you are?'

'DI Malik, Kensington CID. I think we've met before.'

'Aye, I thought I recognised your face. What have you got for us?'

'This is more of a courtesy call. I doubt there will be an investigation. You better come with me,' Malik said, cryptically.

Bayford and McIntosh exchanged a glance as Malik led them along a monoblock path, round the gable end of the house to the rear garden, a large, beautifully landscaped space with a substantial wooden structure backing onto the neighbouring property.

A young PC guarded the front of the closed double doors. Malik nodded and the PC pulled the doors open. Adjusting to the gloom took a few seconds but at the far end, a hefty timber beam spanned the entire width of the garage. From the beam, a man's body hung from a thick rope.

Ex Commander, Jonathan Beswick.

No-one spoke.

After a minute McIntosh nodded to Bayford and they exited the garage and stood in silence on the frost covered rear lawn, shielding their eyes from the emerging morning glare, while Malik conversed with the PC.

Malik joined them. 'Just thought you should be told sir. We don't expect a need for your involvement.'

'Thanks, I appreciate the call. I don't suppose there's any suggestion of foul play?'

'At first glance no, but I expect we'll find out later. Like I said, it was more of a courtesy call.'

McIntosh and Bayford thanked Malik and strolled back to their cars, hands in pockets. McIntosh climbed into his car, switched on the engine and turned the heaters to full blast. Bayford stood at the window. 'You think Beswick finally did the decent thing?'

McIntosh shrugged, 'Either that or he's just a coward,' he said, putting the car into gear. 'Or……. karma's a right bitch,' he added, driving towards the early morning London traffic.

The End

Please leave a review on Amazon or contact me via my website to leave feedback or simply to ask me a question

jerrydye.co.uk

The second instalment in the Angus McIntosh series is currently in the works and should be released later in 2025.

Also available as an eBook.

Printed in Dunstable, United Kingdom